HELEN YENDALL has had dozens of short stories and a serial published in women's magazines over the past twenty years and now writes female-focused WW2 novels. She's a member of the Romantic Novelists' Association.

She studied English and German at Leeds University and has worked in a variety of roles: for a literary festival, a university, a camping club, a children's charity and in marketing and export sales. But her favourite job is the one she still has: teaching creative writing to adults.

Although a proud Brummie by birth, Helen now lives in the North Cotswolds with her husband and cocker spaniel, Bonnie. When she's not teaching or writing, she likes reading, swimming, tennis and walking in the beautiful countryside where she lives.

Also by Helen Yendall

A Wartime Secret

The Highland Girls series

The Highland Girls at War

The Highland Girls on Guard

HELEN YENDALL

ONE PLACE. MANY STORIES

HQ
An imprint of HarperCollins*Publishers* Ltd
1 London Bridge Street
London SE1 9GF

www.harpercollins.co.uk

HarperCollins*Publishers*
Macken House, 39/40 Mayor Street Upper,
Dublin 1 D01 C9W8

This paperback edition 2024

1
First published in Great Britain by
HQ, an imprint of HarperCollins*Publishers* Ltd 2024

ISBN: 9780008603298

MIX
Paper | Supporting
responsible forestry
FSC
www.fsc.org   FSC™ C007454

This book contains FSC™ certified paper and other controlled
sources to ensure responsible forest management.

For more information visit: www.harpercollins.co.uk/green

Printed and Bound in the UK using
100% Renewable Electricity at CPI Group (UK) Ltd

To Alan, with love.

Chapter 1

'Righto, girls!' Seffy said. 'Everyone move back now.'

The lumberjills had gathered round to watch this monster fall. A couple of girls had taken off their berets, respectfully.

The tree had started to creak. Seffy gazed up at it: a huge Douglas fir, towering eighty feet above them, high up into the cerulean sky. There was a gaping white wound in its base, where she'd cut in with the axe. Then she and Morag had taken one end of the crosscut each and sawn expertly through the trunk.

Seffy wiped her brow with the back of her hand. Phew, it was warm work.

She glanced around to check the five other girls were standing well clear. Then she stepped forward and patted the fir's rough bark.

'What're you doin'?' Enid asked.

'I always give them a little thank you for their part in the war effort,' Seffy said.

She smiled as she imagined Morag behind her, tutting and rolling her eyes. Once her little moment of sentimentality was over, she placed both hands on the trunk and gave it a firm shove.

1

The creaking got louder; the tree started to tilt.

Seffy watched, satisfied it was moving in the right direction, then – her favourite part – she cupped her hands around her mouth, lifted her head and yelled, 'TIMBERRRRR!'

Her voice echoed through the forest as, WHOOSH! down it went, gathering pace and falling in exactly the right spot with an almighty crash.

There was nothing quite like it. Even after a year as a lumberjill and with hundreds of trees under her belt, it was still a thrill to fell a tree.

Flora gave a little cheer and Seffy grinned at her.

She didn't look at Morag and Grace. They certainly wouldn't be cheering or grinning. Three weeks ago, Seffy had changed the working pairs around and she wasn't in their best books.

'But you always work with Grace and I always work with Enid!' Morag had complained.

'All the more reason to swap,' Seffy had replied, cheerfully. 'A change is as good as a rest! Don't want to get stuck in a rut, do we?'

Seffy had caught the look of hurt and confusion on Grace's face and had felt a stab of guilt. She'd worked with Grace from the start, and they'd always been a good team, but things had changed. It was simply easier not to be around Grace at the moment.

Morag had muttered something and stomped off but she'd accepted Seffy's decision. She was their leader girl, after all.

Grace hadn't said a word. Seffy knew she wouldn't argue – it wasn't in Grace's nature – but she could see from her slumped shoulders and set mouth that she was upset.

'Is it no' time for a cuppa yet?' Flora asked. The others groaned and laughed. Flora, the youngest at only sixteen, was always ready for a break and seemed to have an internal clock that told her exactly when one was due.

The girls started to down tools but Seffy didn't want to stop. She relished her work these days. It was the perfect distraction.

When she was wielding an axe or a saw, yelling "Timber!",

2

lopping off branches or helping Joey and the other horsewomen to attach chains to the logs, it kept her mind from straying; it stopped her thinking about him.

She looked at her watch. 'Actually, Flora, you're a couple of minutes early.' She nodded at the felled tree. The side branches needed stripping. 'There's still time to pick up an axe and start snedding.'

'Och, it's hardly worth it if there are only two minutes to go,' Enid said. 'And I dunno about the rest of yous but I'm fair gaspin' for a brew!' She grasped her throat in both hands, crossed her eyes and stuck out her tongue.

The others murmured their agreement and looked at Seffy, hopefully.

'Oh, very well.' They'd been working hard all morning, after all, and it was Saturday, a half-day. Not long now and they'd be finished for the weekend.

Seffy fished the whistle out of the pocket of her dungarees and blew three times, long and loud.

Five minutes later, the girls were sitting round the campfire with lumberjills from other gangs and Jock, their kindly foreman, who'd earned Seffy's trust and respect over the past year. Water was boiling in billycans for tea and the air was full of chatter and laughter.

'Miss McEwen!' Enid cried suddenly. 'Golly, where did you spring from?'

Seffy looked up and sure enough, their former supervisor was striding into the clearing. She looked business-like, in her Timber Corps breeches and boots. Whatever was she doing here? She'd been gone since last summer and they'd managed perfectly well without her, with only Jock keeping an eye on them and the occasional visit from the welfare officer.

She'd left to train girls in another camp – terrorise them, more like – and they'd hoped she was gone for good.

'Aye, I'm back,' Miss McEwen said, glaring at them all. 'And not

3

a moment too soon, by the sounds of it! Who was that back there, blowing the whistle like one of those Keystone Kops?'

Seffy bit her lip. That must have been her. She was perhaps a trifle overenthusiastic with the whistle. She tried not to laugh, as Flora nudged her hard in the ribs.

When no one answered, Miss McEwen shook her head.

'Make the most of these tea breaks, girls. If the summer turns out to be as hot as folk are predicting, soon there'll be no campfires allowed!'

Seffy rolled her eyes. The woman was such a killjoy.

'Anyhow,' Miss McEwen went on, 'I have news!'

She waited until the excited murmurs had died down before announcing, 'New girls are coming to join you. In fact, they're on their way!'

New recruits? En route to camp? There were exclamations of surprise, then everyone started talking at once.

Morag looked at Seffy. 'I suppose you knew about this?'

Seffy shook her head and huffed. As leader girl for their hut, someone might've thought to give her the nod before it was announced. Honestly, no one ever told her anything.

'How many?' someone asked.

Miss McEwen sniffed. 'Eight. We can squeeze a few more beds in and we've got vacancies in a couple o' the huts.'

Seffy and the other girls from Macdonald hut glanced at each other. They had two empty beds; that meant two new recruits for them.

'Aww!' Flora said. 'What about me? Can I not fill a gap and move into the hut once and for all?'

'You're too young!' Seffy told her, for the hundredth time.

'You have to stay at home for a wee while yet,' Grace said, in a kinder tone.

'In addition to the new recruits, there are other changes afoot,' Miss McEwen said. 'But I'll save that news for another day.'

'Aye,' Morag said, 'that's probably best. We cannae cope with too much excitement all at once.'

4

Flora squealed. 'Maybe the Canucks are coming back? I know they've only been gone a few weeks—'

'Six weeks tomorrow,' Grace said.

'Aye, well, six weeks, then. But perhaps it was a terrible mistake and they shouldn't have been sent away? It was so much fun when they were here! The dances, the cinema night, the summer fete . . . !'

Miss McEwen rolled her eyes. 'Not forgetting the sweeties, nylons, chocolate and ciggies.'

'Oh yes! The candy! That's what they called it! So many goodies!' Flora agreed.

'NO!' Miss McEwen barked, making some of the girls jump. 'Those Canadian fellas are no' coming back, I'm glad to say. They were a distraction and a bad influence and—'

Enid coughed loudly and nodded at Grace, who was sitting cross-legged near the fire.

'Ah, yes, of course. Miss McGinty,' Miss McEwen said.

'Mrs Johnson,' Seffy corrected. She was enjoying seeing the old dragon flounder and she wasn't the only one. Girls were putting their heads down or covering their mouths, to hide their smiles.

'I don't mean your husband, of course, Mrs . . . er Johnson,' Miss McEwen said. 'He was – is – an exception, I'm sure. But on the whole, those Canadian laddies were bad news.'

Seffy's heart had lifted for a moment when the Canadians had been mentioned. The girls had worked alongside them until recently and there'd been several romances between lumberjills and lumberjacks. Lucky Grace had married her chap but Seffy had fallen hard for someone who wasn't free to love her in return.

She sighed. How silly, getting her hopes up like that. Of course, Number Thirty-Four Company of the Canadian Forestry Corps wasn't coming back. They'd packed up their camp and gone to join the combat troops down in England, leaving broken hearts and tear-stained pillows behind them.

Seffy glanced at Jean who was rubbing Grace's shoulder.

'You must be missing Gordy dreadfully,' Jean said.

Seffy gritted her teeth. It wasn't fair! Everyone was making such a fuss of Grace and no one remembered – or cared – that *she* was missing someone too.

She didn't trust herself to speak nicely to Grace these days. She was supposed to be her chum and it felt horrible, being all twisted up with envy like this. So it was best to keep out of Grace's way and say nothing at all.

Miss McEwen coughed. 'I'll give ye a wee clue to the other news,' she said. 'You're going to be working with new folk very soon.'

"New folk?" Seffy glanced at Jock, but he was puffing away on his pipe and not giving anything away. Oh, this was infuriating. Why didn't the woman simply tell them, instead of playing silly games?

'All will become clear,' Miss McEwen said. 'But now, I need to borrow Miss Wallace for an important errand. Where is she?'

Joey was sitting with the other horsewomen. She waved and got to her feet.

'Jock tells me you can drive the truck,' Miss McEwen said.

'Aye, I can.'

Seffy frowned. Why hadn't she been chosen? She could drive the truck too. Better than Joey, in fact. Joey had only learned to drive a few months ago.

Miss McEwen brought something out from behind her back: a clipboard.

'Good! Here, take this. It's got a list of names on it. Drive to the railway station and collect the new recruits. They're due on the 12.05 from Aberdeen. Make sure you're dressed appropriately! You'll be representing the Timber Corps, so those dirty overalls won't do. You can take someone wi' you, so choose now. And be quick about it!'

Joey's gaze flitted over the girls. A few of them waved and entreated her – laughing – to pick them.

'I choose Seffy!' she said.

Miss McEwen frowned. 'Ah, Miss Mills. Still roughin' it here, then?'

Seffy was so thrilled at being chosen that even Miss McEwen's snarky comment couldn't spoil the moment.

'I am, Miss McEwen, thank you,' she said, standing up and brushing pine needles from her legs.

'Make haste then, you two. Forget your teas and go!'

'I'm only agreeing to this on one condition,' Seffy whispered, as she and Joey hurried from the clearing.

'What's that?'

Seffy snatched the clipboard from Joey's hands with a giggle.

'That I'm in charge of this!'

Chapter 2

Tattie was sitting on the floor of the luggage van, leaning against a large trunk. The porters had pushed it to the back and so hopefully it wouldn't be needed 'til the end of the line.

So far, so good. The train had stopped a few times since Aberdeen and she'd stayed hidden, tucked between the tall trunk and the van wall.

Aw, but it was scary: scarier than anything Gregor had made her do. It wasn't the dark: she'd spent enough time in the blackout. She was used to it. No, it was the fear of being caught that was giving her the heebie-jeebies. It wasn't her fault she didn't have a ticket but she'd still be in trouble without one. They'd throw her off the train, sure as eggs were eggs.

She'd considered hiding in the lav'. That was one sure way of avoiding the ticket fella. But another stowaway might've had the same idea. This luggage van was a safer bet.

Each time the train slowed for a station, her heart started clattering and she found herself gasping for breath. And by the time the train stopped, the doors opened and light flooded in, she felt like she was going to have a heart attack.

The porters – old fellas, by the sounds of them – were only

ever a few feet away. Trollies trundled to and fro and the men grunted with effort as they heaved baggage in and out.

Passengers called out for their luggage.

Please, she thought, don't let anyone ask for, "The big trunk at the back." If they did, she'd be well and truly rumbled.

But each time, the doors had slammed shut, the train had jolted forward and with a clank of chains and a hiss of steam, they'd set off again.

Tattie hugged her knees to her chest, grateful for the dungarees Ma had pressed on her that morning.

'Put these on, hen,' she'd said. 'You'll look the part when you arrive and that's half the battle, eh?'

The dungarees were good for running and climbing. They were warmer than a skirt, too. It'd been sunny when she'd made her way to the station but it was chilly in here and the cold from the floor was seeping into her bones.

They were nearly there. She'd been counting the stops. Not long now.

Joey blinked hard as she steered the lorry towards Farrbridge station. She'd gone dizzy there, for a second. The road, the overhanging trees and the distant green hills had gone blurry.

It happened sometimes, when the nightmares had kept her awake until the early hours.

She took one hand off the wheel and rubbed her eyes, grateful that Seffy was in the back getting changed and couldn't see.

Seffy had gone to fetch the truck when Miss McEwen had dismissed them and there hadn't been time to change out of her overalls.

Joey had nipped back to the hut, put on her own uniform and grabbed Seffy's from the pile on one of the spare beds.

The bed had been Irene's but since she'd left the corps, it had gradually become a dumping ground for other girls' belongings. It was littered with an assortment of hairbrushes, magazines and uniforms.

'I thought you might've asked one of the horsewomen to come with you,' Seffy said, from the back. Her voice was muffled. She was probably pulling clothes over her head.

Joey smiled. The wee Sassenach was always looking for proof she was popular.

'I'd never choose one of them over a Macdonald girl!' she called back.

In truth, she'd chosen Seffy because she could drive, but that wasn't the only reason: she liked her.

The others were all dear to her, but Jean was a tad too bossy, Morag too miserable, Flora and Enid were definitely too daft for an important job like this and Grace was too quiet.

Thinking of Grace reminded Joey of something.

'I've noticed,' she said, carefully, 'that you're not so pally with Grace these days. And I hear you're not sharing the crosscut anymore. Have you fallen out?'

There was silence, then Seffy replied, 'No! Well, not exactly.' Her voice sounded strained.

'Och, don't tell me if you don't want to. I'll still be your pal!'

Seffy's head popped out from the back of the truck. She was smiling and her blonde hair was tousled. She started to climb through into the cab.

'Now it really doesn't matter,' she said, as she sat in the seat next to Joey, 'but this uniform isn't mine. It's about two sizes too small!'

'I'm sorry!' Joey said. 'I was rushing.'

Seffy looked down at her feet. 'At least I've got my own boots and haven't had to cram my size sevens into anything tiny!' She patted Joey's leg. 'Don't worry! I'll survive!'

They drove on for a little while, enjoying the scenery and the bright summer sunshine.

'You were saying,' Joey said. 'About you and Grace?'

Seffy fidgeted in her seat. 'We're not as chummy these days, it's true. But I truly thought it was time we swapped felling partners.

Though, I must admit, working with Morag's not exactly a barrel of laughs.'

Joey made a sympathetic murmur.

It sounded as though Seffy had cut off her nose to spite her face. She didn't want to work with Grace but Morag, unsurprisingly, was no fun at all.

'Morag's a case, isn't she?' Seffy said. 'It's a mystery how the girl snaffled herself a fiancé. A man actually found Morag attractive—'

'A man of sound mind!'

'Yes! And decided he wanted to spend the rest of his life with her! But, to quote my Aunt Dilys, "there's a lid for every pot"!'

'Aw, I like your auntie,' Joey said. 'She's awful scary at times but she's . . .' She cast about for the right expression.

'A good egg?'

'Aye. How is she, anyway?'

'Actually, she's gone to London.'

'London?'

Seffy laughed. 'No need to sound so horrified. It's hardly Timbuktu!'

Joey shrugged. 'Might as well be. You wouldn't catch me down in London. Isn't it terribly dangerous?'

'Probably. She's got pals there and she used to make an annual pilgrimage before Herr Hitler put paid to that. Even Dilys isn't mad enough to go to London during the blitzkrieg! But she's been hankering to go back for ages. "One can't put one's life on hold forever," she says and, "We mustn't let the war get us down, else the Germans are winning before they even get here."'

Seffy had done a passable impression of her aunt but Joey didn't laugh.

'"Before they get here"? Does she think they're going to win the war, then?'

'Oh, I don't know. She's worried, like everyone. She's back next weekend, so I'll ask her. We've been invited to tea with the Lockharts.'

'At Blantyre Castle? Very nice.'

Joey sometimes forgot that Seffy was an actual titled lady, with a titled lady's privileges.

Most girls would give their eyeteeth for an invitation like that – to the home of the laird, no less – but Seffy was wrinkling her nose.

'Her ladyship's cousin is staying in the area, so she wants to hold a tea party, apparently. It'll be deadly dull.'

'Anyhow, about you and Grace,' Joey said. She was starting to think Seffy was deliberately changing the subject.

Seffy sighed. 'Grace has changed, since she got married, don't you think? It's Gordy this and Gordy that. She can't talk or think about anything else!' She gave a hollow laugh.

Sour grapes, Joey thought. It was hardly surprising Grace was missing her new husband. They'd only been married a few days when the Canadian company had packed up and gone. Anyone would be the same. But she judged it wasn't the right time to say it.

They sat in silence for a few moments. There'd been something – a dalliance – between Seffy and one of the Canadian boys but, unlike Grace's romance, it hadn't led to anything. Perhaps he'd thrown her over? Seffy was clearly feeling sore and resentful of Grace's happiness.

'Have you not kept in touch with that Canadian fella? Your sergeant?' Joey asked.

Seffy shook her head and turned to face the window. 'No. It's easier this way.'

Joey laughed. 'Are you sure about that? Because you look terrible and since the Canucks left you've been awful crabbit! Worse than Morag!'

She winced. Perhaps she'd gone too far; sometimes her mouth ran away with her. Seffy didn't reply straight away.

Eventually, she said, 'He was never "my" sergeant. We said goodbye and we agreed, no letters. It was for the best.'

Her voice was small and flat, as though she didn't believe a word of it.

Joey slowed the truck to a halt at the crossroads.

'It's right here, for the railway station,' Seffy said, quietly.

Joey took her time before pulling out. She was waiting for Seffy to say more about the Canadian laddie but the subject was obviously closed.

Joey knew something about heartbreak. Perhaps it was time to admit it; it might make Seffy feel better.

'You know,' she said, 'when I swapped to the Timber Corps from the Land Army, it wasn't only because I wanted to earn more.'

Seffy twisted around in her seat. 'Oh, really? What, then?'

'There was a fella.' Joey swallowed. 'It didn't work out, perhaps the same as you – I don't know but . . .'

'Was this when you were a land girl? I had no idea. I'm sorry.'

'Aye, well I've never told anyone before. No one knew. Only the other land girls I worked with. There were three of us on the farm, living in a rat-infested room above the barn.'

'Rats?'

'Aye. When I was sitting in the bathtub, I had to sing loudly to keep them away!'

'Ugh!'

'I liked it there, though. Aside from the vermin. Eventually we moved into the attic of the farmhouse, when the rats got too bad. I worked with the horses. Monty and Pepper. Aw, I loved them. Walking behind the plough, getting the hay in, all of that. It didn't seem like work at all!'

'And who was the fella?'

'It was the farmer, Hamish. He was awful nice and—'

Seffy gasped. 'The farmer? Was he married?'

Joey shook her head. This was why she didn't tell people: they always jumped to the wrong conclusion.

'Widowed. He had three bairns. His wife had died two years earlier.'

'Oh, that's too bad. Those poor children.'

Joey nodded, remembering their wee wan faces.

'Don't tell anyone, will you?'

Seffy promised.

'When we first got there, Hamish was a dour thing and he wasnae happy about women working on his farm. But it was us or nothing. Gradually he realised we weren't half bad and, we . . . well, me and him, we became close.'

Seffy raised her eyebrows. 'Were you courting? Properly stepping out?'

Joey shrugged. The farm was in the middle of nowhere and apart from the occasional get-together with other land girls, they'd hardly ever seen anyone else. She and Hamish had certainly never gone out anywhere on a proper date.

'Did you kiss and cuddle?'

Joey laughed. 'Of course! What d'you take me for, a nun? But that was all. It never went any further, although I'm not sure the other girls believed that. They were mean. Jealous, I suppose, though he never treated me any different whilst we were working. But you know how girls can be.'

'Oh, yes, I do!'

'Sometimes, the others wouldn't speak to me. At night, if I said summat, one of them would call out to the other, "Did you hear something?" and the other would say, "No. Mebbe it's an owl hootin' outside."'

Joey felt tearful at the memory. It had been a dark time. Although she'd had Hamish, she'd been awful lonely.

'Hamish said I reminded him of his late wife. I was falling for him but another girl, on the next farm, warned me off. She said he was probably looking for a mother for his bairns. It preyed on my mind. I started doubting whether he liked me properly, for myself. He never said. In the end, I decided to cut ma losses and leave.'

Seffy sat back in her seat and exhaled. 'Men! They're the giddy limit, aren't they?'

Joey laughed. 'You're speaking double Dutch again but yes, I'm sure they are!'

There was a moment's silence.

'And what about your fella, Seffy? The sergeant? What happened there? He seemed nice.'

Seffy sighed. 'He was. Very nice. But he wasn't free.' She was looking down, toying with the edge of the seat. 'He was engaged to a girl back home and—' she shrugged '—he took his promise very seriously. Quite right, too!'

There was a quiver in her voice.

'You know, when he turned me down, it was the first time in my life that I hadn't got exactly what I wanted.'

Seffy looked at Joey with sad eyes. Then she forced a laugh.

'It probably did me good but goodness, it was a hard pill to swallow!'

Joey wouldn't say what she was thinking: that a lass like Seffy, with all the advantages she had in life – money, education, good looks – wasn't likely to be without a sweetheart for long. That would be dismissing her feelings; that wasn't what Seffy wanted to hear.

'Anyway!' Seffy said, sitting up. 'Enough of that! I admire you, Joey, for leaving the farm and whatshisname. That was brave. How was he, when you left? Did he seem heartbroken?'

Joey's eyes stung as she remembered her last day on the farm. She'd wandered around in a daze, asking herself whether she was doing the right thing. Saying goodbye to the horses had been heartbreaking. She'd cried, then the nippers had cried, clinging onto her legs, begging her not to go. They'd lost their mother and now she was leaving too. She'd felt rotten. But as for Hamish . . .

'No, he seemed more offended, than anything. How dare I leave him – that kind of attitude. I'd thought, if I left, he might fight for me. But he didn't. He let me go.'

'The rotter!'

She and Seffy were a sorry pair, with their tales of lost love. Joey wasn't sure if talking about it was helping, or if they were merely wallowing in self-pity.

'I'd say you had a jolly lucky escape,' Seffy said. 'You deserve someone better.'

Joey shrugged. 'He knows where I am and he's not far away. If he'd really wanted to see me again, he could've found a way. I miss those fellas though. I'd give anything to see them again.'

Seffy tilted her head. 'The children?'

'No! The horses!'

Seffy burst out laughing and seconds later, Joey joined in.

'Oh, you silly sausage!' Seffy said eventually, wiping a tear from her eye. 'You're as bad as me! I honestly think the motherly instinct has passed me by. I can't cope with babies and their non-stop wailing. I'd rather have a puppy and it sounds as though you'd rather have a horse!'

Joey laughed. This wee chat had definitely lifted her spirits.

'Anyhow,' she said. 'I'm glad I made the move to the Timber Corps because I've met a great group of lassies, including you, you wee Sassenach! And who needs men, in any case?'

'Hear, hear!'

Seffy had cheered her up; Joey wanted to do something in return.

'You know, if you still want to work with the horses, I could have a word with Miss McEwen. Ask if you could transfer and work wi' me? She likes me. I dunno why!'

'Probably because you don't answer back.'

'Aye. I'm not gobby like some of yous!'

'I'd be awfully grateful. I'd love to be in the dragging team with you.'

Seffy looked bashful and Joey wondered if she was remembering the time she'd tried to buy her job with the horses.

There was no denying the cash would've been welcome, but Joey was glad she'd stuck to her guns and turned it down.

'I'll find the right moment and ask the auld dragon,' Joey said. 'One of the girls wants to take a turn at felling, so mebbe you can do a swap. As long as Miss McEwen isn't minded to put one of the new recruits in the dragging team, of course.'

'Isn't it queer to be talking about "new recruits"? It only seems like five minutes since we were new recruits ourselves.'

Joey agreed. What a lot had happened since they'd first arrived in camp. Some good, some bad. They weren't the same people anymore, that was for sure.

Chapter 3

'Farrbridge! This is Farrbridge!'

Tattie's guts did a loop-the-loop as the train juddered to a halt and the guard's voice rang out.

They'd arrived.

She'd stood up a few minutes earlier and stretched her aching limbs. Then, feeling her way in the dark, she'd clambered over suitcases, trunks and boxes, until she'd reached the front of the van.

All this luggage! Folk must have more stuff than they knew what to do with. Here she was, leaving home for goodness knew how long – perhaps, forever – and she'd hardly brought anything.

She could've had a field day in here, opening bags and feeling for treasures. But she'd had enough on her mind and besides, she'd promised Ma.

She crouched behind a couple of mail sacks and hitched her wee bag over her shoulder.

She hadn't thought this part through properly. Gregor would've rolled his eyes at her. 'Always have a plan, hen!'

But Gregor wasn't here. She was on her tod and no one was going to help her: she had to do it herself.

The start of the journey had been easy. She'd given her name to the ministry man, who'd ticked her off his list, then she'd slipped past the other recruits – who were too busy blethering to notice her – and headed down to the platform. She'd waited until the porters were out of sight and jumped into the luggage van.

Getting off was going to be trickier.

Someone pulled open the doors. Tattie held her breath but the man's heavy tread receded down the platform. The porters would be here any moment. If she got her timing right, she could pretend to be a passenger retrieving her bag.

She stepped towards the open doors and peeked out to the right. All along the train, doors were swinging open and passengers were emerging. Without stopping to check the other way, she jumped down onto the platform and almost collided with a uniformed soldier, who'd suddenly appeared from the left.

'Hey! Watch out!'

'S . . . sorry!'

In her panic, Tattie stepped back and tripped over her feet, losing her balance. The soldier had barged past and leaped up into the van. Someone else grabbed Tattie's wrist, just in time to stop her falling. She was roughly yanked up onto her feet and turned to face – the guard!

'Oi, sonny! What d'you think you're doin'?'

He was spraying spittle in her face.

'Aww. Gerroff!' She tried to wriggle away, using her free hand to prise him off. But he was holding her fast and the more she struggled, the tighter his grip.

The soldier suddenly dropped back down onto the platform, making the guard jump.

'Is there a problem?' he asked, hoisting a hessian haversack onto his back.

Ma God, he was braw. Tall and burly, with a strong jaw, a scar on his right cheek and questioning dark eyes.

He looked like a real hero: how she'd always imagined William Wallace. She hadn't learned much in school but she remembered the stories of brave William Wallace and his fight for freedom.

If Ma was here, she'd say, 'You wouldnae want to meet him down a dark alley!' But he wasn't a roughneck. He was well-spoken and he had badges on his tunic. An officer.

'Aye, sir,' the guard said. He was still gripping her wrist and she'd given up struggling now. 'This laddie's been stowing away, if I'm not mistaken. Probably helping himself from the luggage an' all. I'll bet you a penny to a pound he's no ticket.'

Tattie flushed. That part, about the ticket, was true enough but if he made her turn out her pockets, he wouldn't find anything.

She grimaced as her wrist was squeezed again. Should she tell him she was a lass, not a laddie? He might treat her better.

The soldier tightened the straps on his haversack. His sleeves were rolled up and his strong, sinewy arms were covered in dark hair. He pushed down his cap and glanced along the platform.

He was leaving her at the mercy of this horrible fella. God only knew what was going to happen.

He turned his gaze on her, raising his thick eyebrows and Tattie gave him a pleading look.

'He's with me,' he said, sharply. 'Major Ralph Stirling, Royal Scots Guards. And that's my batman you're restraining. Do you mind?'

There was no arguing with that voice and the guard released her instantly.

Tattie could hardly believe her luck.

'Beg pardon, sir. But ye can't be too careful these days,' the guard said, tipping his cap and stepping away.

Tattie hitched her bag onto her shoulder. She was itching to make a dash for it before the guard changed his mind but if she scarpered, she'd be letting him down: William Wallace, her saviour.

He'd undone something from his haversack – a pair of boots, tied together by their laces – and he threw them at her. They hit her hard in the stomach and she let out an "Ugh!"

He rolled his eyes, then gestured towards the exit. 'Come on then, boy! Jump to it!'

As he turned and started to stride towards the exit, she could've sworn there was a faint smile on his face. She ran to catch up with him, which was difficult, with legs as wobbly as jelly.

'Ta ever so, sir!' she managed, hugging his boots. She wouldn't even mind if they were muddy, but they were shiny. She could smell the polish. 'I owe you, sir!'

He nodded and marched on. His haversack was as big as a toddler but he was carrying it like it weighed nothing. He was amazin'! He'd saved her. Perhaps she should forget about joining the Timber Corps and go off wi' this man – if he'd have her – and be his "batman" for real and carry his things until he realised he couldn't do without her and then she'd tell him the truth, that she was a lassie, after all, and—

He was glancing at her, frowning, as though wondering what she was still doing there. He took the boots from her, hardly breaking stride. 'Well, so long then,' he said and broke into a run.

Tattie stopped and watched him go. '"Freedom is best, I tell thee true, of all things to be won!"' she called after him.

A couple walking arm in arm down the platform stared at her and muttered something to each other.

'William Wallace,' she added, quietly. But she was talking to herself.

Chapter 4

'There they are!' Joey said, pointing down at the platform. The lassies were smartly dressed in skirts, stockings, heels and hats. They were standing in a huddle, luggage at their feet, glancing around uncertainly.

Seffy nodded. 'Let's be terribly nice and reassuring. They look totally unsuitable for working outdoors but we were once like that, remember?'

'Speak for yourself!' Joey said, with mock indignation. 'I was a land girl!'

They were tripping down the steps now and Joey was doing her best not to laugh.

Seffy frowned. 'What in heaven's name is the matter with you?'

Joey had stuffed the knuckles of one hand into her mouth.

'It's those wee breeches. They're halfway down your legs. Every time I look at you, I crack up.'

Seffy tapped her on the head with the clipboard. 'Well, DON'T LOOK, then!'

They'd reached the group of girls.

'Good afternoon, Timber Corps recruits!' Seffy said. 'We're Mills and Wallace. Gosh, that sounds like a firm of solicitors! But you can call us Seffy—' she pointed to herself '—and Joey.

We'll use Christian names from the off. We're not terribly formal in the corps.'

Joey was impressed. It'd been the right decision to bring her along: Seffy had struck the right note of business-like-but-friendly.

'But don't call the supervisor anything other than "Miss McEwen" – at least, not to her face,' Joey said. 'Else you'll be for the high jump!'

There was silence. It was a joke but the poor things were clearly terrified. No one even smiled.

'We were standing exactly where you are now, twelve months ago,' Seffy said.

'And look at us now!' Joey pushed up her sleeves, flexed her tanned arms and grinned as she showed off her biceps.

Everyone laughed.

Thank goodness. The ice was broken.

Seffy asked the girls to call out their names and ticked them off the list.

'Hmm,' she said, tapping her pen on the clipboard. 'We're missing two.'

'Might they be in the ladies'?' Joey suggested. She nodded at one of the girls, who must've been sticking her head out of the window on the journey. She had smudges of soot on her face. Perhaps the others had done the same and were in the lavatory, tidying themselves up.

Seffy nudged Joey. 'Look! I expect she's with us. Hello there! Timber Corps? Now, where've you been hiding yourself?'

The girl blushed as everyone stared and one or two girls whispered something behind their hands.

She couldn't have looked more different from the others, with her short hair, bad skin and small frame. And she was wearing dungarees. She looked like a wee street urchin. Joey hoped those spindly arms were stronger than they looked.

But her heart went out to her; the lass was clearly terrified.

'Glad to see you've come dressed for work,' Joey said, and the girl smiled.

'Now,' Seffy said, 'which one are you? Edwards or Buchanan?'

'Edwards. Kathleen Edwards. But everyone calls me Tattie.'

'We didn't see you on the train,' a tall girl said. 'We were all sitting together.'

The lass – Tattie – blushed furiously. 'No, I wasn't in a carriage. I can't stand small places, so I . . . I stayed out in the corridor.'

'Oh, I'm exactly the same with small spaces,' Seffy said. 'Completely claustrophobic. Always have been since school, when . . . well, anyway.' She turned back to the list.

'We're still missing one. "Miss A Buchanan." Was she at the mustering point in Aberdeen?'

The girls shook their heads dolefully. No one knew.

'What'll we do?' Seffy asked Joey. 'The train's gone. We'd have spotted her by now, if she'd got off. Wait much longer and we'll be late for lunch.'

'Let's head off,' Joey said. 'We don't want to miss out on our grub, do we, girls?'

A chorus of 'Noo!' rang out.

The skinny wee Tattie – who looked like she could do with feeding up – said it loudest of all.

Joey asked Seffy if she wouldn't mind driving the truck back to camp.

It was humid and she was so tired, she thought she might fall asleep at the wheel.

She didn't want to put the lorry into a ditch, with their precious cargo of new recruits on board.

As they set off, she yawned loudly.

'Keeping you up, are we?' Seffy teased.

'I didn't sleep well last night.'

'Yes, it's getting warmer. We might end up having to sleep outside at this rate.'

But it wasn't the heat: it was the dreams. She woke from them

24

with a jolt, her whole body bathed in sweat. Then, no matter how many sheep she tried counting, she never got back to sleep until it was almost time to get up.

Seffy was humming a few bars of a tune. 'I don't think we need worry about this lot,' she said.

'What do you mean, worry?'

'That any of them will be . . . I don't know, a threat. The tall one used to be a hairdresser! Imagine! Mind you, that could be handy for a quick shampoo and set. But none of them has experience of forestry. I asked.'

Joey smiled. Seffy fretted about the queerest things.

She wound down the window to let some air in. 'Do you think we'll be allowed to choose the two for our hut?'

Seffy laughed. 'Like games lessons at school when you had to pick teams?'

'Aw, God, I hated that. I always felt sorry for the lassies who got left to the end. The chubbies or the clumsy ones.'

'That was me,' Seffy said. 'Not chubby but definitely clumsy. They called me "Butterfingers".'

'Whenever I was captain, I always picked those girls first. The not-so-good ones. It drove everyone crackers. We always lost, of course, but I didnae mind. I'd have picked you, Butterfingers!'

Seffy frowned. 'That's not why you picked me today, is it? Because you felt sorry for me?'

'No, you daft Sassenach! I picked you because you're the only one, apart from me, who can drive this beast. And,' she added, quickly, 'because I couldn't think of anyone else I'd rather spend time with.'

'Aw, that's nice. Regarding the new girls, I wish we could pick, but you know Miss McEwen, she's far too unreasonable to let us do that!'

There was something – or rather, someone – on the road ahead. Joey frowned and peered through the windscreen.

'Can you see that fella? Running along the side of the road?'

'Yes. We'll stop and give him a lift, shall we?'

They soon caught him up. Seffy drew alongside and slowed the truck to a crawl.

It was a soldier in khaki uniform, loaded up with a knapsack, from which a pair of boots were swinging by their laces. He kept glancing down at a compass in his hand.

Joey leaned out of the window and felt the breeze lift her hair.

'You'll gi' yourself heatstroke, running in this!' she yelled. 'Where're you heading? Jump in the back and we'll gi' you a lift. It's full of lassies from the city though, I'll warn you now!'

She laughed and waited for the fella's eyes to light up. That was an invitation no man could resist, surely?

But he didn't reply. He didn't even look at her.

His face was shiny, there were beads of sweat on his forehead and a hint of five-o'clock shadow on his jaw. There was no denying, he was bonny. Rude, but bonny with it.

'No, thanks,' he said, continuing to pound up the road.

What? Was he turning them down?

Joey turned to Seffy. 'He says no.'

Seffy shrugged and started to accelerate.

'No, wait! He's mebbe shy!'

Joey put her head out again. This was fun; shame the fella had no sense of humour.

'Last chance. Do you want a lift or no'?'

'NO!'

'Aw, come on. We don't bite! Well, most of us. We won't even charge you!'

He continued to stare straight ahead and shook his head; his mouth was firmly set. He had a scar on his right cheek.

'Now look!' Joey said. 'It's starting to rain.'

It was true: even though the sky was still blue, a light shower had suddenly come from nowhere. She could feel the droplets on the back of her hand. Good job they'd got the cover on the truck, else the city lassies would be getting wet.

26

The soldier made a shooing motion. 'Drive on!'

'You may as well put your foot down,' she told Seffy. 'I reckon he's worried we'll kidnap him!'

As Seffy accelerated and the truck pulled away, Joey turned and waved at the fella.

'See you!' she called, wishing she could think of summat wittier to say.

She pulled her head back in and watched him getting ever smaller in the wing mirror.

'There's no pleasing some people,' Seffy said.

Seffy wasn't troubled by his refusal to join them but then, she hadn't seen the fella properly. Joey had been close enough to hear his heavy breathing and the rhythmic slap of his boots and to feel a stirring of something she hadn't felt for a long time; not even when those good-looking Canadians had been around.

She wouldn't even have minded if he'd wanted to squash up here on the front seat with her, sweat an' all.

'What are you smirking about?' Seffy asked.

Joey gestured at the wing mirror.

'Him! He's so cross! Pardon us for trying to help! Now he's wavin'! No – ha! I think maybe he's shaking his fist! What do you think of that?'

But Seffy wasn't listening. The rain was getting heavier now, splattering onto the windscreen. She had to lean forward and strain her eyes to see the road ahead.

'I'm glad it's raining,' Joey said. 'Let's pray for a proper downpour so he gets completely drookit! It'll serve him right, the miserable sod!'

She was laughing but she felt strangely – stupidly – disappointed.

Chapter 5

Tattie sat apart from the other recruits, near the tailgate of the truck, which was open to the elements.

No one had spoken to her since they'd climbed aboard. No matter – she didn't want to talk to them either.

The girls who'd met them at the station – the blonde English lass and the smaller dark-haired one with dimples – were nice, though.

She'd watched as they'd come down onto the platform. They were so pretty, they looked like girls on recruitment posters.

The dark one – Joey – had said something that had made the blonde one pretend to smack her. They'd been laughing so hard it'd made Tattie smile.

She couldn't imagine being pals like that with any of these girls. They'd looked down their noses at her from the moment she'd joined them on the platform.

Their chatter swirled around her. They were talking about how they'd enlisted.

'I went to the Labour Exchange, saw a poster for the Women's Timber Corps and liked the look of it!'

'I wanted to join the WAAF but I was six months too young to enlist and I couldn't bear to wait, so I chose this instead.'

'Gosh, the WAAF!' another girl said. 'What would you have done there?'

'Packed the parachutes, I expect, or armed the guns on the planes.'

Tattie put her head down and hoped no one would ask her. She didn't have a fancy story to tell. She'd wanted to get away from the city and she'd liked the idea of working in the woods. That was it.

When she was wee, Ma used to tell her fairy tales at bedtime. Not from a book because they didn't have books: Ma knew the stories off by heart.

There was always a wood or a forest in the story and kind woodsmen, princes who rescued maidens and trees, bigger than buildings. She'd never been in a forest, but she liked the sound of them.

Ma cleaned at a big house on the other side of town. She'd asked the housekeeper to help them with the enrolment form, so that Tattie could get away and do her bit.

They'd sat in the warm kitchen and the woman had carefully written down everything it asked for.

'"Current occupation"?'

Tattie and Ma had exchanged anxious glances.

'Put, she's been helping me with the bairns,' Ma had said.

The housekeeper had pursed her lips and written it down.

At the interview, Tattie's heart had been in her mouth, in case the housekeeper had written something like, *Don't take her on, not if she's the last lassie in Scotland!*

They'd asked what she'd been doing up to now and Tattie had lied about helping her ma with the weans.

'Now they've been evacuated, I'm at a loose end,' she'd said.

They'd looked doubtful – folk always did – so she'd added, 'I'm a grafter. I know I'm wee but I'm strong and I dunnae mind what I do.'

It'd been all right; she'd been accepted.

She stared out at the passing scenery, relieved to breathe fresh air after so long in that stuffy luggage van.

So, this was the Highlands. She'd heard of it, of course – Bonnie Prince Charlie country – but she'd never been here before. She supposed it was pretty but there was too much space. If enemy planes came, there'd be nowhere to hide.

It had started to rain and a mist was covering the distant hills. Were those patches of dark green the trees? She hoped they wouldn't have to climb a hill every day, to reach them. She'd be worn out before she started.

Suddenly, the truck slowed down, and the girls stopped talking and wondered what was happening.

They could hear someone shouting at the front, but they couldn't make out the words.

The girl who'd almost joined the WAAF stood up and tried to peer through the window into the cab. Suddenly the truck lurched forward and she almost landed on top of the others, which caused much laughter and shrieking.

When Tattie looked out at the road again she saw the officer from the railway station: William Wallace. He was pelting along, loaded up with his kit, looking grim and determined.

She went to wave at him but stopped herself.

'Oh, look! I think they were offering him a lift, but he must've refused,' one of the girls said.

'Too bad!'

'Yes, more's the pity!'

They laughed, someone whistled and they all cheered and whooped.

The officer appeared to lift his hand to them but whether it was a friendly wave or something else, it was hard to tell.

Thank God he'd said no. Imagine if he'd got into the truck and recognised her? Tattie's stomach flipped over at the thought.

Aw, the shame of being thought a laddie, in front of all these snooty types.

The truck was bouncing along the road now, picking up speed.

Tattie kept her eyes fixed on the officer. What had he called himself? Major something or other.

He was William Wallace to her.

She watched, until he was nothing but a dot on the horizon and then the truck hurtled round a bend and he was gone.

Chapter 6

'What's going on?' Seffy asked.

She was standing in the doorway of Macdonald hut, which had been completely rearranged.

'It was dry when we started,' Enid said, 'but the moment we put the last bed out, it started chuckin' it down!'

Jean pushed her glasses up her nose. 'It was my idea, because of the new girls. I thought we should rearrange things, so that no one was sleeping in . . . the empty beds. We carried them outside and moved them around, so no one knew which was which.'

They'd gone about it in a queer way but Seffy supposed it wasn't a bad idea. It meant no one was seen to be taking Irene or Hazel's place.

Poor Hazel had died and her bed had been left pristine, almost like a shrine, since that terrible day.

Seffy would keep her fingers crossed that she didn't end up in a bed next to Grace, though.

She turned at the sound of footsteps. It was Joey, with one of the new recruits.

'Everyone, this is Tattie,' Joey said.

It was the thin, ragamuffin girl in the dungarees. Her arms were full of the Timber Corps clothes with which she'd just been issued.

'Put those things down on that chair for now,' Seffy said. 'You've drawn the lucky straw because Macdonald is the best hut!'

'Aye, come on in,' Jean said, 'and let's get you settled. We're about to draw lots for the beds.'

'Though we can't promise yours won't be slightly damp,' Seffy said.

'"Tattie"?' Enid said. 'What kind of name is that? Is it Gaelic?'

'Is it short for Tatiana?' Morag asked.

'It's . . . it's a nickname,' Tattie said. 'My real name's Kath. Kathleen Edwards.'

'Ah!' Jean said. 'That's the key to it. King Edwards is a type of potato, hence "Tattie". Is it Aberdeen you're from? They call it "Siren City", don't they? You've had it bad there.'

The girl looked surprised. 'I suppose we have.'

'But none of the cities have escaped,' Grace said. 'They've all taken a battering.'

'Aye but Aberdeen's had it worst. All those granite buildings, glinting in the moonlight, show themselves to the bombers,' Jean said.

'You know it, then? Aberdeen?' Tattie asked, shyly.

'Och, no. Never been there in my life. I read about it in the newspaper,' Jean replied.

'She reads everything in the newspaper,' Morag said. 'Look!' She pointed to the cutting on the wall. 'She even pins them up!'

Seffy sighed. That blasted newspaper article. As if it wasn't enough for Grace to get her man and have a lovely wedding, now she was practically a pin-up girl, with her picture on the front of the local rag.

When the journalist and photographer had arrived from *The Courier*, for a feature on the lumberjills, they'd barely spoken to anyone else. It was Grace's story they were interested in, Grace's photograph they'd wanted to take. It had all been most tiresome.

'We'll have to move that now,' Seffy said, waving vaguely at the wall.

Grace bit her lip and turned pink.

'Have I done something to upset you, Seffy?' she asked, quietly.

'Don't be silly!' Seffy said. 'But it's your picture. I thought you'd want it above your new bed. To be frank, I don't think the wall's the best place for it, in any case. It'll fade in the sun and . . .'

Her words dried up.

'It wasn't actually Grace who put it up,' Jean said, tartly. 'I bought two copies of the paper. One for Grace's scrapbook and I put the other cutting up there. But if you don't think—'

'No, no. Leave it. It's fine. I was only thinking of . . . Grace,' Seffy said.

There was an awkward silence.

Then Seffy asked brightly, 'Say, aren't we supposed to have two new girls in here with us? Who's the other one?'

'It's the missing recruit: "Miss A Buchanan",' Joey said. 'If you're drawing lots, Jean, put her name in the hat, just in case. I was expecting Miss McEwen to scream blue murder when we were one girl down but she simply said, "Miss Buchanan will turn up in her own good time." Mind you, she was busy at the time, sorting uniforms and giving the recruits the pep talk.'

'Pep talk?' Enid said.

'You know,' Joey said. 'We all had it, on our first day.' She said it slowly, encouraging them with rapid movements of her hand.

'You're a task force, you're soldiers of the forest—'

'—you're the LUMBERJILLS!' everyone yelled.

That night, as Seffy lay in her new bed, she breathed a sigh of relief that she hadn't been put next to Grace.

Oh, she was a nasty person, permanently tense and crotchety these days. When she thought about Grace's situation or heard her talk about her wonderful husband, she got a horrible twisting sensation in her chest.

Surely, it would pass soon, like a head cold. She simply had to get over it, come out the other side and hopefully everything would be as it used to be.

Seffy's new bed was at the top of the hut. She had Morag on one side and an empty bed on the other. If the Buchanan girl didn't turn up and the bed remained unoccupied, Seffy would have more room for the clothes that were currently crammed into her suitcase.

Fingers crossed that "A Buchanan" had been held up permanently or that she'd decided the Women's Timber Corps was not for her.

Chapter 7

On Monday afternoon, Seffy and a group of other lumberjills were trudging back wearily to their huts. It was quite a trek to reach their felling sites these days: they'd cleared all the trees in the vicinity of the camp. Soon, they'd have to start using the truck to get to and from work.

The sound of a lorry pulling up on the road outside the camp stopped them in their tracks.

'It's the Tallies!' someone yelled.

'The what?' Flora asked.

'Italian POWs,' Seffy said, wondering if Flora walked around with her eyes and ears closed. 'Perhaps their lorry's broken down. Come on, let's go and see!'

The girls were used to trucks shooting past, transporting prisoners to and from the fields in which they worked. The Italian boys invariably hanging out of the back, catcalling, were unmistakeable in their brown uniforms, covered in large red circles, which according to Morag, were "targets, for shootin' them, if they try to escape".

But one of their lorries had never stopped at the camp before.

The girls scampered through the woods and onto the road, suddenly no longer tired.

They were just in time to see a petite, dark-haired girl

lowering herself backwards down the steps of the cab. She was wearing slacks and a short-sleeved shirt; there was a cigarette dangling precariously from her lips.

Seffy felt an instant twist of dislike.

The stranger glanced around, removed the cigarette and flashed the lumberjills a smile.

'I think I might hate her,' Seffy muttered to Joey, who'd just caught them up.

'Aw, gi' the lass a chance! She's probably nice enough.'

Joey always saw the best in people. But if this was who Seffy thought it was, she sensed trouble ahead.

'Who's that?' Grace asked, folding her arms.

'I assume it's the girl who didn't turn up on Saturday,' Seffy said. 'She's awfully late. She's blotted her copybook before she's even started.'

Grace nodded. 'She's not shy, neither.'

The girl had jumped down neatly onto the ground. She was holding her cigarette aloft and calling up to the driver and his mate, presumably thanking them for the lift. They passed her bag down and she hoisted it effortlessly onto her shoulder.

She sauntered round to the back of the truck.

'Why's she going that way?' Grace asked.

The more direct route would've been to walk around the front of the vehicle.

'Because,' Seffy said, 'otherwise, she'd have disappointed her fans.'

When she appeared, the POWs erupted into cheers. She waved back at them, stretching her arm up and wiggling her fingers one at a time, looking for all the world like a film star on the red carpet.

They called out to her in Italian and one of them clutched his chest theatrically.

Seffy had to admit the girl had a certain something. Her nose was a little large and her chin, if one were being particular, was rather pointy, but Seffy had known girls like this before: not classically beautiful but the sort who seemed to send chaps into raptures.

'I wonder what they're saying,' Enid mused. 'They've certainly taken a shine to her!'

Morag sniffed. 'Those fellas'll take a shine to anyone.'

The thud of heavy footsteps came from behind and, as she glanced around, Seffy's heart lifted – for probably the first time – at the sight of Miss McEwen. She was marching towards them, stern-faced. The new recruits, including Tattie, were following close behind.

The girl turned towards Miss McEwen with a smile.

'Right, let's see what the old dragon has to say to this,' Seffy whispered to Joey.

They giggled and waited for the dressing-down that was sure to come.

'Ah, you're here at last. Welcome to Blantyre Forest!' Miss McEwen said.

The girls stared at one another in surprise.

'I don't believe it. She's all sweetness and light!' Joey muttered.

Miss McEwen had spoken in such a familiar tone, it was almost as though she and this new girl were already acquainted.

'Huge apologies, Miss M!' the girl said, cheerfully. 'I couldn't get away on Saturday. Problem in the camp.'

'Aw, don't fret,' Miss McEwen said. 'You're here now.'

She turned to the group of lumberjills.

'This, is Miss Buchanan.'

She couldn't have sounded any prouder if she'd been introducing Princess Elizabeth herself.

'She's clucking round her like a wee mother hen!' Joey said.

'Miss Buchanan is an experienced lumberjill and forewoman who's joining us from a camp in Aberdeenshire. We're extremely fortunate to have her.'

Some of the girls clapped.

Seffy rolled her eyes at Joey.

'Creeps,' she whispered. Miss McEwen's words were ringing in her ears: "experienced lumberjill and forewoman".

She had a bad feeling about this.

'I am ALSO,' Miss McEwen said, 'making her the new leader girl of Stevenson hut with immediate effect!' She shot a triumphant look in Seffy's direction. 'Replacing Miss Mills.'

What? Ouch! That was a blow. Seffy rocked slightly on her feet, as though she'd been hit.

But, hold on, that didn't make sense. Their hut hadn't been called "Stevenson" for yonks. Seffy was confused and judging from the other girls' frowns, she wasn't alone. Was she being replaced by this new girl, or not?

'But Seffy's our leader girl,' Flora said, pouting.

'Forewomen are chosen on merit, based on skills and experience,' Miss McEwen said. 'I decide on the leader girl for each hut and Miss Mills is a long way down ma list!'

'But you can't demote her, just like that!' Enid said.

Miss McEwen pursed her lips. 'I am not demoting her! She was never promoted in the first place. You've been "acting leader girl", Miss Mills, but now it's time for a proper leader girl to take over.'

Seffy had a hard lump in her throat.

"A *proper* leader girl"? As opposed to what? Someone who'd only been play-acting? That stung.

Everyone was staring. Seffy concentrated on keeping her face blank. She wouldn't give Miss McEwen – or, indeed, this newcomer – the satisfaction of seeing her crushing disappointment.

She watched Miss Buchanan for any sign of surprise at the announcement, but there was only that silly smirk. She already knew! This must have all been agreed before today.

Joey nudged her. 'Don't sulk, Seffy, whatever you do. I can see your bottom lip starting to go.'

'Bad luck,' Grace muttered.

'Thank you,' Seffy replied. She felt a stab of shame. She'd been so cold to Grace recently and yet she'd been the first to offer her commiserations.

Jean was waving madly from the back of the group. Perhaps

she was going to lead a rebellion and threaten that if Seffy wasn't kept on, they'd all strike?

'Miss McEwen? Miss Buchanan can't be leader girl in Stevenson hut!' she said.

There! Good old Jean, the brightest and bravest of all her colleagues.

Miss McEwen scowled. 'And can you give me one good reason why not?'

Seffy held her breath.

'Because we actually changed the name, a while back. It's "Macdonald" now.'

Seffy exhaled. So much for a rebellion.

Miss McEwen rolled her eyes. 'Well, I don't know—'

Miss Buchanan interrupted. 'I have to agree that Macdonald is a better name. I'm guessing you chose Macdonald in honour of Flora Macdonald. Am I right?'

'Aye!' Joey called out. 'We did! And it was my idea!'

They smiled at each other.

Et tu, Josephine. Goodness, even her pal was siding with the newcomer.

Miss McEwen waved her hand dismissively. 'Very well, the name can stay.'

'And talking of names, I'm Angie, by the way,' the new girl said.

Goodness, she was like a Cheshire cat. Did she ever stop smirking?

Miss McEwen made a shooing motion at the crowd of girls. 'Come along, you lot, it'll soon be suppertime. Time for a wash and brush-up.'

The lumberjills from the other huts gradually drifted away but the Macdonald girls stayed put.

The truck was moving off now, with a few jolly toots of the horn.

The Italians were hanging out of the back, clambering over one another, blowing kisses and shouting. It was probably a good thing, Seffy thought, that no one could understand them.

Angie gave them a final wave.

'There was no one to meet me at the railway station,' she said, 'so I thumbed a lift with them.'

Seffy's chest tightened. Of course there'd been no one there to meet her: no one had been expecting her!

'You hitched a lift? Most resourceful!' Miss McEwen said.

Seffy and Joey rolled their eyes at each other. *They'd* been warned about the dangers of hitch-hiking, but when Angie Buchanan did it she was apparently being "resourceful".

'Now, come along,' Miss McEwen said. 'Do you have your bag? I'll show you to your accommodation.'

Once Miss McEwen had delivered Angie to the hut and left them alone, Seffy spoke to the new girl for the first time. She was still smarting from losing her position as forewoman and it was a struggle to keep her voice neutral.

'We were expecting you on Saturday. Miss Wallace over there and I drove to the station, to pick you up.'

'Sorry if I put you out, Miss Wallace,' Angie said, pleasantly.

Seffy's mouth dropped open. What about her? Clearly, she didn't merit an apology.

'Aw, nae bother,' Joey said. 'And please, it's Joey.'

Angie was perched on her newly allocated bed, next to Seffy's. And, she was still smoking.

'Actually, do you mind?' Seffy said. 'We don't allow smoking in here. It makes the place smell.'

'Och, I think it's all right, Seffy,' Jean said, quickly. 'All the windows are open, after all.'

Angie smiled. 'I simply couldn't come on Saturday. And there was no time to send a telegram so . . .' She shrugged. 'I had every intention of catching that train but I wasn't able to leave.' She paused. 'It was actually a matter of life or death.'

'Never!' Enid said. She skipped across the hut and threw herself down on Angie's bed. 'What happened?'

'Yes! Tell us!' Flora said.

Everyone's gaze was fixed on the new girl. She certainly had the knack of making herself the centre of attention.

'One of the girls – dear Rosemary—' Angie smiled fondly '—was so distraught at the thought of my leaving, that—' She closed her eyes and shook her head.

'And what? You can't stop the story there!' Joey said.

A "story", that was precisely what it was. But despite herself, Seffy couldn't march off to the washroom now and miss the ending. She wanted to find out what "dear Rosemary" had done, almost as much as anyone else.

Angie lowered her voice so that the girls had to move closer to hear.

'Rosemary said, if I left, she'd do herself in!'

Everyone, except Seffy, gasped.

'How?' Grace asked. 'I mean, how was she going to do it?'

At least Grace sounded the tiniest bit sceptical. The others were lapping it up.

Angie shrugged. 'Throw herself off the bridge, drown herself in the burn, who knows?'

'Och, that's terrible!' Enid said. 'Of course, you couldn't simply up and leave.'

'No, I had to dissuade her from doing anything so silly. I told her we'd keep in touch; I promised to write, that kind of thing.'

'And will you?' Tattie asked. She'd hardly said two words since she'd arrived but she seemed as entranced with Angie as everyone else. 'Will you write?'

'Of course! I never break a promise. But I know Rosemary's going to be all right. I have a feeling for these things.'

Honestly! Now the girl was claiming to have some kind of "sixth sense".

Seffy yawned and grabbed her towel. She couldn't bear to hear another word. The girl hadn't been able to leave her old camp because someone had a pash on her and had threatened to top herself? Pull the other one, as Father liked to say.

Before she slipped out to take a shower, Seffy stood in the doorway and glanced back, hoping to exchange an eye roll or a shake of the head with someone. Surely she couldn't be the only one who had their doubts about Angie Buchanan? But no one was looking in her direction. Even Morag was smiling at Angie, as they all chatted away to her.

They'd accepted her, as a new member of the dorm and, apparently, as their leader girl, too.

Apart from Grace, who'd said it was "too bad", no one had said anything about her demotion or that they thought Seffy should still be in charge. She might as well be invisible.

Gosh, this was grim. How had she so suddenly become *persona non grata*?

It reminded her of when she'd first arrived. She'd stood out as the only non-Scot and she'd had to try awfully hard to win the girls over. She'd jolly well done it, too.

But now, it was almost as though none of that had happened.

It was like being in a game of snakes and ladders. She'd scaled the ladder to get to a certain point, made friends and become a good leader but suddenly, everything had changed.

She'd thrown the dice, landed on a snake and slithered right down to the start again.

Chapter 8

Tattie's first morning as a lumberjill got off to a slow start.

She'd expected to be heaving logs and learning to saw, but instead, she and the other recruits had to sit on tree stumps and listen to Miss McEwen blethering on.

Tattie sat at the back, as the supervisor talked about the history of the corps and other borin' stuff.

The other lassies were straight-backed and attentive. A couple of them were taking notes. And when Miss McEwen talked about "a patriotic calling" they all nodded, as though they knew exactly what she meant.

As the supervisor's voice became a distant drone, like a midge buzzing round her ear, Tattie sighed and gazed around.

A wee bird was flitting about, darting from tree to tree. It was watching her from a branch a few inches away, with black, beady eyes.

'That there's a robin.'

The man's quiet voice had come from behind. It must be Mr Brennan, the foreman – Jock, they'd been told to call him. He was a grizzled old chap with a beard. He'd been waiting in the clearing when Miss McEwen had shepherded them here after breakfast.

Tattie nodded. She didn't know many birds' names, but she knew this one.

'Bonny enough, those wee fellas, aren't they? Aw, but they can be vicious. They'll fight one another to the death.'

The robin was tilting its tiny head. It was hard to believe something so dainty – its legs were like wee sticks – could be a killer.

'What do they fight about?' Tattie asked, curiosity overcoming her shyness.

'Territory, food, women! Isn't that what fights are always about?'

'And NOW!' Miss McEwen said. 'Your foreman will explain how to identify trees by their leaves and bark! To the front, please, Jock! The stage is yours!'

After a few minutes, Tattie's head was spinning. This was like school. She hoped there wasn't going to be a test at the end because she wouldn't be able to do it.

'Don't take on so, hen!'

Jock had paused, holding up a piece of bark. He was looking straight at her. She must look as worried as she felt.

'I promise,' he said, 'it'll soon start to make sense. And when we're finished with the theory, you'll be let loose with the axes!'

Tattie smiled. That was more like it.

'Your axe is your best friend out here,' Jock continued. 'Some of the girls have a favourite. They even give them names!'

'It's all very Anglo Saxon,' Miss McEwen said. 'It's true. Anglo Saxon warriors used to name their swords. They inscribed the name on the hilt or the blade.'

Tattie sat up. She liked tales of fighting and derring-do. She wondered what kinds of names the swords had. She wished Miss McEwen would say more: it was the most interesting thing the woman had said all day.

But the mention of axes had sent the other recruits into a tizzy.

Two of them were talking about Jock.

'Have you seen his hand? He's missing two fingers in the middle!'

'Probably chopped them off in an accident—'

'—with an axe!'

Honest to God, surely they knew they'd be working with sharp tools? Had they expected to use nail files or a pair o' scissors for felling trees?

Tattie had noticed Jock's hand straight away and hadn't given it another thought. She'd seen worse.

But although the work wasn't what she'd hoped for – at least, not yet – the other parts of being a lumberjill were good.

The food, for one thing. The others grumbled that it was too greasy, too dry or that the portions were too small, but she had no complaints.

And it was a treat to have a bed all to herself, even if it had been out in the rain before she arrived.

Then, there was the view. When she tugged back the blackout curtain in the mornings, she could see mist-covered mountains from her bed.

It was peaceful, too. There were no raids here – no wailing sirens, bangs or heart-stopping explosions; she didn't have to traipse outside to the shelter at midnight. At night, apart from the shrieks of creatures and birds, there was silence.

If only she could write and tell Ma everything and let her know she was all right. Mebbe she'd get the chance, one of these days. But not yet.

At morning break, everyone was reunited: the felling and dragging teams, the measurers and the new recruits sat together around the campfire, clutching their brews.

Jock was having a right old laugh and when Joey commented on his good mood, he looked bashful.

'Aye. To tell the truth, I'm celebrating! Ma daughter – ma wee Jennie – had another bairn last night. My first grandson!'

Everyone cheered and several of the girls slapped him hard on the back, until he yelled for mercy.

46

'Well, hearty congratulations from the Timber Corps, Grandpa Jock,' Seffy said. 'Does the little chap have a name yet?'

Tattie listened to Seffy in awe. She was so sure of herself.

Tattie could no more stand up in front of all these people and speak like that, than fly to the moon.

'Aye, he does. They've called him wee Jock, after me.'

There were yet more cheers and cups of tea were raised to toast the new arrival. Tattie smiled at all the happy faces.

Despite the snooty recruits and the boring lessons and the hard graft to come, she was glad she was here.

Later that day, as they followed Miss McEwen back to their huts, things got even better.

The missing girl – Angie Buchanan – had arrived and Tattie's heart had lifted: she wasn't the only new recruit in Macdonald hut anymore.

Angie seemed nice, which was a good thing because she had the bed next to Tattie's.

'You're new too, aren't you?' Angie asked, as she unpacked her things before supper. 'We can help one another out. What do you say? Shall we look out for one another?'

Tattie was so happy she couldn't speak. She nodded.

Angie smiled. 'Was today your first day as a lumberjill?'

'Aye.'

'Are you aching yet? Those boots are rock hard, aren't they? They take a bit of breaking in. Whatever you do, don't pop your blisters! Here, give me your hands.'

Tattie held them out, wincing as she noticed her nails could be cleaner.

'It's difficult to get all the dirt out, I know. I'll give you a tip—' Angie raised her voice '—a tip for all of you! Don't dig under your nails with a file: you'll only push the dirt further down. I soak my hands in *Steradent* once a week.'

'Gosh, do you?' Jean said. 'Any good?'

'I'll let you have some. It whitens and brightens. Look!'

Angie held out her own hands and the other girls came over to admire them.

Only Seffy didn't seem interested. She was lying on her bed on the other side of Angie's.

'*Steradent*?' she said. 'Isn't that for cleaning dentures?'

'Aye, it is,' Joey said. 'My grandpa soaks his falsies in the stuff every night.'

Angie laughed. 'Do I look like someone who needs dentures?' she said.

'No,' Tattie said. 'You've lovely gnashers.'

'Thank you, Tattie,' Angie said. 'Later, you're going to have the first – and biggest – slice of carrot cake.'

'Carrot cake?' Enid asked.

'I've brought one with me. My nana made it,' Angie said. 'I kept it hidden from the girls in my last billet. They'd have devoured it like a swarm of locusts!'

After supper, when the cake was divided up, everyone agreed it was all the more delicious for being saved especially for them.

Seffy didn't have any. Nor one of the barley sugars, which Angie passed around.

'No thanks,' she said, patting her stomach. 'I'm watching my figure!'

Which was a daft thing to say because the girl was as slim as a pencil.

It was clear she was in a sulk and didn't want to accept anything from Angie. It was mean to be so off with her, even if – as Jean explained later – Seffy was upset because she'd lost her position as leader of the hut.

It was hardly Angie's fault.

Seffy was nice, though – especially for an English lassie – and Tattie was sure she'd soon come round. Angie Buchanan was so friendly and kind; it was impossible not to like her.

Chapter 9

When Joey and Seffy returned to the hut a couple of evenings later, there was a throng of girls around Angie's bed.

Angie was sitting next to Belinda from Carlyle hut, who was currently part of the Macdonald felling gang. She was bent over Belinda's hand.

'Has she got a wee skelf?' Joey asked. 'I've got a needle somewhere if you need it.'

'I think you'll find the proper name for those is "splinters",' Seffy said.

It was a game they played: Scots words versus English. As Seffy was outnumbered, the Scottish – as the others would say, the *correct* version – usually won.

'It's not a skelf,' Grace said. She was sitting cross-legged on her bed, writing a letter. 'She's reading Belinda's palm.'

Joey laughed. 'You're joking? Angie's telling fortunes?'

'For goodness' sake!' Seffy muttered. 'The girl's a witch!'

'Shh!' Enid said. 'We can't hear a word, thanks to the racket you lot are making!'

Admonished, Joey and Seffy quickly sat down on the bed, beside Grace.

'Did you no' see her reading Flora's tea leaves in the break today?'

49

Grace whispered. 'Angie told her she's going to meet some "tall men in the forest".'

'Was Flora petrified?' Seffy asked.

'No! She thinks it means the Canucks are coming back. Word's getting round and everyone wants Angie to read their hand. I'm stayin' well out of it.' Grace shuddered. 'My ma would say it's the work of the devil.'

A burst of applause came from Angie's bed, as she finished telling Belinda's fortune. The girls who'd been watching broke into excited chatter.

'Angie's a strange one,' Seffy mused. 'I wonder what made her transfer here.'

Joey tutted. 'Och, you're so suspicious! Mebbe she wanted a change of scene?'

'Aye,' Grace said. 'After all, a change is as good as a rest. You've said so yourself, Seffy.'

Ouch. Those were the words Seffy had used when she'd changed the pairings around. Grace was clearly still smarting.

'Or perhaps she wanted a promotion?' Joey said.

Seffy shook her head. Miss McEwen had called Angie an "experienced lumberjill and forewoman" so she must've already been a leader girl. There had to be another reason for moving camps.

'Belinda looks happy enough,' Joey said. 'What's the harm in it, after all? It's a good way of passing the time.'

'I suppose so,' Seffy said, with a shrug. 'And I expect the novelty will wear off soon enough.'

'I dare say,' Grace said. 'But only once she's run out of girls.'

'Anyone else?' Angie asked, holding up a pack of cards. 'Tarot, anyone? Tattie, how about you?'

Tattie shook her head.

'Perhaps she's got summat to hide,' Morag said, making the poor thing blush scarlet.

'Highly recommended!' Belinda trilled, on her way out. 'She's awful good!'

'Awfully good at making things up,' Seffy said. It was no good; try as she might, she couldn't keep quiet. The whole charade was ridiculous.

'Do we have to cross your palm with silver?' Joey said. 'Because I only have sixpence to last me all week!'

'You're not joining in, are you?' Seffy asked.

Joey shrugged. 'Why not? I'm curious. There's no need to look so outraged!'

Seffy laughed. 'I'm hardly outraged. I simply can't believe everyone's falling for it! This wouldn't have anything to do with that soldier from the other day, would it?' She nudged Joey. 'Admit it: you want to know if you're going to run into him again!'

Joey could protest all she liked but she'd mentioned the chap several times since their encounter on Saturday and that could only mean one thing: she liked him.

Angie was patting the space on the bed next to her. 'No charge! Come on, Joey!'

She shuffled the cards as Joey sat down.

'Now, mind you don't give anything away,' Seffy said. 'Don't say "aye" or shake your head. That's how she gets her information! It's a kind of trickery. It'll be so general, it could apply to anyone. You'll see.'

Angie raised her eyebrows at Seffy. 'Who's rattled your cage? I bet you read your horoscope, don't you? There's no real difference. What star sign are you?'

'If you're so "all-seeing",' Seffy said, 'I'd have thought you could tell me yourself!'

The others cheered, enjoying the sparring.

Angie was smiling too, as though it were all one big joke, but the smile hadn't reached her eyes and there was a tightness around her mouth.

'I'll tell you mine,' Angie said. 'I'm a Leo. A fire sign. Leos are natural leaders.'

So, those were her credentials for being leader girl? The fact that she was born under the sign of Leo! Honestly, why couldn't anyone else see how utterly ridiculous she was?

'I'm not sure what I am,' Flora said, mournfully. 'I'm either the one with the scales or something else. I'm in the middle.'

'On the cusp,' Angie said, nodding absent-mindedly. 'I'd need to do your chart to tell you for sure.' She turned back to Seffy. 'Well, what's your star sign?'

'My birthday's September the nineteenth.'

'Ah, Virgo.'

Seffy felt another flash of irritation: Angie was right.

'Yes, but I don't believe in any of it. So, you may as well save your breath.'

'The Virgo woman,' Angie said, 'is stubborn, hot-headed and highly critical.'

Morag gave a long, low whistle. 'I'd say that's not far off the mark!'

Seffy's mouth dropped open. Was that what they really thought of her?

'Aw, take no notice,' Joey said. 'They're only teasing.'

'Yes, don't take on so!' Angie said. 'You got out of bed the wrong side today, for sure. I bet it's trouble with a fella. It always is! I'll read your cards next and tell you if it's going to work out.'

'Don't trouble yourself!' Seffy said. Even to her own ears, she sounded prim. 'I don't believe in dabbling in the occult.'

Everyone laughed.

'It's only a bit of fun,' Enid said. 'Are we no' to have any fun anymore?'

Seffy shrugged. 'Do what you like but don't expect me to join in. It's complete poppycock!'

Joey was still waiting and the girls around the bed watched, as Angie cut the cards and turned the first one over.

'You're missing someone,' she said.

'Ridiculous!' Seffy said. 'We're all missing someone!'

Grace murmured her agreement but no one else was listening. They were all watching Angie.

The next card was cut and Angie made a few vague comments that had Seffy rolling her eyes and tutting.

But when the final card was turned over and Angie said, 'But you're not sure about the weans, are you?' Joey gave a visible jolt of surprise.

'That meant something, am I right?' Angie asked.

'Aye, it did! Tell us!' Flora said.

But Joey remained tight-lipped. She managed to thank Angie in a small voice, before returning to Grace and Seffy. She looked shaken.

'Did you hear?' she whispered to Seffy. 'About the bairns? She hit the nail on the head there. Remember I told you about the weans in Forres and how I wasnae ready to be their mother? How did she know? Maybe she really does have the gift?'

Angie had overheard. She looked like the cat that had got the cream.

'I do have the gift. My nana—' She stopped and shook her head. 'Sorry, I find it hard to talk about her. She's no longer with us. Summat horrible happened and she never got over the shock.'

Seffy turned away, anticipating another of Angie's stories. But after accepting the condolences of the other girls, she only said, 'My nana was the seventh daughter of a seventh daughter. The gift has been passed down through the generations and from her to me.'

'Cor, that's amazin'!' Flora said.

'How did she know?' Joey asked Seffy again.

'Lucky guess! She probably overheard us talking about Jock's new grandson last night.'

Before lights out, they'd all been discussing wee Jock and babies in general. Some of the girls – including Joey – had said they didn't want to think about marriage and children for ages.

'You probably said something that gave her the idea,' Seffy said. 'She's constantly watching and listening, picking up clues. But she got the first part wrong. She said you were "missing someone" but it wasn't "someone", it was a horse!'

That did, at least, raise a smile.

That was twice Angie had mentioned a beloved nana. Seffy wondered how the woman had managed to make such a perfect carrot cake from beyond the grave, but she said nothing. Perhaps Angie called both of her grandmothers nana.

She was going to get a reputation as a meanie, if she wasn't careful. The other girls were aware of her coolness towards Grace and if she kept criticising Angie she was going to make herself unpopular.

'Anyone else?' Angie asked, deftly shuffling the cards.

'Me!' Morag said. 'I'll do it!'

That was a surprise. Morag was highly sceptical of most things.

When the pack had been cut three times, Angie laid out three picture cards on the bed and stared at them.

'There's a man,' she said.

'Oh, for goodness' sake!' Seffy said. 'You said yourself "it's always a fella"!'

The hut was instantly filled with groans.

'Stop spoiling it!' Enid cried.

'Clear off, Seffy, if all you're going to do is mock!' Jean said.

Seffy sighed. Goodness, they were all totally captivated by Angie's supposed mystical powers. Even sensible, clever Jean had been drawn in. And she'd been on the verge of going to university to study maths, until the war had intervened!

'I don't hold with it, either,' Grace said. 'Whatever the future holds, I can wait and find out.'

Seffy knew Grace was thinking of Gordy and when – if – they'd be reunited. The old Seffy would have squeezed Grace's hand or said something reassuring, but she couldn't bring herself to.

Angie was still talking in riddles about Morag's mysterious man.

'You think he's strong but he's weak,' she declared finally, scooping up the cards.

Everyone looked at Morag, expectantly. She frowned.

'That'll be my da,' she said, finally. 'He's about as much use as a glass hammer!'

Everyone laughed and even Seffy had to smile. Oh, maybe she was being an old stick-in-the-mud. Perhaps it really was only a bit of fun.

But the next day, Morag received a letter from her fiancé. He'd met someone else – an ATS girl – and he was breaking off their engagement.

Morag was devastated.

'Angie's prediction's come true!' Flora said, wide-eyed. 'She thought he was strong, but he was weak!'

And despite herself, a shiver ran down Seffy's spine.

Chapter 10

It was Saturday, the day of Lady Lockhart's tea party, and Seffy was about to leave the camp.

She looked longingly at the patch of grass in front of the huts, where off-duty lumberjills were lying in the sunshine, reading magazines, knitting and snoozing.

She wished she could stay here, lolling about like Enid, who was stretched out with a damp flannel on her forehead. Or like Grace, who was sitting in the shade, writing a letter. No prizes for guessing to whom.

When she saw Grace writing to Gordy every day, looking out for the post and sometimes getting a whole stack of letters at once, it made her cross. And empty. Why couldn't that be her? She thought she'd come to terms with saying goodbye to Callum Fraser, but the truth was, she hadn't.

She pulled herself together. No, it was better to be busy. The problem with doing nothing, was that her mind wandered. And it always came back to him. The only solution was to be fully occupied, in mind, body and soul.

Enid looked up at Seffy and yawned. 'I wish I was coming with you.'

'Do you? Honestly, it'll be frightfully dull. It's in honour of Lady Lockhart's second cousin twice removed or something. Polite chit-chat with ladies of a certain age. And Angie Buchanan isn't the only one who can see the future. I can predict exactly what I'll be asked.'

Angie was sitting nearby, with her back to them. She must've heard her name but she didn't look round.

That was fine. Seffy couldn't stand the girl and the feeling, she was sure, was mutual.

After lunch, Seffy had spotted Angie queuing for the shower. She'd had a towel over her arm and had been tapping her foot impatiently. There'd been at least six girls ahead of her.

'Why don't you cool down with a dip in the burn, instead?' Seffy had suggested. 'That's what we do.'

Angie had turned up her nose. 'No thank you! Goodness knows what's in that water!'

Seffy had been about to say it hadn't done the rest of them any harm, but she'd thought better of it. She didn't have the energy for another spat. Let her stand in a queue, then. She'd simply shrugged and walked on.

Joey propped herself up on her elbow. 'Come on then, tell us what the old dears will ask you!'

Seffy hunched her shoulders and put on a croaky Scots accent. '"What does Daddy do? Are ye courting? And where do you stay, dear, when you're not playing around in the woods?"'

Everyone giggled.

'No' bad,' Joey said. 'You've definitely fine-tuned that Scots brogue.'

Seffy bowed and accepted the compliment. It felt nice, to have the girls' attention and to make them laugh.

She glanced around. Tattie had wandered over to sit with Angie and they were talking intently.

Those two had got awfully pally in the past few days. It made sense, as they were both new, but it was still a most unlikely friendship. Angie was confident and poised and she knew her way around an axe and saw. Tattie, on the other hand, was like a scruffy little mouse. She still had a lot to learn about being a lumberjill.

Someone – Seffy suspected Morag – had placed a bar of soap

at the end of Tattie's bed the other night and Seffy had swiped it away before it was spotted. But the message that she needed a wash had been clear.

Perhaps her new chum, Angie, would steer her in the right direction, before there was an embarrassing scene.

'Seffy, will you have to curtsey to the laird?' Flora asked.

'Of course she won't,' Morag said. 'They're not royalty!'

'Ah, but around here the laird and his lady are as good as royalty!' Jean said.

'Aw, that's nothing to Seffy,' Grace said. 'She's been to Blantyre before, am I right?'

Seffy nodded.

Back in April, she'd invited herself and Captain Graham, the Canadians' commanding officer, to Blantyre Castle. Graham had been withholding consent for Gordy and Grace's wedding. Over tea with Lady Lockhart, during which Seffy had bent the truth somewhat, she'd managed to get Graham to change his mind. Without her, Grace mightn't have got married before the company left.

It was ironic, that she'd been instrumental in getting Grace and Gordy together, and now she envied their happiness. She'd never even told Grace what she'd done for her.

'Oh, that last visit was more business than pleasure,' Seffy said. 'And today's not going to be much fun, either. I'd much rather be staying here, with all of you.'

Of course, she didn't mean Grace – or Angie – but she could hardly say: "with *some* of you".

'But I bet her ladyship puts on a good spread,' Jean said.

Enid sat up. 'Aye! There'll be FOOD!'

Seffy laughed at the way Enid said "fud!"

'And cakes!' Flora said, eyes bright.

'Bring us back a scone?' Enid pleaded.

'I'll do my best!' Seffy said. She patted the sides of her dress and wished it had pockets.

* * *

Aunt Dilys' friend Marigold, was standing outside, leaning against the porch, when Seffy arrived at Ballykinch House.

Seffy had borrowed Jean's bicycle. She started to pedal faster down the drive, calling out, 'Oh, don't say she's not back?'

Gosh, that must've sounded awfully rude. As though Marigold's company wasn't quite going to hit the mark.

'Don't fret, dear,' Marigold said, smiling. 'She's here. She's on the telephone to her new best friends in London! I thought it was too nice a day to wait inside.'

It was, indeed, another beautiful day. The blue sky and mild temperatures had continued and Jock had assured them the good weather was set to stay "for a wee while yet".

'Doesn't this glorious weather make you feel guilty?' Seffy asked. 'How can we enjoy it, when there's a war on?'

Marigold frowned. 'I think the good Lord has sent us this fine day to encourage us. And I also think . . .' she waggled her finger '. . . it'd be a sin to waste it!'

So many things were a sin these days: wasting food, paper, clothing or petrol and yes, Marigold was right – it was surely a sin to waste good weather, too.

Seffy propped the bicycle against the wall. The front door was open and she could hear her aunt's dulcet tones drifting out from the hallway.

'How've you managed without her for a whole fortnight?' Seffy asked.

'Aw, I've been fine. I've had Goldie for company and I've been playing croquet and doing a spot of painting. Ah, now I wanted to show you something.'

Marigold darted inside the house and returned, brandishing a newspaper. 'Have you seen this? You must have!'

Seffy's heart sank; she knew exactly what it was.

'It's the article in *The Courier*,' Marigold said, tapping the front cover. 'Such a lovely piece! And a wonderful photograph of your pal. Marriage obviously suits her!'

Seffy had no choice but to take the newspaper and pretend to admire the picture.

'It caused quite a stir in the village,' Marigold said. 'The shop had oranges that day but that piece in the paper caused even more excitement!'

Seffy had listened to every word of the article read aloud by Jean, more than once. She almost knew the rotten thing off by heart:

'*When 21-year-old Mrs Gordon Johnson (formerly Miss Grace McGinty) joined the WTC last year, little did she know that as well as finding muscles she never knew she had, she'd find herself a husband!*

'*Sadly for the ladies, the lumberjacks of the Canadian Forestry Corps, who'd been working alongside the gallant gals in Blantyre Forest for several months, have now moved on to join their comrades in other parts of the British Isles . . .*'

Seffy smiled. 'Yes, I've seen it. Grace is starting a scrapbook. She's kept cuttings from when she and Gordy got married, too.'

To her own ears, the words sounded forced and insincere, but Marigold didn't seem to notice.

'Super! Aw, but she must be missing her husband terribly, poor lamb.'

Seffy swallowed. 'Yes. But they write every day. And they're trying to arrange to meet up.'

She'd overheard Grace talking about their plans over supper. Gordy would only get a few days' leave so the plan was to meet at the Borders. That was as much as she could bear to hear before she'd moved to a different table.

'Ah, there you are!' It was Dilys, dressed in a yellow frock, with a handbag looped over her arm.

Seffy gave her aunt a peck on the cheek. 'How was London?'

'Marvellous! Lots to tell. But wait until we're in the car. How are things with you?'

'Fine,' Seffy said. She wasn't going to admit she'd been demoted. She couldn't stand the inevitable interrogation. Her aunt would certainly urge her to fight for her job or imply she must've done something to deserve losing it.

Dilys frowned. 'Quite sure?'

'Yes! Except our supervisor's back and she's never liked me and there's a new girl who positively hates me. But otherwise, everything's tickety-boo!'

Dilys tutted. 'Why do you set such store by people liking you, Persephone? It's more important, believe me, that you like yourself.'

Seffy was taken aback. Was that true? Did she always want people to like her?

'I've often found,' Marigold said, 'that once you start to like yourself, others will like you too.'

As Seffy wrestled with these thoughts, Dilys tapped her watch.

'I do hope this car's not going to be late.' She looked Seffy up and down. 'I thought you might have worn your blue frock today, Persephone. Most fetching, that blue.'

Seffy almost choked. Dilys took little interest in her own appearance, let alone anyone else's. Perhaps it was the influence of these new pals in London.

'Oh, the blue needs washing,' she said, airily. In truth, she'd simply pulled the least-creased garment out of her suitcase and thrown it on.

'I think you look lovely, as always, dear,' Marigold said. 'Take no notice of Madame Isobel, there!'

The women cocked their ears at the sound of a trotting horse. Its jaunty clip-clopping was getting louder. It was coming down the drive. A harness jangled, wheels rumbled and the next moment, a pony and trap appeared and pulled up in front of them.

The driver, in smart black livery, tipped his hat.

'Well,' Dilys muttered. 'I assume this is our transport to Blantyre. I thought they might at least have sent a taxi.'

Marigold clapped. 'But this is much better!'

The chestnut pony was a dear little thing, not much bigger

than a Shetland. He had a shaggy mane and his forelock had been tied into a topknot. Seffy stepped forward to give his nose a gentle rub.

The driver got down from his seat, grunting with the effort. He was an elderly chap, rather red in the face and clearly uncomfortable in his stiff uniform.

'Probably the chauffeur,' Marigold whispered to Seffy. 'Downgraded to a cart, since there's no petrol to be had.'

He pulled down a set of wooden steps and gave them each his hand, to climb aboard. Dilys was first and she hesitated but then, with much huffing, she got in.

They made themselves comfortable on the bench seats. Dilys sat on one side and instructed Seffy and Marigold to sit opposite, "for balance".

The driver handed out folded parasols, at which point Dilys brightened a little. 'Very thoughtful,' she murmured, as she opened hers and held it up.

Then, with a jolt and a creak, the cart started to move.

Dilys looked down. 'They haven't exactly pushed the boat out. You can see the ground through the gaps in these slats. I wonder who got the landau? I wouldn't have minded a ride in that.'

'Do stop complaining, Dilys,' Marigold said, 'or I won't allow you a moment to discuss your special project with Lady Lockhart. Every time you broach the subject, I'll distract her.'

Seffy left them to their good-natured bickering and leaned back against the wooden bench, enjoying the gentle bouncing of the cart. She stretched out her legs and turned her face up to the dappled sunlight filtering through the trees.

'You are wearing stockings, aren't you, Persephone?'

'Of course, Aunt,' she said, pulling her legs back in.

In truth, Seffy couldn't remember the last time she'd worn stockings. Or a girdle, for that matter. But her legs were nutmeg-brown and her stomach was as flat as a flounder. She had no need for stockings or girdles these days.

Dilys collapsed her parasol and laid it down at her feet.

'Now, Persephone, tell me what you think about this! Oh, don't listen, Marigold! Count the buttercups in the verges or something. I know you disapprove.'

Marigold looked at Seffy. 'This is something she picked up in London.'

'"Picked up"?' Dilys said. 'Like a dose of influenza?'

Marigold sniffed. 'It's certainly nothing healthy – that's for sure.'

Intrigued, Seffy sat up. 'Go on. I'm all ears.'

'When I was down in England last week,' Dilys said, 'I met some remarkable women—'

'Edith and Venetia,' Marigold interrupted. 'One's an MP as well as a doctor, if you please.'

Dilys ignored her and carried on. 'They're doing something quite remarkable: they've set up a "Women's Home Defence Corps". Like the Home Guard but for women! You know we've never been allowed to join the Home Guard? The morning after Anthony Eden made that request for volunteers on the wireless, I dashed to the police station to offer my services, didn't I, Marigold?'

'You most certainly did.'

'And I – and no doubt, countless others – was flatly refused!' Dilys' nostrils flared. 'The constable actually laughed. "It's men we're wanting," he said, as though I were a piece of rubbish.'

Marigold looked sympathetic. 'It was a long time ago now, Dilys, dear.'

'It was May 1940, almost exactly three years ago. I remember it well.'

Seffy frowned. 'But why won't they allow women to join?'

'Not enough instructors, uniforms or equipment, apparently. That's been their argument for years. It's even been debated in Parliament. They won't let us defend ourselves or our country! Can you imagine, if the Germans were to invade and we had to admit, "I'm awfully sorry but it wasn't considered womanly for me to learn to use a rifle"? Ridiculous! Of course, now they've relented and said we might join but merely as "auxiliaries". Under no circumstance can we bear arms. Back-room only. Well, bugger that, pardon my French!'

'Language, Dilys!' Marigold reprimanded, mildly.

'Some forward-thinking Home Guard units have allowed women to join properly but the laird heads up the Home Guard around here, so that's a non-starter. Anyhoo, I've decided to set one up: a proper Women's Home Defence Corps. WHD for short. Will you join, Persephone? And your lumberjill colleagues?'

Seffy was taken aback.

'But what would we be doing?'

The cart jolted as a wheel hit a rut in the lane and Marigold screamed.

'One more wallop like that,' Dilys said, 'and this contraption will collapse. Now, where was I?'

'You were filling me in, Aunt, on what it would entail.'

Dilys delved into her handbag and brought out her spectacles and a list written on a piece of paper. She read: '*Handling and the use of firearms, musketry, bombing, field craft, Morse code and unarmed combat!*'

Goodness, how radical! "Bombing" and "unarmed combat"! Could women really do that kind of thing?

'What d'you say?' Dilys said. 'We need strong young women, or else it'll be just us old crocks!'

Seffy hesitated. It was a lot to take in. She couldn't answer for the other girls. Any influence she might once have had over them seemed to have gone.

'I'm not sure about my colleagues, but I can ask them. Bribes might help. They're partial to cake.'

'I'm sure cake could be arranged. And we'll need training, of course. And weapons. Do you have opera glasses, Persephone?'

'No! At least, not with me!'

'You see—' Dilys sat back and shook her head '—this is going to be our stumbling block.'

64

'What? A lack of opera glasses?'

'A general lack of equipment!'

'And why are you so against it, Marigold?' Seffy asked, turning in her seat.

'Oh, she's a pacifist; practically a Quaker!' Dilys said.

'I *am* a pacifist, as it happens,' Marigold said. 'It's bad enough that men have gone off to fight, without the gentler sex joining in. Before you know it, there'll be women on the battlefield!'

'But, as I keep telling her,' Dilys said, 'this isn't about fighting, *per se*, it's about defence and resisting the enemy, should the worst happen. But Marigold is worried about the preservation of society!'

'Aye! When this terrible war is over, the men must still have a civilised society to come back to. And we women have an important part to play in that.' Marigold gave a firm nod. 'In any case, no one thinks the Germans are going to invade anymore.'

Dilys tutted. 'I disagree. They're in Norway, a hop, skip and a jump away.'

'Yes, but they're bullies and therefore cowards. They don't have the nerve! So, there's no need for this women's army malarkey!'

Although Seffy could understand Marigold's reservations, Dilys' proposal for a Women's Home Guard sounded just the ticket. It would be the perfect distraction: a way of taking her mind off everything that was currently making her blue.

'So, what do you say, Persephone?' Dilys asked.

'I like the sound of it,' Seffy said. 'Yes, count me in. You've got your first recruit!'

Chapter 11

A footman was conducting the women along a corridor, towards the drawing room at Blantyre Castle.

The sound of tinkling teacups and laughter was getting louder, when Dilys suddenly dived through an open door on the right.

'This way, madam!' the footman cried, without breaking stride.

Seconds later, she re-emerged, looking sheepish.

'What are ye up to?' Marigold muttered. 'Are you on a reconnaissance already?'

Dilys had a twinkle in her eye. She put her finger to her lips and Seffy smothered a giggle. Perhaps this afternoon wasn't going to be such a dull affair, after all.

Lady Lockhart was sitting with a group of ladies. 'Ah, there you are!' she said, standing up as they were announced. 'How did you like your transport?'

Dilys beamed. 'Such a quaint little cart! And that darling pony! We enjoyed every moment. Thank you for arranging it.' She gestured towards Marigold and Seffy. 'Lavinia, I think you know Miss Mackenzie and my niece, Lady Persephone Baxter-Mills?'

Seffy held her breath.

It had only been a couple of months since she'd been here, under cover. Lady Lockhart must surely remember her and the awful Captain Graham? Her ladyship had assumed they were courting and it had been uncomfortable to say the least, when Graham had mentioned his wife back in British Columbia. Twice.

But Lady Lockhart gave no sign of disapproval when she looked at Seffy now. In fact, she beamed. 'Of course. Delighted to see you both!'

Seffy exhaled. That was a relief.

She glanced around, while the women made small talk. The drawing room reminded her of home. It was light and well-proportioned, filled with plush velvet sofas and leather armchairs. There were fireplaces at either end, gold-framed portraits on the walls and sumptuous Persian rugs under foot.

The French doors had been thrown open to allow a warm breeze to float through the room.

On the far side, the laird was standing with a group of women, guffawing loudly. He was the only man here, aside from the elderly footmen, who were bobbing around, handing out plates, retrieving napkins and replacing teacups.

No, she was mistaken: there was another man standing with his back to them. A soldier, judging from his khaki tunic, slacks and leather belt. He was facing a woman who was talking at him, gesticulating madly. From the stillness of his posture, he was either completely fascinated or completely bored.

Lady Lockhart followed Seffy's gaze. 'Now do come and be introduced. Then you must take tea. My cook has rustled up the most divine Dundee cake!'

Moments later, they were lined up in front of the soldier, as though awaiting inspection.

'Ladies, may I introduce my cousin, Major Ralph Stirling? He's a commando, recently posted here. Fighting fit and fit to fight, isn't that right, Ralph?' She tapped her nose. 'Top-secret stuff!'

Seffy gaped. This was the cousin? Not a dull, middle-aged woman but an elite army officer? He seemed rather young for a major. He was older than her, of course, but he couldn't be more than thirty.

Introductions were made and when Seffy extended her hand to shake his, he pressed it firmly.

'How do you do?' she said, determined not to wince.

His gaze was cool and disinterested and Seffy was reminded of the first time she'd met another tall, prickly stranger. But she quickly pushed that thought from her mind.

'Shall we leave the young people to chat?' Lady Lockhart said.

As she guided Dilys and Marigold away, Seffy heard her aunt begin her Women's Home Defence offensive. 'I have something important to discuss with you, Lavinia, if I may . . .'

Seffy smiled at the major and he raised his eyebrows. He was obviously surprised too and not entirely pleased that they'd been left alone.

It was a relief when a maid appeared and offered them refreshments and two armchairs, which faced the garden.

The major shook his head. 'I'd rather stand. If . . . er, that's all right with you, Lady Persephone?'

'Perfectly, thank you.' She'd much rather stand, too. It would be easier to excuse herself and slip away at the earliest opportunity.

In the few minutes it took the maid and a footman to furnish them with a small walnut table, tablecloth, napkins, crockery and cake and to pour tea from the silver teapot, Seffy had time to observe the officer.

Her first thought – that he reminded her of Callum – was completely wrong; she could see that now. The two men were nothing alike.

Although Callum was also tall and strong, there was a litheness about him that this officer lacked. Callum was fair and blue-eyed, while the major was a dark brooding hulk of a man. There was the faintest suggestion of stubble on his chin and a two-inch scar on his right cheek.

When the staff left them, there was a moment's silence before he said, 'Are you local, your ladyship? You certainly don't sound it.'

'Neither do you.' He was a Scot but his accent was so soft it was barely there.

He nodded. 'I'm originally from Edinburgh.'

He pronounced it "Edin-bruh" not, as she said it: "Edin-bor-ough".

'Oh, there's a marvellous castle at Edin . . . burgh—' she tried to replicate his pronunciation '—so I'm told. High up on that rock? Not actually been there myself.'

She was wittering now; he was making her nervous.

He inclined his head and smiled.

Goodness, she hoped Edinburgh Castle was still standing and hadn't been obliterated in a raid. She might've just made a prize booby of herself.

The major's right foot was tapping.

'Do you have somewhere else to be?' Seffy asked.

'I beg your pardon?'

She shook her head. He wasn't even aware he was doing it.

'And you're quite right, Major, I'm not local,' she said. 'We live in Ayrshire but I'm originally from London.'

He nodded again but his eyes were scanning the room behind her. It was most disconcerting. When she was introduced to a man, she didn't usually have to vie for his attention.

At least, while he seemed otherwise engaged, she could do something useful. She opened her handbag, quickly placed two pieces of fruit cake inside, on top of a clean handkerchief, and snapped it shut again.

The noise of the clasp closing made him look back at her.

'A little something for the girls back at camp,' she said, brightly.

He sighed, as though it were an effort to think of something else to say. 'And what brings you to Morayshire?' he asked, finally.

'Work, actually. I'm in the Women's Timber Corps. Doing my bit!' She felt proud. How marvellous to have something positive to say. 'And what about you?' she asked, when he merely pursed his lips.

'Timber Corps, did you say?'

She nodded. He had been listening, after all.

The major put down his cup and cleared his throat. 'You know, I was barracked by some women the other day. I'm fairly sure they were from the Timber Corps.'

Seffy frowned. 'Whatever do you mean?'

'I was heckled, from their truck, as I ran to my posting.'

It hit her then, like a ton of bricks: it was him! The grumpy soldier that Joey had yelled at from the lorry. Seffy had been driving, so he wouldn't have seen her.

'One of the er . . . ladies was most insistent I should have a lift,' he added.

Seffy gulped her tea and glowered at him over the rim of her cup. She wasn't sure she liked the doubtful way he'd said, "ladies".

'But you didn't want to accept their lift?'

'Absolutely not! I had to run the seven miles from the railway station to my new unit within an hour. Under my own steam. I couldn't accept a lift, under any circumstances.'

'Goodness! And if you hadn't managed it . . . ?'

'It's the first test for the cadets under my command. For those who fail, it's RTU.'

'RTU?'

'Returned to Unit. They go straight back to their regiments.' He shrugged. 'It seemed only proper that I should do the run myself.'

'And if you'd failed, you'd have had to send yourself back?'

Golly, she'd actually made him smile. He looked much nicer when he smiled. She must remember to tell Joey.

'I can see how that might have been tiresome,' Seffy said. 'Being bothered by the lumberjills, I mean.'

'Lumberjills?'

'That's our nickname. I'll ask around, if you like, and have a word with the guilty party. Harassment of His Majesty's forces is not acceptable!' She laughed and hoped that was the end of the subject.

'Thank you. I appreciate that.' Goodness, he was so formal, she wouldn't have been surprised if he'd saluted.

70

'Ah, Ralph, my boy, there you are!' A man's voice and the smell of tobacco filled the air.

It was the laird, wearing a navy kilt and smoking a pipe. He strode up to the major and slapped him heartily on the back.

Behind him, a footman was carrying a half-empty bottle of whisky on a silver platter.

The laird leaned in. 'I've drunk enough bloody tea to last a lifetime! Join me in a wee snifter, eh? What d'you say? Glenmorangie. A drop of the good stuff!'

Judging from his flushed face and slurred speech, his lordship had already had a wee snifter or two. Seffy wasn't sure what was funnier: the laird's inebriated state or the major's obvious discomfort.

His lordship suddenly noticed her. His eyes lit up. 'Ah, hello there, young lady!'

He looked from her to the major and back again. He winked. 'Now, how are you two getting along, eh? Lots to talk about? Jolly good. I'm sure my wife will be most interested to know!'

Seffy's stomach dropped. Why would Lady Lockhart be interested? Had she and the major been left together in the hope they'd hit it off? Oh goodness, how mortifying.

She looked down at the carpet. The major probably thought she was in on the plan to snare him. How she'd love to tell him not to worry: she had no intention of setting her cap at him. Or her beret, for that matter.

The footman was pouring whisky into two cut-crystal glasses.

'Cameron!' Lady Lockhart scolded. She was perched on a sofa with Dilys, a few feet away. 'It's only three o'clock! Do come over here a minute, dearie, will you? I need to ask you something.'

The laird looked crestfallen.

'Duty calls!' he said, shuffling away.

The major declined the remaining glass of whisky and the footman disappeared.

Blast. She'd missed her chance to escape. They were facing each other again. She'd have to think of something else to say.

'Did you say you were a commando?'

'No. It was actually Lavinia, my cousin, who said it. But yes. We're training up here, at Blantyre Lodge, on the estate. High altitude and so on. The terrain is . . . erm, suitable.'

Seffy was bursting to know more but she knew better than to ask. No doubt it was all hush-hush.

'You might hear gunfire in the woods from time to time but don't be alarmed. It'll only be us, on exercises. Perhaps you could warn your colleagues? I'd hate to think someone might be frightened.'

Seffy's chest tightened. Yet another man who thought they were timid little women, playing at forestry. 'Oh, I can assure you, it'll take rather more than a few distant bangs to frighten us. We're not made of china!'

They both turned at the sound of raised voices.

'Absolutely NOT!'

The laird was towering over Dilys, Marigold and Lady Lockhart, seated on the sofa. His jaw was clenched. He looked very different from the convivial host of a minute ago.

'Cameron, dearie . . .' Lady Lockhart said, in a placating tone.

'Excuse me, won't you?' Seffy said. She moved to stand behind the sofa, facing the laird. She could guess why he was so irate.

'I'm completely agin it!' the laird said, waving his glass so that the whisky sloshed about. 'A women's militia? Ordinary citizens taking matters into their own fair hands? Completely out of the question!' He looked around. 'Ralph! Come and listen to this hare-brained scheme!'

Oh, no! She'd only just got away from him. And he was bound to take the laird's side.

'Please don't involve poor Ralph,' Lady Lockhart said.

The major appeared at Seffy's side. She didn't look at him but she could feel his presence.

'Women's Home Guard, Ralph! Have you ever heard such nonsense?'

There was a pause, as though the major thought the whole scheme so outrageous, he didn't quite know where to start. 'I . . . I wouldn't exactly recommend it,' he said, 'but if the ladies—'

'Apart from anything,' the laird interrupted, 'you'd be breaking the law!'

Dilys made a scoffing noise.

'It's true! If you create one of these groups and arm yourselves, you'll be raising an illegal army!'

Lady Lockhart gasped and put her hands to her chest. 'I think we should consider the subject closed, Dilys,' she said. 'I admire what you're trying to do but I'm sorry, it doesn't sound particularly sensible.'

'Oh, I'm sure you're right,' Dilys said, throwing up her hands. 'Me and my silly ideas!'

The laird leaned towards her. 'If you're interested in the Home Guard, come along to the village hall on Monday evenings. We always need a hand with typing, making the tea and so forth.'

Seffy noticed Dilys' shoulders stiffen.

'Thank you, your lordship,' Dilys said. 'I may well take you up on that kind offer.'

The laird nodded beatifically at them. It was a wonder, Seffy thought, that he didn't pat them all on the head like so many labradors.

Once he'd wandered off, taking the major with him, and Lady Lockhart was occupied with one of her staff, Seffy bent to whisper in Dilys' ear.

'You're not going to take any notice of that old duffer, are you?'

Dilys tilted her head backwards. 'What do you think?' she said.

Chapter 12

'Would you like to read my *Woman's Weekly*?' Enid asked Tattie, as they lay on blankets in the sun. 'It's got a good piece about skincare.'

Tattie said no, ta. She wanted to get her face up to the sun, like Angie had told her to.

It was a half-day and apart from English Seffy, who'd gone somewhere all dolled-up, everyone was relaxing outside. That suited Tattie. She'd only been a lumberjill for a week but she was fair puggled.

Morag, the lass who'd been thrown over by her fiancé, wasn't around and the others were talking about her.

'I wonder if she'll send the ring back?' Jean said. 'That's what you're supposed to do.'

'Aw, that'd be a shame. It's a lovely wee ring,' Enid said. 'It's an opal.'

'Opals are unlucky,' Angie said, without looking up from her magazine.

'I'd pawn it, if it was me,' Tattie said, and blushed when everyone howled with disapproval.

She tugged at a blade of grass, not wanting to meet anyone's eye. These lassies had probably never been in a hock shop. Half of them probably didn't know what one was.

She remembered the first time Gregor had come out of a bombed-out house, during a raid, his pockets clinking.

He'd shown her his haul: a couple of gold wedding bands, a ruby ring, surrounded by diamonds and some silver signet rings.

Something about those rings had knocked Tattie for six.

They'd been given with love. Whoever had lost them would be heartbroken. They might've been a gift from someone serving; someone who mightn't be coming home.

She wished he'd taken almost anything other than those rings.

Then later, it got worse.

When Ma was trying to persuade Tattie to leave, to get "out of Gregor's clutches", she'd said, 'You know the stuff he takes to the hock shop? Where d'you think that comes from? Folk don't leave precious things like that lying about!' She'd tapped Tattie's head. 'Think on, lass!'

Though she hadn't wanted to believe it, she'd finally realised the truth: Gregor had taken the jewellery from dead bodies, from poor wretches killed in raids.

And that'd been the final straw.

The other girls were still blethering on about Morag's ring.

'She should keep it,' Enid said. 'If she finds another beau, he might propose quicker if she already has a ring. Because it's a nuisance, having to wait. A lassie can hardly do the asking.'

'Not so!' Jean said. 'Queen Victoria proposed to Prince Albert. No one could propose to a reigning monarch; it wasn't the done thing. Victoria loved Albert from the moment she saw him and she did the proposing.'

'And what was his answer?' Flora asked.

Everyone laughed, though Tattie thought it was a fair question.

'He said, yes, of course,' Jean said. 'You don't say no to a queen! Theirs was a real love match. They had about a hundred children, so there's the proof of it! Oh, here comes Morag, now. We'd best change the subject.'

Angie yawned loudly, tossed her magazine to one side and sat up. 'I've got something to ask the felling girls.'

Tattie was irked with her, for the first time. She didn't want to hear about work until Monday morning rolled round again.

'Are you all content with the way things are arranged,' Angie went on, 'or do yous want a change?'

'Me and Morag definitely want to work together again!' Enid said. 'No offence, Grace.'

'None taken,' Grace said, mildly. 'But Seffy's not here. Perhaps we should talk about this when she's back?'

Angie shook her head. 'I cannae wait. I'm a new broom; I want to make changes. Speak now or forever hold your peace!'

Everyone started to talk over one another. Tattie was glad she could stay out of it. It would be a wee while yet before she'd finished her training and could join the Macdonald gang.

Jean, who, as a measurer, wasn't involved in the discussion either, yawned and said she was heading for the burn.

'Coming, Joey?'

'You take Tattie and go on,' Joey said. 'We'll meet you down there by and by.'

Angie's brown kneecaps were bobbing on the surface of the water and she was moving her hands at the sides, like fins. She was sitting and floating at the same time. Tattie frowned. How did she do that?

The other girls were paddling, ankle-deep or, like Angie, treading water. They'd all stripped down to their vests and pants.

Angie called up to Tattie, sitting on the bank with Grace. 'Come on in! Have a wee dip!'

Tattie hesitated. 'Is it deep?'

'No! I can stand up. Look!' She straightened up and put her feet on the bottom. The water only came up to her waist.

'But I'm shorter than you,' Tattie said.

Angie slapped the water hard, sending an ice-cold spray into the air. 'Don't be boring! All work and no play makes Tattie a dull girl!'

Heat rose in Tattie's chest. Angie was right, of course: she was being dull but she was afeared.

'Take no notice of her,' Grace said, wiping water droplets off her arm. 'You don't have to go in if you don't want to.'

But Tattie felt bad. Angie had looked out for her since she'd arrived. She'd given her calamine lotion for her midge bites and arnica for her bruises; she'd told her toothpaste was good for drying out pimples and that if she put her face up to the sun, that'd help too.

'I'm no' dressed for a dip,' Tattie said. 'I need to get—' she was going to say, "changed" but Angie had already turned away, calling out to the others. They were laughing at something or other: Tattie hoped it wasn't her.

She sighed and turned towards Grace, who was reading one of her letters. 'What number is that?'

She'd heard Grace say that she and Gordy had to number their letters because they didn't always arrive in the same order they'd been written.

'This is number forty. If you ever want to write a letter yourself, Tattie, I have plenty of stationery. You only have to ask.'

That was kind and Tattie opened her mouth to say so, but then Morag's voice rang out. 'Hey, Grace! Are you no' coming in? Do you no' feel well?'

The girls in the water were looking up at Grace on the bank.

'Aye, she looks a bit peely-wally!' Enid said. 'You don't think you might be . . . you know, in the family way?'

'Give the girl a chance,' Jean said. 'She only had a two-day honeymoon!'

Tattie would die if anyone spoke about her like that. But Grace was letting the teasing wash over her.

'Two days is plenty long enough!' Joey said. 'There are eight of us and my ma always says my da only had to take off his pyjama bottoms and she caught for another!'

The girls screeched in mock-outrage.

Grace smiled and shook her head. 'I'm not expecting. I wouldn't want to bring a wean into this war, for a start. As for the water, I never go in. Yous all know that.'

Tattie wondered whether, like her, Grace couldn't swim and was too ashamed to admit it.

It was too late now to join them. The girls were climbing out and throwing themselves on the grass, to dry in the sun.

Tattie was relieved when Angie lay down next to her: it meant she still wanted to be her pal.

They lay in silence for a few minutes, eyes closed. The murmurs and chatter of the other girls floated around them.

Tattie's eyes flickered open as she heard Angie turn over onto her front. 'Who's Gregor?' she asked.

Tattie nearly jumped out of her skin.

'Who's . . . ? No one!'

She'd said it too loudly. Grace and Enid had lifted their heads and were watching them.

How did Angie know about Gregor? She'd never mentioned him here.

'Aw, come on. He must be someone,' Angie said.

Tattie's face was burning. 'He's someone from back home.'

'Oi, oi!' Enid said. 'Is it your fella?'

Yuck. The thought of it. Tattie thought she might barf. 'How do you know about him, anyway?' Tattie asked.

'Oh, I know everything!' Angie said, smirking.

'I sleep on the other side of you, remember, Tattie,' Grace said. 'And you talk in your sleep sometimes.' She turned back to her letter. 'I'm only saying.'

Aye, that was it: she must've said his name in her sleep. That's how Angie knew.

Because if Angie knew about Gregor some other, spooky way, it didn't bear thinking about. Angie might know other things about Tattie that she didn't want anyone to know.

Angie started whispering so the other girls couldn't hear. 'Who is he, though? You can tell me. Pals tell each other everything.'

Was that right? Tattie didn't know much about having a pal. 'He's . . . he's my stepfather.'

She couldn't help shuddering, at the thought of him.

Angie put a reassuring hand on her arm. 'He didn't ever hurt you, did he, this Gregor?'

Tattie shook her head. He'd pinched her and wrenched her arm up behind her back and stamped on her foot in a temper but she couldn't say he'd hurt her. Not badly. No more than a bruise or two and goodness, she got enough of those from messing around with her wee brothers.

'I used to work with him,' Tattie said, praying Angie wouldn't ask what kind of work. 'He didn't want me to join the Timber Corps. My papers and travel warrant came in the post and Gregor ripped them up into tiny wee pieces.'

Her chest fluttered at the memory of his raging. None of them – not Ma or the laddies or Tattie herself – had dared say a word, for fear of making things worse. When he got really mad, he'd reach for the belt. And use it.

The travel warrant had gone and there hadn't been time to get another, even if she'd had the nerve to try. The authorities would ask what she'd done with the first and she'd be too ashamed to tell them.

She and Ma had decided she'd still join the Timber Corps but without a ticket, she'd have to stow away on the train.

'But he'll go berserk!' she'd said to Ma. 'What'll you tell him, when he asks where I've gone?'

'I'll say you must've slipped away in the night, that your things have gone and you've taken the only bag we had.'

They'd had it all worked out but in the end, it wasn't necessary. The police had knocked on the door that very evening and Gregor had been arrested.

'They'll be coming for you next, ma girl,' Ma had said. 'The wee boys are too young but you're not. Get on that train tomorrow and make a new start. Keep your neb out of trouble and don't be taking anything that doesn't belong to you, d'you hear?'

Angie's eyes were fixed on Tattie's face now. 'If this Gregor ripped up your warrant, how did you get here?'

'I hid in the luggage van.'

Angie looked impressed. 'Good for you.'

She frowned, as though something else had occurred to her. 'And you're not afraid he might come looking for you?'

Tattie opened her mouth and closed it again. She'd never thought of that. Gregor had been carted off by the police. With any luck, he'd been put away for a good wee while.

But what if he wasn't? What if he'd got away with it and was back home and up to his old tricks? He was slippery, Ma always said.

'I . . . well, he doesn't know where I am.' Tattie looked around at the miles of countryside, the big sky, the nothingness everywhere. 'Where would he start looking?'

'You're right,' Angie said. 'He could never find you here.'

Tattie exhaled. It should've felt like a weight had been lifted, to have finally told someone the truth. But it didn't.

'I won't breathe a word,' Angie whispered. 'Thanks for trusting me. After all, that's what pals are for.'

Chapter 13

The women were subdued on the return journey to Ballykinch House.

The pony trotted all the way back – clearly the driver wanted to get home for his dinner – and Dilys complained that the rattling cart was making her teeth shake.

'It's darned annoying,' she said.

'It is rather jolty,' Marigold agreed.

'No, not this. That!' Dilys waved at Blantyre Castle, receding into the distance. 'The scuppering of my plans! I was relying on Lavinia to help with weapons. And ammo.'

'Ammo?' Seffy laughed.

'Ammunition, dear! Do keep up!'

'I know what it means. It's only – oh, never mind.'

'I wanted to show you something, Persephone, but we didn't get chance. There are rifles hanging up in one of the castle rooms.'

'Aha! That's where you disappeared to!' Marigold said.

'I spotted them once before, at some do or other. They're antiques, of course, but they might've done the trick. We'll never find out now though. I should have realised Lavinia would ask her husband's permission. She's as good as banned from any involvement. I know the woman: she won't disobey.'

'He is head of the Home Guard,' Marigold pointed out. 'Highly decorated, saw action at Gallipoli last time.'

'Yes, yes, all of that,' Dilys snapped. 'He obviously has visions of us rampaging through the streets, armed with knitting needles and heaven knows what. Edith and Venetia have faced the same issues. Men don't think we can be trusted!' She sniffed. 'They're the ones not to be trusted! To defend us, I mean. I'm not sitting around, relying on them to save the day. I want to be able to do it for myself!'

Seffy raised her eyebrows at Marigold. It would require some careful handling, to get Dilys out of this funk.

They sat in silence for a few minutes, as the pony trotted on.

'What did you think of Major Stirling?' Dilys asked suddenly. 'I expected him to be as critical as the laird but he kept his own counsel, did you notice?'

Seffy narrowed her eyes. That was a curious – and sudden – change of subject. Unless . . . yes, it all made sense! Her aunt must have been in cahoots with Lady Lockhart, to bring her and the major together!

'It hardly matters what I think of him,' she said. 'I'm quite sure he has a very low opinion of me.'

'But why?'

'Because we were clearly left to take our tea together for a reason. And he probably thought I was involved in the plan. It was excruciating! Was that your idea?'

Dilys looked indignant for a moment, then her face relaxed. '*Mea culpa*,' she said. 'I can't deny it.'

'You know,' Seffy said, 'if this Women's Home Defence idea doesn't take off, you and her ladyship could always set up a marriage bureau. I believe there's one on Bond Street that does awfully well.'

'Oh, drat!' Dilys said. 'I thought he'd be your sort. By all accounts, he's not had a good time of it lately and you're awfully glum, too, since your Canadian chappie left. It was done with the very best of intentions. And Lavinia said he looked like a matinee idol and I must say, I agree.'

'Even with the . . .' Marigold stroked her cheek and whispered: 'scar.'

Seffy sighed. 'Well, your plan failed. The fellow couldn't wait to get away from me. Kept tapping his foot. Most irritating.'

'That'll be on account of his injuries,' Dilys said. 'He was practically blown up, a while back. Spent some considerable time in hospital. He's only recently gone back into active service.'

Seffy grimaced. She felt rotten now.

'And he's had a failed love affair,' Dilys said. 'But Lavinia doesn't know much about that.'

Honestly! Lady Lockhart was a dear old trout but she was rather indiscreet. Although, admittedly, the love affair had suddenly made the major slightly more interesting.

'Look,' Seffy said, 'I know I'm rather peevish these days but I really don't need you to find me a beau, Aunt. And you might want to tell her ladyship that her cousin almost certainly feels the same way.'

'I expect he's far too busy soldiering to think about affairs of the heart, in any case,' Marigold said.

'Yes, quite. If I need a boyfriend – which I don't, incidentally – I'm perfectly capable of finding one myself. Will you promise not to do that again?'

Dilys looked suitably chastened. She promised.

'Good, now let's get back to the Women's Home Defence,' Seffy said. 'I'm still as keen as mustard, if you are?'

'Most certainly! I'm planning to infiltrate the Home Guard. I've been invited by the laird himself, as you heard, although if they think I'm going to be making the tea—'

'She makes terrible tea,' Marigold said.

'—they've got another think coming. I shall find out what they do and get some ideas. Although we still need to recruit, of course. And it looks as though we're going to need subterfuge.'

The pony was trotting down the drive of Ballykinch House now.

'Will you be at church tomorrow, Persephone?'

It was Angie's first Sunday as leader girl and she'd decided they should all attend the service in Farrbridge, so the answer was yes.

'Can you get there early?' Dilys asked. 'Jolly good! I've got a plan.'

When Seffy arrived back in camp, the girls were lying on the grass, exactly where she'd left them.

She distributed the Dundee cake to those most in need: Enid and Tattie. The slices had got slightly squashed in her handbag but they were still eminently edible. Judging from Enid's cries of ecstasy, they were as delicious as Lady Lockhart had promised.

'You look as though you haven't moved all day,' Seffy said.

'We were down at the burn for a wee while,' Joey said.

'All of you? Did our leader girl go in?'

Joey nodded.

Angie was sitting a few yards away, her back against a tree.

'I say!' Seffy called over. 'I thought you didn't want to go into the burn!'

Angie frowned and did a good impression of looking mystified. 'What are you talking about?'

Seffy sighed. 'Earlier on, when you were queuing up for the shower? I said you might want to cool down in the burn instead but you said you didn't trust the water.'

Angie frowned. 'You're mixing me up with someone else. Why on earth would I say that?'

She looked at the others and tapped her head. There were a few awkward smiles, as the girls looked from Angie to Seffy, clearly unsure whom to believe.

The atmosphere was strange.

Tattie and Enid, in particular, Seffy noticed, were looking at her as though she'd gone quite mad.

She clenched her fists. She hadn't mixed her up, she remembered it quite clearly! Angie had turned up her nose and said, 'Goodness knows what's in that water!'

Why was she lying, so blatantly? And making Seffy out to be some kind of mischief-maker?

Joey stood up and tugged Seffy's arm. 'Come on. Don't start rowing. Let it be. Are you coming to supper in that frock or are you going to change? A little bird's told me it's shepherd's pie tonight, your favourite. You don't want to miss that!'

Chapter 14

The next morning, when Seffy arrived at church, her aunt was in the vestibule, distributing hymn books to the first members of the congregation to arrive.

'Morning!' Seffy said. 'Need some help?' She grabbed the nearest hymn book.

'Yes! No! Put that down!'

A smartly dressed couple were mounting the steps towards them.

The man took a hymn book but the woman declined, waving her gloved hand with a smile. 'We'll share, thank you,' she said.

Dilys nodded but once they'd entered the church, she muttered under her breath. Clearly, something wasn't going to plan.

'Where's Marigold?' Seffy asked, glancing down the aisle.

'Won't play any part in this. She's at home, dabbling with paint. Now, Persephone, quickly, before anyone else arrives: do not, under any circumstances, mix up the hymn books! These on the left are for the men, those on the right – because we are in the right, that's how to remember – are for the women.

'If they insist on sharing, like that pair, it won't work, so do press a book on the women!'

Seffy nodded, uncertainly.

'When they turn to the first hymn,' Dilys went on, 'which

you can see from the board up there, is number 238 – that's "Be Thou My Vision", a terrible dirge, by the way – the women will see the note I've left them.'

Seffy picked up a hymn book and started flicking through it.

Meanwhile, Dilys gazed around the church, suddenly miles away. 'You know, Marigold and I were here – sitting on that very pew – when war was declared and the minister stopped the service to announce the news. Then we sang "Oh God Our Help in Ages Past" and there were quite a few tears, I can tell you. And not only from the women.'

'Gosh, how ingenious!' Seffy said. She'd found Dilys' carefully typed note. It was an actual advertisement!

The heading read:

Mothers' Union Meeting!

Seffy frowned. '"Mothers' Union"?'

'I had to call it something. Read on. All will become clear!'

Seffy turned back to the note and read:

FEMALES OF FARRBRIDGE!

Your Country Needs YOU!

Come and be educated in the art of

DEFENDING

yourself, your home, your family, your country!

All WOMEN welcome. Inaugural meeting:

Farrbridge Village Hall, 2pm, Saturday 26th June 1943

'What do you think?' Dilys asked. 'Too many exclamation marks? Marigold calls them "howlers". She also wanted me to change "females" to "ladies" but I like the alliteration.'

If anything, there were perhaps too many capital letters. It rather felt as though one were being shouted at. But perhaps that was deliberate.

'It's very stirring, Aunt. Who could say no to an invitation like this? But you haven't mentioned the "Women's Home Defence Corps".'

'At this stage I'm calling it a "Mothers' Union Meeting" because nobody can take exception to that. We've got until Saturday to drum up support. Have you asked your pals yet?'

Seffy winced. She hadn't, partly because she still couldn't decide whether to include Angie. It would be nigh on impossible to keep the project from her if the other girls got involved, but could she be trusted not to spill the beans to Miss McEwen? Or "Miss M" as she insisted on calling her? Their supervisor would probably ban them from any involvement.

'Morning, Reverend!' Dilys said.

The minister was gliding down the aisle, his black gown billowing like a sail.

'Is he in on it?' Seffy whispered.

Dilys shook her head.

'Morning, ladies! So kind of you to help out! Ah, a lumberjill! I hear you're getting more help in the forest very soon!'

He swept past, to take up his position at the top of the steps.

'"More help"? What does he mean?' Seffy asked.

But there was no chance to discuss it: a breathless elderly woman had shuffled up to them and accepted a hymn book from Dilys.

They waited until she was out of earshot before speaking.

'I hate to be a wet blanket,' Seffy said, 'but I've spotted the tiniest flaw in your plan. Won't the older ladies, in particular, know the hymns off by heart? They mightn't even bother opening the hymn book.'

Dilys shrugged. 'If that happens, all well and good! Because I don't actually want to recruit oldies. Not unless they've got some vim! It's a kind of natural selection. I want to attract young women to the cause! I assume the other lumberjills are coming today?'

Seffy nodded. 'They're under strict instructions from—' She stopped herself just in time; she'd almost said: "the new leader girl".

Dilys was busy rearranging the hymn books on the table and only half listening.

'Yes,' Seffy said firmly. 'Have no doubt, they'll be here.'

Tattie was excited about this morning's outing. Not the borin' church part but the dressing up.

It was the first chance she'd had to wear her smart Timber Corps uniform.

When she'd been issued with her new clothes, she'd laid them out on her bed, hardly able to believe her luck.

It was like Christmas and ten birthdays, rolled into one.

She hadn't noticed the others watching her, at first. What must they have thought, as she ran her hand over the nap of the corduroy breeches and the soft wool of the green jumper?

It was only when she'd heard a giggle, that she'd looked up and seen them.

'Someone's happy!' Morag had said.

Tattie had shrugged. 'Aye. The uniform's no' bad.'

The beret was the best part: it even came with a nice wee badge, with a fir tree on it and a crown. She wasn't sure how to wear the beret but this morning, Angie had fixed it properly on her head.

'There! You look the part!' she'd said and Tattie had smiled. Those were almost the exact words Ma had used, when she'd given her the dungarees. "You'll look the part, hen, and isn't that half the battle?"

'Can you make sure everyone's up and ready on time?' Angie had asked Tattie last night. Tattie was turning into Angie's deputy. It made her feel important.

But now, while everyone else was up and getting ready, Joey was still curled up in bed, fast asleep.

Tattie stood over her, a hand hovering over Joey's shoulder. She should give her a wee shake to wake her up. Aw, but she looked done in. She was so pretty but there were dark circles under her eyes, like she could do with a few more hours' kip.

'Shall I leave her be?' Tattie asked.

'No,' Angie said. 'She needs to come. I'll no' have anyone say Macdonald hut was a girl down!'

Chapter 15

As the other girls filed out at the end of the service, Joey stayed behind, to light a candle for Hazel.

Her hand was shaking so much that the first match burned out before the tiny wick caught alight.

She sighed.

'Here, let me,' Seffy said, appearing at her side. She took the box of matches, struck one and they joined hands to light the candle.

'Do you think about her often?' Seffy asked, gently.

'Always.' Joey's eyes had filled with tears. 'I dream about her, too. I can't stop replaying what happened, over in my head, like a film, you know?'

Seffy bit her lip and nodded.

'I blame myself,' Joey said. 'Because I couldn't manage Nelson. You were so brave, Seffy, grabbing his harness and calming him down. I remember that noise so well . . .'

She could still hear it: the dreadful rumble and roar as Hazel scaled the lorry and the logs rolled off the back, taking the poor lass with them.

Seffy sighed but said nothing.

They watched the candle burning for a minute, then they walked out of the church, bidding farewell to Seffy's aunt, who was collecting up the hymn books.

Joey felt better, once they were out in the fresh air. She and Seffy linked arms as they tripped down the stone steps and started to walk along the leafy lane. The other lumberjills were ahead of them, walking in twos and threes.

'You know,' Seffy said, 'Marigold says fine days like this are sent from above to comfort and encourage us. I rather like that idea, don't you?'

She didn't seem to be expecting an answer, which was a comfort in itself. Joey nodded and let Seffy rabbit on.

'Now, did you see the note in the hymn book? Inspired, wasn't it? Not my idea, I hasten to add! So, what d'you think? Will you come along? Of course, it's not a Mothers' Union meeting at all!'

Joey rubbed her eyes. She was so tired, she'd dozed for half the service. She hadn't even had the energy to sing. She'd stood up when required and mimed. She must've missed summat.

'You don't have the foggiest what I'm talking about, do you?' Seffy said. 'I'll explain. Oh, but first, I must tell something. You'll never guess who I met at the tea party yesterday? A friend of yours!'

Joey frowned. A friend? She knew quite a few land girls; perhaps it was one of them. They were always being moved around. But she couldn't imagine any of them being invited somewhere as grand as Blantyre Castle.

Seffy looked as though she might burst.

'Go on, then,' Joey said. 'Tell me.'

'Remember the soldier we met, coming back from the railway station? The one who caught your eye?'

Joey's heart gave a jolt. 'Sure. How could I forget Mr Rude?'

It had been a week and a day since they'd seen him and she couldn't get the fella out of her mind. She got butterflies in her stomach just imagining how things might've turned out if he'd actually accepted their offer of a lift.

Seffy was laughing. 'Well, it was him!'

No! That couldn't be right. She must be mistaken.

'Are you sure? What was he doing there? Guarding the place?'

'No, he was actually the guest of honour. He – this is so droll – turned out to be Lady Lockhart's cousin! Oh, honestly, Joey, your face is a picture!'

It wasn't possible! The braw soldier had turned up at Blantyre and Seffy had met him! Yesterday! Why had the wee Sassenach waited all this time before telling her?

The fuzziness in her head had gone. She was alert now and she wanted every detail: what he'd said and done, how he'd looked, what he'd eaten. Everything.

But all in good time. On their way to the station, she'd as good as told Seffy she'd sworn off men forever and she'd been so scathing about the fella. Seffy was quite sure Joey had taken a shine to him; she certainly wasn't going to admit it now.

'Aw, that's a turn-up for the books, eh?' Joey said. 'Had he taken off his backpack and stopped sweatin'?'

She knew that would make Seffy laugh and she duly obliged, squeezing Joey's arm at the same time.

'Apparently he couldn't accept a lift from us because he had to run to his new posting at full tilt, under his own steam.'

Joey nodded. That explained his rudeness.

'And I must say, he looked terribly smart. Which was why it didn't even cross my mind it could be the same man. It was only when he mentioned being "barracked" by the Timber Corps that I put two and two together.'

It was Joey's turn to laugh. '"Barracked?"'

'Yes, he was most put out! He's probably not used to such disrespect! He's actually a major.'

A major! Joey wasn't surprised. He'd had an air of something special about him. 'Aw, I don't care what rank he is,' she said. 'He's evidently never learned any manners!'

'He's fairly civilised. He managed to hold a teacup and a conversation, all at the same time. And he does have a nice smile.'

'Aye, well I didnae get to see him smile, remember!'

'It was a tad embarrassing though, because my aunt and Lady Lockhart had conspired to pair us off.'

Joey swallowed. 'And er . . . did you hit it off, like?'

'Goodness, no! He was quite haughty, especially when he found out I was a lumberjill. I found myself promising to seek out whoever had heckled him and have a word!' She nudged Joey. 'So, consider yourself told!'

There was so much to take in but at least – oh, the relief – Seffy hadnae taken a fancy to him.

'He's ancient, of course,' Seffy said.

'Is he?'

'Hmm. Nearer thirty than twenty, I'd say. And he's got a scar, here.' She tapped her cheek. 'But he's not bad-looking.'

Not bad-looking? Joey almost choked at the understatement. But better that, than have Seffy swooning over him.

She felt rotten, pretending like this, but the ribbing she'd get now, if she confessed to liking him! And Seffy would wonder why she hadn't said anything before. No, she'd best keep her feelings to herself.

They were catching the other girls up. She didn't want to talk about the major in front of them, so she had to be quick.

'What's . . . did you find out his name?' Joey asked.

'Now, let me think . . .'

Aw, Seffy, come on. Please don't say you can't remember!

'It's Ralph something or other. Same as my father, actually. Yes, got it: it's "Ralph Stirling". And he comes from good Edinburgh stock!'

Joey felt light-headed at the thought of him: Major Ralph Stirling.

Oh, but what was the point?

She wasn't likely to bump into him again. Seffy might – at another society event – but Joey wouldn't be there. He was a toff, from a different world. And even if she did come across him, he wouldn't be interested in an ordinary lass like her.

'Anyway, on to more important news,' Seffy said. 'This "Mothers' Union" business.'

Joey nodded and swallowed her disappointment. The discussion of the major was over.

'I may as well tell everyone at the same time,' Seffy said. 'It's my aunt's new venture. It's going to be tremendous fun!'

She unlinked her arm from Joey's and gestured to the girls fifty yards ahead.

'Come on, run!' she said. 'Let's catch them up!'

Chapter 16

The next day, after work, Seffy strolled through the woods to meet Joey at the stables.

It was so peaceful. Occasionally, she passed trees daubed with white circles, destined to be telegraph poles but otherwise there was no sign that anyone had ever been in this part of the forest.

She was feeling particularly perky.

Yesterday, she'd bitten the bullet and explained Dilys' plans to the other girls – including Angie – on their way back from church.

And to her surprise, Angie had been most enthusiastic and had agreed everyone should attend Saturday's meeting. It could all be a cunning ruse, of course, but Angie had certainly given no indication that she'd be running off to Miss McEwen to tell tales.

Seffy suspected that some of the girls had only agreed to go to the meeting because she'd promised them cake. But hopefully, once fired up by her aunt, they'd see it made perfect sense to join the WHD, regardless of refreshments.

It was quiet at the yard. Seffy wondered for a moment whether she'd missed her pal.

The three horses were hanging their heads over the stable doors. They pricked up their ears when they saw her.

'Halloo, the house!' she called.

'Hullo!' came a reply from inside the grey's stall.

Seffy looked over the half-door. Joey was bending down, using a hoof pick on the horse's near hind leg.

'All alone?'

'Aye,' Joey said. 'I sent the others back to camp. I'm almost done here.'

'That's all right. I can wait. Remind me who this is.'

'This is Storm.'

Seffy swatted away a couple of flies that were buzzing around the horse's eyes and ran her hand down his warm neck.

'He's a darling. I always did have a soft spot for a grey.'

'Me too,' Joey said, straightening up. She came to the door, her face flushed. 'I worked with a grey called Monty once. Best horse in the world! He was gettin' on but he'd do anything for you. That horse taught me how to steer a plough!'

Seffy moved along to the next stable, where the horse was stretching out its neck, hoping for a tit-bit.

'That's Nippy.'

Seffy pulled her hand in. 'Crikes! Does it nip, then?'

Joey laughed. 'No! She's Nippy because she's agile, despite her size.'

Reassured, Seffy patted the mare and stretched up to scratch her head underneath her forelock.

'Oh, you like that, don't you, miss?'

Another bluebottle landed on Seffy's hand and she swiped it off. 'Pity about the blasted flies. Annoying little blighters.'

'Aye. They're a pain in the you-know-where.'

The flies were gathering in the corners of the horses' eyes; they had to constantly shake their heads to get rid of them.

'It's a pity they can't cool down in the burn, like us,' Seffy said.

Joey opened the stable door and came out into the yard, carrying a bucket.

'I haven't forgotten my promise,' she said, as she shot the

bolt. 'I'm waiting for the right moment to ask Miss McEwen if you can work with us. When she doesn't have a face like a wet weekend!'

'In that case, we might be waiting forever and a day!' Seffy laughed even though the mention of Miss McEwen had made her stomach twist. She was still smarting from the humiliation of being demoted by the woman, so publicly.

She looked around. 'I'd love to work here and get away from Angie Buchanan. I can't take to her at all.'

'Really? I'd never have guessed! But remember, we weren't awful keen on you, when you first arrived!'

That was true. But she'd been so different from the rest of them, with her English accent and – yes, she could admit it now – her rather uppity attitude.

'The lass probably feels uncomfortable,' Joey said. 'She's come to a camp where she knows no one and she's immediately given your job. Everyone could easily have been agin her.'

Yes, but they weren't against her; that was the whole point. Angie had smiled her smarmy smile, dished out goodies, told their fortunes and made them feel good about themselves. They'd all fallen under her spell.

Joey picked up a broom and started to sweep the yard. 'But they should've at least paid you the extra, for the months you were leader girl.'

'I'm more browned off about losing my position,' Seffy said. 'You know me, I like being in charge! I'm not bothered about the money. I won a stash from my brother in a bet. I'm rather flush at the moment.'

'Lucky you! I'd have fought for that extra money, if it were me,' Joey said. 'I send what I can spare from my wages home each month. There are a lot of mouths to feed.'

Seffy winced. She should try to remember that most of the girls – and Joey, in particular – were hard up. Money – or the lack of it – was always a sore point.

'I'm going to treat us all to a night out, very soon!' she said. 'Perhaps we could go into Inverness? I think we all need cheering up!'

Joey nodded. 'That'd be nice.'

Seffy's gaze landed on the last of the three horses. It was Nelson, the chestnut Suffolk punch who'd been misbehaving just before Hazel's accident.

She had no desire to fuss him, although he was looking at her hopefully. He gave a gentle snicker. She turned away and caught Joey watching her.

'Aw, don't be like that,' she said, leaning on the broom handle. 'What happened wasn't his fault. Here – gi' him this.'

She dug into her pocket and held out a piece of carrot. 'I kept it from supper last night.'

Seffy took it and pressed it between her fingers. 'It's all squidgy!'

'He won't mind.'

Nelson was kicking the stable door. He stopped when Seffy held the carrot out and took it from her gently, brushing her palm with his lips.

'Yikes,' she said. 'I'd forgotten how big he is. He must be seventeen hands.'

'Yes, he's about that. He's the biggest of the three, anyway.'

There was a pause, then Seffy said, 'And is he behaving himself, these days?'

'He's more of a handful than these two for sure, but he's no' bad.' Joey carried on sweeping, with vigorous strokes.

Seffy knew she was thinking about the accident again.

It hadn't been Joey's fault, but there was no point in saying it. Everyone had said it to Seffy too, after Hazel's death, and it had taken a long time before she'd believed it.

Joey propped the broom against a wall and started carrying buckets of water into the stables.

'Do you want some help?' Seffy asked.

'No,' she said. 'It won't take long.'

When Joey had finished, she wiped her hands on the front of her breeches and hesitated before she spoke.

Seffy braced herself. This was going to be about Hazel again.

'It's only,' Joey said, 'the other girls.' She shook her head. 'I dunno. I'm not saying they've forgotten—' she took a deep breath '—about Hazel. But . . .'

'They don't talk about her? And they seem all right? As though they're getting on with their lives?'

Joey nodded. 'Remember the ceilidh? I didn't dance that night, not once. I had this beautiful red frock. Irene had altered it, so it fitted like a glove. I'd never worn anything like it but . . . how could I dance? It had only been three months since Hazel had gone.'

Seffy felt winded. She hadn't known any of this. Why had no one told her? Perhaps they'd all been enjoying themselves too much to notice Joey sitting out? Which, if true, was doubly awful.

The ceilidh had been held for Dilys' birthday but it was also meant to cheer everyone up. Death was all around them but life, as her aunt had told Seffy, had to go on.

But it hadn't cheered up Joey.

'I was rather tied up that night,' Seffy said, with a wry smile. 'With Irene. So, I didn't notice you weren't dancing. I'm sorry.'

Tears were streaming down Joey's face. Seffy pulled out a handkerchief and handed it to her.

She blew her nose. Now Joey had started talking, it was as though she couldn't stop. But her voice was flat and lifeless. Seffy simply stood and listened.

'And now,' Joey said, sniffing, 'the new girls have come. And they're grand. Aw, I know you don't like Angie but she'll grow on you—'

Seffy doubted that but she nodded.

'—but it's like the gap that Hazel left has closed up.' Joey clasped her hands together. 'And everyone's moving on. Everyone but me.'

Seffy's heart ached for her pal. What kind of a friend had

she been? She'd had no idea that Joey was still consumed by the accident.

It had been different for her. She'd gone to Aunt Dilys' house to recover and she'd been encouraged to talk.

Joey had clearly never talked about it to anyone.

'One of the things my aunt told me is that grief is a visitor,' Seffy said. 'It comes and goes. Sometimes you'll feel terrible and other times you won't. And when you don't, you mustn't feel guilty.'

Joey nodded but she didn't look convinced.

Oh, bother, Seffy thought. She was useless at this. There must be something she could do to cheer Joey up. She glanced around, looking for inspiration.

Apart from the unwanted flies, it was a perfect, late afternoon. The air was warm, the sun was glinting through the trees and it wouldn't get dark for hours.

'I know!' she said, as a ridiculous half-baked idea occurred to her. 'This'll buck us up no end.'

Buck? Whoops, bad choice of words. She hoped that wasn't a premonition.

'It'll mean missing supper but we can probably beg leftovers from the kitchen.'

'Tell me, then!' Joey said.

Seffy smiled. 'How are you at riding bareback?'

Chapter 17

Joey looked at Seffy uncertainly.

'You want us to ride Storm and Nippy to the loch? Without any tack?'

'Yes! Actually, we don't have any!' Seffy shrugged. 'But they'll have their headcollars on and I can cobble together some reins out of lead ropes. We'll only be plodding. It'll get them away from these dratted flies.'

Joey was tempted.

But they shouldn't. They weren't allowed to ride the horses for pleasure and besides, riding bareback wasn't safe.

'We'll be in trouble if anyone sees us,' Joey said.

'True. There'll be the almightiest stink. Miss McEwen will lecture us on how the horses are "government property, not playthings!" but who's going to see? Come on! Are you a man or a mouse?'

It was a dilemma. If they were caught and her pay got docked as punishment, it would be a disaster. Her folks needed the money she sent. And besides, she wasn't too sure about this bareback riding lark.

Seffy had probably learned to ride before she could walk. She'd had her own ponies and all sorts. No one had ever taught Joey. She'd simply picked it up, during her time on the farm.

The sensible option would be to say no.

She sighed.

But sensible was dull; she was tired of playing safe, of acting like someone middle-aged when she wasn't even twenty-one. And it would be a caper to let the horses splash around in the loch. They worked hard; didn't they deserve some fun too?

She looked at Seffy and shook her head. 'You're a wee rebel, Miss Mills, a bad influence! But . . . aw, go on then, let's gi' it a go.'

The horses stood quietly, as Seffy gave Joey a leg-up onto Storm and then stood on a tree stump, to mount Nippy.

Joey's head was spinning. Were they really doing this? Working with the horses was dangerous enough but this – sitting high up on Storm, her legs dangling down and not even a proper bridle or reins to steer with – was madness.

'Wait!' Joey said. 'What's that noise?'

It was Nelson, kicking his stable door. Seconds later, he started whinnying: making desperate, ear-splitting shrieks that must be carrying for miles.

'If they hear that racket in camp and come to investigate, the game'll be up!' Seffy said. She started walking Nippy back towards the stables. 'We'll have to take Nelson instead.'

Joey's stomach clenched. Och, she wasn't sure about that, at all. What if he misbehaved? A hundred awful scenarios flashed through her mind. 'Do you think you can manage him, Seffy?' she called after her.

But Seffy was already leading Nelson out. 'Look, he's calmer now. He didn't want to miss out. It's a shame for Nippy but we'll take her next time.'

Next time? Joey gritted her teeth and grasped the makeshift reins that were lying across Storm's neck.

Let's get through this first, she thought, *before we start thinking about "next time".*

*   *   *

After twenty minutes, mostly spent walking sedately through the forest and along a few deserted lanes, they reached the loch.

It hadn't been too bad, Joey had to admit. The horses had been as good as gold.

The only hairy moments had been when Storm had broken into a trot to catch up with Nelson, who had a longer stride. Joey had bounced and jiggled and, for a few heart-stopping moments, had thought she might slip off his back.

'Grip with your thighs, knees and seat!' Seffy had shouted.

Joey wasn't sure how you were meant to grip with your "seat" – which was, presumably, your bahoochie – but she'd done her best. At least she'd managed to stay on.

And now, here they were. Apart from a few ducks bobbing on the surface of the water, the place was deserted.

The only movement came from the light wind, which was making wavelets on the loch and rippling through the horses' manes. Joey's hair flapped around her face; she should've tied it back.

'It's wonderfully cool,' Seffy said. 'And that breeze will keep the midges away.'

They brought the horses to a halt. Joey gazed out across the wide expanse of water, to the purple hills on the opposite shore. 'Remember when we crossed this loch in rowing boats, to get to that dance?'

Seffy smiled. 'I certainly do! It was the nineteenth of September, my twenty-first birthday, and I saw the Northern Lights.'

'Aye, and I missed them because I came back on the truck with the Canucks. That still smarts!' Joey laughed.

Seffy's smile faltered then, as though the memory was tinged with sadness. But then she seemed to pull herself together. She looked down the beach and nudged Nelson with her heels to ask him to walk on.

'Let's get past all this shingle,' she said. 'There's sand over there. It'll be much better for a gallop.'

Joey gasped. 'You're joking? No one said anything about galloping!'

'It'll be fine,' Seffy said. 'These are carthorses, not hunters or steeplechasers. They can't go very fast. It'll be like sitting in an armchair! But if you don't think you can manage it . . . ?'

The challenge hung in the air.

Joey sighed. If she backed out now, as well as looking like a prize softie, she'd spoil everyone's fun. It wasn't only Seffy who was filled with anticipation: the horses were throwing up their heads and refusing to stand still.

Maybe she simply needed to let go? She'd been like a coiled spring for so long. If she fell off, then so be it. Hopefully, the sand would make a soft landing.

She nodded. 'All right, let's do it.'

'Good-o! Now, they'll take off as soon as we give them their heads, so you need to be ready.'

Joey felt a surge of something rise up from her stomach. Perhaps it was excitement but it could also be fear.

'But listen,' Seffy added, 'if you do take a tumble, keep hold of the reins. We mustn't lose these chaps, whatever happens!'

When they reached the sand and the horses had a clear view of the long empty beach, they started snorting and side-stepping. Storm pawed the ground; Nelson gave a little buck and almost unseated Seffy.

Seffy laughed and turned him in a circle. 'He can't wait for the off! Just tell me when you're ready!'

Joey felt strangely calm. She gazed down the beach. The pale sand was the colour of sawdust. 'Aw, to heck wi' it!' she yelled. 'Whit's fur ye'll no go by ye!'

'I have no idea—'

Joey didn't hear the rest. Seffy's words were left behind and carried away on the wind.

As soon as she'd relaxed her hold on the reins, Storm had taken off, like a rocket.

Seffy gave a small yelp of surprise and seconds later, Joey heard the drumming of hooves as Nelson started to catch them up. In no time, the horses were galloping side by side along the beach.

Joey leaned forward and gripped Storm's mane.

The wind was making her eyes water and her hair was streaming out behind her. She stole a glance at Seffy and they grinned at one another. It felt amazing! The power of the horse beneath her, the speed and the wind in her hair. It was impossible not to smile.

'Yeehaa!' Seffy yelled, as she and Nelson surged ahead and streaked towards the water's edge. Joey and Storm tucked in behind them, keeping well clear of Nelson's powerful hindquarters.

Water splashed over them, like an icy rain shower. The girls squealed in delight and the horses tossed their heads and tails.

They galloped like that for a few hundred yards. Then they moved out to deeper water and slowed to a gentle canter.

Joey didn't care if she fell off now; the water would break her fall.

'Whoa up!' Seffy called.

They started to trot – oh, that was bouncy – and, finally, they were wading through the crystal-clear water at a walk.

The girls were panting, too breathless to speak and the horses were blowing. Joey was sure she could feel the thudding of Storm's heart.

'Oh, ma God!' she managed, finally. 'That was out of this world!'

Seffy laughed. 'Wasn't it? Well done, you! It was like you'd been glued on!'

They laughed and, when they couldn't find any more words to express how joyful it had been, simply shook their heads in wonder.

Joey leaned forward, rested her cheek on Storm's thick neck and hugged him.

'Good fella,' she said. She should never have doubted he'd look after her. She sat up straight again. 'Have you galloped on a beach before, Seffy?'

She was sure the answer would be yes. Seffy had done everything, been everywhere. But she shook her head.

'No, I never have. But I've always wanted to! So that's a lifelong ambition realised!'

Joey laughed. The lass did have a funny way with words. 'The others'll be green with envy,' Joey said.

'Don't tell them! Someone's bound to go running to Miss McEwen and we'll get it in the neck!'

Joey frowned. 'Do you think any of them would drop us in it like that?'

Seffy must be thinking of Angie. None of the others, not even Morag, would tell; she was sure of it.

'They might let it slip by accident,' Seffy said. 'Best keep it secret.'

She swung her leg over Nelson's back but as she dismounted, she staggered and fell backwards, shrieking. She lay helplessly in the shallows and when she finally managed to stand – weak with laughter – she was completely soaked. 'I'm fair drookit!' she said, proudly, as she led Nelson out of the loch.

Joey rode Storm up onto the beach and dismounted there.

When her feet touched the sand, water squelched in her boots and her knees almost buckled beneath her.

They stood back to allow the horses to shake themselves. Water was streaming down their legs and flanks.

'I bet they feel better for that,' Joey said.

'And I'll bet you ten shillings they're about to roll,' Seffy said. She tugged at Joey's arm. 'There they go! Stand back.'

Nelson – and then Storm – bent their front legs and thumped down inelegantly onto the sand. Then they rolled onto their backs, huge legs flaying, snorting and grunting with pleasure.

When they stood up, they were covered in sand. They shook themselves but most of it was still stuck to them.

'We'll have to brush that off when we get back,' Seffy said.

They weren't going to get any supper. If they had to groom the horses before settling them in for the night, the camp kitchen would be long closed. But Joey didn't care; it had been worth it.

The girls flopped down on the sand. They pulled off their boots, poured the water out, then peeled off their socks and laid them out on the ground to dry.

'We must look such a state!' Seffy said, running her fingers through her hair, which was plastered down on her head like a helmet. 'Good job no one can see us!'

Joey agreed. Her hair was hanging down around her shoulders in sopping tendrils.

Seffy stripped off down to her vest and laid her white shirt out to dry on a nearby rock.

The horses had started to forage, nibbling at weeds and bits of grass between the rocks.

'Do you think we should bring them nearer?' Joey asked. 'And tether them somewhere?'

'No, let them wander for a while. They never get the chance, stuck in a stable all day. Besides, they'll be tired after all that galloping. They won't go anywhere.'

Joey supposed Seffy was right. Nelson and Storm seemed perfectly calm and the conditions here were perfect. The cool breeze was coming over the loch and there wasn't a pesky midge or fly anywhere.

Seffy was stretched out, one hand behind her head. She patted the sand next to her. 'Why don't you lie down and dry out? That sun's still warm. It's heavenly.'

Joey nodded and did as she suggested. The tight knot that was always inside her had loosened a little. She could hear the cawing of a bird way up in the sky and chomping sounds from Nelson, as he grazed between the rocks.

Seffy's stomach rumbled loudly, making them laugh. 'I'm ravenous! I wish I'd got an apple or a jammy piece.'

Joey lay on her side, letting the sand fall through her fingers.

'Listen to you, with your "jammy piece"! You're a real Scots lass these days, hen!'

Seffy looked thoughtful. 'Whenever anyone calls me "hen" it reminds me of Irene.'

'Ah yes, Mrs Calder. I wonder how she's gettin' on, with her bairn and life in Glasgow? Hey, you're not wishing Irene was here now instead of me, are you?' Joey asked, pretending to be affronted.

'No, silly. You're my best pal up here. Besides, I can't imagine Irene on a horse, can you?'

'Never! Not unless she could ride side-saddle! So who's your other pal, then, if I'm only the "best up here"?'

'It's Emmie. Emerald. We've been best friends since we were eleven. We've done everything together. Not so much these days, though. She's a married lady, expecting her first child and I'm a working . . .' She searched for the word.

'Spinster?' Joey suggested, laughing.

'Oh, don't. I detest that word! But I'm sure she and I will always be pals, no matter what life throws at us.'

'It's a pretty name, "Emerald".'

'Isn't it? But yours is, too.' Seffy said.

'What, Joey? A baby kangaroo?'

'No, silly. I meant "Josephine." Does anyone ever call you that?'

'Not unless I'm in very big trouble!'

'Same here! My aunt's the only one who calls me "Persephone" and I always imagine she's cross with me!'

They were still laughing when the first gunshot rang out.

Chapter 18

The gunfire had come from further up the beach, behind them. It was immediately followed by an almighty bang, like a bomb exploding.

They screamed. Seffy swore under her breath and pulled Joey behind the cover of the rock on which she'd draped her shirt. They covered their heads with their arms.

Several more shots were fired, making them jump each time. Joey's ears were ringing. 'Jerries!' she said, breathlessly. 'How did they get here?'

'Oh, no! The horses!' Seffy said.

They scrambled to their feet but it was too late. There was a thunder of hooves, then Nelson, followed by Storm, galloped past in a flash of brown and grey. Their makeshift reins were trailing, their eyes wide in terror.

'Noo!' Joey cried, watching helplessly as they tore down the beach. Nelson suddenly swerved and headed for the trees on the right. Storm followed him.

More gunfire sounded and they threw themselves back down behind the rock.

'They've gone into the woods!' Joey said.

Seffy was pulling on her boots. 'At least they'll be safe in there.'

She moved slowly from a crouched position and peered over the rock.

'Blast!' she said, dropping down again. 'We're right in the middle of an army training exercise.'

Joey exhaled. 'Not Jerry, then?'

'Someone warned me about this. That major chap, actually. But he said they'd be in the woods.'

Joey's stomach lurched. The major? Was he involved in this? 'So, they're our fellas?' she asked. 'Do you think they'll help us get the horses back?'

Seffy made a hopeless gesture. 'We daren't risk going to ask them. We'll be gunned down! Oh, wait!' She reached up, grabbed her wet shirt from the rock and started waving it above her head.

'What're you doing?'

'Surrendering! My shirt'll look like a white flag.'

They waited for a minute until Seffy was red in the face from the exertion and the gunfire seemed to have stopped.

'I think it's done the trick,' Seffy said, struggling to put her wet shirt back on over her vest. She pulled it down as best she could and stood up.

'You stay here, in case the horses come back. Keep your head down!'

She set off down the beach towards the section of woods into which the horses had disappeared.

Joey groaned and squeezed her forehead, which had started to throb.

She might have known, the moment she let her guard down, something like this would happen. What a disaster!

What did she think she'd been doing, galloping bareback on the beach like the Queen of Sheba? It'd been stupid and reckless and now she was paying the price.

All the terrible things that could happen flashed through her mind.

The horses might gallop out of the woods and onto a road and meet one of those crazy POW trucks on a bend.

Or someone might steal them.

And if – when – Miss McEwen or Jock found out, she'd lose her job. She'd be hauled in front of someone official and sacked.

She cocked her head and listened. The gunfire hadn't resumed.

Men's voices were carrying on the breeze. Joey looked out across the water. Half a dozen soldiers in battledress were pushing a raft out from the shore.

They were shouting at one another, heaving themselves on board and pulling up those still in the water. Then they started paddling furiously and the raft inched out towards the middle of the loch.

'Aw, I can't stay here like a rabbit in a hole!' Joey cried, to no one in particular.

She stood up, ran around the rock in her bare feet and sprinted towards the part of the beach where the exercise was still in progress.

A group of men was marching in strict formation over the sand, heading, strangely, for the loch. She watched them for a second and then—

'OW!'

She'd run slap bang into a grim-faced soldier with a chest as hard as a rockface.

She sprang back, rubbing her nose.

'Hey!' he yelled. 'What do you think you're doing?'

He held up one hand in a "stay there" gesture, turned and waved a red flag at the men on the raft.

What was *she* doing? What was he doing, more like! He was clearly in charge and was, therefore, responsible for this whole mess.

'Will you stop this now?' Joey yelled. Her eyes were smarting. It'd hurt when she'd run into him. 'Cease fire!' she added, for good measure.

'No need to shout, miss. I've called a halt to the exercise.'

Joey looked at his rugged face and the scar on his right cheek and felt a jolt of recognition. It was him! The soldier from the road. The major, as he'd turned out to be. Ralph Stirling. Honest to God, the man got everywhere!

He was as big and braw as she remembered. But he wasn't as tetchy. This time, she was the one who was cross.

As he stared at her, Joey saw herself through his eyes: soaking wet, barefoot, covered in sand, with damp hair flying about her face and screaming blue murder. He must think she was some kind of harpy.

'Are there any more of you?' he asked, looking down the beach.

Seffy! She'd forgotten Seffy.

'Aye. My pal's away after the horses. They took fright, thanks to your banging nonsense and God knows if we'll ever find them and you might at least help us get them back . . .'

Her voice trailed off. She was gabbling now. He was infuriatingly calm.

Major Stirling swallowed, his Adam's apple bobbed and she wasn't sure whether he was trying not to smile or not to lose his temper.

'The banging nonsense, miss,' he said, firmly, 'is a military exercise. We're on manoeuvres. Or rather, we were until someone waved a white flag.'

'Aye, that was my pal. And a good thing she did, else you might've blown us to pieces!'

She was jabbing her finger at him and as he stepped nearer she thought for a moment he was going to reach out and grab it.

She'd spotted a movement out of the corner of her eye. The men on the raft were paddling back into shore but the troops on the beach were still marching. They'd carried on into the loch and the water was now up to their thighs.

She nodded at them. 'Are those fellas meant to be going for a swim?'

The major wheeled round and muttered something unintelligible. 'HALT!' he yelled, making Joey wince and hold a hand to her ear.

The men stopped.

He exhaled, ordered them to turn, march and halt again and finally, 'At ease!'

His troops were sopping wet from the waist down but they marched back up the beach, eyes front, mouths set, as though nothing untoward had happened. Daft so-and-sos.

'What were they doing?' Joey asked.

'Obeying orders. I told them to march and they couldn't stop until I gave the order to do so.'

'Even if they ended up chin-deep in the water?' Joey laughed. 'I've never heard anything so stupid in ma whole life!'

He managed a small smile, as though he agreed. 'This isn't possible,' he said, slowly, 'but I feel as though we've—'

'—met before?'

His eyes widened in surprise. 'Yes.'

'I—' She started to say. Then she heard the thud of hooves behind her.

Seffy! Oh, thank God.

She was panting and red-faced but, hallelujah, she was riding Storm. He was skittish: tossing his head and sweating. So much for cooling him down at the loch. But otherwise, he looked in fine fettle.

Joey beckoned Seffy nearer. 'Well done! Dunnae fret, they've stopped shooting and drowning themselves. No luck finding Nelson?'

'Not yet.'

Seffy looked down at the soldier, who'd backed off. 'Oh, hullo. We meet again, Major Stirling.'

He pulled off his cap and Joey tried not to mind that he hadn't done that for her.

He nodded, an ironic smile on his lips. 'Lady Persephone. Fate has conspired to bring us together again. Or are your aunt and my cousin behind this?'

He turned to Joey. 'And I've placed you now, miss. Those dimples gave it away. You were the one barracking me from the lorry.'

She nodded. 'So—' She'd started to say "sorry" but stopped herself. What did she have to apologise for? 'So what?' she said. 'It was me, aye, I cannae deny it!'

She sounded brash but inside, she was dying. He'd remembered her – that was something – but now he must think she was loud and rough.

He only had eyes for "Lady Persephone".

'Thanks for calling a halt to things,' Seffy said, as though none of this was out of the ordinary. 'But we really must dash. We're still a horse down. Joey, jump up behind me, then the major can continue with his exercise.'

Joey looked at Storm. How was she supposed to get up there? She needed summat to stand on. Oh, what did she have to lose? She turned to the major.

'Sir, would you mind givin' me a leg up?'

Sir? Where had that come from? The man had sent her doolally.

He looked startled, as though she'd suggested something improper and, despite everything, Joey wanted to laugh.

'I cannae get on, else,' she said, nodding at the horse, towering above her.

The major's cool confidence seemed to desert him. He looked at Storm and grimaced.

'You don't like horses, right?' Joey asked.

'It's more that they don't like me.'

She felt like using the words Seffy had used on her earlier: "Are you a man or a mouse?"

But then he changed his mind.

'Very well,' he said, stepping forward. He reached down and tapped her left leg. 'Bend this. No, wait. Don't you have any shoes?'

Oh, crumbs! She'd completely forgotten she was barefoot.

She ran back to the rock, stuffed her wet socks in her pockets and put on her boots as fast as she could. She was all fingers and thumbs, as she tied the laces in a double knot. When she returned, Seffy and the major were chattering away like old pals. Of course they were.

Joey had to cough to get their attention. Then she stood at Storm's side, bent her leg and before she could even take a breath, the major heaved her up behind Seffy, as though she weighed no more than a bag of flour.

'Thank you!' Seffy said and, while Joey was still reeling from everything that had just happened, they cantered away down the beach.

Joey gripped Seffy's waist. She could feel the major's eyes on them and she prayed they wouldn't fall off, like a couple of clowns.

She leaned in against Seffy's cold back. Her shirt was still wet.

'He likes you!' she said.

'He does not!' Seffy called back, but she sounded pleased. 'He thinks I'm part of his cousin's conspiracy to pair us off!'

This had all been one big hoot for Seffy. Never mind they'd almost been shot or that they'd lost the horses and might still be in terrible trouble. Did the girl never fret about anything?

'Mind you,' Seffy said. 'He's definitely more interesting when he's not at a stuffy tea party. He's a man of action! He would be quite a distraction, wouldn't he?'

Joey's heart sank. He'd be a delicious distraction. So Seffy did fancy him, after all. She supposed she could hardly blame her.

They slowed down to a trot and headed for the trees.

'Aye,' Joey said, reluctantly. 'He'd certainly take your mind off the Canadian fella.'

She could imagine the major and Seffy together. They'd make a handsome pair. They were both toffs; they spoke each other's language. And why should it matter to her, if Seffy started stepping out with him? She had no chance with him herself: that was just wishful thinking.

Seffy was giggling and saying something Joey couldn't catch; her words were lost on the breeze.

'What did you say?' she asked.

'I said I'll have to engineer another meeting. One that doesn't involve blasts and bullets!'

'Aye. Good idea.'

Joey felt suddenly flat and hungry She wanted to find Nelson and head back to camp.

She had no doubt Seffy would get her man. It gave her a dull ache in her chest, thinking about it.

But she would try to be happy for her friend.

Chapter 19

Tattie was rinsing out her clothes in the sink, when Seffy burst into the washroom.

'Where is everyone?' she demanded.

'Out,' Tattie said. 'They're away to see wee Jock, the new bairn in the village.'

Seffy nodded. 'Why didn't you go?'

Tattie looked down at the sopping clothes in her hands. 'I had a bit o' washing to do.'

In truth, she'd been shamed into "tidying herself up" by Angie.

Seffy ran her hands through her hair. 'We're in an awful pickle! Can you help, Tattie?'

As they ran towards the woods, Seffy explained how she and Joey had lost a horse. They'd lost two, in fact, but they'd found one. Joey was riding it to the stables now, in case its pal had found its own way home. It might've done if it had enough sense and a homing instinct.

'Like a pigeon?' Tattie asked.

'Yes. Listen, you mustn't tell Angie. I know you're as thick as thieves but she'll be honour-bound to tell the bosses. And Joey and I will be in trouble.'

Tattie's heart sank but she nodded.

She was between a rock and a hard place. If Angie found out she'd kept a secret from her, she'd be cross. Whatever she did, someone would be put out.

Before they split up to start searching, Tattie asked what the horse looked like.

'He's a chestnut Suffolk punch.'

'What?'

'He's brown,' Seffy said. 'Chestnut. The colour of a conker? Look, never mind. He's a hulking great horse. You can't miss him! There won't be another big brown creature in the forest! If you find him, hold onto him and yell for me. Now, go!'

They ran off in different directions.

After a short while, Tattie stopped to catch her breath. Row upon row of identical fir trees stretched in every direction. It was dusk, the sun was setting, it would be easy to get lost.

If this was a fairy tale, she'd have scattered a trail of breadcrumbs behind her, so she could find her way back.

She took a deep breath and set off again.

After she'd been searching for a while, with no luck, she heard sounds up ahead. Voices. Or was it the wind, whistling through the treetops? She listened hard: it was definitely men's voices.

A twig cracked and she spun round.

'Oh!' She gave a little start.

The horse! There he was, quite unexpectedly. Big and brown, exactly as Seffy had said and standing only a few feet away.

But he wasn't alone.

A giant of a man – well over six feet tall – was at his shoulder, holding the rein. He was in his twenties, with a suntanned face. He was wearing a brown uniform.

His eyes met hers and Tattie wasn't afraid. She'd been in plenty of lonely places where meeting a stranger like this would've filled her with terror but not now.

It was a relief to stop running. She didn't actually have the horse yet but she had no doubt the man would hand it over.

'Is you?' he asked, gesturing to the horse.

'Err, yes. Ta very much. That's who – what – I'm lookin' for.'

He smiled and patted the horse's neck. 'Is *bello. Un cavallo molto bello.*'

Tattie smiled uncertainly. What was all this "*bello*" business? Perhaps that was the horse's name but how would this fella know that?

The horse was a big brute and it kept putting its head down, yanking the man's arm. Maybe she should ask him to hold on to it, until she could find Seffy?

Tattie licked her lips, raised her fingers to her mouth and whistled, long and loud up into the treetops.

The horse's ears flicked back; the man looked impressed.

'*Brava!*' he said.

They listened but there was no answering call. The only sound was the men's voices – and laughter – up ahead.

'You come?' the man asked, pointing down the track. He set off, leading the horse, who went with him quite happily.

Tattie had no choice but to follow them.

The voices got louder and she could smell woodsmoke and something else, too. It was a rich, good smell. She breathed in hard but she couldn't work out what it was.

'Please,' the man said, bowing. They'd stopped in a clearing. He made a sweeping gesture, like he was welcoming Tattie into his home.

The voices fell silent.

Tattie blinked hard.

In front of her was a campfire and a dozen men, all wearing the same brown uniform as the man who'd led her here.

Aw, but they were bonny lads. And they were smiling at her.

One fella was tending a teapot on a metal stand over the fire. He straightened up and a couple of the others got to their feet, respectfully.

One of the men said something in a foreign language, which made them all laugh.

120

It felt like the best kind of dream. Perhaps, as she'd hastened through the woods, a branch had fallen on her head and now she was in heaven?

'*Bella!*' one of the men said.

Bello, bella. There they went again.

Tattie noticed a soldier, sitting with his back pressed up against a tree. He looked nothing like these fellas: he was small and pale, a ghost of a man. His rifle was hanging loosely around his neck by its strap.

Of course! These were Italian prisoners. She'd seen them – or fellas like them – when Angie had arrived in the truck.

The guard looked up at her and yawned. He took a drag of his ciggie and blew a cloud of blue smoke into the air.

'Do you know what they're saying?' she asked him.

'They say you beautiful,' he said, in a monotone voice.

Tattie felt her ears turn pink. 'Don't be daft.'

'No, is right. They like all ladies.'

Och, he was being silly now. Although, when she looked at the men smiling at her, she had to admit, they were paying her a lot of attention. Maybe it was a while since they'd seen a lassie.

Tattie had never been called beautiful before. Probably because she wasn't. Her face was as dotty as a set o' dominoes, though her skin was better these days, thanks to the fresh air and sunshine. And she wasn't womanly. She was skinny and folk often thought she was a laddie: not only on account of her short hair but because she went straight up and down and had no chest to speak of.

But even if it wasn't true, it was still nice to be called beautiful.

She sat down on the forest floor near the guard and folded her legs underneath her.

A pair of robins flew past, chasing one another. One of them landed on a nearby branch and cocked its head at them.

The guard had seen it too.

'This bird is *rudzik* in my language,' he said. 'And in English? Is what?'

'It's called a robin.'

'Robin,' he repeated and nodded.

'*Rud*—' she tried to remember the word he'd used.

'*Rudzik.*'

'*Rudzik.*'

They nodded at each other.

'TATTIE?' Seffy was yelling from somewhere nearby. 'Where in heaven's name are you?'

Tattie quickly stood up.

'Over here! I've got the horse!'

Aw, but had she? She'd forgotten all about it in the excitement of seeing these fellas and being called beautiful. But it was still there, standing quietly with the tall man.

The men were muttering amongst themselves and looking around. *Oh, you wait, fellas,* Tattie thought, *now you're really going to see someone bonny.*

They burst into excited chatter when Seffy appeared. There were yet more cries of '*Bella!*'

'Oh, hello, chaps,' Seffy said, scratching her head. 'Ah, there he is!'

She ran up to the horse and took the rein from the man. 'Well done, Tattie! And – erm, you, sir. *Grazie!* Gosh, what a relief!'

Seffy inhaled deeply and closed her eyes for a second, as though smelling something good.

She opened them again and smiled at the Italians. 'Now, which one of you is brewing coffee?'

'And then I said, "And more to the point, might I have a cup?"' Seffy said, making the other girls laugh.

It was later that night, a few minutes before lights out. Everyone was tucked up in bed and Joey had assured Tattie, in a whisper, that both horses were safely tucked up in their stables, too.

Seffy was relating how she and Tattie had come across the Italian POWs, brewing coffee.

'How do they get coffee?' Seffy asked. 'We don't even have any!'

'They probably get Red Cross parcels from home,' Jean said. 'Did they give you some?'

'Oh yes! They were quite happy to share it, weren't they, Tattie? It was divine! I can't remember the last time I tasted anything so good.'

Tattie nodded. The coffee had been too bitter for her taste. She'd been tempted to hold her nose, to get it down.

'Never mind the coffee,' Morag said. 'What were POWs doing in the woods?'

'They had a bonfire,' Tattie said.

'Yes, they were burning brushwood,' Seffy said. 'Which they must have collected. So, if I'm not very much mistaken—'

Jean gasped. 'They're the "new folk" who'll be working alongside us?'

'Exactly!' Seffy said. 'The mystery is solved!'

'I'm not sure I like this,' Enid said. 'Will it be safe? They're the enemy, after all!'

Jean and Seffy reassured her that the authorities wouldn't let the Italians work in the woods if they posed any kind of threat.

'And besides, they have guards with them,' Seffy added.

Tattie bit her lip. The guard she'd spoken to – that skinny pale lad – wouldn't be able to put up much of a fight, if anything went wrong.

'It'll make a nice change to have some chaps around the forest again,' Seffy said.

Angie shifted in her bed. 'Aye, well I wouldn't get too excited. You won't be working alongside them.'

Seffy's smile faded. 'Won't I?'

'No. I'm rearranging things. Enid and Morag, I'm putting you back together—'

Enid cheered and thumped her pillow in delight.

'Grace, you can go with Flora and I'll be working with Belinda.'

Tattie felt a thud of disappointment. She wasn't included. She was still a little way off being able to join the felling gang.

'And what about me?' Seffy asked.

'You'll be working with the horses,' Angie said.

Seffy looked across at Joey and mouthed 'Thank you!'

'I don't know why you're thanking her,' Angie said. Tattie winced at the tartness in her voice. 'Joey said you wouldn't mind swapping but it was me who cleared it with Miss M. She took some persuading!'

There was silence; everyone was waiting for Seffy's response.

'Thank you,' she mumbled, eventually.

'What were you the two of you doing in the woods, anyway?' Angie asked.

Tattie swallowed, stuck for words.

'We were gathering firewood for the stove,' Seffy said, quickly. 'Who knows when the nights will turn chilly again? This is Scotland, after all!'

Angie narrowed her eyes at Tattie and harrumphed, as though she didn't believe a word of it.

Thankfully, someone turned out the light and it was pitch-black in the hut.

Tattie heard Angie shift in her bed.

'You should've come with us tonight, to see the bairn,' Angie whispered. 'Don't keep to yourself so much. Try to make pals with the other girls, eh?'

Tattie was confused. 'But you said I should do ma washing and not come wi' you.'

'Night, night!' Jean called out.

'Don't let the bed bugs bite!' Enid called back.

In the darkness, Tattie stretched a hand towards Angie's bed and shook the edge of her mattress. 'You said it! You DID!'

But Angie didn't answer. She must, Tattie supposed, already be asleep.

Chapter 20

'I hate being in her debt,' Seffy said, glaring at Angie, who was sitting at the next table.

Joey sighed. They were at breakfast, the morning after Angie had announced the changes to the teams and Seffy hadn't stopped moaning.

'Look, I'm sorry I didn't get to Miss McEwen before her,' Joey said, swallowing a mouthful of toast. 'But does it matter? You've been hankering after working with the horses for a year! And now you've got the job but you're still no' happy!'

She rubbed at her temple; she had the start of a headache.

She hadn't slept well again last night but this time, it wasn't nightmares that had kept her awake but thoughts of yesterday, at the loch.

It was a blow, not being able to tell the others how she'd galloped bareback, escaped gunfire and explosions, lost and found the horses and had an encounter with a dashing commando.

It was like something out of an adventure story.

'What are you smiling about?' Grace asked, from across the table.

But before Joey could answer, Jock stood up and started rattling a spoon in a saucepan.

'Listen up, lumberjills! I have news! Some of the Eyeties have been taken off the farms and brought in to help us out.'

The Macdonald girls exchanged glances and satisfied nods. They'd guessed right.

Jock laughed. 'Stunned silence? Now, there's a novelty! The fellas are being billeted in part of the Canadians' old camp, up the road.'

'Don't suppose there's any chance of the dances or the cinema nights startin' up again, is there?' Enid asked and everyone laughed.

'But why do we need fellas?' Morag asked. 'Do the authorities think we cannae cope?'

'No one's saying that,' Jock said. 'But the Canucks are gone and there are still plenty o' trees wantin' felling. Don't be afeared. The Eyeties won't be any trouble.' He winked. 'Ye might even grow to like them!'

Miss McEwen stepped forward and put her hand up for silence. 'Calm down, girls! I hardly need remind you, these men are prisoners of war! I strongly advise against romantic attachments! Most will be married or have sweethearts. When the war's over, they'll head home without so much as an *arrivederci*!'

The girls erupted into excited chatter.

Joey rolled her eyes at Seffy. 'So much for "calm down",' she said. 'Now all they can think about is falling in love with a Tallie.'

Not her, though. She could think of no other man but the major. She glanced at Seffy, sitting next to her and wondered if she felt the same way.

'The Eyeties are starting today!' Jock yelled. 'So, look sharp!'

'Angie knew!' Enid said, eyes wide. 'She saw it in the stars! Angie, didn't you tell Flora she'd soon be meeting tall men in the woods?'

Angie nodded and a few girls exchanged knowing smiles, as though they weren't surprised at all.

'I bet she found out when she thumbed the lift to camp,' Seffy said. 'She was in the cab with the guards. They most likely let it slip.'

'Aye, you're probably right.' Joey pushed her chair back and stood up. She wasn't in the mood to hear more grumbles about Angie.

'Are you ready, Seffy? Come on, I'd like to take a look at the

Tallies before we head off to the stables. Show me the one who found Nelson. I've got an idea.'

When they arrived at the felling site, the Italians were already there. It was the first time most of the lumberjills had seen them at ground level and not hanging out of a truck, catcalling.

They were quiet and respectful. The girls and Jock stood a little way apart and the men looked back at them, warily.

'Not quite so sure of themselves now, are they?' Jean said.

'Aye, not half as fresh!' Morag said.

'*Buon giorno*,' a few of them murmured.

'See the tall chap at the back?' Seffy said to Joey. 'He's the one who found Nelson. But why d'you want to know?'

Joey looked at the fella. He was standing quietly, his arms crossed. Perhaps he would do.

'Because I'm thinking of asking Jock if we can have one of these fellas to work with us. But do you think it's safe?'

'They've only got one guard,' Jean said, nodding at a soldier standing nearby. 'And they're wearing white armbands, which means they're harmless.'

'Most are safe,' the guard confirmed.

'Most?' Joey said. 'What about the rest?'

'Others not allowed,' the guard said. 'Fascists.'

'Aw, don't you fret about them,' Jock said, quickly. 'The bad lads are all locked up.'

'What do the different armbands mean?' Joey asked.

'White's harmless,' Jock said, 'and grey's a wee bit less harmless but nothing to fret about. The black armband brigade are the Fascist fellas he just mentioned. They won't be allowed to work near you lassies.'

'I dunnae think I could work near them if they were Germans,' Enid said. 'They're the real foe, right?'

'Not the ordinary German folk,' Jean said. 'They probably hate the war as much as us. You mean the Nazis. I'd say they're worse than the Eyeties.'

Seffy had been quiet up to now but she suddenly spoke up. 'I don't think we should call them "Eyeties",' she said.

'I agree!' Angie said.

Joey smiled at the shocked look on Seffy's face. For once, she and Angie weren't at loggerheads.

'Why not?' Morag asked. 'That's their name.'

Seffy shook her head. 'I don't think it's particularly nice. Nicknames often aren't.'

Joey frowned. All the lumberjills were listening now and a few were muttering to each other. Any minute, someone would probably accuse Seffy of being unpatriotic, sticking up for the enemy. She might find herself getting into a row.

But Seffy either hadn't noticed or didn't care.

'Imagine if our boys were prisoners in a foreign land,' she said. 'Wouldn't we hope that even if those in charge weren't kind to them, that the ordinary folk would be?'

Everyone was quiet, thinking about their loved ones. All the girls knew fellas who were serving king and country: friends, sweethearts, cousins or brothers, facing all kinds of peril. The thought of any of the men Joey knew being held prisoner or mistreated made her feel lousy.

Seffy was talking sense again. That whole anti-Angie business was daft, of course, but now she'd put that silliness aside, Joey felt nothing but pride in her pal.

'We are the ordinary folk for these captured men,' Seffy said. 'So, let's be kind, shall we? And that starts with what we call them. Do we agree not to say "Eyeties" from now on?'

Jock was scratching his beard but he didn't object.

A few girls nodded and said, 'Aye!'

'What shall we call them, then?' Flora asked. Everyone knew Flora's pa was serving and she'd listened, pale-faced, as Seffy had made her wee speech.

'"Tallies" is all right, isn't it?' Grace said. 'We all call them that.'

Seffy wrinkled her nose. 'Not really. Not now they're going to be working alongside us. I was thinking, we could—' She glanced over at the POWs, who were watching from a few yards away. Whether or not they could understand was anyone's guess.

Seffy exhaled. 'Well, this might seem rather radical but perhaps we could actually ask them their names? And use those?'

At afternoon tea break, as they sat around the campfire, Flora proudly announced that she'd learned quite a few names already.

Seffy was pleased: the girl had been paying attention, for once, although as she started to reel them off, Seffy had to ask her to keep her voice down. The Italians' fire was only across the clearing and it wouldn't do for them to hear.

Flora lowered her voice. 'Private Giovanni Alessi!' she said. 'That's one of them.'

'You know "Giovanni" is the equivalent of John, in English,' Jean said.

'Aw, is that right?' Flora said. 'Anyhow, I shall call him "Gio" for short.'

Angie tutted. 'They're soldiers. You should use their rank.'

Flora shrugged. 'No, they said it's all right. We're all on first-name terms!'

She cast a sly look at Enid. 'I think someone's already sweet on Gio!'

'Aw, get away with you!' Enid said. But she was giggling and pink.

'The one with the curly moustache is Mattias,' Flora continued. 'I suppose that's Matthew, in English. He showed me a photograph of his wife and baby. He's had to stop kissing it because he was wearing away the picture.

'There's another called Luigi and in English, that's . . .'

The girls laughed as Flora almost went cross-eyed trying to work out the English equivalent.

'I don't think there is one,' she said, finally.

'And you've found a fella who speaks good English, haven't you?' Grace prompted.

'Aye! Sergeant Paolo Cigno! That means Paul Swan, in English,' he said. 'He was a school teacher before he got cons – whatever it's called—'

'Conscripted,' Jean said.

'He said none of them wanted to fight in a war but they had no choice. Isn't that right, Grace?'

Grace looked sheepish: clearly she and her partner Flora had spent some time getting to know the men.

Seffy glanced at Angie but rather than looking cross, as she might have expected, the girl was nodding and smiling at Flora. Wonders would never cease.

'Yes,' Grace said. 'They weren't in uniform at all 'til they got drafted. They were office workers and carpenters, builders and chefs and the like.'

'And Paolo said they're glad to be out of it,' Flora said. 'They thought it'd rain all the time in Scotland, so the weather's better than they'd expected. They're homesick, of course but they'd rather be here than on a submarine.'

'A submarine?' Jean said. 'Not the desert in North Africa?'

'Some of them were captured in the desert,' Grace said. 'but others were on a submarine.' She smiled. 'Paolo didn't know the English word for "submarine", so he mimed being underwater.'

'It was hysterical!' Flora said, laughing. 'You should've seen it.'

'Goodness,' Seffy said, with a shudder. 'The thought of being incarcerated in a tin can at the bottom of the sea is bringing me out in a cold sweat.'

'I think I'd like it,' Flora mused. 'Watching all the fishes swimming by.'

'When I was about seven,' Seffy said, 'someone shut me in a trunk, at school, as a prank. I was in there for hours and it was quite terrifying. I've never been able to stand small spaces like that – where I can't get out or see the exit – ever since.'

The other girls were quiet.

'What kind of school did you go to?' Jean asked. 'That's barbaric!'

Seffy laughed but stopped when she saw the looks of pity on the other girls' faces. 'It's what happened at boarding school,' she said, with a shrug. 'One got used to it after a while. But before that—' her voice cracked '—it was rather lonely. I mean, until one made pals. You need allies in a place like that. Once you've got pals, it's not so bad. The bullies can't get you!'

'I can't imagine you ever being bullied,' Joey said.

'Ah, well, you don't know everything about me! I am a woman of mystery!' Seffy laughed again, a little too loudly this time.

She was glad when Angie stood up and announced it was time to get back to work.

Chapter 21

It was Saturday afternoon. Seffy and the other Macdonald girls were on their way to the village hall for the inaugural meeting of the Women's Home Defence Corps.

They wouldn't see the Italians again until Monday and Enid wondered what they'd be doing over the weekend.

'Playing football and going to church,' Angie said.

'How does she know so much about it?' Seffy muttered to Joey.

'I hear she's got quite pally with one of them,' Joey replied. 'Luigi. The one with the cap. Grace says she's always nipping off for a chat wi' him.'

Fancy that. Miss Angie Buchanan wasn't as perfect as she liked to make out. Imagine if Miss McEwen found out she was slacking and had to have a word? It would make Seffy's day.

'Oh, we're the first to arrive!' Jean said, as they walked into the empty hall.

Aunt Dilys and Marigold were sitting disconsolately at a table near the stage, facing rows of empty seats.

Dilys had a face like thunder. It wasn't a good start. At least Seffy had done her bit: she'd brought all the Macdonald girls.

Thanks to Angie's encouragement, they'd all been keen to come, including Flora, who had no idea what the WHD entailed but didn't want to miss out.

'It's no bad thing if we're the only ones,' Enid said. 'There'll be more cake for us!' She looked around. 'Where is it?'

'It's in the kitchen, dear,' Marigold said. 'For later. After the main business of the day!'

Joey nudged Seffy. 'That girl never stops eating. My ma would say she's got worms.'

Seffy laughed. 'I love how you say that.' She tried it out. 'Worrr-ums.'

'What kind of cake is it?' Flora asked.

Aunt Dilys thumped the table. 'Forget about the confounded cake! Come here, girls, and take a seat. Well done, Persephone, for rallying the troops but there are dozens of lumberjills at your camp. Couldn't you have persuaded any more?'

Gosh, her aunt was such an ingrate. How about, "Thank you, Persephone, excellent recruiting!"? Why was nothing she did ever quite good enough?

Seffy rubbed her nose. 'I did ask around but everyone was too busy or too tired.'

'Tired? We're all tired! I'm exhausted but I'm about three times their age! They're not too tired to go dancing though, I'll wager!'

'Belinda said she might join,' Joey said. 'But most girls are too fagged out, like Seffy said. Or they don't want to give up their half-day, even if it is in defence of the realm.'

Dilys turned her attention to the girls who had, at least, shown willing.

'Now, don't sit at the back. Come to the front row, where I can look you in the eye!'

It was a joke but some of the girls – Tattie for example, who'd never met Dilys before – were looking rather nervous.

'Here, let's bring these seats nearer the front,' Dilys said.

While the seating was being rearranged, Seffy turned to Marigold.

'Didn't she manage to recruit any women from church? Via the hymn books?'

Marigold rolled her eyes. 'A few were interested but their husbands were agin it. Dilys hasn't stopped gurning about it. "Do we live in the Middle Ages? Are women still in servitude to their lords and masters?" I'm sick of it!'

Seffy could understand her aunt's disappointment. They could hardly have a proper defence corps if no one joined from the village.

'What's this I hear about you working with POWs now?' Marigold asked, eyes bright. 'How exciting!'

Seffy smiled. "Exciting" wasn't the word she'd have used, although some of the girls were definitely thrilled by the new development.

She felt sorry for the Italians. She couldn't think of anything worse than being held captive, separated from loved ones and with no idea of when one's situation might change. So, she'd be polite and respectful but she'd be keeping her distance from the POWs.

The last time a group of foreigners had worked alongside the lumberjills, it had ended in tears.

A memory of Callum Fraser popped into her head and she pushed it away. She had to stop thinking about him or she'd go stark-staring mad.

The girls were settling down on the front row of seats.

'Did you go to the Home Guard meeting, Aunt?' Seffy asked.

'Oh, that! What a rabble! Bickering and squabbling over whether hay bales make a decent road block or the best way to disable a bicycle. Honestly, it was worse than the WI!'

'Dilys was asked to leave the WI,' Marigold said.

Seffy sighed. 'A complete waste of time then?'

'No, actually, I learned quite a bit. You'll see! Now, do sit down, Persephone. I'm going to start.'

Joey had saved Seffy a seat and she sat down as Dilys thumped the table.

'LADIES! Thank you for coming today for what I hope will be the first of many meetings. I've been in London recently, where I was inspired by women who've set up female combat groups.

They're like the Home Guard but run for, and by, women, to defend home, hearth and country. Now, we may be a long way from the capital—'

'Thank God,' Joey muttered.

'—but we don't live in a backwater!'

Everyone looked at Dilys doubtfully.

'And even if we do, we don't have to be backward and behind! I want to set up something similar here. Those London women don't have any particular skills or accomplishments. In fact, they're less well-equipped than you. You're young, strong and fit as fleas! They don't have any physical advantage over you, they merely have knowledge – which we can obtain – and access to firearms, which is, I'll admit, a stumbling block at present.'

The hall door creaked open and Lady Lockhart slipped inside. She was wearing a headscarf, pleated skirt, twinset and pearls. 'Cameron thinks I'm at bridge, so I can't stay long. I came in the pony and trap. Such fun! I'm not promising to join but I wanted to show my support and at least attend the first meeting.'

'Same here!' Marigold said, wilting slightly under Dilys' glare. 'I'm only here today to bring the cake.'

The girls shuffled along and made room for Lady Lockhart at the end of a row.

Dilys pointed at her. 'Don't dash off at the end before I've spoken to you about rifles, Lavinia.'

Lady Lockhart's eyes widened. 'Very well. But do you really think this is absolutely necessary? Isn't invasion unlikely now? That's what Cameron thinks.'

'Yes, that's right,' Jean said. She pushed her glasses up her nose. 'Hitler's turned his attention to the East.'

'And the Americans have joined in now, of course,' Lady Lockhart said. 'I don't think Herr Hitler would try it.'

'But that's exactly what the wily little creep wants us to think!' Dilys said. 'He wants to lull us into a false sense of security and before you know it, we'll be overrun with Nazis!

135

Has the Home Guard been stood down? No, it jolly well has not! Which tells you something!' She tapped the side of her nose. 'The government knows more than it's letting on.'

'But—' Jean started but Dilys was off again.

'Until the war's over, no one knows what might happen. Inverness isn't a million miles away. Jerry could drop down in parachutes, aiming for the city and get blown off course. Who knows what terrible deeds he's planning?

'Weren't any of you in the Girl Guides? "Be prepared" – isn't that the motto? Those countries on the continent who've been invaded were taken by surprise. If their populations had been better prepared, they mightn't now be living under Nazi rule. Let's not make the same mistake!'

"Nazi rule". It was a chilling thought. There were a few murmurs of agreement. Lady Lockhart's thoughtful "Hmm" was the loudest of all.

'So, are you with me?' Dilys asked. 'We need to train and be prepared and we need to start now!'

Angie stood up. Her chair made a loud scraping noise on the floor. 'I think I can speak for all of us, your ladyship, when I say we're with you all the way!'

Joey nudged Seffy. 'Ladyship? She's getting mixed up.'

'No, my aunt's a lady too.' Seffy giggled. 'We're ten a penny round here.'

'Those in agreement,' Angie said, 'say "Aye!"'

'AYE!'

Seffy gave her "aye" along with everyone else but for her aunt's sake, not Angie's. It was galling to hear Angie making speeches and being the leader. That used to be her job.

'Good!' Dilys said. 'And thank you for that vote of confidence. But do dispense with the "ladyship" business, gals. It's really not necessary.'

Angie was still standing. She frowned. 'But we need to call you something.'

'How about "Captain"?' Jean suggested.

Dilys started to object, rather half-heartedly.

'Excellent idea!' Seffy said. 'Those in favour, say "Aye!"'

'AYE!' everyone yelled.

Seffy smiled to herself, as Angie's face fell and she dropped back down in her seat.

Chapter 22

During the first part of the meeting, Dilys attempted to teach the girls Morse code.

'One second for a dot, three seconds for a dash and if you don't have a torch, gals, you can use a compact mirror!' she said.

Marigold handed out Morse code alphabet charts and torches and within a few minutes, they'd all learned to flash and to tap "SOS".

'That's your homework for today,' Dilys said. 'Learn the Morse code alphabet! I'll be testing you at future meetings! And now, please put all the seats away and stack them in the stockroom at the back!'

'Is this part of the training?' Flora asked, grimacing as she carried a wooden chair in each hand.

Once the hall was clear, Dilys reached into a wicker basket and brought something out. She held it up. 'We're going to start with these! Beanbags! Take one and hurl it as far as you can. And shout! Anything you like, as long as it's clean. Shouting helps!'

The girls glanced at one another, uncertainly.

Angie stepped forward. She picked up a beanbag, bounced it lightly on her palm, put her arm back and hurled it towards the stage, letting out a loud 'Aagh!'

'Marvellous!' Dilys said. 'And not a bad throw! Now, the rest of you have seen how it's done, so off you go!'

They didn't need to be asked twice.

'Take that, you brute!' Seffy shouted at an imaginary foe, as her beanbag flew high up towards the rafters.

Once all the beanbags had been thrown, there was a temporary lull in proceedings as Marigold and Tattie ran around picking them up and refilling the basket.

'What's the point of this?' Morag asked.

'Aye,' Joey said. 'It's fun but I cannae see how it's going to help if we meet an enemy soldier. Are we meant to take him out wi' one of these?'

Marigold was passing, her arms full of beanbags. 'It's practice for throwing hand grenades,' she said. 'And Molotov cocktails.'

Seffy knew all about cocktails, of course. She'd been taught to mix them at finishing school and she was still rather partial to a G&T. But a Molotov cocktail meant nothing.

'Chin, chin!' she said, as she threw another beanbag. 'Whoops! Sorreee!' she called, as she hit Jean on the shoulder.

'I can't throw for toffee,' Flora said as her arm flapped ineffectually and the beanbag landed a couple of feet away.

'Utter rot! It's mind over matter. Look at Lavinia!' Dilys said. 'Do stop, everyone, and look at her ladyship's technique. She's got it off to a tee!'

Lady Lockhart was able to pull her arm back and flick her wrist so that the beanbag sailed to the other end of the hall. One even landed on the stage, to a general cheer.

'Tennis!' her ladyship said. 'Hours on the court, perfecting that dratted serve. It's the same action, you see. Who'd have thought it would've equipped me for life as a saboteur?'

'Who indeed?' Dilys said.

She winked at Seffy, who guessed her aunt was having the same thought as her – that her ladyship was showing a surprising aptitude for the WHD.

The door opened and a young woman stepped in, carrying a chubby, red-faced baby. She looked around uncertainly, while the baby chewed his fist. His little head started to move back and forth, as he watched the flying beanbags.

Seffy and Dilys went across to speak to her.

'Hello,' Dilys said. 'Do you want to join the Women's Defence Corps?'

'Aye. Me and my pal Jennie McIlroy. She's no' here but—'

'Jennie McIlroy? Isn't that Jock's daughter?' Seffy said. 'She's only just had a baby!'

'Aye, that's right.'

'All the more reason for learning how to protect herself and the infant,' Dilys said. 'Now, my dear, you're very welcome, but—' She looked at the baby and raised her eyebrows.

The girl shifted the child onto her shoulder. 'I've got three little 'uns and I cannae leave them. Is there no chance of bringing them wi' me?'

'Completely out of the question,' Dilys said. 'We can't have children running about the place. You don't have a mother who could care for them for a couple of hours each week?'

The girl shook her head. 'Ma other weans are with my pal for now but I cannae leave them with her for long; they'll drive her to distraction.'

That was such a shame, Seffy thought. There might be plenty of young women in Farrbridge who'd like to join the WHD but who couldn't leave their children at home alone.

There was a frantic knocking on the window behind them. More recruits, with a bit of luck.

But Marigold's face fell.

'Goodness, it's Mr Strachan.' She glanced at the clock. 'It's not time yet. We've still got another hour.'

She waved at him and pointed to the door and seconds later, an officious-looking chap burst in. He was short and stocky, with a thatch of grey hair and thick-rimmed glasses.

140

'What's going on?' he said. Everyone had stopped what they were doing and turned at the sound of his angry voice.

Seffy glimpsed Dilys and Lady Lockhart diving into the kitchen at the back, leaving her and Marigold to face the music.

'Miss Mackenzie,' the man said, 'I hired you this hall in good faith for a mothers' meeting!'

Marigold opened her mouth but nothing came out.

'But instead, I see something that looks very much like military training!'

Marigold twisted her hands but before Seffy could stick up for her, Angie spoke. 'I can assure you, sir, this is a mothers' union meeting. We may not be mothers yet but, God willing, one day we will be and we're training for that happy day.'

Joey and Seffy frowned at one another. A couple of the girls giggled.

The man huffed and puffed. 'Now, miss, I wasnae born yesterday. What I was seeing, only a minute ago—' he glanced around but all the beanbags had been quietly gathered up '— looked like training for throwing Molotov cocktails! We were doing it ourselves in the Home Guard only this week.'

'Molly what?' Angie said. 'I honestly have no idea what you're talking about. We were doing arm-strengthening exercises. It's very heavy lugging a bairn around!'

The girl with the baby said, 'Aye, it is! Sometimes I can't put this one down for hours, else he screams the place down!'

Right on cue, the youngster started to grizzle.

'Here!' the girl said. 'See for yourself!'

She thrust the baby into Mr Strachan's arms and he had no option but to take him. The baby immediately made a high-pitched screech that echoed around the hall.

'Aye, I see what you mean,' Mr Strachan said. He was holding the baby out with straight arms and looked relieved when the mother took him back.

'Very well,' he said. 'For today, I'll let ye stay but I'll be checking!

If there are any more military meetings, I shall cancel all future bookings forthwith!'

That was it, then. Another nail in the coffin of the Women's Home Defence Corps.

'Thank you,' Marigold said. 'Come and see next week and you'll find this hall filled with weans. We're starting a nursery!'

'Are we?' Dilys asked, when Mr Strachan had left and she and Lady Lockhart emerged from the kitchen. 'Are we starting a nursery?'

'Yes!' Marigold said.

She was smiling at the baby. He was sitting on his mother's lap and Flora was kneeling in front of him, playing "peekaboo" behind her hands. He was gurgling with pleasure.

'You're not allowed to meet here any longer,' Marigold said, 'so I suppose you'd better decamp to Ballykinch House.'

She put up her hand to quell Dilys' cry of surprise.

'I know what I said! But as long as I don't have to witness it, I can pretend it's not happening. I'll ask some friends to help me run a nursery from here on Saturday afternoons. Which means the young mothers of the village can join your "Amazons Club" or whatever you're going to call yourselves.'

'Amazons Club?' Dilys said, frowning.

'Thank you, Marigold!' Seffy said, quickly. 'That's a marvellous offer! We accept, don't we, Aunt Dilys?'

It was perfect: no one would be excluded from the WHD simply because they didn't have anyone to care for their children.

'Do you think Strachan spotted me?' Lady Lockhart asked Seffy. 'He's my husband's right-hand man in the Home Guard, so I didn't want to be seen! And neither did Dilys.'

'He was so busy being cross, he didn't look at any of us very closely,' Seffy said. 'Else he might have noticed that we already have rather strong arms!'

Joey laughed. 'Imagine any of us needing "arm-strengthening exercises"!'

'I do.' The small voice had come from Tattie. She'd rolled up her sleeves and her spindly little arms were clear to see.

Joey put an arm around her. 'Mebbe so, but dinnae fret, lass. You'll soon catch us up!'

Marigold announced it was time for tea and there was almost a stampede to the kitchen.

Dilys patted Angie's shoulder. 'Well done, my dear. I could hear you talking to Mr Strachan from the kitchen. He'd have thrown us out on the spot without your quick thinking!'

Yippee doo, Seffy thought. Dear, clever Angie had saved the day.

A little while later, as they finished off their tea and cake, Dilys said, 'Next time, we'll be learning "unarmed combat"!'

'What is that, exactly?' Morag asked.

'All will be revealed!' Dilys said.

Seffy nudged Joey and whispered, 'That means she's yet to learn about it from the Home Guard!'

'I'm assuming it's not very ladylike?' Lady Lockhart said.

'Count me out if it's wrestling!' Enid said.

'I'm not sure I like the sound of it,' Grace said.

Dilys shook her head crossly, as the objections rained down.

'I'll do it.' It was Jean. Blushing scarlet, she said, 'If none of you wants to do it, that's your business, but I'd like to be able to defend myself against a man. Any man.' She nodded firmly. 'It doesn't have to be a Nazi.'

Seffy and Grace exchanged glances. Jean had been attacked last year and it had only been Grace's quick thinking that had saved her. It was no surprise that she wanted to learn how to give a good account of herself.

'Aye,' Grace said. 'Jean's right. We may not be invaded – please God, we won't – but it wouldn't do any harm to learn how to fight off a foe.'

'That's settled, then,' Seffy said. 'We'll do it! Unarmed combat, here we come. We'll learn to heave a man over our shoulders, whatever it takes!'

Chapter 23

Joey's instinct about tall Italian Alonzo had been right. Jock agreed he could work with the dragging team and he soon proved his worth.

He was good with the horses. He spoke to them softly in Italian and their ears flickered as they listened.

'They like it,' Seffy said, as she and Joey watched him one morning.

'Who wouldn't?' Joey said.

'I wonder if he's married? He's not wearing a wedding ring, like some of the others, so maybe not.'

Joey laughed. 'Oh, aye! Interested, are we?'

'Don't be silly,' Seffy said. 'I just want to try to make conversation.'

Like most of the POWs, Alonzo only spoke a few words of English and the girls didn't speak any Italian, so they communicated through mime and a rudimentary kind of sign language.

'Alonzo?' Seffy said. Once she had his attention, she touched the ring finger on her left hand, followed by the left side of her chest and finally, she rocked an imaginary baby in her arms.

Then she gave what she hoped was a questioning glance and tried to ignore Joey's giggles.

Alonzo nodded enthusiastically and rattled something off,

smiling and throwing his arms theatrically in the air. When he finally stopped, the three of them stared blankly at one another.

'I think he was saying he is married,' Seffy said, 'but as for the rest . . . ! Oh, this is hopeless!'

During tea break, they tracked down Paolo and asked him to translate.

'Yes, he is married,' Paolo said. 'He has two children: a boy of seven years and a girl three years.'

Alonzo was looking down at his left hand and shaking his head.

'He has no wedding ring no more because British boys take rings – and watches and money and everything – when they capture us.'

Seffy's hand flew to her mouth. 'Oh, I'm sorry.'

She felt as though she'd been punched in the gut. She'd never thought about it before but of course, their boys weren't perfect. They could be mean too.

Tattie was on cloud nine. Finally, she was being allowed to join the Macdonald felling team.

'Ideally, you'd be spending longer with me,' Miss McEwen said, when she released the new recruits. 'But I'm needed to teach the Tallies.'

Life got even better when Angie sent Belinda back to the Carlyle gang to make way for her. Tattie was finally partnering Angie.

But it only took a day or two for her delight to turn to disappointment. Half the time, when they were supposed to be working together, Angie disappeared.

She was the leader girl, so Tattie supposed she had to keep an eye on the others, but she spent an awful lot of time with the Italians.

Her favourite was the dark and brooding Luigi. She was always off, talking to him. He looked like a miserable so-and-so to Tattie, but if Angie liked him, she supposed he must be all right.

'They're missing their folks, poor fellas,' Angie told Tattie once when she returned, smelling of ciggies. 'They're wondering if they'll ever be free. It's hard for them.'

'Could you not read their palms and give them some good news?' Tattie suggested. 'Summat to look forward to?'

A cloud crossed Angie's face. She wasn't so keen on fortune-telling these days.

'We're not allowed to get that close and besides, I wouldn't dare. What if I saw something bad? Best not, eh?'

Tattie agreed. Sometimes it was best not to know what lay ahead. When she lay in bed at night, a whirligig of thoughts spinning through her mind, she often wondered whether Angie really could see the future and if that was a blessing or a curse.

Did she know the outcome of the war? Did she know some of the things Tattie had done? Did she know whether Gregor had gone to gaol or if he was going to come and look for her?

It was tea break and the lumberjills and Italians were in close proximity again.

A few of the chaps had strayed from their own fire and were sitting nearby. Seffy racked her brains to think of some Italian. The odd word would do, to show willing and extend the hand of friendship.

She'd never been to Italy and she hadn't learned the language at school. She was starting to wonder whether she'd ever learned anything in that stupid school of hers that was of any earthly use.

Opera! That was the only exposure she'd had to Italian.

She turned to the nearest POW and said the first thing that came to mind.

'*Così fan tutte*?'

The man's eyes lit up and he rattled off an incomprehensible string of Italian phrases, grinning and gesturing. His voice went up at the end of a sentence. He'd asked her a question.

Oh, dear.

Some more men had gathered around now and Seffy had to shrug apologetically at them. There was to be no conversation, after all. Their faces fell.

'What did you say to him?' Joey asked.

Seffy winced. 'It's the name of an opera. But I don't even know what it means!'

'You've been to the opera?' Flora said. 'Cor! What's it like?'

Seffy wrinkled her nose and wished she'd never mentioned it. 'Oh, it's terribly overrated!'

'I've never been,' Flora said. 'But I have been to a pantomime and that was fabulous!'

'Do you know any more operas?' Joey asked. 'Try another one.'

'*La Traviata*!' Seffy said and there was a moment's silence before the Italians burst out laughing. Oh, cripes. What had she said?

To her relief, Paolo had appeared. There was a smile dancing on his lips. He cleared his throat.

'*Così fan tutte* means "so do they all"', he said.

Seffy frowned. Goodness, that didn't even make sense.

'And *La Traviata*,' he said, 'means . . . how do you say . . . ? "The Fallen Woman".'

Whoops. That was something of a faux pas.

But everyone – except sour-faced Angie – seemed to find the whole episode highly amusing. If she'd done nothing else today, at least she'd made them all laugh.

Chapter 24

Seffy had good news for her aunt: she'd persuaded Belinda and two other lumberjills to join the WHD. She could hardly wait to tell her.

But when the girls arrived at Ballykinch House for their next meeting, Dilys was nowhere to be seen.

The housekeeper let them in and sent them out into the garden, where the air was still and clammy, with no hint of a breeze.

It hadn't rained for weeks. Not since that sudden and short-lived downpour on the day the new recruits had arrived.

Enid and Flora had even tried doing a rain dance, careering like lunatics on the parched grass outside the huts. It had entertained everyone but it hadn't worked: the hot, dry spell looked set to stay.

In the garden, mallets and balls from a croquet set were scattered about on the lawn but it was too hot to even contemplate a game.

'I can't breathe!' Seffy declared, lying inert on the ground, arms above her head. 'I shan't complain about being cold, ever again!'

Angie wrinkled her nose. 'You will. Come winter, when you've got chilblains and there's ice inside the windows, you'll be moaning as much as the rest of us!'

Oh, do be quiet, Seffy thought. What an awful prospect: Angie, still amongst them at the year end. It'd ruin Christmas. She didn't think she could bear it.

'I vote we have a siesta,' Morag said. 'I bet those Italian fellas have one.'

'Maybe they do back in Italy,' Jean said. 'but I doubt POWs would be allowed to sleep in the middle of the day.'

Goldie the retriever barked, as more WHD recruits were shown into the garden. It was a group of cheery young mothers from the village, including Jock's daughter, Jennie. They'd presumably dropped their offspring off with Marigold at the new nursery and were buoyed up by the thought of an afternoon free of responsibility.

In Dilys' absence, Seffy acted as hostess and introduced everyone, taking great pleasure in the scowl on Angie's face as she did so.

'Who's that fella?' someone asked.

A six-foot scarecrow had been erected in one of the flower beds.

'I expect that's for target practice,' Jean said. 'Although, as we still don't have any firearms, he might remain unscathed.'

'We could always chuck beanbags at him,' Morag suggested, dryly.

A few minutes later, Lady Lockhart arrived. She was wearing her customary twinset and pearls and a large straw sunhat, as though she were going to a summer fete.

'Who's that fella?' Grace asked.

Seffy turned, assuming it was the scarecrow again, but her ladyship had brought someone with her.

'What's he doing here?' Angie asked. 'I thought this was women only.'

Gracious, it was Major Stirling.

Joey had spotted him, too. She rushed across the lawn to mutter in Seffy's ear, 'He'd better not let the cat out of the bag.'

It had been almost a fortnight since their escapade at the loch and the girls had assumed they'd got away with it.

149

The major was looking around, stern-faced. When his gaze landed on Seffy, she surreptitiously raised a finger to her lips. He gave an almost imperceptible nod and his gaze moved on.

'I thought we could do with some help today, ladies,' Lady Lockhart said. 'So, I asked my cousin here if he wouldn't mind giving us some pointers, vis-à-vis this . . . what's it called again?'

'Unarmed combat,' Seffy said.

'Yes. Prompted, I must admit, by erm . . . Dilys' accident.'

'Accident?' Seffy said. 'What accident?'

'Does anyone know how she is?' Lady Lockhart asked.

'I'm in better shape than my target, that's for sure!' Dilys said, emerging through the back door.

She was wearing a neck brace.

Lady Lockhart winced. 'Your target? Oh dear! Don't tell me she's injured too!'

'He,' Dilys corrected.

Seffy stifled a giggle as she pictured Dilys wrestling some poor unsuspecting chap to the ground.

Dilys had brightened at the sight of the major.

'Excellent! Good to have you here, major. Obviously, I shan't be taking part but I shall watch and learn! Shall we start?'

She spotted the croquet set and tutted. 'I asked Marigold to put that away. She's obsessed. Can someone—?' She waved her hands and the girls busied themselves, moving the sticks, hoops and balls to one side.

They sat in a circle on the lawn. Dilys pulled up a chair and placed herself beside Seffy and Joey.

Despite the heat, the appearance of a handsome soldier had livened everyone up.

'Gosh, the gals are rather skittish,' Dilys muttered.

Except Tattie. She was staring at the major, open-mouthed.

'Look at her! She's almost droolin'' Joey said and Seffy laughed.

The major clapped once to get everyone's attention and licked his lips. Was he perhaps the tiniest bit nervous? He probably had little experience of teaching women. He was wearing his army tunic, which must be warm. He was probably about to get even hotter under the collar.

'Would you like a glass of water, Major?' Seffy asked. 'It's awfully humid.'

'I'll get it!' Joey said. She stood up and dashed into the house.

'Have you spotted the new girls?' Seffy asked Dilys. 'I managed to get three more to join.'

'Good-o,' Dilys said. 'Mavis Imrie's in, too. From the village.'

Seffy sighed. Praise from her aunt was always on the ration. But of course, she'd hurt herself; she might well be in pain.

'What happened to your neck?' Seffy asked.

Dilys pulled a face. 'Home Guard the other night. I should never have got involved.'

'Well, hopefully nothing like that's going to happen today.' Seffy nodded at the major, who was chatting to the village women on the far side of the lawn. 'With him in charge, I mean. It's jolly good of him to help us out.'

'Hmm. I do wonder whether he had an ulterior motive.'

'Oh, please don't start that again!' Seffy protested, nonetheless feeling a flicker of satisfaction at the idea that Major Stirling might be here on her account.

'Actually, I should tread with caution, where he's concerned, Persephone.'

'Goodness, you've changed your tune.'

Dilys sniffed. 'Commandos. The laird gave me the low-down at the Home Guard meeting.' She touched her neck brace. 'Before I did this. They're all as mad as a box of frogs, apparently. Rebels, daredevils, the lot of them. Who knows what foolhardy missions they'll be sent on or—' she lowered her voice '—whether they'll come back?'

Joey had delivered the glass of water and sat down again, next to Seffy.

The major thanked her and knocked it back in one continuous

gulp. The girls cheered as he finished and, laughing, held up the empty glass.

'See?' Dilys said. 'Everything's a challenge.'

He wiped his mouth with the back of his hand and put the glass down on the lawn. 'Ah, that's better. Now, good afternoon, members of the Women's Home Defence Corps!'

Gosh, he'd got their name exactly right. Impressive.

'Unarmed combat! It sounds like a marvellous idea but get it wrong and you can do more harm than good. You can really hurt yourselves. Therefore, my advice is, do it properly, or not at all!'

He was studiously avoiding looking at her aunt: a prime example of how it could all go wrong.

'Unarmed combat will give you confidence, ladies!' he said.

The girls had stopped giggling now and were listening.

'Confidence,' he continued, 'that you can be in control of any unpleasant situation, regardless of your weight, build or strength.'

Seffy and Joey nodded at one another. That sounded just the ticket.

'Can anyone give me an example of an unpleasant situation in which you might find yourselves?'

'Wandering hands!' Bonnie, one of the village girls, said. 'I'd like a defence against those!'

'Aye, in the cinema, it always happens to me!' another said.

The major coughed, removed his cap and placed it on the ground.

'Very well. Would someone like to help me demonstrate?'

There was a moment's hesitation, then half a dozen hands shot into the air.

Chapter 25

Joey's hand was up in a flash.

She stared at the major, willing him to pick her and not caring who else might have volunteered.

The moment he'd appeared in the garden, her heart had started racing and she'd felt a little breathless. She'd offered to get him a glass of water because she needed time alone: a minute to calm herself down.

Fate had brought them together again. First on the road, then at the loch and now, here. Third time lucky. This time, she wouldn't yell at him. She'd take a leaf out of Seffy's book and prove she could be demure and ladylike.

He was looking straight at her. 'You,' he said, pointing briefly. 'Miss – er?'

'Wallace,' Joey said, stunned.

She was shaking. Someone pinch her; she must be dreaming. Perhaps she'd been the first to raise her hand and he was only being fair? Oh, no matter why – he'd picked her!

She got to her feet, suddenly self-conscious. Everyone was looking at her.

They sat side by side on chairs in the middle of the circle, so close, she could feel the heat from his body.

'Right,' the major said. 'The scenario is, you're sitting in the cinema or theatre and someone—'

'A dirty old man!' Morag said.

'—puts their hand on your knee.' He looked at Joey. 'May I?'

She nodded, expecting whoops and catcalls from the other girls but there was nothing but a respectful silence.

He laid his hand lightly on her knee. They'd come straight from work, still wearing their dungarees rolled up into shorts. It might've been prudent to have rolled hers down. He was touching bare flesh. She felt a little frisson course up her thigh and swallowed hard, only just managing not to squeal.

It was a relief when he started speaking again.

'Now, grab this errant hand of mine in yours – no, grip harder – and pull my arm across your body. Yes, that's it! Now, twist my hand and arm away from you and seize my elbow from above.'

It seemed awful complicated but she did as he said, moving slowly and carefully.

'Perfect!' he said, struggling to speak with his head upside down. 'Press on the elbow, force my arm down then twist it in your right hand.'

She had him in an armlock! He couldn't move.

Everyone applauded and Joey reluctantly released her captive. He straightened, his face slightly flushed and gave his arm a cursory rub.

'Well done!' he said. 'Now, ladies, obviously, for demonstration purposes, that scenario played out as though we were sitting in the front row of a theatre. If that had happened in another row, the opponent's head – my head, in this case – would've been smashed on the back of the seats in front.'

Wild cheering broke out and the major looked slightly taken aback.

Joey thanked him for the lesson. 'It'll come in handy if there are any dirty sods in the cinema,' she said, cursing herself for saying "sods". 'Because . . . erm, we're off to the pictures in Inverness soon.'

'Oh really? What are you going to see?'

'Next Saturday night, in fact!' What was she saying? How forward! And it wasn't even true. As for the film, her mind had gone blank. She couldn't think of one.

'Um, it's something with John Mills,' she said.

Major Stirling nodded. Their eyes met. Was it her imagination or had something passed between them?

Joey stood up to make way for someone else but the major shook his head and gestured to the seat.

As soon as she sat back down, he started to run through another set of moves. No one else got the chance to demonstrate; he didn't ask for any other volunteers.

He taught them what to do if an assailant grabbed them in a bear hug.

'Stamp on his feet, kick him in the shins, bump him in the face with the back of your head!'

'But what if he grabs you from the front?' Jean asked.

'It's almost the same. Stamp on his feet, kick him in the shins, bump him in the face with the front of your head and—' he raised a finger '—knee him in the pit of the stomach!'

The girls frowned.

'The pit of the stomach? Where's that, exactly?' Grace asked, looking down at her own belly.

'I think the major means – but is perhaps too polite to say – the groin area,' Dilys said. 'Am I right?'

He lowered his eyes and nodded.

'Aye!' Tattie said. 'He'll no' try that again, if you knee him in the—'

'ANYHOO!' Dilys interrupted. 'Any more moves we should be aware of, Major?'

He rubbed his face as though debating with himself whether it was wise, then he said, 'There is one other, that might be useful.

It's called "the chin jab". But it needs to be used with extreme caution! It can render an assailant unconscious.'

'Ooh yes!' Dilys said, rubbing her hands. 'That's the kind of thing, eh, gals? Do show!'

Tattie couldn't take her eyes off him.

It was her very own William Wallace. Only that wasn't his name. It was major something or other but he'd always be William Wallace to her.

He looked exactly as she remembered him from that day at the railway station. He probably wouldn't remember her but she hadn't put her hand up to volunteer, just in case.

Besides, she was more than happy to watch. She leaned back on her elbows and stretched out her legs. It was quite something, the way he turned his body this way and that and instructed Joey on how to move hers.

'It's like ballet!' Jean said.

The major explained how you had to take it easy at first but then you could speed up, once you knew the ropes.

Tattie knew some of the ropes already. She'd kneed a few fellas in the "pit of the stomach" afore, although she hadn't known that's what it was called.

The girls were put into pairs, to practise the moves. Tattie's partner was a wee stout woman called Mrs Imrie.

Tattie had her in a good, firm neck hold, waiting for the major to reach them. He was inspecting everyone, wiping his brow, frowning and looking fair mithered.

He'd made the girls howl with laughter when he'd talked about grabbing your assailant by the "pinkie". He'd had to wait for a wee while for everyone to quieten down, before he could explain he meant his little finger.

He'd gone as red as a beetroot and she'd felt for him.

Tattie knew about being eaten up with shame like that. And it must be tricky, being the only man here. Women could be fresh and loud when they got going. Even without a drink inside them.

'NO! Stop right there!' he yelled when he reached Tattie. 'For heaven's sake, you're going to break her neck!'

Seffy's aunt – Captain, as they now called her – was sitting nearby.

'Isn't that rather the point?' she said.

He wheeled around. 'Yes, if she were an enemy invader but as Mrs Imrie runs the post office and we'd all be rather lost without her, perhaps a lighter touch would be preferable?'

Tattie released Mrs Imrie, whose face had gone a wee bit purple. 'Sorry, missus,' Tattie said.

But even though she'd overdone it, she was pleased with herself. Perhaps all that chopping and sawing in the forest was doin' her some good, after all. Mrs Imrie was hefty and yet, she'd managed to get a good hold of her.

When the lesson was over, the housekeeper came out with jugs of lemonade. It wasn't like any lemonade Tattie had ever tasted but the air was claggy and she was as dry as a bone, so she drank it gratefully.

Some of the girls were playing a game on the grass, with sticks and balls, and Angie was there, in the middle of them. It didn't look as though there was room for her, so Tattie took her drink and sat down near Seffy, Joey and the major. The old dears were nearby: Captain and Lady Lockhart, who spoke like someone on the wireless.

'Now, about those antique rifles, Lavinia,' Captain Dilys said. 'They're hanging on the wall in an unused room and it's such a waste! We could put them to much better use. Have you thought about my request? Might we borrow them?'

Lady Lockhart tilted her straw hat and frowned. 'I'd let you have them in an instant but Cameron wouldn't hear of it! It's not even worth asking him.'

'We could break in and get 'em?' Tattie suggested.

Aw no! Had she said that out loud? She'd only been thinking it but the way everyone was gawping at her, she must've said it.

They were waiting. Aw well, in for a penny . . .

'If we take 'em,' she said, 'there's no need to ask this Cameron fella. He doesn't have to know.'

It was a daft suggestion and they all thought so too – she could tell by the way they laughed.

'Are you serious?' Lady Lockhart said.

'Aye. Choose a time when everyone's away from home.' Tattie shrugged. 'Else do it under cover of darkness.'

Captain laughed. 'Oh, I do like you! What's your name, dear?'

'I . . .' She could feel herself blushing. Please don't let William Wallace remember her as the wee laddie at the station. 'I'm . . . it's Tattie.'

'Well, Miss Tattie,' Lady Lockhart said, 'that mightn't be such a bad idea. I'll give it some thought.'

Tattie had an urge to laugh. If only Ma could hear this. It was a rum new world she was living in. She'd never been invited to break and enter before. And a big house too, with rooms that never even got used.

Captain was holding up her finger. 'Right, that's potentially the rifle problem solved but what about ammo?'

William Wallace, who'd been listening with a queer look on his face, laughed. 'If you're serious about this, ladies – and no offence meant, of course you are – then, I can get you some ammunition.' He lowered his voice. 'But for God's sake, don't shoot anyone, or yourselves, will you? Keep it under lock and key outside target practice.'

Dilys assured him she would.

He nodded at the scarecrow. 'You'll be using that for target practice, I assume?'

'We should give him a name,' Seffy said.

'No!' Captain said. 'No names! This is not the time to get slushy and sentimental. Once we've got the rifles—' she nodded at Lady Lockhart '—and the ammo—' she nodded at the major '—I want to see that thing blasted to kingdom come!'

Chapter 26

At breakfast on Sunday, as Tattie was scraping the last spoonful of porridge from her bowl, Angie asked if she wanted to come to mass.

Mass? She couldn't think what that meant.

Jean looked across the table. 'Ah! You're wanting to go to the Catholic church to see the Italians, am I right?'

Angie nodded. 'Correct!'

Och, no. Not more church. Tattie had hoped for another Sunday off.

Grace frowned. 'Ma mother would kill me if I went there, with all the papists.'

'I expect we'll survive,' Angie said. 'It's the same God, you know. They're hardly devil worshippers!'

Some of the girls laughed. Not Grace, nor Seffy. Mind you, Seffy never laughed at anything Angie said. They weren't exactly pally, that pair.

'We used to be the same,' Joey said. 'Remember how keen we were to go to church when the Canadians were here? Church parade, first Sunday of the month?'

That cheered Grace up. 'Oh aye, I do,' she said, smiling. 'Mind you, it wasn't *that* church.'

Enid sighed. 'It was heaven! Two hours of goggling at them in their uniforms and their utter gorgeousness! I'll come wi' you, Angie, if I may?'

'Sure, the more the merrier!' Angie said. 'Anyone else?'

'I'll come,' Tattie said. If Enid was going, she wasn't going to stay behind. She was Angie's special pal, after all. 'But I ain't . . . I mean, I'm not one of them.'

Angie threw her head back and laughed. 'A "papist"? Doesn't matter a jot. I promise, no one's going to ask you for ID!'

It was a long walk to St Mary's in the next village. The priest droned on summat rotten – even longer than the reverend in Farrbridge – but the Italians were there, so Enid and Angie were happy.

Tattie spent most of the service shifting uncomfortably on the hard wooden pew and gazing up at the pretty stained-glass windows.

Afterwards, the congregation filed out and milled around outside the church in the sunshine. The guards didn't seem in any rush to get the POWs back in the truck, so the fellas stood around, chatting and smoking.

Angie and Enid had made a beeline for their favourites – Luigi and Giovanni – and as Tattie stood alone on the edge of the crowd, a guard meandered over. It was the small, pale fella she'd met that time in the woods. His rifle was slung over his shoulder and he was holding a ciggie.

'You are different,' he said, looking her up and down. 'In these clothes.'

She was wearing her smart Timber Corps uniform, quite a change from her grubby dungarees. She was surprised he remembered her at all.

'What're they selling?' she asked. She'd spotted that the POWs and villagers were bartering but she was too far away to see exactly what.

'Prisoners make wooden carvings, pictures and boxes for jewels. They swap for cigarettes, apples or pennies.'

Fair enough. It was good of the guards to turn a blind eye to it:

not only to the selling but to the wood the Italians must be taking from the forest.

'Your first time at this church?' he asked.

'Aye. My pal wanted to see her fella.'

Angie and Luigi were standing inches apart, talking intently. Luigi was wearing the worn peaked cap he always wore, pulled down low, and Angie was gazing up at him with a soppy look on her face.

'And you? You want to see your fella too?'

'Och, no one in particular. I came to keep her company.'

He nodded.

They were the same, her and him: standing on the outside, watching everyone else enjoying themselves.

She'd spotted him going up for communion during the service. He must be Catholic, too.

'Where are you from?' she asked.

'I am from camp, of course! "Former Canadian barracks".'

She laughed. 'No, silly. You know what I mean.'

'I am from Polska. Poland.'

He stood a little straighter and a look of pride flashed across his face. She didn't know where Poland was, only that it must be a good way away.

'You know?' he asked.

As Tattie shook her head, he dropped to the ground, letting his rifle fall. He stubbed out his ciggie and started to draw in the dust with his finger.

'Look, here is Scotland.' He drew a long box and pointed to the top of it. Tattie laughed. She'd been expecting something more like a real map. But she shouldn't mock. She couldn't draw either and he was so keen to make her understand.

'Here is English Channel—' He sketched two parallel lines. 'Here is France. Here, Germany—' he pretended to spit out of the side of his mouth '—and here—' he tapped the square he'd just drawn '—is my country. Poland!'

He stood up, dusted down his trews and straightened his

tunic. Finally, he bent to pick up his rifle, as though suddenly remembering why he was there. He slung it back over his shoulder.

Tattie bit her lip. Should she ask him something about his country? She was useless at this conversation lark. What would Seffy say? Or Jean?

She thought fast. 'Poland,' she said, finally. 'You've had it bad there, haven't you?'

'Yes,' he said, staring straight at her. He swallowed. 'Very bad.'

Oh God, his eyes had filled with tears. He was a soldier; he was supposed to be strong and brave and yet she'd made him cry.

She looked down, at a loss for what to do or say.

He sniffed a couple of times and then seemed all right again. 'There is football game tomorrow night, at camp,' he said. 'Six o'clock. Come and see, if you like.'

Tattie looked up and smiled. 'Football? Good! I like football.'

'Village against these men.' He nodded at the Italians.

'But would we be allowed in the camp?'

'No, not allowed. You sit on grass near fence and look.' His face was perfectly serious as he mimed looking through a gap, gripping an imaginary barrier with both hands and pushing his head forward.

Tattie laughed. He wasn't trying to be funny – he just was.

'All right. I'll ask the others.'

'My name is Tomasz,' he said, touching his chest. 'That is Jakub.' He pointed to the bigger guard, who was heaving himself up into the truck. He looked at her. 'And you?'

'I'm Tattie.'

'Tattie.' He nodded.

Jakub had started the lorry's engine and he was sounding the horn. It was time to leave.

Tomasz turned away without another word and began calling out to the men, ordering them back into the lorry.

Tattie watched as Luigi quickly kissed Angie on each cheek, tapped her gently on the nose and, with obvious reluctance, turned to go.

Enid was standing on the church steps talking to a couple of land girls. Angie had spotted them in the congregation during the service and pointed them out to Tattie.

Enid would probably be a while. Once she started gabbing, there was no stopping the girl.

Tattie put her hands in her pockets and waited. She watched as Angie waved off the POW truck and the locals called farewell to one another and drifted away. Some of them were carrying carved jewellery boxes and pictures.

Eventually, Angie joined Tattie. She was quiet.

When Enid finally made her way over, she brought one of the land girls with her.

'This is Cora,' Enid said. 'And guess what? She knows Joey! Fancy that, eh?'

'Aye, that's right,' the girl said, 'we used to work together.'

Angie flashed her a quick smile. 'My, it's a small world. Good friends, were you?'

'Och, not especially.' There was an awkward silence. The girl started to turn away. 'Well, anyway, it was nice to meet you all.'

'You too,' Angie said. 'Cora, is that your name? I'm Angie and this—' she turned towards Tattie '—this is my sister, Tattie.'

The girl's eyes widened in surprise as she looked from Angie to Tattie.

Tattie's stomach plunged. What was she talking about?

'Sisters? Is tha' right? You don't look much alike, do you?'

Angie laughed. 'We're adopted.'

Enid had turned away, covering her mouth with her hand. 'You're mad! What did you go and say that for?' she asked, when the land girl had run off to join her pals. 'I mean to say, it was funny, but—'

Angie shrugged. 'I suppose I was bored. Why be dull, eh?'

Enid and Tattie smiled in agreement but in truth, Tattie thought it'd been queer. Where had that come from – that "sisters" idea – so out of the blue?

'Look, let's keep this morning to ourselves, shall we?' Angie said. 'The others didnae want to come. In fact, they laughed at us. I was especially disappointed in Grace. So bigoted!'

'Bigoted?' Enid said.

Tattie thought Enid probably didn't know what that meant either. Whatever it was, it was summat Angie disapproved of.

'Aye,' Angie said, her cheeks suddenly flushed. 'It's attitudes like hers that cause problems; that start wars! If the others want to know what it's like here, let them come and find out for themselves!'

'Sure,' Enid said. 'They'll not get a peep out of us, right, Tattie? Oh!' She patted her head. 'My beret! I've lost it again! I must've left it in the church. Wait for me. I'll only be a minute!'

They watched Enid tear up the church steps.

'You don't have a sister, do you?' Angie asked. 'No, silly me, of course you don't. You've told me. Me neither.'

Some of the girls, like Jean and Joey, came from big families and talked about them all the time. But Angie, like Tattie, never talked about home.

'I've always hankered after a sister,' Angie said. 'Do you want to be mine? My sister?'

Tattie started to laugh and then stopped. Angie was deadly serious.

She swallowed. The air felt thick with possibility, as though this was some kind of test and she needed to make sure she gave the right answer. 'Sure,' Tattie said. 'But how can we?'

'Aw, don't fret!' Angie punched her playfully on the shoulder. 'I'm not gonna make you slit your wrist and swap blood with me!'

That was a relief. Because sometimes, where Angie was concerned, nothing would surprise her.

'No,' Angie said, smiling. 'We'll simply decide that we are. Like I told that lass a minute ago. If we want to be sisters, we can be!'

'All right,' Tattie said, slowly. 'Sisters, then.'

She was waiting for a catch but, for the time being at least, there didn't seem to be one.

164

Chapter 27

'What do you think about our friend the major now, then?' Seffy asked, feigning nonchalance.

She and Joey were the only girls left sitting in the dining hall. The others had already gobbled down their supper of pilchards and tomatoes on toast and dashed off to watch the football match.

It was the first chance Seffy had had for a quiet chat with Joey since the unarmed combat training.

'Who? Oh, him,' Joey said, looking down at her empty plate. 'He's no' so bad, when you get to know him, I suppose.'

'I was surprised when you volunteered,' Seffy said. 'I thought you couldn't stand the chap!'

She strongly suspected that Joey did rather like him, or at least, that he was growing on her. She'd been all of a fluster when he'd turned up at the WHD meeting. But trying to get Joey to admit it, was like getting blood out of a stone.

Joey shrugged. 'Aw, you know me: I'm not one for sitting on the sidelines. I thought it'd be more interesting, to actually do summat.'

'And was it? More interesting?' Seffy was like a dog with a bone: she was absolutely not going to let this one drop.

'Oh aye,' Joey said. 'The training was good. It might come in handy one day.'

'You were awfully calm and collected when he was demonstrating on you. Considering . . .'

Joey's head jerked up. 'Considering what?'

Seffy laughed. 'Considering there were limbs and hands everywhere! My aunt and Lady Lockhart watched with mouths agog! And, if I'm not mistaken, with a certain amount of envy!'

'Aw, stop!' Joey said. She reached across for Seffy's empty plate and stacked it on top of hers. 'What about you? What do you think about the fella now?'

Seffy shook her head. Major Stirling definitely hadn't come to Ballykinch House on Saturday to see her. After their initial eye contact when she'd put her finger to her lips and he'd nodded, he'd barely looked at her. And now that she thought about it, she really didn't mind. There was no denying he was a handsome chap. Quite a catch. But not for her. No other man could match Callum Fraser or the way he'd made her feel. She wondered if anyone ever would.

'Funnily enough, my aunt's warned me off him now,' Seffy said. 'After all her matchmaking efforts! But it's immaterial, in any case. I think he's taken a shine to you, my girl!'

She wasn't the first to say it. Since the weekend, everyone had been teasing Joey something rotten.

'I had ma hand up first, that's all!' Joey said, for the umpteenth time. 'Anyhow, why did your aunt warn you off him?'

Blast. Seffy didn't want to put Joey off the chap by telling her what Dilys had said about commandos being reckless.

She stood up. 'Oh, it was something and nothing,' she mumbled. 'Come on, we'd better take these to the hatch, or they'll be locking us in for the night.'

Once they'd delivered their plates and crockery to the kitchen, Joey said, 'I wanted to ask you something, Seffy. That night out you've promised us, in Inverness? Are you still game?'

'Of course! If everyone likes the idea.'

'I'm sure they will. Why don't we go on Saturday night?'

Seffy agreed that sounded like an excellent idea but before they could start making plans, the door of the dining hut flew open and Miss McEwen's head appeared.

'FIRE!' she yelled. 'All hands on deck! NOW!'

They rushed outside and immediately smelled burning. There was a cloud of black smoke in the sky behind the huts.

They could feel the heat well before they reached the fire. A patch of undergrowth was alight. At least it wasn't any of the buildings. Not yet, in any case.

Through the thick smoke they could just make out a row of lumberjills, who were bashing the flames with beaters and shovels. Every few seconds they had to jump back as the flames came too close.

Their pal Belinda was amongst them. She looked around at Joey and Seffy, as they charged up.

'It's nearly under control,' she said, panting. She put her hand up to her mouth and coughed. 'Miss McEwen thinks someone dropped a ciggie. The ground's so dry, that's all it takes. We're making a chain, to bring water up from the burn. Look out, behind you!'

A girl was staggering towards them, struggling with a heavy pail of water. She tottered forwards, holding the handle with both hands and as Seffy ran to take it from her, the girl let go too soon. The bucket slipped from Seffy's grasp, banged against her leg and half the water sloshed onto the ground.

'Nooo!' Seffy groaned.

Miss McEwen chose that moment to reappear. 'Aw, well done, Miss Mills! I sent you out here to help but you're more of a liability!'

'Ignore the sarky so-and-so,' Joey muttered. 'Let's join the chain. There's someone else with a bucket now. Grab a hold o' that one!'

After a few minutes heaving the unwieldy buckets to the girls at the front who were dousing the flames, the fire was finally out.

Joey and Seffy stood with the others, coughing and rubbing

their stinging eyes. The earth around them was scorched and still smouldering. They were too worn out to even speak.

'And that,' Belinda managed at last, 'wasn't even a big fire. No trees went up. Can you imagine, if it had been a proper one?'

Seffy shook her head. It didn't bear thinking about.

Miss McEwen was striding along the edge of the singed undergrowth, inspecting their work.

'Aye, you've not made a bad job of that, girls. You have to put 'em out good and proper, else fires can go underground and spring up again.' She put her hands on her hips. 'I'll be introducing some changes from tomorrow. Fire-watching rotas – day and night – no more burning brush and campfires will be banned!'

She turned to go.

Something that had been smouldering, like a fire itself, in Seffy's chest for nearly three weeks, suddenly rose to the surface. 'Miss McEwen, might I ask you something?'

She could feel Joey tense beside her and the other girls' chatter stopped.

The supervisor wheeled around and raised an eyebrow. 'What is it?'

'Would you mind explaining why you thought fit to replace me? Why you didn't think I was good enough to be a leader girl?'

She heard Joey's sharp intake of breath. No doubt, her chum thought she was overstepping the mark. But there was no going back now.

Miss McEwen tilted her chin and stepped closer.

Seffy stood up straight, determined not to be intimidated. She would stand her ground.

Miss McEwen fixed her with a hard gaze and crossed her arms. Seffy did the same.

'You were never promoted to that position.' She said each word clearly, as though she were talking to someone stupid.

'But she did it for months, after Irene left,' Joey said. 'And she was good!'

Seffy shot a small grateful smile at Joey.

'Irene Calder had no right – no *authority* – to make you leader girl, Miss Mills,' Miss McEwen said, ignoring Joey. 'And I hardly need remind you, she didn't exactly cover herself in glory whilst she was here.'

Oh, that was mean. Especially as Irene wasn't here to defend herself.

'But you chose her, out of everyone, to be leader girl!' Seffy said. Her polite tone had vanished and she didn't care.

'Aye, I did! And I'll thank you to remember who you're speaking to! I got it wrong.' Miss McEwen glanced at the watching girls. 'See, I'm big enough to admit my mistakes! But I shan't make the same mistake again!'

'But—' Seffy started.

'Wheesht!' Miss McEwen was rattled now; there was a red flush creeping up her neck. 'I wasnae going to bring this up, Miss Mills but you leave me no choice. You had a breakdown!'

The words were like a slap across the face.

'I . . . I didn't!'

Was that true? Had she had a breakdown?

There was silence.

Miss McEwen sighed. 'At the end of last year, did you or did you not prove to be incapable of working? For weeks?'

Seffy's head swam. She'd holed up with Aunt Dilys after Hazel's accident. She'd lost track of time. 'I don't know how long—' she started.

'It was three weeks,' Joey said.

Three weeks wasn't so bad, was it? It had included Christmas. Not that they'd celebrated, of course. Christmas had been cancelled. Oh, it was all so foggy in her mind. If only she could remember!

'It's no' your fault, I suppose, if you suffer with your nerves,' Miss McEwen said, coldly. 'But a leader girl needs a backbone of steel!'

And with that parting shot – and one last glare – she turned on her heels and left.

169

The other lumberjills were still gawping. Apart from Belinda, none of them were particular friends. Some were whispering to one another.

At least Angie hadn't been there to witness her total humiliation. Or Grace. It could've been worse.

Seffy blew out her cheeks. Her hands were trembling. She was in shock. 'Gosh,' she said.

'All right, girls!' Joey called out. 'The show's over.' She shook Seffy's arm gently. 'Come on, take no notice of the auld dragon and her nonsense.'

'Now, if she'd accused me of being a butterfingers,' Seffy said, 'I couldn't have argued. I did drop the bucket, after all.' She gave a hollow laugh.

Why hadn't she simply kept her mouth shut? That attempt to stand up for herself, to find out why she'd been demoted, had failed, quite spectacularly. She'd got nowhere. In fact, she felt worse than ever.

She'd had a breakdown; the implication was that she was weak and lily-livered, not deserving of a position of responsibility. Not good enough.

'Let's go and clean ourselves up,' Joey said, holding out her sooty hands. 'Then, let's go and see the football match. We've missed the first half but I never see the point of that. It's only excitin' at the end. What d'you say?'

It was the last thing Seffy wanted. She didn't want to do anything, except perhaps throw herself on her bed, bash the pillow and howl.

But Joey meant well; she was trying to buck her up. She forced a smile. 'All right,' she said. 'Super idea.'

Chapter 28

'Who're we supporting?' Tattie asked, when they arrived at the POW camp and settled down to watch the game.

There was already quite a crowd here: mostly women and children from the village and other lumberjills. They were spread out on the ground, behind rows of barbed wire fencing stretched between tall wooden poles.

Tattie would rather have been directly behind one of the goals but Angie had chosen where they sat and it was halfway down, facing the middle of the asphalt pitch.

'I'm on the villagers' side, of course!' Flora said.

'I'm staying neutral,' Grace said.

Enid nodded. 'Aye, me too. I cannae choose between them. Especially as Jock's in goal.'

'Jock's good for his age, isn't he?' Flora said. 'My grandad just sits in his armchair all day, smokin' his pipe.'

Morag rolled her eyes. 'I know you're only a wean yourself, Flora, but Jock's not as ancient as you might think.'

But Flora wasn't listening; she'd caught sight of fellas she knew.

'Aw, there's ma uncle Willy. He's the blacksmith in Farrbridge. And those lads there are my cousins, Gilbert and David. The baldie fella is Mr Russell. I used to work wi' him in the ironmonger's. Cooee!'

She waved through the fence and the men waved back. They were clustered together, chatting and laughing, dressed in an array of shirts and vests, long and short trousers. What a rag-tag bunch they looked: old fellas and wee laddies.

The Italians looked more like a proper team, in their matching brown uniforms. They were warming up: running up and down the pitch or standing with their legs wide, twisting from the waist, one way, then the other.

Tattie knew which team she'd put her money on.

'It's not fair that the Italians have to wear their uniforms,' Enid said. 'They'll get hot.'

'Aye,' Tattie said. 'But they're younger than most of the village fellas, so it'll even things out.'

'I predict a win for the Italians,' Angie said.

Jean laughed. 'I think we could all predict that, even without the gift of second sight!'

Luigi, Angie's beau, had spotted her. He jogged up to the fence, shouting something in Italian and holding up his arms triumphantly, even though the game hadn't started.

'What's he goin' on about?' Morag asked.

Angie laughed. 'No idea! Probably something like, "We're going to send these Scottish laddies running for the hills!"' She gave Tattie a sly smile.

As well as Luigi, the girls recognised a few of the Italians, including gentle giant Alonzo, who was in goal, Paolo, the fella who spoke good English, and Enid's favourite, Giovanni.

But there were a couple of POWs they'd never seen before. One in particular, who had a black patch over one eye, looked fierce. Like a pirate, Tattie thought.

She called the guard, Tomasz, over to the fence. 'Who're they?'

'Officers,' Tomasz said, curling his lip. 'They do not work in woods.'

He strode off before she could ask any more.

'Probably not befitting their rank,' Jean said. 'Or they might even be part of the black armband brigade.'

Tattie frowned. She'd overheard the others talking about the armbands the Italians wore when they were working but she couldn't remember what the different colours meant.

No matter: the game was about to begin.

Jakub, the portly Polish guard, was acting as referee. He was red-faced within minutes.

'He's no' gonna last!' Tattie said. 'The state of him! He'll be keeling over before the end. Ooh, bad tackle! Is the ref asleep? How did he no' see that?' She was standing up now. She could see better and yell better, too.

Everyone – even clever Jean – started asking her questions about the game and, for once, Tattie knew more than everyone else about something.

By half-time, there was still no score.

The players – flushed and sweaty – scooped water from buckets and drank thirstily. Some of the Italians poured it over their heads, which made everyone laugh.

Seffy and Joey arrived just as the second half was starting.

'Nice of you to join us,' Angie said, sounding anything but pleased.

'We've been putting out a fire, while yous have all been lounging about here,' Joey said.

'A fire?' Enid shrieked.

'Don't panic; no one was hurt,' Seffy said. 'Miss McEwen suspects one of the smokers of starting it.' She shot Angie a dirty look.

Angie held up her hands. 'Don't look at me!'

'What happened?' Jean asked.

'We'll tell you later,' Joey said. 'But the bad news is, all campfires are banned. No more tea for a wee while!'

There were groans all round.

'I cannae live without a brew!' Enid complained.

Joey nodded at one of the Italians, who was taking a corner. 'What's the score?'

'It's nil-nil,' Grace said, yawning. 'This is why I don't like football. Apart from a lot of running up and down, nothing much happens.'

Suddenly, Jakub blew his whistle and stopped the game.

No one could understand it. There hadn't been a foul and the ball hadn't been kicked out of play.

Jakub strode across the pitch to reprimand an Italian. The girls could clearly hear him accuse the player of swearing.

Angie started to laugh. 'Every time that fella loses the ball, he yells, "*Basta*!"' she said.

Jean winced. 'It certainly does sound like a curse.'

'It's not,' Angie said, firmly.

While Jakub was giving the player a stern talking-to, the fella was scratching his head, puzzled.

'Get Paolo to translate!' Angie yelled. 'He's no' swearing!'

She turned to the girls. '*Basta* means "enough". He's just saying he's had enough!'

While the game was at a standstill, Luigi passed near the wire and said something to Angie.

'Ooh, what was that?' Enid said. 'I wonder what he said?'

Angie pursed her lips. 'He said I have the face of an angel.'

Enid laughed. 'Aye, you hope, eh?'

'You seem to understand a lot of Italian,' Seffy said. She was looking at Angie through narrowed eyes.

Angie shrugged. 'I'm a bright girl. I pick things up easily.'

'It's true, Angie's awful clever,' Enid said. 'Miss McEwen wouldn't have made her leader girl, else, would she?'

Seffy's face twisted and she turned away, looking sour. Enid must've hit a raw nerve.

Tattie knew nothing about learning a foreign language but given how much time Angie spent hanging around the POWs – and Luigi in particular – it was hardly surprising she'd learned some Italian.

'She must have known some before,' Seffy said, sticking out her bottom lip, but no one paid her any attention.

The issue over the swearing had been cleared up. Paolo had been brought in to translate and Angie must've been right because the fella had been allowed to play on. The game had restarted.

Seconds in, the fella in the eye patch – the pirate – sent Flora's cousin Gilbert sprawling onto the ground, with a nasty tackle.

'Foul!' Tattie shouted.

Jakub blew his whistle and the village players raced over to the lad. He was face down on the bare earth, hardly moving.

'Oh, ma God!' Flora yelled. 'Someone help him!'

Gilbert was tougher than he looked. Within a minute, he was sitting up, although he did look rather peely-wally. After much chin rubbing and discussion, he was helped off the pitch.

The Farrbridge team was down to ten men.

'That's it,' Morag said. 'They've no chance now.'

Tattie peered at the far end of the pitch. 'Do they no' have substitutes?'

Morag laughed. 'You're no' at Pittodrie Stadium! I expect the villagers only just managed to scrape a team together, never mind extra players.'

'I'll play!' Tattie said. She'd blurted it out, without even thinking. 'I could!' she added, as the other girls stared at her.

'Oh aye, sure you could,' Morag said.

Jean stood up and touched Tattie's arm. 'It's very rough. You saw what just happened to that young fella and he's twice your size.'

Tattie pulled her arm away. 'But I've played in the street wi' wee laddies all my life.'

'But these are hardly wee laddies!' Jean said.

Tattie rolled up her sleeves and started running on the spot, as she'd seen some of the Italian fellas doing. Then she called out to Jock, who was standing near the fence, with a couple of men from the village team. 'I can play for yous! Go on! Gi' me a chance!'

'A lassie, playing football? I've never heard the like!' one of the older fellas said.

Angie stood up and faced him across the wire. 'Aye, well you'd never heard of lassies felling trees until last year and you've seen we can do that, right?'

Jock slapped the naysayer on the shoulder. 'They certainly can,' he said, winking at Angie.

Angie turned to Tattie. 'Can you really play?'

'Aye.'

'Then you should. Oi! Let her in at the gate! You've a new player, fellas!'

There were a few shrugs and one or two of the men muttered something under their breath, but no one raised a firm objection.

Tattie's stomach swooped away.

Oh ma God, what had she let herself in for? They were actually going to let her play.

'Take care in there, Tattie,' Grace said. 'I think you're awful brave.'

Brave or simply daft?

Angie walked with her along the fence as far as the camp's main gate, where one of the guards was waiting to let her in.

'Have a good look round while you're in there,' Angie said. 'Get your bearings.'

What was that supposed to mean? What did that have to do with playing football?

Angie's words swirled around Tattie's head for the first few minutes of play. She couldn't think straight. She missed a few easy passes, stumbled, forgot to mark her opponent and let the ball sail past her.

The Farrbridge men didn't look surprised: they'd expected it. One or two smiled at her, though and shouted words of encouragement.

She caught some of the Italians smirking. They were probably thinking: *what do you expect, from a lass?*

But then, gradually, Tattie pulled herself together. She put Angie's queer instruction firmly to the back of her mind and put everything into the game.

Aye, that was better, she was getting into a rhythm now. No wonder she'd been useless at the start – she hadnae warmed up.

She dribbled the ball up the field, passed it to the right when someone called to her, then raced forward and as the ball was passed back, she stopped it neatly with her right foot.

There was a rival player close behind, pounding towards her. Tattie glanced at the goal – two jumpers laid out on the ground – and whacked the ball with all her might.

She sent it to the right, the goalie threw himself the other way and . . . GOAL!

She'd done it, she'd scored!

The crowd erupted. Everyone rose to their feet, cheering and applauding.

Even some of the Italians smiled and said, '*Brava*!' which Tattie knew meant "well done".

She caught Tomasz's eye. He was clapping too and there was the faintest smile on his lips. He was looking at her, she was sure, with a kind of respect.

She was blushing but there was a lightness inside her too, a thrill that she couldn't remember ever feeling before.

She'd shown the lot of them! Everyone had doubted her – even the other lumberjills – but she'd proved 'em all wrong. She mightn't be as good as them at lots of things but by golly, she could kick a ball.

But the thrill of taking the village team to a 1–0 lead didn't last long.

Now they'd seen what she could do, the Italians had her in their sights. Particularly the two she'd never seen before today: the pirate with the black eyepatch and his crony: the short, thuggish one.

The pirate didn't let her get more than a foot away; he was close on her heels all the time and no matter how much she dodged and weaved, one of them was always there. They muttered at her – and shouted sometimes too. They were cursing; she could tell by the venom in their voices.

They weren't going to let her score again but if the village team could hold tight and defend their lead, a 1–0 victory would do.

One of the lads passed Tattie the ball and she started to dribble it down the pitch. She was glancing around, looking for someone to knock it to, when Luigi appeared out of nowhere.

The next moment, Tattie's feet went from under her. She hit the ground hard and landed on her front with a sickening thud. The mean sod had tripped her up! She was winded so badly, she thought she might barf.

The girls behind the fence booed and yelled.

Luigi shrugged and held up his hands, as if to say, he hadn't meant it.

Paolo left his goal, raced over to Luigi and barged against his shoulder, so that he almost fell too and then they were in a scuffle, which was threatening to turn into an all-out scrap.

The guards and some of the other players had to break it up, holding the men back by their arms as they traded insults.

In the meantime, Jock helped Tattie up.

'These fellas are getting too heavy-handed for my liking,' he said. 'How about calling it a day now, eh?'

She'd only been playing for half an hour. She didnae want to come off. 'But I'm no' hurt!'

It wasn't true. Her overalls were torn at the knee and there was blood seeping through the rip.

'You're no' hurt *yet*,' Jock said, steering her by the shoulders towards the gate. 'Come on, away wi' you.'

Reluctantly, Tattie left the game, to huge applause and although her knee was sore and she wasn't happy about having to stop, she was pleased with herself, too.

After that, they had to watch as the Italians quickly scored two goals. They celebrated by slapping each other on the back, jumping in the air and doing a victory lap around the pitch, to muted applause.

Only Enid and Angie were clapping from the lumberjills side of the fence.

Jakub blew the whistle. It was all over.

Angie and Tattie let the others go ahead and made their way slowly back to camp. Tattie's knee was sore and she was limping.

'Here, lean on my arm,' Angie said.

Tattie shook her head and said she could manage, ta very much. But it was kind of Angie to offer. She was being especially nice to her since yesterday, when Tattie had agreed to be her sister.

'The Italians won the match but you won the moral victory,' Angie said. 'You were up against men twice your size and you scored a goal!'

It was true. She'd been good and no one could take that away from her.

'They were worried about you, for sure!' Angie said.

'I suppose that's why Luigi sent me flying.'

Angie laughed. 'I'm sure he didn't mean to be rough. He forgot himself in the moment! You should take it as a compliment. He wasn't treating you any differently to the rest of the team.'

That was one way of looking at it.

In truth, Luigi hadn't been the worst of the bunch. Those two horrible brutes had been worse. A tiny part of Tattie had been glad to stop playing because those fellas had been scary.

She shivered when she remembered the way they'd snarled at her. Like wolves.

Chapter 29

It was late on Saturday afternoon and the girls were on their way to Inverness, squashed together on the back row, as the bus bounced along.

'Seffy?' Morag asked. 'Have you ever been on a bus before?'

Everyone laughed and Seffy rolled her eyes. 'Have I ever . . . ? Oh, silly, of course I have!'

Joey nudged her. 'Have you though? Truly?'

Seffy had a pal once – a terrible snob, she now realised – who used to call buses "peasant carriers". It was probably best not to mention that to the others.

She shrugged. 'I've been on a double decker in London once or twice but you know me, I'm more of a taxi girl.' She glanced out of the side window. 'This is much more fun!'

The Macdonald girls were dressed up to the nines, in frocks and heels. They'd shared what little make-up they had and there'd been non-stop activity in the hut from the moment they'd returned from their WHD meeting ("map and compass reading") until it was time to make a dash for the bus stop.

When the bus had pulled in and they'd leaped aboard, the driver had whistled at them appreciatively. Giggling, they'd hurled themselves down the aisle, to claim the back row.

As they'd jostled one another and thrown themselves down on the seats, Seffy had reflected how they might look like ladies but they were – thank goodness – still silly schoolgirls at heart.

Oh, she needed this! An evening away from camp and awful Miss McEwen; time to forget about her "nerves" and simply have some fun.

The bus rolled and rattled along the lanes, swinging round bends and making the girls squeal and groan.

'This is like being on a boat!' Grace said.

'Aye, in the middle of a storm!' Morag agreed.

Flora was holding her stomach. 'And I'm gonna be seasick if it doesn't stop soon!'

They were being awfully loud. And probably very irritating. Seffy glanced at the other passengers but everyone was ignoring them, except a girl of about their age, sitting on an aisle seat. She was with an older woman who was probably her mother and she kept glancing at them with something like wistfulness.

The clippie – a woman in slacks, with a ticket machine slung across her chest – was swaying down the bus towards them.

'Let's be havin' you, then!' she said.

Seffy held out the money. 'I'm paying. Seven returns to Inverness, please.'

The clippie started turning the handle on her ticket machine.

'Lady Bountiful here is splashing out,' Morag said.

'Take no notice,' Jean said, glaring at Morag. 'I'm sure we all appreciate it.'

Seffy had insisted on treating the girls. She'd explained, without going into detail, that she'd come into some money. 'A little nest egg. Ten pounds, to be precise.'

'Shouldn't you be saving it?' Grace had asked.

'Goodness, no!' Seffy had said. 'You might be a sensible married woman, Grace, but some of us are still young and carefree. The future can look after itself!'

Grace had bitten her lip and looked hurt and Seffy had

181

immediately regretted her words. But there'd been no chance to take them back. Jean had quickly jumped in.

'Perhaps you could buy some war bonds,' she'd said. 'Don't be a squander bug!'

'No, I want us to have a night out. There'll be plenty left over. I can always save that,' Seffy had said, although she had no intention of doing so. She'd stuffed the rest of the money into her suitcase under the bed. She still wasn't getting her allowance from Father and lumberjill wages were meagre. It would be handy to have some extra cash for a rainy day.

Everyone from Macdonald hut had been invited tonight. Flora, who still lived at home, had been included on condition she had her mother's permission and promised to stick to the others like glue.

'It's a shame Angie and Tattie aren't here,' Enid said, mournfully.

Angie had declined the invitation, much to Seffy's delight. She wouldn't have minded Tattie coming along but those two were joined at the hip. You couldn't have one without the other.

Apparently, Angie and Tattie had "other plans". Seffy hadn't enquired what they were. Quite frankly, she didn't care.

'Now,' Seffy said, 'what shall we do first when we get there? Cinema or fish and chips?'

'We'll starve if we don't eat until after the picture,' Joey said. 'Let's have supper first and then go on to the Playhouse. After the film, we should still have time for a dance somewhere.'

'That sounds perfect!' Enid said. 'I can't wait!'

They'd arrived in Inverness.

It felt most peculiar to be in a bustling town, after so long in the still of the forest.

'There's so much sky!' Seffy said and the others agreed. They were used to seeing the leafy canopy of trees above them.

'And so many folk!' Grace said.

There was a long queue outside the fish and chip shop but they didn't mind waiting. It was a warm evening and standing outside, in happy anticipation of their treat, wasn't too shabby.

The delicious sharp smells of vinegar and hot fat, coming from the shop, were soon making their mouths water.

Enid and Flora started chatting to a group of fellas in uniform who'd joined the queue behind them. They didn't sound Scottish. Their English was good but they had accents.

'There's seven o' them and seven o' us,' Flora said, eyes bright. 'One each!'

'Where do you go after supper, ladies? Do you like to dance?' one of the fellas asked.

The girls looked at one another, clearly tempted.

'Sorry, chaps,' Joey butted in. 'But we're off to the pictures.'

'We might see you after the film, though,' Jean said. 'It's on at the Playhouse on Academy Street.'

Gosh, Jean was being awfully brazen. She blushed a little, as she caught Seffy's eye and they smiled at one another.

Once they'd been served, they waved goodbye to the men from the queue and found a wall to sit on, to eat their supper. The portions had been doused in plenty of salt and vinegar and were simply delicious.

'These chips are exactly how I like them: soft and soggy!' Joey said, holding one up before popping it into her mouth.

'The batter's the best bit: nice and crispy,' Jean said.

Seffy shook her head. 'If my mother could see me now. Perish the thought! Eating in the street, out of newspaper, with my fingers! Like some kind of tramp!'

'Don't tell me you've never eaten fish and chips like this before,' Jean said.

'Honestly, Seffy, you've never lived!' Joey said, putting her head back and throwing another chip into her mouth.

Seffy laughed. She'd done lots of things the others hadn't but in many ways she supposed she had led a sheltered life.

Once she'd finished eating, Jean started to read out the headlines from the newspaper in which her supper had been wrapped.

Seffy put up her hand. 'Stop, please! I honestly can't bear to hear another word about blasted air assaults or Flying Fortresses or U-boats!'

The others murmured their agreement.

Jean nodded. 'Aye, you're right,' she said. She pushed her glasses up her nose. 'Let's have a night off from it all.'

In the cinema, the girls stood for the national anthem and sat through the newsreel. So much, Seffy thought wryly, for forgetting about the war. Finally the main picture began.

But after only a few minutes, Joey tensed in her seat. 'What's that?' She looked up at the ceiling.

Seffy sighed and moved her head, as the couple in front stood up, blocking her view of the screen.

'There!' Joey said. 'Can you hear it?'

At first, Seffy could hear nothing apart from the actors' voices, then, with a sinking heart, she recognised the wail of the siren.

The other girls had heard it too and were picking up their handbags and preparing to leave.

'Aw, must we go?' Enid asked. 'We're going to miss the film!'

Around them, people were filing along the rows of seats and heading for the exits.

'Come on! There's a raid. We have to go,' Seffy said. 'The projectionist won't be hanging around, either, so you won't miss anything. Say, where's Flora? Oh, there you are. Now, everyone, do get a move on! If it doesn't last long, they might start the film again from the beginning.'

It had been cool and dark in the cinema but it was warm outside and the light made them blink. The sirens were louder out here. Seffy hadn't heard that awful sound for yonks but it hadn't lost its ability to make her feel sick to the stomach.

'Shelter's that way!' an ARP officer shouted, as he rushed past. 'Don't run, now. Stay calm!'

They joined a throng of people hurrying in the same direction.

'Here, let's hold hands !' Seffy said. 'We don't want to lose anyone!'

They didn't have a clue where they were going, after all.

Seffy grabbed Flora's hand and then Joey's and held them tightly.

Darn it, the night was ruined! They'd planned one special evening – their first proper night out for ages – and the stupid Luftwaffe had to come and spoil it.

Chapter 30

'Good! That's them gone and they won't be back 'til late,' Angie said with a satisfied nod.

After the chaos of this afternoon, when the others had prepared for their night out in a frenzy of make-up, hair and clothes, the hut seemed awful quiet.

Tattie felt flat. She and Angie were missing out. She'd wanted to go to Inverness more than anything but hadn't dared say so.

The pictures and fish and chips! It'd sounded like the best night ever. But Angie hadn't wanted to go and it was only right that she, her best pal – her "sister" – should stay with her.

'What'll we do?' Tattie asked. 'I might do some washing. Do you have anything you'd like me to rinse through?'

Angie laughed. 'Are you serious? On a Saturday night? We most certainly won't be doing our laundry! You're a weird wee thing at times.'

Weird? Aw, she was a numpty, all right. She might've known Angie would have something planned. She should think before she spoke.

'That lot are not the only ones who're going out!' Angie said. She grabbed her towel and marched towards the washroom. 'But first, I need to get ready!'

'Where are we going?' Tattie asked. She didn't have money for going out and she wasn't keen on dancing, if that was what Angie had in mind.

But Angie had gone.

Tattie sighed and flopped down on her bed. She had a bad feeling about this. Truth be told, she'd rather stay here.

An hour later, Angie was ready. She looked a picture, in a pretty red frock and matching lipstick. She ran her hands through her hair and fluffed it up.

'Will I do?'

Tattie nodded. 'Aye. You look . . . very nice.'

Angie rolled her eyes. 'Is that it?'

'I'm not a great one for dancing,' Tattie said, finally plucking up the courage to say it. 'But I'll come wi' you if you want to go. Is there a dance in the village tonight?'

Angie waved her hand. 'No, it's nothing like that. But I need your help. This won't work without you. Will you help me?'

Tattie nodded. Finally, she had the chance to pay Angie back for all her kindness.

But Angie seemed to be having second thoughts. She bit her bottom lip. 'No, I can't ask you. It's too much.' She reached behind her neck and started to undo her necklace. 'Whatever was I thinking? You can't do it.'

'Aw, please! Let me! At least tell me what it is,' Tattie said.

She was near enough beggin' Angie now and she didn't even know what the girl wanted her to do.

Angie pursed her lips. 'Can I trust you? And do you trust me?'

'Wi' my life! We're sisters, aren't we?'

Angie pondered for a few seconds, then she nodded. 'Very well.'

'But what about me? Don't I need to get ready?' Tattie looked down. She was still wearing her work clothes.

'No,' Angie said, 'you'll do fine as you are.'

Chapter 31

Joey held tightly on to Seffy's hand as they headed for the shelter.

It wouldn't get dark for hours but it would be easy to get lost in this surging, rushing crowd.

'Hallo, girls!'

The foreign men from the chip shop queue had appeared in front of them.

'Not that way, lovely ladies!' The fella was grinning, walking backwards and stretching out his arms in a half-hearted attempt to block their path. 'We cannot let you go again!'

'Oh, no!' another said, waggling his finger and making Flora giggle.

After the disappointment of missing the film, Joey's heart lifted. This was more like it. Spending time with these fellas might brighten up the evening.

But then, she heard another voice coming from behind and her heart almost stopped and then immediately soared.

'Ladies, why don't you come with us?'

Was that really . . . ? Joey turned – pulling Seffy round with her – and almost jumped for joy. It was him: Major Stirling! She'd never been so pleased to see anyone in her life.

'Hullo, you,' she said, grinning at him.

'Goodness!' Seffy said, doing a double take. 'What a shock!'

'What're you doing here?' Flora screeched.

When Joey had told him they'd be in Inverness tonight – even before she'd engineered the outing – the major had appeared to be paying close attention but she hadn't been sure whether he'd take the bait. But clearly, he had! He'd followed them to Inverness and now he was inviting them to go with him and these other fellas.

'Listen, we know somewhere we can go,' he said, raising his voice over the waxing and waning of the siren. 'It won't be as busy as the shelter. You'll be packed in like sardines in there.'

Joey nodded at the other men – mostly tall and blonde – who were surrounding the girls. 'Are they with you?'

'Yes, they're part of my section.'

Folk were still rushing past. Every few seconds Joey's shoulder was buffeted and a woman tutted loudly as she swerved to avoid her.

'Come along,' the major said. 'It's quite safe.'

They all looked at Seffy. She was in charge, after all.

Please say yes, Joey thought.

'Lead on, Macduff!' Seffy said, which must've been some kind of joke because the major – who, as Flora pointed out, was definitely not called Macduff – nodded and the next minute, the girls were being bustled away, in the opposite direction to the one they'd been heading.

They hurried along the road with the men, going against the tide of people heading for the shelter. The rolling drone of the sirens went on.

The major led them down an empty side street to the place of safety: a pub.

Joey stole a glance at him, as he stood at the top of the stairs and ushered everyone down into the cellar.

He looked calm and in control. More relaxed, in fact, than the last time she'd been with him, at Ballykinch House.

Her stomach flipped as she remembered that afternoon and his touch, as they'd oh-so-gently grappled with one another:

189

hands on waists, necks and backs and their faces, at times, only inches apart.

'Yikes!' Seffy said, as they clattered down the wooden stairs in semi-darkness. 'Don't tell my mother! She takes a jolly dim view of women who frequent public houses!'

Joey laughed. 'Relax! One night in a pub's hardly going to turn you into a lady of the night!'

She couldn't admit it but Joey was thrilled at the thought of being incarcerated with these fellas – and more specifically, with the major – for who knew how long. They might be down here all night.

In the basement, they sat on benches between huge beer barrels. It smelled damp and yeasty but it was comfortable enough. Someone had thought to light candles and place them on the tops of the barrels. They threw shadows on the walls and gave just enough light to see by.

There were plenty of locals down here, too. Everyone was in good spirits, helped, no doubt, by a bottle of whisky that was being passed around.

The girls squeezed up together on one of the benches. The major stood nearby.

'I can't believe we've bumped into you like this!' Seffy said. She had to shout over the noise of so many folk, talking and laughing. 'What are the chances?'

The major cleared his throat. 'I must admit, a little birdie told me you'd be in Inverness tonight. I thought it sounded like a good idea for a night out.'

'It would've been,' Seffy agreed. 'If this hadn't happened!'

'We were in the pictures,' Joey said, conscious that she was the "little birdie" and praying the major wouldn't reveal it. 'We're hoping to get back in later.'

What was she saying? She didn't care tuppence for the film now. It was a shame for Seffy, who'd wasted all that money, but this was much more exciting.

190

'Why are the Luftwaffe targeting Inverness?' Jean asked.

'They might just be flying over,' the major said. 'In which case, we won't be here long. Or they could be trying to get a fix on the aluminium factory to the east.'

Who cared if there were bombers overhead and danger all around? Joey felt perfectly safe, here, with Major Stirling standing right beside her, like her own personal bodyguard.

She couldn't think of anywhere she'd rather be.

Chapter 32

Angie led Tattie through the woods, stumbling a few times in her high heels. She was hardly dressed for a wee stroll and Tattie couldn't understand why she'd brought them here.

Finally, they stopped at the edge of the Italians' camp. They weren't far from where they'd watched the football match.

Angie pointed to the barbed wire fence a few yards away. 'There's a loose section of wire there. Luigi's been whittling away at it when they're let out for exercise. None of the guards has noticed.'

'Loose wire? So the fellas could all escape?'

Angie gave a hollow laugh. 'But why would they? Where would they go? Unless they had money and weapons, they'd soon be rounded up. None of them wants to go on the run. But a night out, on the town, with me? Now that's a different matter!'

Tattie shook her head. None of this made sense.

Angie sighed, as though Tattie must be daft. 'Luigi wants to take me out on a date.'

Oh, him. Tattie had never warmed to the brooding hulk, but since the football match, when he'd shown his true colours, she had even less time for him.

But each to their own. He was probably different with Angie.

'A date? Aw, that's nice,' she said. 'Perhaps one day, he'll—'

'No!' Angie snapped. She softened her voice and said, 'No, silly, he really wants to take me out. But we need your help.'

A horrible realisation was creeping over Tattie, like a sea mist rolling in. 'Here's the plan,' Angie said. 'You're going to swap places with Luigi. Just for a few hours.'

Tattie gave a jolt, as though someone had hit her.

'I'm going to . . . ? When?'

'Tonight, of course. Why d'you think I've got all dressed up and we've tramped all this way?'

Angie couldn't be serious. She'd made it sound easy, like a jaunt to the corner shop. But Angie wanted her to go into a prison. A prison full of men.

Tattie had done her fair share of break-ins. The most terrifying had been that big house on Bayview Road where three big dogs roamed the ground floor and had nearly caught her.

But she'd done nothing like this. Gregor had asked her to do some ridiculous things but this took the biscuit.

'But . . . what if I'm caught?' she said.

'You won't be caught! It's fool-proof.'

That was daft; nothing was fool-proof.

'After supper,' Angie said, 'the prisoners are allowed out for a last walk and a ciggie. It's the most relaxed time of day. Only about a dozen of them bother to go out and the guards hardly pay them any attention. But they do count them back in.' She patted Tattie's shoulder. 'And that's where you come in, sis.'

Tattie swallowed. She was running out of objections.

'But I dunnae look anything like Luigi! He's at least a foot taller than me.'

'I'm not asking you to impersonate him! You're there to make up the numbers, that's all. So that when they do a headcount, it'll be the right number.'

Tattie bit her lip and looked down at the forest floor. She'd got the raw end of the deal here. No wonder Angie hadn't wanted to go to Inverness. She'd had this all mapped out.

'What'll you be doing?'

She knew she sounded sulky and Angie would get cross but she couldnae help it.

Angie sighed. 'I'll be having some precious time alone with my fella. We're going for a quiet drink, somewhere no one knows us.' She placed her finger under Tattie's chin and tilted her head, until their eyes met. 'Is that too much to ask? After all I've done for you?'

'Here he comes now,' Angie whispered. There was an unmistakeable thrill in her voice.

Tattie watched, with a thumping heart, as Luigi sauntered over to the fence in his brown POW uniform. He was wearing his peaked cap and had a ciggie in one hand.

'How did he know we were here?' Tattie asked.

'I signalled to him.'

Angie showed Tattie her compact mirror and then slipped it back into her handbag. 'Quite handy, those women's defence classes,' she said, with a giggle.

Luigi bent down, gave the barbed wire a yank and slid under it in one swift movement.

Tattie gave a start. This was all happening so fast. She hadn't even agreed to do it and here was Luigi, out of the camp and on their side of the fence.

'Quick!' Angie said, slapping Tattie on the shoulder. 'Go!'

She had no choice, it seemed, but to run forward. Luigi was grimacing as he held up the taut wire and she crawled under, snagging her shirt on a metal barb on the way.

Luigi let the wire go and it pinged back into place. He tossed his cap at her. It landed on the dusty soil in front of her face. Then he'd gone, without saying a word.

Tattie was shaking, despite the warm evening. She slowly got to her feet, put on the cap and looked around.

The woods behind her were silent. Angie and Luigi had already slipped away.

She was at one end of the prison yard. The last time she'd been here, she'd been playing football. That had been scary enough – she shivered when she thought about the wolf-men and how they'd pursued her – but at least she'd been surrounded by other people and some of them had been on her side.

She was completely alone here. She'd be happy to have anyone – even Gregor – with her now.

In the distance, she could just make out a group of POWs and behind them, a cluster of wooden huts.

Surely, any moment now, someone would spot her.

The evening sun had gone behind a bank of clouds and it was suddenly chilly.

Tattie looked back at the barbed wire fence. She was tempted to try lifting the wire by herself. Perhaps, if she quickly squeezed under, she could get out before anyone saw her?

But then the headcount would be wrong and Luigi and Angie would get into terrible trouble. Angie might even be sacked from the corps and she'd probably drag Tattie down with her.

She had no choice: she had to do this.

Oh, ma God. She gave a little whimper as she spotted two Italians walking slowly and deliberately across the yard towards her.

Tattie recognised them but they weren't any of the fellas the girls were particularly friendly with. She prayed they were pals of Luigi's and that they were in on the plan. Otherwise, how would she even start to explain what the heck she was doing here?

Chapter 33

When the all-clear sounded, Seffy exhaled and felt her shoulders drop. She ran a finger over her top lip. Goodness, she was actually perspiring.

The landlord had been sitting at the top of the stairs, listening at the hatch. He stood up and clapped his hands.

'That's it, folks! Jerry's gone on his merry way. Up the stairs wi' you. Mind your heads! Let's all have a bevvy to celebrate still being alive.'

There was a collective sigh of relief and everyone started to stand up.

'Hurrah!' Flora cried, storming up the stairs, with Enid close behind. 'I've never been in a raid before but it wasn't so bad.'

It was hardly the thing to say to city dwellers, who were most likely in and out of shelters all the time.

The major laughed. 'She's right. As raids go, it wasn't half bad. We've only been here an hour.'

'Are you all right, Seffy?' Joey asked. 'You look pale.'

'I'm not keen on small spaces,' she said. 'I'll be fine once we get upstairs.'

The close confines had been bad enough but Seffy had also been desperately worried. This expedition had been her idea and if anything truly awful had happened she'd never have forgiven herself.

'We're not going back to the cinema, are we?' Joey asked.

'Och no,' Morag said. 'Let's stay here with these fellas.'

'Can we?' Jean pleaded.

Seffy hesitated. Strictly speaking, nice girls didn't drink in pubs and this wasn't even an officers' pub. But it was the girls' night out and she didn't want to spoil it, so she agreed they could stay.

In the bar, everyone settled down at tables, pints were pulled and someone started to play the piano.

Jean gave a cry of delight, as she spotted room for dancing at the far end, where the tables had been pushed back. There was even a gramophone and enough space for two or three couples. In no time, Enid and Jean had been whisked onto the floor and were happily dancing with two of the foreign soldiers.

Joey and Seffy sat near the bar, where the major and a couple of the commandos were ordering pints.

'Rather dishy, aren't they?' Joey said, quietly.

They were, undoubtedly. They looked tall and strong, as though nothing would be too much trouble for them. A couple of the blonde chaps had the most exquisite bone structure.

'Yes,' Seffy said. 'But I'd steer well clear, if I were you.'

Joey frowned. 'What do you mean?'

'I tried to tell you the other day. They'll be doing awfully perilous stuff. They might not . . . well, they might not make it. We've already had our hearts broken once.'

Joey looked unconvinced but before Seffy could say any more, the major called to them from the bar. 'Ladies, can I tempt you with a wee dram?'

The girls looked at one another.

'Oh, why not?' Seffy said. "We have just been through a raid, after all!'

'Yes, please!' she called back. 'But I'll tell you now, I've never had whisky in my life!'

A local leaning on the bar turned towards the girls with a lascivious grin on his face. 'Oi! A whisky virgin, eh!' He was slurring his words. He leered at them and raised his glass. 'About to be deflowered!'

He guffawed and took a slug of his pint.

The barman winced before turning away to pull a bottle from the shelf. Seffy thought afterwards that he'd probably guessed what was about to happen.

The major must've given a signal to two of his men, because, as one, they stepped towards the drunkard, took an arm each and wordlessly dragged him outside. In seconds, he'd gone and he hadn't even had chance to protest. Seffy and Joey looked at one another, eyes wide.

No one else in the pub seemed to have noticed. The tinkling of the piano continued, the gramophone still played and couples – three of them now – were still dancing.

'Sorry about that, ladies,' the major said, smoothly. 'Now, where were we? Ah, yes, a wee dram! Miss Wallace, will you join us?'

'Aye, I will, ta.' She turned to Seffy. 'I hardly dare say no, after that performance!'

As he placed the glass of whisky in front of her, the major whispered in Joey's ear, 'Don't fret, Miss Wallace. You're perfectly safe.'

His voice made her earlobe gently vibrate and his warm breath on her neck made her tingle all over. She was blushing.

She glanced at Seffy to see if she'd noticed, but she was peering suspiciously at her glass of whisky.

The commandos had returned, presumably having deposited the man on the pavement outside. They picked up their pints and their conversations, as though nothing had happened.

The major threw himself down on the seat between her and Seffy.

Joey toyed with her glass, not daring to look up. Seffy could warn her off all she liked but she couldn't help it: she liked the fella. More than liked; she was smitten. She'd never felt like this about anyone before. She burned for him. She was conscious of him sitting just inches away, with every nerve in her body. It must be written all over her face.

'Have you had whisky before, Miss Wallace?' he asked.

Joey nodded and kept her head down. She wouldn't tell him she'd only had the occasional sip, on special occasions. Whisky was a rare treat in her house.

'You must smell it properly,' he said to Seffy. 'Inhale deeply.'

Seffy put her nose to the glass and immediately pulled back. 'That's atrocious! It smells like our hallway when Mrs O'Reilly's been round with the mop.'

They laughed.

'It is rather peaty,' the major agreed. 'Something of an acquired taste, perhaps. Look, as we're all off duty now and we're . . . well, I hope we're friends, do please call me Ralph.'

Joey's stomach twisted. Friends? She looked at Seffy, hoping she'd respond.

Seffy nodded. 'Very well. I'm Seffy, this is Joey. The three up dancing are Enid, Morag and Jean and the others are somewhere around. Ah yes, there they are, with a couple of your chaps over at that table. That's Flora—'

'The gobby one,' Joey said and then wished she hadn't said "gobby".

'And that's Grace. I think that's everyone.'

He frowned. 'Aren't there a couple missing? The dark-haired girl and the wee one, with short hair?'

'Angie and Tattie,' Joey said. Gosh, he didn't miss a trick.

'I'm sure I've come across the little one somewhere before,' he said. 'I never forget a face.'

'Those two had other plans tonight,' Seffy said. 'Too bad. They've missed the fun!'

She held up the glass.

'Ready?' Ralph – as they'd now been told to call him – said. 'Don't down it in one. You must sip it and savour it.'

Seffy looked reluctant so Joey offered to go first.

She took a sip. 'Aye, it's no' bad at all. Come on, give it a try.'

Seffy took a few cautious sips. 'It still tastes disgusting but the effect is rather nice.'

Joey agreed. A warm glow was spreading from her stomach through her limbs. It was relaxing.

'Don't get a taste for it, will you?' Ralph said, laughing. 'That's twenty-five-year-old finest malt.'

'Goodness,' Seffy said, with a giggle. 'It's older than me!'

One of the blonde men joined them, pulling up a chair next to the major who – strangely – made no move to introduce him.

'You're not Scots or English, are you?' Seffy said. 'Where are you from?'

Without a word, the fella rose abruptly from his seat and headed back to the bar. They watched as he slapped another man on the back, said something that made them both laugh and ordered another pint of beer.

'Did I say something wrong?' Seffy asked.

Ralph glanced around before he spoke. His voice was low; they had to lean in, to hear him. 'There are other nationals being trained at the lodge. That man – I can't tell you his name; as far as you're concerned, he doesn't have one – is Norwegian. He's part of the Resistance.'

'Gosh,' Seffy said, raising her eyebrows at Joey.

'It's imperative that no one knows they're here,' Ralph said. 'They hardly ever go out. Tonight's a special occasion and it's turning into a longer night than we expected. If the Nazis discover they're training in the Highlands, their families – possibly their whole villages, back in Norway – will be in mortal danger.'

'What do you mean?' Seffy asked.

Ralph drew his hand slowly across his throat.

Joey swallowed. Ma God, that was shocking.

She glanced around the pub. The men were dancing, laughing

200

and drinking, as though they didn't have a care in the world and perhaps, for these few hours, they didn't.

'But why have they come here to be trained?' Seffy whispered.

'The Cairngorms are like Norway. Similar weather and terrain. It makes perfect sense.'

Ralph fixed his gaze on them. He looked deadly serious.

'I'm trusting you, ladies, with that information. It's vital no one knows they're here. Don't breathe a word to anyone.'

'Oh, we won't, will we, Joey?'

Joey shook her head.

'It's easy to forget when you're so far away from the action up here, but we are at war. And there's no telling who is friend and who is foe.'

The Norwegian fella was back again. This time he did say something. He asked Joey whether she'd like to dance.

Her heart sank.

She tried to look pleased but it was the last thing she wanted to do. Why hadn't he asked Seffy instead? She could hardly say no.

She stood up. 'All right then,' she said. 'Thank you.'

And she stepped away from Ralph.

Chapter 34

As Joey got up to dance, Seffy looked across the table at Ralph. It was yonks since a chap had twirled her around a dance floor. She wouldn't say no, if he asked her.

But he inclined his head and looked faintly embarrassed. 'I'm afraid I can't afford you the same compliment. I don't dance.'

Seffy smiled. 'No need to apologise. One of our gals is exactly the same. Grace over there, with the long dark hair? She never dances, either.'

Perhaps it was for the best. Despite Joey's feeble attempts to appear disinterested, she was clearly carrying a torch for Ralph Stirling. She mightn't be too pleased if Seffy had started dancing with him.

He'd turned in his seat and was watching the dancers, tapping his foot in time to the music. There was no denying he was very handsome, in a rough and rugged kind of way. And his confidence and devil-may-care attitude would turn a lot of girls' heads.

But Seffy felt nothing for him, except a friendly warmth.

Rather like the feeling she'd got from the whisky.

It was a relief. It would've been a bore if she and Joey had been rivals for the same man; it might have ruined their friendship. And besides, she couldn't face the ups and downs of falling in love again. Thoughts of Callum popped into her head and she pushed them away. Goodness, it was exhausting.

No, this was better; it was liberating. She could just relax and be herself.

'My aunt says you've had a rough time of it recently,' she said.

Ralph turned back to her and thought for a moment before replying. 'Yes, I was laid up for a while in the infirmary.'

Seffy guessed it had been something more serious than his casual tone implied, but she let it pass.

'And there was a nurse,' he added, with a wry smile.

'Ah. You've had your heart broken.'

'No, you misunderstand. I was the one doing the breaking of the heart.' He drained his glass. 'My parents didn't approve.'

'Why ever not?'

She was undoubtedly overstepping the mark but the wee dram had made her bold.

Ralph grimaced and rubbed his face. 'They didn't think she was quite up to the mark. She wasn't absolutely squeaky clean.' He shrugged and toyed with his empty glass. 'In their estimation.'

Seffy nodded. Not good enough for him – not from the right stock. She'd imagined it might be something like that.

He looked up at her. 'They rather had someone like you in mind as the future Mrs Stirling.'

'Heavens! Hence, the tea party?'

'Yes.'

'Couldn't you make it up with her? The nurse?'

But he said no, there was no going back and Seffy understood. Sometimes, she agreed, you had to simply let things go. Too many obstacles, simply not meant to be. She was thinking about Callum, of course. When was she not?

She was rather surprised that someone like Ralph – surely, master of his own destiny – would be swayed by his parents' opinion on anything, but she didn't ask any more. Families, as she knew from her own, could be funny old things.

'And you?' he asked.

'Oh,' Seffy said airily, 'I fell for someone but he was already spoken for.'

'Married?'

'Engaged.'

'So not completely off limits, then?'

'What do you mean?'

'Engagements can be broken off. Much easier than getting a divorce.'

Seffy frowned. It had crossed her mind, of course, that Callum might call time on his engagement, but knowing the man, that would never happen.

'No,' she said, firmly. 'He wouldn't break a promise. He's rather committed.'

Ralph smiled sympathetically. 'His loss.'

'Quite!'

They clinked their empty glasses in solidarity. Ralph stood up to get another round.

While he was at the bar, something niggled at the corner of Seffy's mind. It was clear that Joey liked Ralph and Seffy suspected the feeling was mutual. No one else had got a look-in at the unarmed combat demonstrations, after all.

But would he be influenced by his parents again? If they wanted him to marry a girl with "breeding", that counted Joey out.

She was a lovely girl but she came from a humble background and, like the nurse, might be considered unsuitable. The last thing Joey needed was more upset. Seffy's stomach twisted. How could one tell a dear friend that she wasn't quite good enough? And that, charming though he was, the man she had her eye on was awfully well-bred and his family were snobs?

Perhaps nothing would come of their brief flirtation after all, and that might be for the best. Seffy didn't relish the thought of having to dissuade Joey from setting her cap at Ralph Stirling.

She looked down the room. Joey was still dancing with the Norwegian but every few seconds she glanced their way. She was clearly looking for the major. Perhaps it was already too late.

Joey was doing the foxtrot with the Norwegian chap.

'Benny Goodman!' he cried, when the record started to play. '"Moonglow"!'

As they spun around, she couldn't help glancing across the pub, at Seffy and Ralph.

She should never have left them alone.

They were a long way back and the pub was packed by now, but it looked as though they were getting along. They were chatting away nineteen to the dozen and laughing.

She shouldn't be surprised, of course.

'Hey?' Her partner had moved his head, to block her view. 'Am I not so interesting?'

'Sorry!' Joey said.

She was being rude. He was right to point it out.

She apologised again and smiled at him. She would dance with him all night, if he liked. She'd give him all her attention and try to put Seffy and Ralph Stirling right to the back of her mind.

Chapter 35

The two POWs stopped a few feet away from her and Tattie took an uncertain step backwards.

They didn't look threatening but they didn't look overly friendly either. Perhaps they were frettin' about this just as much as her.

One of them beckoned her forward and murmured something in Italian. He pointed towards the wooden huts at the end of the yard. It was clear they'd come to take her into the camp.

For a moment, they stared at one another.

Tattie swallowed. She was afeared. These men were strangers and they were taking her to a strange place. But if she stayed out here much longer, one of the guards would spot her. She'd have to trust them.

She gave the smallest of nods, pushed Luigi's cap further down on her head and moved towards them.

They walked in silence, Tattie in the middle, an Italian on either side.

Evening break must be over: the other prisoners were filing out of the yard, through a gate and making their way towards the huts.

She peered around as much as she dared, while still keeping her head down. She couldn't spot a single friendly face.

Where were the nice fellas? She'd give anything to see Paolo or Giovanni.

Her heart was pounding as they joined the throng of men, jostling to get through the narrow gate. There were supposed to be about a dozen men here but it was more like twenty. What other fibs had Angie told her?

Tattie tried to remember to breathe. Even with the two men shielding her, this was going to be a crush. Someone was bound to touch her, even if only by accident. She gritted her teeth. Whatever happened, she mustn't make any kind of noise. A girl's voice, amongst all these men, would be heard in an instant.

They were filing past the guard now. Tattie was in the middle of the crowd of men. She could smell sweat. She kept her head down as they shuffled forward, praying it would soon be over.

The guard was standing on tiptoe, straining to see everyone and counting heads. She fixed her gaze on the mass of black boots moving steadily forward. She was holding her breath. Any second now, the guard might stop counting and shout, "Hey, you!"

At least it wasn't Tomasz. Tomasz might have recognised her.

And then – oh, the relief – they'd got past the guard and were heading towards a hut. No one had laid a hand on her; no one had called out.

She'd done it. This part, at least.

They stepped into a huge wooden hangar, filled with rows of bunk beds.

It was dim in here and air was dank and stale. Why didn't someone open a window?

She looked around at the wooden walls and realised why: there were no windows.

So this was where they lived when they weren't in the forest: in huts like the lumberjills but much more cramped. There were clothes hung on the ends of beds, crumpled sheets and a feeling of neglect.

No wonder the Italians liked being out in the woods, where they could sing and drink coffee and breathe fresh air.

There were so many men here. And instead of their uniforms, they were wearing white vests, some cleaner than others. Most of their muscled, tanned arms were covered in tattoos.

Tattie felt herself shrink as dozens of eyes turned on her. None of them looked particularly pally.

She supposed, if they tried anything, she could shout for help. Mebbe a guard would come. And mebbe not.

She swallowed. It didn't bear thinking about. What on earth was she doing here? She must have been out of her mind to have agreed to this. Not that she'd ever really agreed; it'd just happened.

'Welcome, signorina,' one of the men said, with a horrible leer.

Tattie thought she might faint but Paolo suddenly appeared in front of her, like an angel. Thank God. She could've hugged him.

'Do not worry,' he said, taking her hand and guiding her away from the man. 'I take care of you. Though it is a very dangerous thing you do, no?'

She was too shaken to even smile but she nodded at him and hoped he realised how grateful she was.

They weaved their way through the rows of bunk beds. The POWs were lying on their cots, snoozing or smoking. They stared as she and Paolo walked past, muttering and murmuring and saying things she couldn't understand.

Occasionally, Paolo yelled something back at them. Presumably, he was telling them to shut up.

Finally, they reached the end of the hut, where a few tables and chairs were laid out. Five or six Italians were playing dominoes and cards. This was better: these men seemed more interested in their games than in her.

Paolo pulled out a chair for Tattie and she sat down.

'Do not worry,' he said, 'black armbands are in high security, another place in the barracks. Not here, not in forest.' He grinned and mimed turning a key. 'Locked up!'

One of the men at the next table shouted something and Tattie turned. He was holding up some kind of box or board. She frowned. She couldn't work out what it was.

'Is a chessboard,' Paolo said. 'He made his self.'

'Chess?'

'*Sì!*' Paolo's eyes were bright. 'Chess in here is like magic carpet, you know?' He stretched his arm up to the ceiling. 'It takes you away, far away, to another place. Do you play?'

Was he joking? She knew nothing about chess: only that you had to be awful clever to play it. So that counted her out.

Tattie shook her head. She'd started to shiver.

Paolo smiled at her. 'Is OK,' he said.

She thought she might be about to burst into tears. She couldn't sit here like this all night. She glanced up at the clock on the wall. When was Luigi coming back? They hadn't even agreed a time. What if he didn't return? Mebbe he and Angie had planned to elope and this was all simply a trick, to give them longer to get away?

A fella with a handlebar moustache held up a pack of cards and called, '*Signorina*?'

Seeing the pack reminded Tattie of Angie, reading those stupid cards when they'd first arrived at camp. But these weren't tarot cards; these were proper cards, with kings and queens, knaves and aces.

He was asking if she wanted to play.

Tattie nodded. The fella sat down opposite and she pulled her chair in. She mightn't be able to play chess but she could manage a game of cards. And it might help take her mind off things.

'Deal!' she said.

'SNAP!' Tattie yelled, slamming her hand down on the table and making the men roar with laughter.

There were four of them around the table now and they'd been playing for so long, she'd lost track of time. She was still quicker than any of them.

One of the POWs gently took hold of her wrist and held up her hand. He said something in a surprised tone, which made the others laugh.

'He says your fingers very fast. Lots of practice, maybe?' Paolo said.

Tattie nodded. She'd lost count of the number of pockets she'd picked. She supposed that was why she was nimble.

She'd just won another game. She picked up the pile of cards and started to shuffle them. Someone behind her called out a greeting and she looked round. It was him, the surly so-and-so. Luigi was back.

Heaven only knew how he'd dodged the guards and got back into the hangar without being seen. Surely at least some of the doors would be locked? Maybe he could pick them. Aw, well, no matter. He was here; that was the important thing. And now, she could leave.

Luigi was grinning and exchanging quips with the other men. He'd clearly had a good evening. He might at least have said thank you, but he barely looked at Tattie and just grunted when she gave him back his cap.

She stood up, nodded her thanks to the other card players and pressed Paolo's hand.

These men had been kind but she didn't want to stay here a moment longer.

Paolo went with her to the door of the hangar, opened it cautiously and peered out. Once he'd checked the coast was clear, he beckoned Tattie forward and pointed down the shadowy corridor.

He whispered his assurances that she'd be able to find her way back to the exercise yard that way. Tattie nodded. That was all very well but what if she couldn't find that loose part of wire again? It would be dark out there by now and she didn't have a torch.

Paolo must've noticed the worried look on her face.

'There is a full moon tonight,' he said. 'Be careful. It will help you to see. But also the guards, yes?'

Tattie's heart started to beat ten to the dozen again The guards. Oh, golly. How was she going to get past them? At least they didn't have any dogs. It would be all right.

She wasn't quite so full of dread as she'd been earlier this evening. God willing, a few more minutes and she'd be out of here. She'd be free.

Chapter 36

'GIRLS!' Jean's panicked voice filled the pub.

Morag, who'd been dancing next to Joey gave a loud 'Aww!' as the music stopped abruptly.

'My watch must've stopped!' Jean cried. 'We've missed the last bus home!'

The girls looked at each other in dismay.

'If we run, perhaps we could still make it?' Joey said.

Jean shook her head. 'It left five minutes ago!'

'My ma'll never let me out again!' Flora wailed.

Joey's head started to spin. How were they going to get back to camp? The Norwegian fella grinned at her. They'd been dancing for ages and she still didn't know his name.

'No problem,' he said. 'You can get a ride back with us.'

It was dark outside but thanks to the full moon, it wasn't pitch-black.

As the fellas escorted the girls to their truck, which was parked in a nearby street, Ralph appeared at Joey's side and walked quietly beside her.

She'd deliberately hung back, hoping he might appear. The Norwegian fella had melted away as soon as they'd left the pub and Seffy was ahead, with Flora and Enid.

When they reached the truck, Joey peered inside. Where on earth was she going to sit? The commandos were burly fellas and it would be a squash to fit everyone in.

'It's a terrible sacrifice but I'm prepared to do it!' Enid said, plonking herself down on the lap of a blonde Dutchman who laughed and held up his hands in surrender.

'No room in the inn!' another fella said to Joey.

'You can come back with me,' Ralph said softly. 'If you like.'

Joey's stomach flipped over and she was glad he couldn't see her face.

'You've got transport, then?' She sounded calmer than she felt.

'Yes. I travelled here separately. I had some work to do before I could get away.'

That would explain why he wasn't there earlier, at the queue for fish and chips.

'It's not a penny-farthing or something daft, is it?'

He laughed. 'Not quite. I'll fetch it and you can tell me what you think.'

'Are you getting in, Joey?' Morag called from inside the truck.

Everyone was waiting. She shook her head, her mind already made up.

'No, I'm going with the – with Ralph.'

Some of the men whistled.

'Who's Ralph?' Flora asked.

'Has he got a car, then?' Enid asked.

'No, he has something better than a car!' the Dutchman said.

Joey turned to look down the street. Ralph was heading back and he was wheeling something. It was a motorcycle, all silver metal gleaming in the moonlight.

She'd hadn't expected that.

As he reached her, the blood started pounding in her ears. Was he serious, about taking her back to camp on this?

The motorcycle had a long black leather seat. She'd have to sit behind him and hold on, somehow. But she was hardly dressed for it, in this close-fitting dress. No, she couldn't possibly.

'Beautiful, eh?' one of the commandos said.

'The bike's not bad either!' another replied.

'It's a Triumph Tiger 100,' Ralph said. 'They don't make them anymore. The Germans bombed the factory.'

Enid half stood up, to get a better look and gasped. 'I will, if you won't, Joey!'

'Well?' Ralph swung his leg over the seat and started the engine. 'Not afraid are you? The girl who rides horses bareback?'

'Shhh!' Joey tapped her lips. The others weren't supposed to know about that. Fortunately, they were all too busy talking to hear.

He'd got her all wrong. He thought she was reckless and brave. She could hardly tell him it'd been Seffy's idea to gallop bareback around the loch and if it'd been up to her, they'd never have done it. If he knew the real her, he probably wouldn't be interested.

'Are you coming?' Ralph asked. 'You'd better decide: the truck's about to leave.'

Joey pouted and pretended to think. 'I'm not sure. When we offered you a lift that time, we were snubbed!'

He laughed. 'You were, indeed.'

He handed her a pair of goggles. 'Here, put these on. They'll keep the dust out of your eyes.'

He wasn't taking no for an answer, then. Oh, what the heck.

'Drive on!' Joey said, to everyone in the truck. 'I'm doin' it. I'm going on the motorcycle!'

There were loud whoops and catcalls. Joey laughed and told them to hush. Any minute, windows on the street would start opening and folk would yell at them to be quiet.

She waved at the other girls until the truck had trundled down the street and out of sight.

She'd never been on a motorcycle before. She had to hitch her dress right up before she could swing her leg over the seat. Thank goodness Ralph had his back to her.

There was nothing to hold on to. Except him.

'Put your hands around my waist and hold tight!' he said. 'No, tighter than that! You don't want to fall off, do you?'

Joey's stomach lurched. It wasn't only the thought of falling off: it was being this close to him and being ordered to hold on as hard as she could.

She pushed herself closer to him and wrapped her arms around his torso. He felt reassuringly solid.

'That's better!' he said.

As they set off, Joey was jolted forwards into his broad back and she stayed there, pressing the side of her face against him, feeling his muscles flex as he steered the motorcycle. It was the strangest feeling: fast and bumpy and the air was cool on her face and legs. But she felt perfectly safe.

They soon caught up with the truck and followed it most of the way back, winding down the dark lanes. Joey kept expecting him to release the throttle, overtake the truck and roar away but she was grateful he didn't. She'd had enough of feeling out of control to last her a little while, thank you very much.

Even if they'd wanted to, they couldn't have spoken – the roar of the engine was too loud – but Joey was happy to sit in silence, trying to hold on to every moment of tonight.

When they reached Farrbridge, the truck turned off to drop Flora at her ma's and at that point, Ralph accelerated away. The driver of the truck hooted his horn as they left the others behind.

Before long, they'd arrived in camp and Ralph brought the motorcycle to a halt and cut the engine. There was a light on in Macdonald hut but the other huts were in darkness.

They had a few minutes to themselves, before the truck would catch them up.

Joey dismounted and pulled her dress down. Her bare legs would be covered in midge bites tomorrow but she didn't care. It'd been worth it.

215

She pulled off the goggles and handed them to Ralph. He flicked the stand out and propped up the motorcycle and they stood together in the moonlight, admiring it.

'Why didn't you ride this to your unit instead of running with that great pack on your back? It would've been easier,' Joey said.

He laughed. 'I was on an exercise! And besides, I didn't have the motorcycle then. I got someone to bring it across later.'

Joey nodded. That made sense. He and Seffy were two of a kind: they were used to folk fetching and carrying for them.

'In any case,' he said, 'if I'd done that, I wouldn't have met you.'

Her stomach plunged. He'd made it sound like something special. In the future, if anyone asked how they'd met, would that be the tale they'd tell? That Ralph was running down the road and she'd yelled at him from a truck?

She pushed the thought from her mind. She was being stupid now, she was living in a fantasy world.

'What did you think, that first time you saw me?' she asked.

'Hanging out of the truck? Honestly?'

'Yes.'

'I thought you were loud and brash. Something of a fishwife, in fact.'

Joey shrieked, pretending to be outraged.

'I rest my case,' he said, spreading his hands. 'A fishwife!'

Joey shrieked again, making him cover his ears. A light went on in one of the other huts. They were both laughing now. She thumped him on the arm and he exclaimed and pretended it was sore.

'But when I saw you at the loch—' he said, slowly '—you looked like . . .'

'Something the cat had dragged in?' She'd say it before him. She must've looked a sight, with sopping clothes and bare feet, her hair hanging in tendrils like seaweed.

'I'm a soldier, Miss Wallace—'

'You're supposed to be calling me Joey now.'

He nodded. 'Short for Josephine?'

'Aye.' She wouldn't say the only person who called her that was Ma, when she was cross. He could call her Josephine, if he liked.

'I'm a plain soldier, Josephine. I can't speak poetry or—'

Goodness, what was he goin' on about? As if she wanted any of that!

He'd stopped speaking. Perhaps he'd heard her sigh.

'—but when I saw you on that beach,' he continued, 'I thought you looked like a mermaid.'

Joey gazed up at him. A mermaid? How much of that whisky had he drunk?

'It's not what you're thinking. Truly, it's not the drink talking!'

'A mermaid, eh?'

She couldn't look at him. She traced her finger along the motorcycle seat.

'And you know what mermaids do . . . ?' he said.

The question hung in the air. Joey's mind raced. What did they do? She couldn't think. And now it was too late: the truck was coming along the lane.

'Aw, that's the others back.' She felt suddenly shy. 'I'd best be going. Thanks for the lift.'

She turned and started to walk away because what else was there to do? But it was disappointing. She didn't want the night to end like this.

Neither, apparently, did he. He grabbed her hand and before she could turn, he gently lifted her hair at the back and kissed the nape of her neck so softly that it set her skin alight and she shivered with pleasure.

She turned towards him and he took her in his arms and pressed his warm lips on hers and then they were kissing. She stood on tiptoe to reach up to him and his hands were in her hair and every time she thought they would stop, the kiss went on.

Finally, they came up for air, breathless, as the lorry trundled into camp. Any second now, the lights would be on them.

Joey thought afterwards, that it must have been blind panic that made her say it. And embarrassment. Because she'd never kissed anyone like that before, with such passion. The stupid words were out and she couldn't take them back.

Chapter 37

Tattie crept silently down the passageway, keeping close to the wall. It was half-lit by the moon outside and full of shadows. If she got out of here in one piece, she'd never do anything as daft again in her whole life. No matter who was telling her to do it.

As she turned a corner, she heard a faint click of metal and almost collided with someone.

Tomasz.

She gasped. They froze, inches apart and stared at one another in horror. His face had turned even whiter, as though he'd seen a ghost.

He muttered something under his breath, grabbed her by the sleeve and pushed her roughly behind a door.

Tattie's head banged against the wall and she was suddenly more frightened than she'd been the whole night.

'What . . . ?' he said in an urgent whisper, barely able to get the words out. 'What you do here? How you get in?'

His shock had turned to anger. He'd almost spat out the words.

Tattie didn't trust herself to speak: she might start sobbing and as he shook her by the shoulders, she gritted her teeth and prayed he'd stop. She braced herself. Was he going to hit her?

He suddenly released her, as though coming to his senses. He must have realised he was terrifying her.

'What you do here?' Tomasz whispered again. 'Never, NEVER do this again. Do you hear?'

He was shaking, too. She could see the tremble in his hand.

'If you come again, I must tell,' he said. 'Is first time here, yes? Promise?'

Tattie promised.

Tomasz's face was waxy and shiny with sweat and she felt a stab of guilt that she'd been the cause of it. She'd put him in danger too. He might get a dressing-down – or worse – for not doing his job. He could get into terrible trouble because of her.

She felt rotten. Tomasz was a nice fella and she'd let him down.

'Are other girls here?' he asked. His eyes were burning into hers.

She shook her head. That was the truth. But she couldn't say any more.

He mustn't know that Angie was involved. Or Luigi. If he knew that Luigi had been out of the camp tonight! Her heart nearly stopped at the thought of it.

Tomasz cocked his head, listening. Satisfied, he put his finger to his lips, then grabbed the back of Tattie's shirt and propelled her in front of him. They marched so fast down the corridor that Tattie's feet hardly touched the ground.

They turned down another passageway. He was taking her a different way out. Unless he wasn't taking her out at all but steering her to a prison cell, before he called the police?

They saw no one and heard only the faint shouts of men in other parts of the camp.

Finally, Tomasz unlocked a door with a key from a bunch that hung from his waist. He shooed her out, as though he were putting the cat out for the night. A cat that he couldn't stand the sight of.

She expected him to slam the door behind her but he waited for a moment, as she looked around, trying to get her bearings. She was near the camp's main gate and the sentry boxes. There would be guards out there, surely. She'd be spotted if she went that way.

There was a line of sweat on Tomasz's upper lip. He glanced at his watch. 'You have one minute until new guard comes to replace me out there. Now, go!'

They nodded at each other and then he shut the door.

Tattie slipped out past the sentry boxes, keeping close to the fence, and braced for a sudden flash of torchlight and the shouts of a guard.

But there was nothing except the gentle hooting of an owl in the trees.

She dared to exhale, to believe that she might actually do this. She made her way around the perimeter of the fence, heading for the point where she'd entered the camp.

Tomasz probably thought she was sweet on one of the POWs. Which couldn't be further from the truth. Aw, never mind that now. She had to accept that Tomasz thought less of her. He'd liked her, before – she was sure of it – but now he didn't. It wasn't her fault and it wasn't fair but she'd learned a long time ago that life wasnae fair, especially for the likes of her.

Angie was standing at the edge of the trees.

'There you are,' she said, as though she'd been waiting a while.

She didn't ask how she'd got on, nor did she seem surprised that Tattie had come around the outside of the fence and not from across the yard.

On the way back to camp, all Angie could talk about was her evening with Luigi. Tattie tried to listen but it was hard to concentrate. She supposed going on a date must be exciting. She'd never been on one herself, mind.

It had been terrifying, getting into that camp. And getting out again. She could still hardly believe she'd done it.

But it was over now and she could finally breathe. She'd made Angie happy and that was all that mattered.

As Angie led the way back through the woods, shining her

torch on the trail between the trees, Tattie caught glimpses of the fat, full moon, shining like an orb in the black sky.

'Same time next week, then,' Angie called back, as though it was all agreed.

Tattie's throat closed up. She couldn't speak for a second.

But then she took a deep breath. 'No, I'd better not. It worked out this time but I reckon I'd be pushing ma luck if I tried it again.'

Angie didn't say anything at first. Tattie knew that silence. Angie was irked. She braced herself for what would come next.

'I'll tell on you,' Angie said, finally.

'Tell what?' That didn't make sense. If Angie spilled the beans on Tattie, she'd be spilling the beans on herself too.

'I'll tell Miss M how you sold your travel warrant on the black market.'

'Black market?' Tattie almost laughed. She was joking, wasn't she?

The path had widened and Tattie stepped forward, so they were walking side by side. Angie's mouth was set. She was serious.

'Aw, but that's no' true!' Tattie said. 'I told you, Gregor ripped it up. I didn't sell it. I wouldn't even know how to try.'

Mebbe Angie had been drinking. She was acting awful strange. Tattie knew the girl had a mean streak but not with her, surely? Not with her own sister?

Angie's voice was cold and she stared straight ahead, as they walked on and she said, 'I'll swear to it. On the Holy Bible.'

Tattie bit her lip. So that was her game: blackmail. If Tattie didn't go back into the camp, Angie would fib and tell Miss McEwen she'd sold her travel warrant. Tattie would be sunk. She might even be sacked from the corps. *Ma God!* And she'd trusted Angie: she thought she was her pal.

'You do understand don't you?' Angie said. 'I'm leader girl – they'll believe me.'

Angie had played her trump card but Tattie had one too. She hadn't dared say it before because of how cross it'd make Angie, but now she had no choice. 'One o' the guards saw me,' she said.

222

Angie stopped and grabbed her arm, none too gently. 'A guard?'

'Aye. He spoke to me, an' all.'

She had Angie's full attention now. Finally, she looked worried. 'What did you tell him?' Angie asked.

Tattie pulled her arm away. 'Nothing. It was Tomasz. He's all right; he won't tell. But he made me promise never to do it again. If he catches me, he'll dob me in.'

They started walking again. Angie was quiet; Tattie could almost hear her mind whirring.

'We can't go to church tomorrow, then,' she said. 'That's a – that's a blow. But this Tomasz fella's bound to be there. We can't risk any awkward questions.'

Tattie's heart lifted. No church! Summat good had come out of it, then. And Angie wasn't talking about a return trip to the camp anymore. For now, at least.

'Aye,' Tattie said, keeping her voice level. 'You're right. Best keep our heads down for a wee while.'

Later that night, they'd got into bed and there was still no sign of the others.

Angie was flicking through magazines, turning the pages so fast she couldn't possibly be reading them.

Tattie tucked her hands behind her head. Her heart rate still hadn't gone back to normal. Try as she might, she'd never be able to sleep – not in a month of Sundays.

Angie looked across at her, sighed and put the magazine down. 'What's up with you?'

'I can't drop off. My mind's too busy.'

Angie sighed again. 'Would you like me to tell you a story?'

'A story?'

Angie had never offered to do anything like that before. Perhaps she felt rotten about the way she'd spoken to Tattie tonight and wanted to make amends.

'All right, then,' Tattie said. 'I'm listening.'

223

Angie hesitated, as though unsure of how to begin.

'It's best to start with "Once upon a time".'

Angie gave a little snort but then she propped herself up on her side and began.

'Once upon a time, there was an old woman who ran an ice cream café.'

Tattie sat up. 'What's that?'

'It's a place that sells ice cream in the summer and chips in the winter.'

Tattie liked the sound of that. What a place! She wondered what the woman's name was. It was good to give people names in stories, but she thought better of interrupting again.

'The old woman ran her business without any bother and although she was a widow, she had a big family who helped out. They all looked after one another.'

Tattie felt her eyes starting to close.

But the next minute, the story changed. It wasn't so nice anymore.

'When the Italians declared war – do you remember that, Tattie – youths ran amok down the street and threw bricks through the window of the ice cream café.'

Tattie was wide awake now. 'Why would they do that?'

'Because the old woman was from Italy, a long time ago. And everyone hated the Italians. They were the enemy. The old woman had a stroke and was never the same again. And then—'

'There's more?'

'Aye, it gets worse,' Angie said. 'Her two sons were sent away on a ship because they were Italian too and no one wanted them here and the ship got torpedoed and they were lost.'

'Lost?'

'Killed,' Angie said. 'And the old woman died of a broken heart.'

'Is that the end?' Tattie asked.

It was a queer kind of story. There was no happily ever after.

'What do you think?' Angie asked, flopping back down in her bed.

'Where did you hear it?'

Angie shook her head. 'Someone told me. It's a true story.'

'It was good,' Tattie said, carefully. 'But it was awful sad. That poor old woman and those poor fellas. Me, I like a happy ending.'

Angie huffed. 'Sometimes there are no happy endings. I thought you of all people would know that, Tattie. Life's not a fairy tale.'

Chapter 38

'Look at you!' Enid declared, when Joey followed the other girls into the hut. 'Your hair's a state!'

Joey patted it down. 'It was awful windy on that motorcycle,' she said. There was also the small matter of Ralph running his hands through it, as they'd kissed, but she wasn't about to admit that.

Tattie and Angie were already tucked up in bed, half asleep.

'They say they've been here all night, reading magazines,' Grace muttered, as she walked past Joey towards the washroom. 'But I don't believe it.'

Joey frowned. That did seem odd. Weren't they supposed to have had plans for this evening?

'We missed the last bus,' Jean was telling Angie. 'But we got a lift with Major Stirling's men.'

'Not all of us,' Seffy said, raising her eyebrows in Joey's direction.

'Joey got a ride on the major's motorcycle,' Enid said. 'There's no doubt about it: he fancies her something rotten!'

Joey wrinkled her nose. 'Och, don't be too sure. I think I've ruined things. Mebbe I was too keen?'

'No!' Enid said, pulling her nightie over her head. 'You cannae be keen enough! Else some daft lads don't catch on.'

'Major Stirling's hardly a daft lad!' Grace said.

Morag was walking around the hut, opening all the windows. 'My nan says men like to do the chasin',' she said. 'If you're too keen, it's no fun and they give up.'

The girls' discussion, about how much you should show a fella you liked him, provoked much raucous laughter.

Joey joined in even though she was feeling rotten.

She'd spoiled everything. What an idiotic thing to say. What had she been thinking?

The shame of it was making her squirm inside. She would forget for a minute, then the memory would hit her again and her anguish was almost like a physical pain.

He was probably wishing he'd taken Seffy on the motorcycle instead.

They'd make a good match. They were both tall and posh and Seffy wouldn't make daft blunders. She was cool and collected and Joey knew she liked Ralph. Hadn't she said he'd make "the perfect distraction" after they'd met him at the loch?

He wouldn't have dared kiss Seffy the way he'd kissed her.

And that was another thing: perhaps that had been a mistake, kissing him like that, with abandon, in a way she'd never kissed any fella before.

As the truck had roared into the camp and Ralph had pulled away from that final, long embrace, Joey had said, 'You'll have to marry me now!'

It had been a silly, stupid joke.

But it hadn't been the time for joshing. And it hadn't been the thing to say to a man who'd just kissed you so hard that your lips were stinging.

She'd been intoxicated. Not with whisky but with the excitement and the newness of it all.

Ralph's face had been in shadow and as she'd stood there, aghast, wishing she could take the words back, there was no telling what he was thinking.

He'd released his hold on her, touched her cheek gently.

'Goodnight, Josephine Wallace,' he'd said, stepping away. She'd fancied she could hear a smile in his voice.

'Goodnight . . .' she'd started to say.

'Whee!' Enid had screeched, jumping out of the truck. 'There yous are! How was it? Did you go fast? Oh – look!'

Enid had peered up into her face. 'Joey, you've circles round your eyes, from the wee goggles. Now, Major, you must promise to take me next time!'

The moment had been well and truly over.

Now, in the hut, as someone turned off the Tilley lamp, Joey pushed away thoughts of that last, daft comment and remembered something else.

'You know mermaids?' she called into the darkness.

Morag said, 'I cannae say I know any personally but what about them?'

'Well . . .' Gosh, this was going to sound weird. 'What do they do, exactly?'

'Is this a real question, Joey or are you tiddly?' Seffy asked.

'They swim around with their big floppy tails,' Morag said.

'Aye and they eat fish,' Grace said.

'Yuck, raw fish? They must stink to high heaven!' Seffy said.

The girls laughed. Aw, this was useless. They were all still giddy from travelling back pressed up against those braw commandos.

'I know,' someone piped up in a quiet voice. It was Tattie, from the other side of the hut. 'Mermaids can sing; they have beautiful voices.'

That counted her out, then. Joey couldn't sing: she had an awful voice. She wasn't a mermaid, after all. What had Ralph been going on about?

'Anything else?' she asked.

'They rescue drowning sailors and drag them into shore,' Tattie said. 'They lure men. They cast a spell on them.'

Joey's heart lifted. That was more like it.

'Satisfied?' Morag asked.

'Aye,' Joey said, smiling to herself.

She turned over and pulled the sheet around her. She was drifting off to sleep and that daft thing she'd said was already fading from her mind. Please let her dreams be full of Ralph Stirling: the sound of him, the feel of him, the taste of him.

She'd solved the riddle: she was like a mermaid who'd cast a spell on him. That must be what he'd meant. And that would do very nicely.

Chapter 39

It was Sunday morning of the following week. Angie had decided they should all go to church and everyone was duly getting ready.

'Me, Tattie and Enid are away to St Mary's again but you can take your pick: papist or protestant!' She shot Grace a look. 'Just so long as you go! After all, none of us went last week. You were all too fagged out after your jaunt to Inverness!'

Joey wondered why Angie had missed church last Sunday. It wasn't like her to pass up a chance to see her precious Luigi and she hadn't got home after midnight, like the rest of them.

Aw, but she couldn't be bothered to enquire. What did it matter?

She had enough to think about, waiting and wondering if she would ever see Ralph Stirling again, or feel the touch of his lips on hers.

He hadn't appeared at their WHD meeting yesterday, which had been disappointing.

She'd hoped for a chance to talk to Seffy about him, but her pal had been quiet on the subject and Joey didn't like to raise it. She'd got the impression that Seffy disapproved.

'Has anyone seen my armband?' Morag yelled.

'And I've lost my beret!' Enid said.

Joey rolled her eyes, glad she'd got ready early. It was the usual mad scramble for uniforms. Trying to get eight girls dressed and out of the hut on time for church was always a tall order.

'There's someone here for you, Joey!' Tattie called, from the window. 'It's him! It's the major!'

Joey's heart skipped a beat. If Tattie was playing a prank, she didn't think she couldn't bear it. She cocked her head and listened. Yes! There was the throb of his motorcycle engine.

'Aw, that's put a wee smile on your face,' Enid said. 'He's come to call for you! "Can Joey come out to play?"'

Enid and Grace ran to join Tattie at the window, all thoughts of getting ready for church forgotten.

Joey swallowed.

'It mightn't be that—' she started but she was shouted down.

'Get away!' Jean said. 'There's only one reason he's here!'

'Maybe he's come to give you some personal unarmed combat training,' Morag said.

'I wouldnae say no to that,' Tattie said, and then blushed as the others laughed.

The windows were wide open and Ralph had turned the engine off. Joey wished the girls would pipe down: he could probably hear their excited calls and chatter.

Angie was sitting on her bed, arms folded. 'What time does he call this? Sunday morning is hardly the time to call on anyone. Did you know he was coming, Joey? You'd best tell him you're away to church.'

Was that an order? It'd certainly sounded like one.

Joey raised her eyebrows at Seffy, who was marching in from the washroom, wrapped in a towel.

'You can't expect Joey to turn him down for church, Angie,' Seffy said. 'You wouldn't! If whatisname—'

'Luigi,' Tattie said.

'If Luigi turned up now in a wheelbarrow, never mind a motorcycle, you'd be through that door in a flash! You certainly wouldn't be thinking about your immortal soul!'

Everyone laughed.

'In a wheelbarrow!' Enid repeated, slapping her thigh.

Angie's mouth was set; she didn't like being contradicted, or laughed at.

'Off you go, Joey,' Jean said. 'We'll say a prayer on your behalf.'

As Joey walked across the grass towards Ralph, she was conscious of dozens of eyes on her. Lumberjills from the other huts were gazing out of their windows, too. Some had even come outside, to see what all the fuss was about.

Ralph's goggles were hiding his eyes, so she couldn't read the expression on his face but when he pulled them off and smiled at her, the eight days since they'd seen one another instantly disappeared.

'Good morning, Josephine.'

Her stomach flipped as he said her name.

'Vehicles aren't supposed to come up here,' she said, putting her hands on her hips.

He tilted his head to one side. 'I do apologise. Are you going to call the police? Or perhaps – in that very smart uniform – you are the police?'

It was no good: she started laughing.

'Are you getting on?' he asked.

She glanced back at Macdonald hut. The girls were watching at the windows. She couldn't make out their expressions from here but she could guess who'd be smiling and who'd be glaring.

'Actually, I have plans this morning,' she said. 'I'm off to church.'

She had no intention of going to church if there was a chance of spending time with him. But it wouldn't do any harm to pretend she hadn't simply been hanging around, waiting for him.

Ralph raised his eyebrows. 'I see. Well, if I'm taking second place to—' he looked skywards '—Him upstairs, then I've no chance!'

Joey laughed again. 'Where were you yesterday?' she asked. 'We could've done with your help in the fieldcraft lesson. Captain – that's Seffy's auntie – did her best, but she kept getting mixed up between the catwalk and the kitten crawl.'

'Sorry, we've been on manoeuvres. We're off soon, so got to keep at it.'

Joey swallowed. "Off"? What did that mean? Goodness, this might be the last time she'd see him for a while.

She swung her leg over the seat and sat behind him. At least, this time, she was wearing her sensible breeches and not a daft dress.

'Come on, then,' she said. 'Where are we going?'

'Ooh, she's just got on the motorcycle!' Enid said.

Jean sighed. 'Isn't it romantic?'

'Aye,' Grace said, wistfully.

Seffy was throwing her clothes on. She glanced at Angie, who was standing at the window with her arms crossed. She was positively seething.

Well done, Ralph! And Joey, too, for taking no notice of Angie's demand that she should turn the chap away.

There'd been no sign of Ralph all week and Joey had been like a bear with a sore head. Seffy had said nothing but she'd been worried for her friend. If Ralph was toying with Joey, she'd quite happily throttle him. But now, he was back – and hopefully with good reason for his absence – and his timing today couldn't have been better.

Seffy was conscious she was happy for Joey – and Ralph – in a way that she couldn't be for Grace. Which was spiteful. She sighed. She should really try to be kinder to Grace. She could start by asking her about Gordy. Yes, she would. Not today, but very soon.

'I say, does anyone have a ribbon?' Seffy asked.

'Here,' Grace said, pulling one out of her hair.

Seffy put on her boots and ran outside, just as the motorcycle was starting to move off.

'Hey, wait a sec!' she called.

* * *

233

Joey's heart sank at the sight of Seffy.

She'd been grateful for her support a few minutes earlier but had she changed her mind? Was Seffy about to try to persuade her not to go with Ralph?

'Here, tie your hair back with this,' Seffy said, holding up a ribbon. 'Last time you went on that thing you came back looking like a gorgon!'

Joey felt a swell of warmth for her pal. Seffy was on her side, after all.

'And take no notice of misery guts Angie. She's just wishing she could go out like this, at the drop of a hat, with her beau.'

Her beau? Was Ralph her beau? Joey's heart soared: she was starting to believe that maybe he was.

Seffy turned to go. 'Mind you take good care of her!'

'Yes, Mother!' Ralph said. 'Ready?' he asked Joey.

She pulled herself towards him and clasped him tighter around the waist.

Everyone was still watching them and she suddenly felt like the luckiest girl in the world.

'Ready!' she said.

Half an hour into the journey, as they travelled down a country lane, Joey slapped Ralph on the shoulder.

'Hey, stop a minute!'

He slowed down and pulled over.

Joey had spotted a grey horse in a nearby field. It looked like Monty.

She jumped off the motorcycle the moment it stopped and ran to the fence, calling his name. The horse lifted its head and stared at her.

Was it him? He was too far away to be sure. But then the horse snickered and started to trot towards her. Yes! She'd know those dappled hindquarters and those large, trusting eyes – one darker than the other – anywhere.

'It *is* him!' she cried. 'I knew this horse in Forres! He's a lovely old boy. I can't believe he's here!'

Ralph was still sitting on the motorcycle, staying well back.

'He certainly seems to remember you.'

Monty had reached the fence and Joey leaned over and wrapped her arms around his neck. He even smelled the same. She drew back and stroked his velvety pink muzzle.

'You can come nearer; he won't bite,' she said.

Ralph shook his head. 'I'm not scared. I'm not great with horses. They bring me out in a rash. But you carry on.'

He probably thought she was silly, getting all soppy over a nag, but Joey couldn't help herself.

This was turning into a glorious day. Firstly, Ralph had arrived out of the blue, after she'd almost given up on him, and now here was Monty, her favourite horse in the world.

'They must have retired him,' she said.

'Farmers don't usually retire their horses, do they?'

'Aw, I love his fella!' She landed a kiss on his nose.

'Well, now I'm jealous,' Ralph said. 'Of a horse.'

Joey laughed. 'You'd love him too, if you got to know him. And if he didn't make you sneeze. He's such a character. I wish we had somethin' for him. Look, he's sniffing my pockets. I always had titbits for him.'

She reached down and tugged at the long grass near her feet and held out a clump of it to him. He nibbled at it gently.

'I'll bring summat for you next time, boy,' she said, 'I promise.'

'Oh, there's to be a next time is there?' Ralph dismounted, pushed down the stand and walked over to her. 'That's rather forward, Miss Wallace. Aren't I supposed to do the asking?'

She turned towards him and, leaning back against the fence, tilted her chin and lifted her mouth.

'Be quiet,' she said, 'and kiss me.'

Chapter 40

Angie was fuming on the walk to church.

Enid, who didn't recognise the signals – the set mouth and sarkiness – in the same way as Tattie, wasn't helping matters.

'Aw, the way he turned up like that on his motorcycle! Like a knight on a horse, coming to see his lady!' she said.

Secretly, Tattie agreed. Joey and her William Wallace was turning into a lovely wee story. But she kept quiet.

'Joey's face just now! Aw, she looked so happy!' Enid continued.

Tattie couldn't blame Joey for being on cloud nine. If that man had come and whisked her away like that, she'd be the same.

'Aye, you've said, Enid,' Angie said. 'Can you gi' it a rest now?'

Tattie had realised summat about Angie: she was as nice as pie, if you agreed with her and did what she asked. But if not, she could quickly turn agin you. She'd threatened to fib to Miss McEwen about the travel warrant unless Tattie went back into the camp, so there was the proof of it. And now Joey had disobeyed her, in front of everyone. She'd be in Angie's bad books forever.

The Italians' truck was parked outside the church. They must already be inside.

Tattie's stomach started to churn. It would be the first time she'd had a proper chance to speak to Tomasz since he'd caught her inside the camp.

They'd glimpsed each other in the forest, at work, but any time she'd got near enough to say something, Tomasz had moved away. He must still be angry with her.

She didn't want him think badly of her. She liked him. Every time she saw a wee robin, she thought of him. *Rudzik*. But she couldn't tell him the truth about the night she'd gone into the camp: Angie and Luigi would be in the most terrible trouble and she wasnae a snitch.

But at least she could try to patch things up with him. Tattie patted the pocket of her breeches. She'd bought him a packet of fags from the village shop. A peace offering.

But there was a different guard with Jakub today. There was no sign of Tomasz, in the church or afterwards, when the congregation spilled out onto the steps.

Angie must have seen her eyes scanning the crowd.

'Is your wee pal not here today?' Then, without waiting for an answer, she turned to Enid. 'Is that girl here again?' she asked. 'The land girl from the other week?'

'Cora? Aye, look there she is, talking to the priest.'

Angie nodded. 'You two wait here. I'm away to have a quick word.'

Enid made a beeline for Gio, leaving Tattie alone. She sat on the wall.

It was quite summat to watch that pair. Gio spoke no English, Enid spoke no Italian and yet they seemed to manage well enough with gestures, smiles and – when the guards weren't looking – the occasional kiss.

Tattie felt flat.

She hoped Tomasz hadn't got into trouble on her account. He'd let her off, after all. What if someone had found out and he'd been sacked? He might've been sent away and she'd never see him again.

Later that day, Angie had a strange request. Another one.

'Will you get me some flour from the camp kitchen, Tattie? I only need a couple of spoonfuls, in a cup. Mum's the word. Think you can do it?'

Tattie was so relieved it wasn't anything worse, that it didn't even cross her mind to ask what she wanted it for.

Knowing Angie, it was for summat devious. Maybe she wanted to make a flour bomb.

'Of course, I can,' she said. 'Nae problem.'

Chapter 41

Seffy and Joey were driving back from the sawmill.

'Don't forget Monty!' Joey said.

Seffy shook her head. She hardly needed to be reminded. This would be the third time they'd been to see the horse; the detour had become part of their routine.

Strictly speaking, they were supposed to go straight back to camp after each delivery of logs to the mill but Monty's field was only a short diversion and it cheered Joey up no end to see him.

Ralph had been away for almost a week, on some kind of secret – and undoubtedly, dangerous – mission. Joey had been unable to eat or sleep, for worrying.

The pair were quite the couple, now. They'd been out a few times before he left and Joey was besotted.

Seffy felt torn. She didn't want to pour cold water on their romance but it troubled her, all the same.

Ralph Stirling worked in special operations. It was awfully risky.

Something dreadful might happen to him. How on earth would Joey cope? And on top of that, Seffy had a niggling feeling he wasn't serious about Joey: that she, like so much else in his life, was just another challenge.

And if that were true, it would break Joey's heart.

And even if Seffy were wrong about all that – oh, please let her be wrong – what if Ralph's family didn't approve and he threw Joey over? She'd never told her friend about the fate of the nurse who hadn't quite come up to scratch.

She sighed. No, despite her misgivings, it wasn't her place to say anything. She'd simply have to hope none of her worries came true and if they did, be there to pick up the pieces.

They'd arrived at the field and Joey pointed out a farm lad who was filling up Monty's water bucket.

'He won't mind you giving the horse a few titbits, will he?' Seffy asked.

'Och no, I've chatted to him here before. See you in a couple o' minutes!'

Joey got out of the truck and Seffy drove up the narrow lane until she reached a farm track where she could turn around. It was quite a feat, involving two-handed gear changes and all her strength to manoeuvre the huge steering wheel. Good job she had biceps like a man these days.

On her return, Seffy could tell immediately that something was wrong.

Joey was leaning against the fence with her head in her hands. She was crying.

'What on earth's the matter?' Seffy asked as Joey climbed into the truck. 'Did that boy say something?'

Joey struggled to speak for a moment. 'It's Monty,' she said, eventually, between sniffs. 'The lad said . . . they're sending him to the knacker's yard.'

Seffy's hands flew to her face. 'Oh, no! That's beastly! Why would they do such a thing?'

Joey shrugged. 'He's old. He's not earning his keep.'

Seffy stared into the field, where poor old Monty – oblivious to his fate – was happily grazing. There must be something they could do.

'Can't he join the dragging team? We could do with another horse and I know there's no fourth stable but . . .'

She trailed off as Joey shook her head.

'He's too old, Seffy. The corps wouldn't have him. He's past his best.'

She was right. Oh, but it was a blow. Seffy hardly knew what to say to console her. It was so unfair. Just as Joey had found the horse again, she was going to lose him.

'At least you got to see him a few more times,' she said, gently. 'You made him happy towards . . . the end.'

It wasn't much but what else could she say?

She resolved to add the horse to her prayer list; it couldn't do any harm.

She didn't really believe in God and heaven, but she'd started her nightly prayers at the outbreak of war and they'd been a comfort. She couldn't stop now.

The list of names was long.

The parents were at the top, of course, followed by the twins, then Trixie (was that terrible, to list a dog before human beings?), Emerald and Bertie, Teddy Fortesque (he might be her former beau but she still thought of him fondly) and a whole host of other chums.

And last but certainly not least, even though she shouldn't because she was supposed to be forgetting him, but to leave him off or put a line through his name – God forbid – might jinx him: Sergeant Callum Fraser.

Chapter 42

'Special delivery for you, Captain!' Seffy said, saluting her aunt at the door of Ballykinch House.

They'd come straight from their mission at the castle.

'Eight rifles, eight lumberjills, one new and improved Lady Lockhart—' Seffy turned at the sound of Ralph's motorcycle roaring down the drive '—and one major!'

Thank goodness he was back and, by the looks of him, perfectly hale and hearty.

Joey had already jumped down from the back of the truck and was running into his arms. Seffy didn't blame her for breaking ranks. Even Dilys' face had softened at the sight.

The other girls were clambering out of the truck, passing down their contraband. They'd got here well before the other members of the WHD, who would be arriving for training later. The fewer people who knew the origin of the rifles, the better.

Lady Lockhart opened the passenger door and jumped onto the gravel. She was wearing a pair of figure-hugging jodhpurs and boots.

'I say, Lavinia! Most fetching!' Dilys said, standing to one side to let the girls into the house.

'Thanks awfully! Found these at the back of a wardrobe. Bit

moth-eaten. Ancient old things! But—' Lady Lockhart slapped her rear with a grin '—they still fit!'

'Excellent!' Dilys said. 'Hullo, Major, glad you could join us. Have you brought the ammo? Jolly good! Do come in. Girls, take those rifles into the dining room. Any problems?'

'Nae problem at all!' Tattie said. 'We managed to nick the lot!'

'Erm . . . smashing,' Dilys said, clearly taken aback by Tattie's efficient summary of the deed.

Ralph looked impressed and Seffy smiled to herself. Tattie was obviously no stranger to the shadier side of life. Her suggestion that they should break into the castle and steal the rifles hadn't been as ridiculous as it had first seemed. They'd simply had to wait for the day of the Highland Games, when everyone would be out.

Lady Lockhart had left a back door ajar and had been busy tending her plants in the hothouse when the girls carried out the raid. That way, if it were ever discovered, she could say, with a clear conscience, that she saw and heard nothing.

'No trouble getting the lorry?' Dilys asked.

Seffy shook her head.

'Jock's at the games, with everyone else,' she said. 'It won't be missed.'

'And I told Cameron I had one of my heads,' Lady Lockhart said. 'And that there was no cure but to stay at home, in the dark. He'll be out for hours, as will all the staff. We always give them the day off for the games.'

'And, will he miss these?' Dilys asked, as Grace brought the last rifle through.

'I doubt it. They've seen better days, mind. I only hope they work, after all this!'

'May I?' Ralph asked, taking the rifle from Grace. 'Goodness, it's practically a musket!'

He tested the trigger and peered down the barrel. 'Needs a good clean. And then we'll see.'

* * *

Tattie was enjoying herself.

It had been a hoot, robbing the rifles in broad daylight. Getting them down from the wall hadn't been easy, though. She'd had to climb up onto a glass cabinet to reach the ones at the very top.

Then they'd hightailed it in the truck to Ballykinch House, laughing like lunatics all the way.

Once the guns had been cleaned and loaded, William Wallace – the major – had tested them and to everyone's surprise, they worked. So the raid – and Lady Lockhart risking divorce from his lordship (or so she said) – had been worth it and now they were armed, just like the Home Guard.

Later, when the rest of the WHD arrived – the village women and lumberjills from other huts – they wanted to know where the firearms had come from. Seffy's auntie put her finger to her lips and said, "That's for me to know and you to find out!" and they'd seemed satisfied with that.

And then, Tattie had been allowed to have a go at shootin'. Gregor would've given his eye teeth to get his hands on a loaded rifle and she'd had one handed to her!

Only two girls were allowed on the firing range at a time. They stood behind two deckchairs fifty yards from the target, which was the scarecrow. While the shooting was in progress, everyone had to stand well clear. They were using live bullets, after all.

Tattie and Angie had been first up and Angie had taken it all very seriously. She'd been irked when Tattie turned out to be a better shot than her. Aye, she hadn't been half bad at the shootin', though it jarred your shoulder something rotten when the gun sprang back.

William Wallace had smiled when she'd returned the rifle and his hand had brushed hers. He didn't remember her, of course, but she'd met him before any of these lassies – including his sweetheart, Joey. Tattie hugged that little secret to herself.

Now she and Angie were sitting on deckchairs, watching the others shoot.

'Seffy's up next, with Joey!' Lady Lockhart announced, looking at her list.

'If Joey can bear to let go of the major's hand for five minutes,' Angie said. 'Honestly, the girl's making such a show of herself.'

Tattie frowned. Was she? The fella had been away for a week, doing derring-do; you could hardly blame them for being lovey-dovey.

Angie had had it in for Joey ever since that Sunday a couple of weeks ago, when she'd ducked out of church and gone out with the major instead. Every time he'd turned up on his motorbike after that, Angie had muttered something snide under her breath.

They watched as Seffy and Joey took their positions behind the deckchairs and the major showed them how to stand and take aim.

Angie sniffed. 'I wouldn't mind but he's not even that attractive.'

That was rubbish but Tattie said nothing.

In the next breath, Angie added, 'I need you to do something for me.'

Tattie's stomach dropped like a stone. *Aw, God, what now?* She ran around after Angie like a wee skivvy.

'Don't look at me like that! It's a simple task.'

'Why can't you do it, then?' Tattie asked. She said it in a jokey way but a flash of annoyance crossed Angie's face.

Tattie sighed. 'All right. What is it?'

'I want you to post a letter. There. I told you it was easy.'

'When I give the command . . .' Captain Dilys yelled.

Joey and Seffy were leaning on the back of the deckchairs, pointing the rifles at the scarecrow.

Joey wasn't sure she was holding the gun right. She wished Ralph would check her stance before they started shooting but he'd been accosted by Lady Lockhart, who was asking about safe storage of the ammunition.

'Oh, hold on a sec'!' Captain said. 'Hold fire! His head's coming off.'

The girls straightened up as Dilys ran forward to fix the scarecrow. It had been battered by a fair few bullets already.

Seffy looked down at her gun.

'My brothers are crack shots. I should've learned to shoot with them. But girls didn't do that kind of thing back then.'

'It's never too late to learn,' Joey said. 'You're doing it now, aren't you?'

Dilys had called for reinforcements and it took another minute for Tattie to appear, carrying a garden chair, followed by Angie, with a hammer.

Joey and Seffy watched as Angie climbed onto the chair and whacked the scarecrow's head back down on the nail.

'I don't think she should get her hands on a rifle,' Seffy said. 'I don't trust her as far as I could throw her.'

Joey sighed. Not this again. Why couldn't they all simply get along and have a nice day? She blinked hard, a few times.

'Have you got something in your eye?' Seffy asked.

'No. It's . . . I've only just realised something: I can only wink with one eye.'

Seffy laughed. 'Show me!'

Joey demonstrated. 'See? I can do this one but not this one. And that's the one I need to close when I take aim.'

Seffy nodded and pursed her lips. 'And you can hardly hold your eye closed when you're shooting. You'll have to get an eye-shield. Perhaps you could knit one?'

Joey tried closing her eyes one at a time. No, she simply couldn't manage it.

Seffy laughed again. 'If the Jerries come, you'll have to ask them to wait, while you put your eye-shield on!'

Ralph was still talking to Lady Lockhart. Joey wished they'd hurry up. It was torture, having him so near but not being able to speak to him.

Seffy must've heard her sigh.

'Happy to have him back?'

'Oh aye, of course.'

She was trying not to be smug. Grace was missing her fella – and Seffy too, although she kept that to herself most of the time; Morag had been given the heave-ho by her fiancé and a couple of the lassies were doting on Italians, which was a non-starter, of course. She was the only one lucky enough to actually see her fella – between army commitments – and she wasn't about to start rubbing the others' noses in it.

'But listen,' Joey said, 'I'm not going to tell Ralph the bad news about Monty. We have little enough time together and I don't want us to dwell on sad things.'

'I was going to make a suggestion about Monty, actually—' Seffy started but Captain Dilys interrupted.

'Ready, girls?' she yelled.

The scarecrow had been repaired and the stretch of lawn around it was clear again.

'On my command . . . three, two, one, FIRE!'

Seffy and Dilys were reclining in deckchairs, watching Enid and Flora on the shooting range. The major, to Seffy's relief, was supervising operations.

'I wasn't too sure about the wisdom of letting those two loose with guns,' Seffy said. 'They can be a tad childish. And silly.'

Dilys frowned. 'I'd say they're doing a perfectly good job, for a first go. In fact, the older one – is it Enid – handles the rifle very well. She's not a crack shot like you, my dear, but she's not half bad. The danger with pigeonholing people, Persephone, is that it's very hard to see them in another light. If, say, they change.'

Seffy bit her lip. After the unexpected compliment about her shooting prowess, she could now feel a lecture coming on.

Her aunt cleared her throat. 'Take you, for example. When you first came, you were—'

'Oh, I know! Uppity and spoilt and all those things. Blah, blah, blah.'

Was she never going to be allowed to forget her failings?

'Yes, but look at you now. You're mucking down, you're an excellent lumberjill, by all accounts. Goodness, you're in charge! You're a leader girl!'

'I'm not!' Seffy blurted out. She glared at Angie, on the far side of the lawn. 'She is.'

Dilys looked dumbfounded. 'What? Angie's taken your place? When did this happen?'

Seffy shrugged. 'About six weeks ago.'

She was already regretting telling Dilys. This was going to be like the Spanish Inquisition.

Dilys frowned at Angie. 'She's capable, I suppose and helpful in the WHD but—' She turned in her seat towards Seffy. 'This is a test, Persephone! Prove yourself the better woman, get your job back! Anyhoo, why have you been demoted?'

Seffy took a deep breath. 'Because the supervisor thinks I'm lily-livered and lacking in backbone because I . . .' she could hardly bring herself to say it '. . . because when Hazel . . . had her accident, I had a breakdown.'

There, she'd said it.

She braced herself but Dilys didn't fly off the handle. She sat back in her seat and, when she spoke, her voice was measured and surprisingly gentle.

'But my dear, you were very sick. People get sick; it's a fact of life. Has no one else in the camp been ill? No TB, pneumonia or rheumatic fever?'

'Yes, of course. Last winter there were lots of—'

'And what happened to them?'

'They were sent away to recover in hospital or at home. And when – if – they got better, they came back.'

'And you suffered from an illness too,' Dilys said, firmly. 'In here.' She touched Seffy's forehead. 'Where no one could see.'

Seffy had never thought of it like that. But it was true: she had been sick. Miss McEwen had implied she'd been shirking, but that wasn't right. She'd wanted to get back to work but she hadn't been able to. She'd felt as though she were wading through a never-ending black tunnel. There'd been days when she hadn't even been able to get out of bed.

'And she said I suffer with my nerves,' Seffy said.

Dilys gave a hollow laugh. 'Persephone, my dear girl, we're living through a terrible war! It's hardly the best time to be alive. I doubt there's a woman – or man, for that matter – in the whole country, who isn't currently suffering with their nerves.'

Seffy smiled. 'Good point,' she said.

Chapter 43

Seffy was running alongside Nippy, as the mare swerved between the trees, dragging a log behind her.

The log bounced and skidded on the hard ground, ricocheting occasionally against a trunk. As well as looking ahead, Seffy had to keep half an eye on the log, in case she suddenly needed to leap over it.

She loved this part of the job. You had to be quick and nimble to avoid getting whacked by logs, caught up in chains or stamped on by hooves the size of dinner plates.

The blue funk she'd been in ever since Miss McEwen had implied she was "nervy", had almost completely lifted. Her aunt was right: after Hazel's accident, Seffy had been sick and unable to work but that didn't make her weak or incompetent.

Look at her now! She pumped her arms a little harder. She was fit and strong enough to keep up with a trotting horse, which was certainly more than stout Miss McEwen could do.

'Whoa up, girl,' Seffy said, as they finally reached the clearing. Nippy knew the ropes. She slowed to a walk and then came to a standstill, with a jangle of chains.

Jean and Joey were standing next to the stack of logs, deep in conversation. As they turned towards her, Seffy could tell immediately something was wrong. Despite the warm air, a chill went through her.

'Tell me!' she said, racing over to them.

Joey shook her head. 'Don't fret – no one's badly hurt.'

'What, then?'

Jean rolled her eyes. 'Flora dropped a log on Grace's foot.'

Trust Flora, the silly girl! Seffy felt a stab of guilt. If Grace had still been working with her, that would never have happened.

'She was so busy flirting with the Italians, that she wasn't paying proper attention,' Joey said. 'Hopefully it's only bruised because Grace is off soon.'

'Off soon?' Seffy asked.

'The day after tomorrow,' Jean said, with a firm nod.

Seffy swallowed. Of course, they meant Grace's trip to the Borders to meet Gordy. She hadn't realised it was so soon but she could hardly admit it. The other girls were almost as excited as Grace about her second honeymoon; they'd talked of little else for weeks.

When Jock brought Grace back to the hut from the cottage hospital later, everyone watched with bated breath as she hobbled in on crutches.

Her right foot was bandaged and she was in floods of tears.

'Ma big toe's broken,' she said.

'Ouch!' Angie said. 'Come and sit down and put your foot up on this chair.'

Once Grace had managed to manoeuvre herself sufficiently to take a seat, Seffy moved the crutches and propped them against the wall.

'Well done,' she said and immediately felt rotten. Those were probably the nicest words she'd said to Grace for months.

Seffy pulled a face at the others, who grimaced back. They were all, no doubt, thinking the same: how on earth was Grace going to get to the Borders now?

251

Grace started to cry again, in rasping great sobs that shook her whole body. No one could console her.

Finally, she blew her nose. 'It's no good – I can't go to meet Gordy.'

There was stunned silence in the hut.

'There isn't even time to send him a wire. I'm supposed to meet him on Wednesday and he'll already . . .' Grace dissolved into tears again.

'Aye,' Jean said. 'She's right. He'll already have set off.'

'But you have to go!' Tattie said. She looked at the others. 'Doesn't she?'

Angie sighed. 'But she can hardly move with those crutches. How will she carry a suitcase?'

'Or manage steps, change trains or cross platforms?' Jean said.

Seffy's chest tightened. Oh, why didn't they all shush? This was a total disaster and they were simply adding salt to the wound.

'One of yous will have to go with her,' Morag said. 'Don't look at me. I've no leave left.'

'I've got some leave owing,' Joey said. 'I could go.'

Grace shook her head vigorously. 'No! There's the train fare and the board and lodgings, too. It's too costly.'

Joey bit her lip. She was probably regretting her offer, Seffy thought. Joey couldn't afford a trip to the Borders and besides, she had little enough time with Ralph as it was. No, Joey needed to stay here.

Seffy was in turmoil. If she hadn't been so determined to keep away from Grace, they'd probably have still been working together. The accident would never have happened.

It was all her fault.

She'd been leaning against the wall. She stepped nearer now and joined the circle of girls clustered around Grace.

'I'll go with you, Grace,' she said. 'I've enough leave and I can . . . well, I've got the money, too. I can carry your suitcase and help you on and off the train and . . .' She trailed off and gave a small shrug.

Everyone was looking at her, clearly surprised. Seffy hardly dared look at Grace. She wouldn't blame her if she turned her down flat. After all, why would she want to travel all that way with someone who'd been so nasty?

'Aw, but that's a super offer!' Jean said, grinning. 'Isn't it, Grace?'

'You'll have to get Miss M's permission,' Angie said. 'It's short notice and remember, we all have a duty to ask, "Is your journey really necessary?" But I can have a word.'

Seffy felt the urge to say something sarky but she bit her tongue. Like it or not, she might actually need Angie's help if they were going to pull this off.

Everyone was waiting for Grace's reply.

She sniffed and looked up at Seffy through tear-stained eyes. 'If you're sure? That's so kind. I can't thank you enough, Seffy.'

'Oh, it's nothing,' she said. But actually, it was everything.

Joey looked across the hut and gave her a thumbs up.

'Well done, Seffy,' Jean said. 'You've saved the day.'

Seffy winced. She didn't deserve that. Everyone thought she was being an absolute brick but she'd made her offer out of guilt, pure and simple.

She'd behaved so badly: this was what she had to do, to put things right.

Chapter 44

'Gretna Green?' Seffy said, gazing in disbelief at her ticket.

She and Grace were sitting opposite one another in a packed carriage, on the train heading south. Seffy's head had been in a whirl since they'd left the ticket office, ten minutes earlier.

Someone must have mentioned the lovebirds' rendezvous before today, but Seffy had avoided all discussion of the trip, so she'd been in the dark.

'Isn't Gretna Green where all the runaway weddings take place?' she asked.

Grace laughed. She was probably enjoying this.

'Aye. In olden times, youngsters eloped to Gretna because you could get hitched in Scotland without your parents' say-so. And it's still a popular place for weddings.'

'But why did Gordy choose there?'

'Aw, who knows? Mebbe he thought it'd be romantic! Or funny!'

Yes, it was hilarious. Seffy sighed and sat back in her seat. Being a total gooseberry was going to be bad enough, but she'd be surrounded by newly-weds and soon-to-be-marrieds too. It was as though someone were playing a terrible prank.

Well, it was no more than she deserved. She'd packed a couple of romances and her knitting. It was only three days; she'd simply have to lump it.

'Apparently, there's a famous anvil in the smithy and if you touch it, you'll be lucky in love,' Grace said.

Seffy smiled. 'Now you sound like spooky Angie. But perhaps I'll try it. I could do with some luck in that department!'

Grace looked suddenly serious. 'Seffy, I hope you didn't offer to come because you thought . . .' she swallowed. '. . . that Gordy might bring Callum?'

Seffy's breath caught in her throat. 'No!'

She'd almost shouted. The man beside Grace lowered his newspaper and glowered at her.

'No, of course not,' Seffy said, dropping her voice. 'I came because you needed me and because I'm sorry . . . for the way I've behaved.'

Gosh, this was excruciating. And everyone else in the compartment was almost certainly tuning in now.

Grace reached out with both hands. Seffy took them and squeezed, gently. They smiled at one another. This was hardly the place for apologies or explanations but perhaps that had been enough.

Seffy cleared her throat. 'How's . . . how's Gordy getting on down in England?'

It was the first time she'd asked Grace anything about him and her voice had sounded stilted and wrong.

Grace smiled. 'He doesn't mind it too much. He'd rather be in Scotland of course, but the locals are friendly. Rather too friendly with some of the fellas, he says. Apparently, Jean-Paul is up to his usual.'

They rolled their eyes at one another.

Jean-Paul was a love rat of the first order. He'd got their former colleague, Irene, in the family way and then wanted nothing more to do with her.

Seffy wondered whether Callum had got friendly with any of

the locals. Her stomach swooped at the thought. She'd rather not know.

'Anyway, Grace, you don't have to worry about friendly locals,' she said. 'Gordy worships the ground you walk on.'

'Or rather, the ground I hobble on!' Grace looked up at the crutches in the luggage rack and winced. 'Wait until he sees those.'

Oh, the relief: she and Grace were pals again. There was still a little awkwardness but that would fade in time, Seffy was sure. She'd slayed the green-eyed monster! But although she wasn't jealous anymore, she did feel something else: a kind of painful wistfulness.

If things had been different, she and Grace would've planned this trip to see their men, together. Instead, she was merely accompanying Grace, like a maiden aunt or a chaperone.

And although thoughts of him still swirled constantly around her mind, her memories of Callum were getting fainter by the day.

She could still picture his blue eyes and that twitch of his lips as he tried not to smile. And she had the newspaper cutting: a slightly blurred photograph taken at Grace's wedding, in which Callum was in the front row of a group of CFC men.

But the memory of his lovely, deep, Canadian drawl, had gone. It was torture, not being able to remember the sound of his voice.

Despite her injured foot, Grace could hardly keep still. She jiggled in her seat, sighed and closed the book she'd been trying to read. 'I cannae concentrate!'

'I've noticed!'

They smiled at one another. Seffy could only imagine how excited Grace must be. She hadn't seen Gordy for three whole months.

When the train finally pulled in at Gretna Green, Seffy got off first with their luggage, leaving Grace standing inside the door, leaning on her crutches.

Seffy stood on tiptoe to see over the heads of the passengers swarming down the platform.

There he was! She'd know that CFC uniform anywhere.

'Gordy!' she cried, waving.

Grace peered around the door as best she could. Goodness, Seffy thought, don't fall now.

Gordy was racing towards them at full pelt, cap in hand, dodging passengers and porters. He leaped over a stack of luggage. As he got nearer, his grin faded. He must be wondering why Seffy was there, instead of his wife.

'It's all right! She's here!' Seffy said, as Gordy reached them. 'But she needs a hand down.'

His face fell. 'What in tarnation . . . ?' He stared at the crutches and then leaned in and hugged Grace. 'This wasn't the plan, honey! What's happened?'

'I've broken ma big toe! It's no' funny!'

Gordy had started to laugh. He cupped Grace's chin in his hand and kissed her. 'Oh, boy. It kinda is, though,' he said, when they finally drew apart. 'Bet it's sore as hell ain't it? Come on, I'll lift you down. Did you drop summat on it?'

Seffy had stepped to the side, to give them some privacy.

'Say, Seffy,' Gordy said, 'you need to take better care of my wife!'

Oh, please don't say Grace had told Gordy how mean she'd been since the company had left. She couldn't bear it.

'Without Seffy,' Grace said, 'you'd be standing here alone because I wouldn't have been able to come.'

'Is that right? Oh Jeez, then—' Gordy stepped forward and landed a kiss on Seffy's cheek, 'I take it all back. Thanks a million! It's good to see ya! Now, I brought someone with me too. Where's he got to?'

The steam had almost cleared from the platform and Seffy's eye was caught by another man in green CFC uniform, taking long, loping strides towards them.

Her heart almost stopped. Was it? Could it be . . . ? For a few thrilling and terrifying seconds, she imagined it was Callum. The figure had a similar build and the same slow walk.

257

But as he got nearer, she could see it wasn't him. The disappointment was like a punch in the stomach.

This man's face was rounder, his cheeks were redder and there was no cleft chin. She knew instantly he was the opposite of Callum Fraser in every way.

'This here's Private Wally Mitchell, girls. We travelled up from England together. Wally, this is my wife, Gracie, and her buddy, Miss Seffy Mills.'

Private Mitchell had a serious, intense gaze and as they shook hands, he held Seffy's for longer than strictly necessary and stared into her eyes.

Oh, no. Please don't let this chap – whom she already resented for not being Callum – assume this was some kind of double-date situation.

'What've you got planned for the next couple of days, pretty lady?' He had the most awful, nasal voice.

'Me? Oh, I'm going to be very busy,' Seffy said. She glanced at Grace hopefully, but she and Gordy were nestled close, rubbing noses.

'Erm, how about you?' she asked.

He tapped the binoculars strung around his neck. 'Bird-spotting!'

'Good for you!'

'Outta town.'

'Excellent!'

She exhaled as he lifted the binoculars and started scanning the cloudless blue sky. Maybe it would be all right. As long as he didn't start spying on her with those darned things.

'Shall we go and find the boarding house?' Seffy suggested, when Grace and Gordy came up for air.

'Wally and me've already checked in. And Gracie, our room is on the ground floor, so I can carry my beautiful bride over the threshold! But hey, can you walk that far? It's about a half a mile.'

'She can't possibly,' Seffy said. 'We'll have to get a taxi. I can pay.'

Gordy laughed. 'That's real kind, ma'am, but this ain't London town! No taxis to be had, leastways none that I've seen.'

Actually, that was no bad thing. Seffy didn't have that much cash. It was peculiar but when she'd retrieved her suitcase from under the bed, in order to pack but also to get the money she'd need for this trip, she could've sworn there was some missing. There should have been a stash of pound notes but some were definitely gone.

Perhaps she'd put some of the money in another place and had forgotten? She'd have a proper look in her locker and under the bed when she got back.

She wanted to offer some of her stash to Joey, to buy Monty and save him from the knacker's yard. But she knew she had to choose her moment – and her words – carefully. Joey was proud and her first reaction would almost certainly be to say no.

'Wally, you bring the cases,' Gordy said. 'Seffy, can you manage the crutches? And I'll carry Gracie.'

Grace winced and Seffy's heart went out to her. Grace was self-conscious about her height – she was taller than Gordy – and her weight.

But when Gordy swept her effortlessly up into his arms – oh, lucky, lucky, Grace – she visibly relaxed and put her arms around his neck.

Then their odd little party set off down the road, towards their billet.

That evening, they ate in a small restaurant near their lodgings and after the meal, they moved to a nearby pub.

Of all the men in Thirty-Four company, why oh why did Gordy have to bring sniffling, whining, dreary Wally Mitchell?

If he told her one more time that he missed home and wished he'd never enlisted and how he hated everything about this place – except the birds – she might have to clock him one, as Joey would say.

259

His CFC uniform was very smart, though. Even he couldn't ruin that. It reminded Seffy so much of Callum. She was bursting to ask about him. This might be her only chance.

It was ridiculous, but she couldn't seem to pluck up the courage. She was afraid of using the wrong words and not striking the right, casual tone.

However, after her second port and lemon, she felt braver.

While Gordy and Grace were engrossed in one another, she took a deep breath and turned to Wally.

'I knew someone from your company when you worked near us, in Morayshire.'

'Uh-huh?' Wally's eyes were fixed on the darts game in the corner of the bar. She'd been grateful for it, until now.

'Sergeant Callum Fraser,' she said. Her mouth was dry. That was the first time she'd said his name out loud, for so long.

Wally gasped as one of the darts struck the bullseye. 'Good throw!' he muttered.

'Sergeant Fraser?' Seffy said. Her foot was tapping. 'Can you tell me . . . ? That's to say, how is he?'

He looked at her, finally. He frowned, sniffed and seemed to be considering his answer. How difficult could it be? They were in the same company. Surely, he must know Callum?

'Sergeant Fraser?' he repeated. He scratched his nose, infuriatingly, then exhaled.

'I was only wondering,' Seffy said. 'We haven't been in touch, since the company left, and—'

'Oh, he's no more,' Wally said, solemnly.

It was just as well she was sitting down because her knees would surely have buckled. As it was, her stomach plunged and she almost knocked her drink over. She scrambled around, just managing to grab the glass before it fell.

'Wh – what do you mean?'

Her hand was gripping the glass so tightly, she half expected it to shatter.

'He means,' Gordy interrupted, shooting Wally an exasperated look, 'that Sergeant Fraser is now *Staff* Sergeant Fraser.' He grinned. 'He's climbing the ladder! He's still "Sarge" to us, though.'

The relief was total. Seffy gave a short laugh, which sounded queer, even to her own ears and took a long drink, to hide her embarrassment.

Grace smiled across the table at her, with soft eyes. She put her hand on Gordy's arm. 'You didn't tell me Callum had been promoted.'

Gordy shrugged. 'I wrote you, Gracie. You probably ain't got the letter yet. But I did tell ya!'

Seffy exhaled. Callum was all right. Better than all right: he'd been promoted; he was thriving. She felt as though she could hug everyone in the place. Except Wally Mitchell, whom she could quite happily slap, for almost giving her a seizure.

Gordy and Grace were watching her, expectantly.

'That's excellent news,' Seffy said. 'Do . . . do give him my best, won't you, Gordy?'

'Sure,' Gordy said. 'He almost came on this trip, to tell the truth. Then you coulda told him yourself, huh?'

The room seemed to swoop away.

Gordy stood up, held out his empty glass and gestured to Wally, asking if he wanted another pint.

'Did . . . did he?' Seffy said.

'Yeah.' Gordy watched while Wally downed the last dregs of his beer. Once the glass was empty, he took it and made to go towards the bar. 'Ladies, anything else for you?'

Seffy and Grace shook their heads.

'What happened?' Grace asked, not taking her eyes off Seffy. 'Why didn't he come?'

'He'd gotten leave same time as me,' Gordy said. 'I reckon he was thinking 'bout going to see his folks. His Ma's family lives round these parts.'

'So . . . did he change his mind?' Seffy asked.

She wanted to grab Gordy by the lapels and yell, 'Tell me!' but she had to wait, trying to eke the information out of him.

'Yeah. We don't get much leave. I guess it's the same for you girls. You have to use it real careful, right?'

Tears were pricking the backs of Seffy's eyes. Oh, yes, leave was precious. And she was wasting days of it here. What on earth had she been thinking?

Gordy still hadn't made the move to the bar. He was looking at her, a curious, unfathomable expression on his face. 'Guess you'd have liked to have seen him, huh?'

She couldn't deny it; her disappointment must be written all over her face.

'Yes,' Seffy said, smiling through quivering lips. 'I would.'

Chapter 45

Joey was whistling as she filled the hay rack in Storm's stable. She was alone in the yard; she'd sent Alonzo and the other girls to get their lunch. This was her last task and then the weekend would begin.

It felt queer, being here without Seffy. The wee Sassenach had been away since Wednesday and Joey missed her. This was usually her favourite part of the day, when she and Seffy settled the horses down together.

But her pal had done the right thing, offering to accompany Grace. With any luck, when they came back later today, the girls would be the best of friends again.

She looked round at the unmistakeable sound of Ralph's motorcycle. Her heart lifted and then sank again. She hadn't seen him since last weekend and they were due to go to the dance tonight, at the Farrbridge Hotel. Perhaps he'd come to say he couldn't make it, after all?

She gazed over the stable door. Every time she looked at him, she wanted to pinch herself. He was perfection: braw and solid and strong. And all hers.

Ralph cut the engine and dismounted.

'Well, well. What brings you here, Major Stirling? Couldn't wait a few more hours to see me, eh?'

He pulled off his goggles and wiped his brow. He looked troubled. She hoped it wasn't bad news. Please don't say someone in his unit had been injured. Or worse.

'Are you alone?' he asked.

'Aye, lucky fella.' Joey came out of the stable, pitchfork in hand and shot the bolt on the door. 'You've got me all to yourself! And your timing's spot on: I've just finished here.'

He seemed determined not to match her jolly mood. He had another mission coming up in the next few days. Perhaps he was mithering about that.

'Josephine,' he said, sounding so serious that she jumped. 'Is there somewhere we can go?'

The hayloft sprang to mind. She wouldn't mind a quick, wee tumble up there. But now wasn't the time to say it. 'What kind of place?'

'Somewhere quiet and—' Ralph touched his nose to prevent a sneeze '—not so horsey. I need to ask you something.'

She nodded. She knew exactly where to take him.

As Joey led the way along a narrow path through the woods, she let her hand swing behind, hoping – in vain – that Ralph might reach out and take it. He was preoccupied. She tried not to mind; all would be revealed, soon enough.

'Will this do?'

She'd brought him to a quiet glade, a few minutes' walk from the stables. It was on the edge of an escarpment, with breathtaking views across the valley. You could see as far as the sapphire-blue loch, which glinted in the afternoon sun.

She spread out the rug she'd brought from the yard and sat down, leaving room for him beside her. But he didn't sit. He started to pace up and down.

She sighed. 'What is it, for heaven's sake?'

Ralph stopped pacing and looked down at her. 'Josephine—'

Her heart almost stopped. He sounded so formal, not like him at all. *Oh, ma God.* Was he going to . . . ? Right, here, now?

No, this was too soon; she wasn't ready. Her hands were filthy. Goodness, her nails were black. If she'd had an inkling this might happen, she'd have dunked her hands in a bucket of water, at the very least. She wiped them quickly on her breeches and tried to look curious. And happy.

Ralph was reaching into the inside pocket of his jacket.

She'd guessed right. He was getting the ring! No, this couldn't be happening.

But she could hardly stop him now, just because she was grubby. She wanted it and she didn't, all at the same time. They hadn't been stepping out long enough; they hardly knew one another. But if she didn't say yes, he mightn't ask her again.

She forced herself to take a deep breath and calm down.

There was no time to think of something witty to say. When the moment came, she'd simply say 'Yes, yes, yes!' and throw herself into his arms.

'Josephine?'

'Yes?' Her voice had cracked. She was suddenly so nervous; it was as though they were strangers.

But he'd let his hand fall. He'd changed his mind.

Not a proposal, then.

Ralph rubbed his face. 'I . . . there's no easy way to say this.'

Joey waited, as he gazed out over the valley. He couldn't even look at her. It was summat bad; not what she'd thought, at all.

Joey stood up, feeling cross and let down. She couldn't talk to him properly sitting on a blanket, for all the world like they were about to have a picnic. 'You'd best come out with it, whatever it is.'

She had a horrible feeling of foreboding. Her breath was coming in shallow bursts. Surely he wasn't about to throw her over? They were happy – weren't they?

Ralph reached into his pocket again with a heavy sigh and drew something out. A piece of paper, folded over. 'You should read this. It concerns you.'

A letter, then. The page was wrinkled and thick and covered in big, uneven lettering, like something a child might do. The letters had been cut from magazines and stuck to the paper.

Joey glanced up at him. Was this some kind of joke? But his brow was furrowed; he was deadly serious.

The words danced before her eyes. She had to force herself to focus.

BEFORE YOU GET TOO INVOLVED
ASK I ABOUT THE MAN SHE
LIVED WITH AS MAN AND WIFE
IN FORRES
  FROM
  A WELL-WISHER

Joey gulped and read it again.

'"A well-wisher"? It's hardly that!' Her legs had gone weak. She might have to sit down again. 'Where did you get this?'

'I found it in my jacket pocket on Sunday,' Ralph said. 'Someone must have put it there the day before, during rifle training.'

She felt as though her chest was in a vice.

That couldn't be right. Had someone in the WHD, one of her so-called friends, done this? But who could possibly hate her that much?

Another horrible thought struck her: she and Ralph had been out for a drink last Saturday evening. The letter must've been in his pocket all that time. Like a ticking bomb, waiting to explode.

He'd had it since Sunday. Almost a week. He must've been mulling over it all that time.

Joey felt sick. She scrunched up the paper in her fist and looked at him, her eyes blurry with tears. 'You don't believe it, do you?'

Ralph shrugged. 'I don't know. But – I can't help thinking, there's no smoke without fire. Do you have any idea who might've sent it?'

She felt a flare of anger. Never mind "who might've sent it", why wasn't he asking, 'Who might've sent *this lie*?'

'Didn't you live in Forres? I'm sure you told me . . . isn't that where the horse came from?'

Ma God, she was on trial.

'Yes, I lived in Forres! And yes, there was a man! I was . . .' How could she explain what she'd had with Hamish and how it'd been nothing compared to what they had – her and Ralph?

'I was fond o' him. But I did nothing wrong! Nothing that would make you doubt me or my honour or whatever you want to call it!'

He stared at the ground and then back at her. He looked pained and Joey could tell he was wrestling with this. But he was erring on the side of whoever had written the letter.

"What about this "man and wife" business?'

'That's no' true!' Joey cursed herself for blushing. She was angry and humiliated but it must look like guilt. How could she even start to explain the queer arrangement in that farmhouse in Forres?

'You don't deny that you lived in the man's home?'

'I did live there. But not with him, not like that! There were three of us, billeted in the attic. Sometimes I went down into the house because I could hear the weans crying. Their mother had died; they missed her. I did nothing wrong! What do you take me for?'

Hot tears were streaming down her face. She might've known this was all too good to be true. And she'd thought he was about to propose! How stupid! Lassies like her didn't marry men like him.

'I'm truly sorry,' Ralph said, shaking his head. He reached out for her but she pushed him away.

'Don't touch me!'

Did he really think he could accuse her like that and in the next breath, act as though nothing had happened? Who did he think he was?

'Josephine, I should never have doubted you. I believe you.'

Ralph rubbed his forehead and held out his hand. 'Here, let

me rip that up, right now, and we'll never speak of it again, as long as we live.'

'NO! How could you doubt me? How could you believe this rubbish—' Joey shook the balled-up letter at him '—instead of me?'

'I don't! I'm so sorry—' He started, but she cut him off.

'It's over with us.'

There was a grim satisfaction in seeing his face fall.

She gave a hollow laugh. 'All this time, I've been thinking that mebbe I wasn't good enough for you when . . .' she jabbed her finger at him '. . . the truth is, Ralph Stirling – you're no' good enough for me!'

Chapter 46

Time in Gretna Green moved so slowly, Seffy wanted to scream.

She'd thought having nothing to do might be an enjoyable novelty, but killing time in teashops, to allow Grace and Gordy to be alone, was actually tiresome.

Thank goodness it was their last afternoon.

She was tucked away in a corner of her favourite café, making a pot of tea, a scone and her romance novel last as long as possible.

In a couple of hours, she and Grace would be on the train back to Morayshire. Poor Grace would be devastated, but for Seffy, it couldn't come soon enough.

The bell above the door jangled and she glanced up.

Blast! Wally Mitchell had tracked her down again.

She lifted the book to hide her face and braced herself for, 'Why, there you are, little lady!' but he strode past without spotting her.

She quickly placed some coins on the table, picked up her book and handbag and slid noiselessly towards the exit.

She'd done it! She burst out onto the high street, letting the door slam behind her. Of course, Wally might still have spotted her leaving. He could've reached the door in three or four long strides and might be right on her tail. Seffy pushed past the two or three customers who'd been on their way in.

'Charmed, I'm sure!' a woman said.

There was no chance to apologise. A strong arm suddenly wrapped itself around Seffy's waist from behind, bringing her to a standstill with a jerk.

'Whoa there, miss! Hold your horses!'

A man. But not Wally. This voice was deep and as smooth as honey.

'What d'you—?' Seffy started to say, swivelling to confront her captor.

She stopped, open-mouthed.

'—think you're doing?' she finished, faintly.

It was Callum Fraser.

Except, it couldn't be.

He was holding her close, smiling down at her. There were dots of blue stubble on his jaw; there was that cleft chin she knew so well. She could feel his warm breath on her face. He smelled exactly the same: musky and delicious.

Her breath caught in her throat. If he hadn't been holding her so tightly, she'd have fallen.

What was he doing here?

She vaguely registered people brushing past and stepping around them, entering and exiting the teashop, making the doorbell ring.

Before either of them could speak again, Wally Mitchell appeared.

'Aw, hi there, Sarge,' he said, apparently unsurprised to find Seffy in Callum's arms. 'Ain't this a turn-up!'

'Quite,' Seffy murmured, not taking her eyes off Callum. He was staring right back at her, still smiling.

She'd never been so shocked. Or so joyful. It couldn't really be him and yet, it was! She was filled with lightness, as though she were full of bubbles. This was madness! She thought she might burst into uncontrollable laughter.

The last time they'd been together, she'd left him sitting under a tree. She'd walked away without a backward glance, imagining she'd never see him again.

But dreams did come true. Here he was.

Callum indicated with the smallest movement of his head, that they should move. He released her and, pressing his hand gently into the small of her back, steered her, until they were clear of the teashop doorway.

His shirt sleeves were pushed up and Seffy prodded his tanned arm.

'You,' she said, shaking her head. 'I'm checking you're real.'

He couldn't be a figment of her imagination: she'd felt muscle in that warm, sinewy arm: the arm that, a minute ago, had been wrapped so tightly around her. She touched her waist, remembering how it had felt, wishing it were still there.

'Say, I've been looking all over for you, Miss Mills,' Wally said. He was following them, like an unwelcome wasp at a picnic.

'Private Mitchell, have you been making a nuisance of yourself?' Callum asked, narrowing his eyes.

'No, I haven't! Have I, miss?'

She swallowed. He'd actually been a complete pain in the you-know-where, as Joey would say. But now his superior was here – and Seffy's head was still spinning at the thought – she felt rather sorry for him.

'The thing is . . .' she said, looking anywhere but at Callum. He was grinning and if she caught his eye, she knew she'd laugh.

This had to be a dream. She often dreamed about him and this was one of those rare, especially wonderful dreams in which he appeared, exactly as she remembered him, and rescued her.

Oh, but if it were a dream, any second now, she'd wake up and he would melt away.

'. . . well, Gretna Green is a small place,' she continued, 'and Private Mitchell's path has crossed with mine on a fairly regular basis.'

Seffy held up the romance she'd been reading. 'And I really would like to find out if the hero gets his girl.'

Callum's lips twitched. Was she being too obvious? But to heck with it: if this were a dream then it hardly mattered; she could be as obvious as she liked. Heavens, she could pull him towards her and kiss the lips off him – right here, in the street – and no one would turn a hair.

'D'you wanna get a beer, Sarge?' Wally asked. 'I mean, if the little lady wants to get back to her book, then—'

Callum looked at her. Seffy pulled a face.

'Private, aren't you here for our feathered friends?' Callum tugged, none too gently, at the binocular strap around Wally's neck.

'Yeah, Sarge, but—'

'Oh, the birds are all moulting,' Seffy said. 'I know all about it. At this time of year, they're losing feathers. Shame Private Mitchell didn't realise that before he made the journey here. Because when they're moulting, they don't fly as much. Consequently, there aren't so many to see.'

Wally Mitchell was looking impressed, as though Seffy were his bird-watching protégée.

Callum sighed. 'Mitchell, there were some twitchers on my train and they were headed this way to see the rare something or other out on the marshes. Couple of miles thaddaway.' He nodded down the street. 'D'you know anything about that?'

Wally grabbed his binoculars. 'No! What kinda bird? Did they say?'

'Somethin' like a do—'

'A dotterel?' Wally's face lit up. 'Gee! A dotterel? I didn't think they came this far south but – hey – I sure would like to see one of them fellas and tick it off my list.' He patted Seffy's arm. 'I'm real sorry, ma'am, but I have to go see this.'

Wally stepped backwards off the kerb, wheeled his arms to stop himself falling, then raced away down the street.

Seffy turned to Callum. 'Marshes? Are there—?'

His eyes opened wide. 'I have absolutely no idea.'

'And the bird?'

He shook his head. 'I was gonna say a dodo but he didn't give me chance, so . . .'

'Dotterel it is.'

They looked at each other. Seffy's mouth was dry. She licked her lips.

'He's been bothering you some, ain't he?' Callum said.

Seffy laughed. 'Oh, I'm a big girl now; I can look after myself.'

'Look, d'you wanna get a drink? Is there someplace round here we can go?'

Thank goodness she knew the pubs of Gretna almost as well as the teashops. 'Yes,' Seffy said. 'But I can't stay long.'

That had sounded as though she were playing hard to get. Which perhaps wasn't an altogether bad thing. Of course, she wanted to go for a drink with him! If Callum Fraser suggested jumping off a cliff, she'd probably agree.

They walked through the streets, so close that every few steps, their hands and arms touched and Seffy got goose bumps. There were courting couples everywhere, holding hands or draped around each other. A pair stopped in front of them, for a smooch and she and Callum had to split up and walk around them.

'This feels peculiar,' Seffy said. 'I don't think I've ever seen you outside a forest!'

Callum frowned. 'Hey, that's not right. Let's see . . . you've seen me in a rowing boat, you've seen me in a dance hall, you've seen me at your auntie's castle, dancing the Gay Gordons.' He raised a finger. 'You've even seen me in a bothy.'

She laughed, flushing slightly as she remembered that very chaste night they'd spent together.

'You're right. I suppose I meant I've never seen you in a town.'

She hardly knew – or cared – what she was saying. Her heart was fit to burst. He wasn't a phantom or a figment of her imagination. Callum Fraser really was here. He was flesh and

273

blood, six-feet one inch of solid Canadian and he hadn't forgotten her or the good times they'd shared.

The pub was half empty and they chose a table near the window. Seffy sat facing the bar, so she could watch as Callum ordered the drinks.

She gazed at him unashamedly, admiring his broad back, his narrow waist and long legs. Suddenly, from wanting time to race past, she desperately wanted it to stop.

'Thank you. I need this!' she said, when he placed their drinks down. 'For the shock!'

He pulled his chair close, so that their knees were just touching.

'Not a bad kinda shock, I hope? If I interrupted you and Private Mitchell back there—'

She slapped his hand. 'Stop it! Now, tell me what you're doing here! I'm guessing you've come to see your relatives? How long have you been in Gretna?'

He laughed. 'One question at a time, please, Miss Mills!'

'Sorry.' She sipped her port and lemon.

'I only got off the train ten minutes before I saw you come stormin' outta that café, pushing folk out the way, left, right and centre. Yep, I thought, that sure looks like Seffy!'

She never imagined thinking it, but thank goodness for Wally Mitchell: he was the cause of her storming out.

'But weren't you surprised to see me?'

He must've been; she wasn't meant to be in Gretna. But then, neither was he. It was all so wonderfully weird.

Callum toyed with his pint glass and didn't meet her eye.

'Heck, I'm not surprised by anything these days. But I knew Grace was meeting up with Gordy and there was always a chance she'd bring a pal, so . . .' He shrugged and drank a mouthful of beer.

'It's a long way to come to visit family,' Seffy said.

'Not so far. Back home, a few hundred miles is nothing. And if you really wanna see someone . . .' his blue eyes – oh goodness, they really were awfully blue – looked right at her '. . . distance is meaningless.'

She wasn't going to waste any more time on the whys and wherefores. Nothing mattered except he was here, like a gift from a benevolent God. Maybe all those prayers hadn't been a waste of time.

'How—'

'How—'

They'd said it at the same time.

'You first,' Seffy said.

'How've you been? I mean, you look great.'

'Oh, I'm absolutely top hole! And you?'

Callum smiled. 'I'm guessing that means "good", right?'

He hadn't changed; there was still that teasing tone in his voice.

'I'm good, too,' he said. 'How're all the girls and your aunt?'

'All well. Long story but my aunt's got us involved in all sorts. Unarmed combat! Step out of line, Sergeant Fraser, and I'll have you in an armlock!'

He laughed. 'Gordy said Grace had written him 'bout that but I thought he was kidding.'

'Oh, no, it's deadly serious. We're even learning to shoot! And I'm not bad, I'll have you know.'

'Good for you. Give my aunt your best, won't you? She didn't think much of me but I liked her and her British bulldog spirit. Hers is the kinda attitude that's gonna win us the war.'

Seffy nodded. Oh, this was hopeless! Why were they talking about other people? She wanted to talk about *them* – about him and her – and gauge whether there was the remotest possibility of them ever being together. But they were dancing around each other, being so dreadfully cautious.

Only a few months ago, they'd been so comfortable with one another, so close. What were they now – mere friends?

Seffy's chest felt tight. She had to steer this conversation in the right direction. 'How's your fiancée?' she asked.

She knew the girl's name was Missy but she wouldn't use it.

'Missy? Oh, she's doing just fine. She's doin' her bit. She's joined the Red Cross Corps as a volunteer. She's driving, doing office work, stuff like that.'

Seffy felt a jolt of surprise. She'd imagined Missy to be a homely girl, who wore aprons and baked apple pies and was waiting for Callum to return so she could plan their wedding. Perhaps there was more to her than that.

'You must be proud.'

He nodded. 'And how's your fella doin'?'

'Oh, he's . . . as far as I know, he's all right.'

There. She'd bitten the bullet and as good as told him. Not that it was of any consequence, but why should she pretend she was still courting, when she'd ended her relationship with Teddy Fortesque months ago? Because of Callum, in fact. Because she'd thought they were going to be together.

He seemed taken aback. 'You're not—?'

'No.'

He lifted her left hand for inspection. 'I expected you to be engaged by now, at least. But you're—?'

'Footloose and fancy free!'

He was still holding her hand gently in his, stroking her fingers with his thumb and sending shivers up her arm. 'Okay . . .' he said, slowly.

Seffy swallowed. Her whole body tensed. Was it her imagination or did he seem to be coming to some kind of decision?

Callum cleared his throat. 'Seffy, listen, I just wanna say—'

'Excuse me?'

A girl was standing in the pub doorway, calling out to them. She was dressed in a smart cream suit and was carrying a small bouquet of flowers. A soldier appeared behind her.

'We're getting married,' she said.

'Congratulations.' Callum raised his glass.

'We need a couple of witnesses, fella, at the registry,' the soldier said. 'Would you mind? It won't take long.'

Seffy and Callum looked at one another. It would be churlish to refuse but it was a blow.

'Yes, of course,' Seffy said. 'We'll come, won't we, Callum?'

It was so frustrating. He'd been about to say something important; she was certain of it.

'Sure,' he said. He put down his half-finished pint and let go of her hand.

When the short ceremony was over, Seffy found herself in the ladies' with the bride.

They stood in front of the mirror, reapplying their lipstick, and the girl giggled as she practised saying her new name, over and over.

'Are you married yourselves?' she asked. 'You and the American chappie? Mebbe you can tell me the secret of wedded bliss.'

Hadn't the girl been listening when Callum had introduced them? "Staff Sergeant Fraser and Miss Mills" hardly sounded like a married couple. But she'd probably been too excited to pay proper attention.

Seffy glanced down at her left hand as though she couldn't quite remember. 'Oh, no. We're not married.'

'Well, I'm surprised, I must say. You look very comfortable together!' She patted Seffy's shoulder and looked at her reflection in the mirror. 'Chin up, dearie, it'll happen to you too, one day!'

Seffy tossed her lipstick into her handbag and snapped it shut. What was she doing in this awful place, full of newly-weds and romantic dreams? She could swing for Grace. Of all the places to bring her!

In the lobby, when pressed to go for a celebratory drink with the couple, Callum apologised and said they had a train to catch. Which wasn't a complete fib. Seffy was relieved. She didn't think she could bear any more probing questions.

Callum shook the groom's hand and kissed the bride on the cheek.

Seffy wished them a lifetime of happiness, kissed them both and got quite teary for a moment.

Then, they were gone.

Seffy glanced at her watch. Their time was up. 'Drat! I've got to head back to the boarding house. Our train leaves soon. Will you come?'

'Sure,' Callum said.

'Look who I've found!' Seffy shouted, as she approached Grace and Gordy's room.

They'd rushed through the streets of Gretna Green and there'd been no chance for a heart-to-heart. That moment, back in the pub, when she'd been sure Callum was going to say something meaningful, was gone forever.

When Grace emerged on her crutches and saw Callum, she almost toppled over. 'Gordy!' she called over her shoulder. 'You'll never guess who's here!'

As Gordy and Callum greeted one another, Grace mouthed, *Did you know he was here?*

'No! It was a total shock! I'll tell you everything later. I've still got to pack! We got held up. Someone asked us to witness their wedding.'

Grace nodded. 'Aye, well, you both look so smart and respectable. Someone was bound to.'

In that case, Seffy wished they'd been dressed in their work dungarees and covered in tree sap: they might've been left alone.

It was queer to think of her name and Callum's, side by side in that marriage register, perhaps forever.

She wasn't sure how she felt about that.

Chapter 47

The moment Joey burst into the hut, sobbing, and threw herself down on her bed, Tattie knew it must be all her fault. Hers and Angie's.

'What's happened?' Jean asked. 'Is it Ralph?'

'Has he thrown you over?' Morag asked, sounding hopeful.

'No, I've thrown him over!' Joey said, her voice muffled against the pillow. 'I'm done wi' men forever!'

'Where is he now?' Tattie asked, looking out of the window.

Joey turned a tear-stained face towards her. 'In the woods, where I left him. Lost, hopefully! Serves him right!'

Was the lassie mad? She'd abandoned William Wallace? He didn't know the woods like they did. Tattie had half a mind to run off and try to find him. He'd saved her, after all, that time at the railway station. She owed him.

Work was finished for the weekend. Some of the girls had been dozing on their beds or changing out of their overalls when Joey had burst in. Now they gathered around her. Angie gave her a handkerchief.

'Now, sit up and tell us everything,' Angie said. She sounded full of concern, as if she truly had no idea what might've happened.

Joey blew her nose. She fished a crumpled piece of paper out of her pocket and smacked it down on the bed. 'Someone evil sent him this!'

Jean snatched up the letter and the others clamoured for her to read it aloud.

Tattie swallowed hard. She felt sick. That must be the letter she'd delivered for Angie at Ballykinch House. She hadn't asked what it was all about. Nothin' to do with her. She'd been grateful that, for once, it'd been a simple task.

The envelope hadn't even been sealed. The major's jacket had been hanging over the back of a chair and before she'd slipped the letter into a pocket, she could've peeped inside.

But she hadn't, of course.

'Gosh! It's a poison pen letter!' Jean said. 'Like something out of Agatha Christie! The letters have been cut out of magazines and stuck on.'

Stuck on? That explained why Angie had wanted flour. Mix it with water and you had glue.

Everyone gasped as Jean read the letter aloud. Someone had accused Joey of having lived with a fella "as man and wife".

Angie's face was blank, even as she asked for the letter and examined it with a shake of her head.

'It's a horrid fib,' Joey said.

Tattie believed her. But why would Angie make up something like that?

She was filled with panic. Any second, someone would wonder why she was hanging back. She must look so guilty.

'Who would do this?' Enid asked. 'Who could be so nasty?'

Angie, that's who. And Tattie had helped her.

But Angie wasn't skulking at the back of the hut, like her, shame-faced. She was in the thick of it, doing a good job of looking shocked and consoling Joey.

She was enjoying herself.

'It doesn't even make sense,' Angie said. 'What's Forres?'

Joey rubbed her eyes. 'It's a place I worked when I was in the

280

Land Army. I had a sweetheart there – that part is true. But I didnae live with him! I don't understand. No one here even knew about Hamish.'

'Did you tell Ralph it wasn't true?' Jean asked.

'Aye! He said he was sorry in the end but he never should've believed it in the first place! Not if he really loved me! It's over wi' him! I hate him!'

'Aye and we all hate him too, don't we, girls?' Enid said.

'NO!' Tattie said.

Everyone turned and gawped at her. Angie rolled her eyes.

'No!' Tattie said again. 'You two are meant to be together.' She was blushing but she had to say it. 'It's – I dunno, it's written in the stars!'

Joey groaned. 'Aw, don't start that fortune-telling business again.'

'I don't mean it like that,' Tattie said. 'See, I've always known it. I knew from the moment I heard your surname. It's Wallace, right?'

Joey nodded, wearily.

'And your fella, the major, I . . . well, he's like my hero, William Wallace.' She felt daft, admitting that but at least no one laughed. 'It's the same name as yours. You and him: it's meant to be.'

'It was only a bit of fun,' Angie whispered, a few minutes later, when Tattie cornered her in the washroom.

The girls were off to the WHD meeting this afternoon and everyone was getting ready to leave.

Fun? The lass had a strange idea of fun.

'But they've rowed somethin' terrible!' Tattie said. 'They were in love and now they're not and all because of . . .'

She daren't say any more.

Angie looked at her reflection in the mirror and ran a hand through her hair. 'Look, it's common knowledge that you've got a crush on the major. Folk might think you're jealous of Joey and that little speech of yours was the result of a guilty conscience.'

Tattie's mouth fell open. What was she goin' on about?

'I'd be careful, if I were you, Tattie, else the finger of suspicion might start pointing at you.'

Tattie swallowed. She'd gone dizzy there for a second. She held on to one of the sinks for support.

'Anyhow, fallings-out are good for a relationship,' Angie continued. 'You might find out yourself, one day.' She pouted in the mirror and giggled. 'And making up is the very best part!'

Chapter 48

The others were waiting in the hallway when Seffy emerged from her room, carrying her suitcase. She'd never packed so fast, berating herself the whole time for not doing it earlier. She'd wasted precious minutes that could've been spent with Callum.

Gordy tapped his watch. 'Ladies, the train leaves in twenty minutes. We gotta make haste!'

He scooped Grace up into his arms, Seffy grabbed the crutches and Callum picked up the suitcases. He was coming with them, then. That was something.

As they hurtled through the town, dodging happy couples and wedding parties one last time, the sun came out.

Seffy couldn't have imagined ever being sorry to leave this place but so much had changed in two short hours. Now, Gretna Green would always be linked in her mind with happiness. And with Callum.

She wouldn't even mind if they missed the train. And judging from Grace's downcast face, she wouldn't either. But they'd have an awfully long wait for the next one. And Joey was picking them up at the other end. On second thoughts, they'd better not miss it.

Seffy glanced at Callum, marching along beside her, swinging the suitcases and wrapped up in his own thoughts. He felt her gaze and smiled at her.

Were those different stripes on his tunic sleeve? She suddenly remembered she hadn't congratulated him on his promotion. 'Oh, I meant to say—' she started and then immediately thought better of it. She had another idea.

'Yeah?'

She couldn't stop there or he'd think she was a prize idiot, so she said the first thing that came into her head. 'It's only . . . well, if I forget to say it at the station – I wanted to say, it's been marvellous seeing you.' There was a hard lump in her throat.

'Likewise,' he said. 'I only wish—'

'Jeez, we've got two minutes!' Gordy yelled, from behind. 'Come on, run!'

There were a few servicemen still boarding the train but otherwise, the platform was empty and the guard was walking backwards, with his whistle in his mouth.

The train was about to pull out.

'Hurry!' Gordy said.

'No, that's first class!' Seffy said, as Callum opened a carriage door. 'We're further down.'

He turned and she saw that familiar twitch of his lips.

'You'll always be first class to me,' he murmured.

'Cheesy,' she said.

'But true.'

They grinned at each other.

'Come on, you two!'

Gordy had carried Grace further down the platform and they were waiting next to an open door.

The next couple of minutes were a mad scramble, to get cases, crutches and girls on board.

In the train corridor, Gordy kissed Seffy's cheek, Callum kissed

Grace's, then he gave Seffy the same quick peck before Gordy grabbed his arm and pulled him away.

The moment the chaps jumped down onto the platform and slammed the carriage door, the guard blew the whistle.

The train started to move.

Seffy stepped back from the door, so that, as Gordy walked alongside the train, he and Grace could say their final goodbyes through the window. Callum was behind Gordy, peering in. Was he looking for her?

She froze. She had no idea what to do.

Who knew when – and if – she'd ever see him again? This hollowness was worse than the first time they'd parted.

Grace was suddenly speaking to her.

'Callum's there, Seffy! Go to him!' she said. 'And if you don't have a proper goodbye kiss, I swear I'll pull the communication cord!'

Seffy raced down the corridor to the next window and put her head out.

The train was picking up speed but Callum was already running towards her, pumping his arms and ignoring the guard's cries of, 'Stand clear of the train!'

Seffy squealed as he leaped up onto the running board and suddenly, there he was, right in front of her.

He gripped the window frame with one hand and with the other, he cupped the back of her neck, leaned in and kissed her, with warm, soft lips, until Seffy reluctantly pulled away.

'The platform!' she said, breathlessly. 'It'll disappear any second.'

Callum pressed something into her hand. 'Here, I wanted to give you this. I have nothin' to give you except that. And this—'

He didn't take his eyes off her as he thumped his chest, hard, above his heart.

Then he jumped backwards off the train and Seffy gasped as he stumbled and almost fell. He righted himself in seconds, grinned and they waved and waved until the train rounded a bend and he'd gone.

For the time being, at least, the girls had a compartment to themselves, which was a pleasant surprise.

Once Grace had stopped sobbing, she looked across at Seffy. 'That's a nice smile. You might want to wipe the soot off your cheek though. Do you feel all right?'

Seffy nodded. She didn't trust herself to speak; she was so choked up.

'Aw, that must've been some kiss,' Grace said. 'It's taken away the power of speech!'

They laughed.

It had been some kiss – that was true. All the more marvellous for being so unexpected. Seffy opened her hand. 'Look. He gave me this.'

It was a circular brass badge with a crown at the top and the words 'Canadian Forestry Corps' embossed around the side.

'That's his cap badge,' Grace said.

'Goodness, won't he need it?'

'Perhaps he's expecting to get it back one day.'

It was the loveliest gift Seffy had ever received. It was all he'd had to give her. That and his heart.

'I thought I might write to him,' Seffy said. 'And congratulate him on his promotion.' She wrinkled her nose. 'But maybe I shouldn't? Maybe it's best to leave things be?'

Grace sat back in her seat and sighed. 'I shouldn't say this, what with Callum being engaged to someone else an' all . . .'

'But?'

'I was watching the two of you as we did that route march to the railway station and you . . . you look right together.'

Please don't say nice things, Seffy thought. If she started crying now, she'd never stop.

She painted on a smile. 'It feels right, too. You know, I'm definitely the woman for him; he just hasn't realised it yet!' She

286

laughed, a little too loudly and then they were both fumbling for their handkerchiefs.

'I've had the best time of my life,' Grace said, sniffing.

Seffy blew her nose. 'Me too!'

Those first miserable days in Gretna were a distant memory now.

'I'm so happy,' Grace said, tears running down her face. 'I'm very lucky – I know that.'

Seffy wondered if her face was as red and blotchy as Grace's. She fished in her handbag for powder.

There was flash of khaki in the corridor and the compartment door slid open with a loud clunk.

Troops. At any other time it might've been a lark to share the journey with some soldiers but not now.

The private looked at them and his bright smile disappeared. He turned to the men behind him, who were jostling each other for a better look at the girls.

'Sorry, lads, but there's a couple o' women in here greetin' summat awful. I cannae abide it.'

He looked at the girls. 'Sorry for your loss, ladies, but ... no—'

He pulled the door shut and the troops filed past, looking for somewhere else to sit.

The girls waited until the men had gone and then burst out laughing.

'There are some benefits to being a blubbering wreck!' Seffy said. 'With a bit of luck, at this rate, we'll be left alone for the whole journey!'

Chapter 49

Joey was fifteen minutes late arriving at the station and the girls were waiting on a bench outside.

Seffy was nudging Grace, teasing her about something and they were laughing. Joey was glad – for Grace's sake – that they were pals again but she'd soon be wiping the smile off the wee Sassenach's face.

She'd been thinking about that letter the whole way here. Once she'd put her mind to it, working out the guilty party was easy. It was like a stab to the heart – almost as bad as breaking up with Ralph – but the only person who could've written it was Seffy.

Jean, who fancied herself as a detective, had said "the perpetrator must've had means, motive and opportunity". Seffy had all those, plus, she had knowledge. Joey hadn't told anyone else about Hamish.

As she stepped down from the cab, Seffy called out, 'Oh, hullo, stranger. We thought you'd forgotten us!'

But when the girls saw her face, their laughter died.

Seffy stood up, letting her handbag fall. 'Whatever's happened?'

'Is everything all right?' Grace asked.

Joey picked up their cases and tossed them into the truck. 'Oh aye. Everything's just fine and dandy!'

'Well, it clearly isn't,' Seffy said, all uppity.

Joey was tempted to thrust the letter at her and ask Seffy to explain herself but this wasn't the right time or place. She needed to be calm, not seething with rage.

They helped Grace up into the cab and as they set off, there was silence in the truck.

Eventually, Joey said. 'So, Grace, how was it? Did you have a good time?'

'Aw, it was wonderful!'

'Was Gordy well?'

'Aye. Still the same lovely man I married!' Grace glanced at Seffy, sitting beside her. 'Oh and you'll never guess who—'

Seffy had nudged her and Joey saw a look pass between them.

'What?' she said.

'Someone asked me to witness their wedding,' Seffy said, quickly. 'That's all.'

Joey nodded.

'Anyhow . . .' Grace said. 'Any news? Has Flora stopped greetin' about breaking ma toe, yet?'

'Oh aye. You know Flora. Nothing troubles the lass for long.'

They were making small talk. Which was awkward. And Seffy must've noticed that Joey wasn't talking to her.

'How's Ralph?' Seffy asked, suddenly.

There! She was giving herself away. Why would she ask that, unless she knew there was likely to be trouble with him?

'Aw, well it's funny you should ask,' Joey said, slowly. She scowled. 'In actual fact, we've broken up.'

But you'd probably guessed that, she thought. *It's what you wanted.*

Grace gasped and put her hand to her mouth.

'Why? When?' Seffy asked. The girl was a good actress – Joey'd give her that.

She shrugged. 'We had a row. It's all over wi' him.'

Seffy laughed. She actually *laughed*. 'Ah, a lover's tiff!'

'No! It's more than that. I hate him!'

'Well, you know what they say: love and hate are closely aligned. Strong emotions!' Seffy leaned across Grace and patted Joey's leg, making her flinch. 'You'll be back together in no time. I'd put money on it. You're made for each other!'

Seffy was still reeling when they arrived at Ballykinch House.

Joey and Ralph had broken up! What on earth could have caused that? They'd seemed rock solid when she'd left for Gretna Green. No wonder Joey was cross and sarky, which was so unlike her. And she looked dreadful: her face, normally so pretty, was pale and puffy.

Trying to jolly her along probably hadn't been the best approach but when Joey had told them the news, Seffy had been almost lost for words. Thank goodness she'd stopped Grace from mentioning Callum. It definitely hadn't been the right time for that.

And now they had this blasted WHD meeting to get through. After that long train journey, Seffy wanted nothing other than a cup of tea and a nap but Aunt Dilys had been adamant that everyone should attend. It was the last meeting before their expedition next weekend – the culmination of seven weeks of training – and the briefing was today.

As they reached the front door at Ballykinch House, it was flung open and Grace was swallowed up by Enid, Morag and Flora, keen to hear about her trip.

'We want to know everything!' Enid cried.

'Not quite everything,' Morag said.

Seffy started to follow them in but Joey caught her arm.

'I need a word,' she said.

Seffy nodded. Now she'd find out what had really happened with Ralph. Joey probably hadn't wanted to say too much in front of Grace. She was Joey's best friend, after all.

They stood beside the truck on the drive and wordlessly, Joey passed Seffy a piece of paper. It was a message. A childish, mean trick.

290

'Who the hell wrote this?' Seffy asked.

'Someone put it in Ralph's pocket.'

'My God! Is this why you and he quarrelled?'

Joey was silent. When Seffy looked up from the letter, she was startled by the look on Joey's face.

'You . . . you don't think I had anything to do with this, do you?'

Joey crossed her arms. Her mouth twisted. 'Aye, I do!'

Seffy's stomach plunged. 'But why would I?'

'Because you cannae bear to see anyone else happy! You're . . . you're not a nice person. The way you were with Grace . . .'

'But Grace and I are friends now!'

'You gave Grace the cold shoulder because she'd found someone and you hadn't and you couldn't stand it!'

Joey was shouting. Seffy glanced towards the house. The girls – or Aunt Dilys – might hear them and come out to ask what was going on. Seffy couldn't bear for the whole WHD to know about this.

'It's true,' Seffy said, in a small voice. 'Not the letter, but everything else you've just said. I'm a horrible person, I know. I wasn't nice to Grace and I wish I could turn the clock back but as for this—' She waved the letter at Joey. 'It's got nothing to do with me!'

She was exhausted. Her emotions had been up and down – from glum to ecstatic and back again – all day. Now her throat was hurting, as she tried not to cry.

The house door opened and Tattie put her head out.

'Captain says can you come in now, please? Everyone else is here and she's waiting to start.'

'One minute,' Joey said, and Tattie disappeared back inside.

Seffy took a deep breath. 'Anyhow, I couldn't have done this. See how the letters are all higgledy-piggledy across the page? You know me, I'd have lined them up perfectly.'

Joey didn't smile. 'Aye, I thought o' that. But mebbe you did that to throw me off the scent? Because you're the only one who knew about me and Hamish! Have you told anyone else?'

'No! I promised not to! But I swear, on my life and everything I hold dear, I did not do this!'

What else could she say, to make Joey believe her?

'Mebbe you want him for yourself,' Joey muttered. 'And you wanted to break us up.'

'What?'

'Ralph! You've always liked him. You said once, he'd be a distraction!'

Seffy frowned. 'Did I? Well, if I did, I didn't mean it. Listen, I'm going to tell you something now. Callum, my Canadian sergeant, was in Gretna Green. I saw him. Today!'

Joey frowned. 'Your fella? The one who wasn't free?'

'Yes. And he's still not free and, of course, he's not mine but . . . oh, I adore him! And, quite frankly, no other chap stands a chance. I have no interest in Ralph Stirling. Never will! Although I'm sure he is – was – a poppet.'

There! Joey had to believe her now.

'He was there? In Gretna Green?'

'Yes! What are the chances?'

Joey narrowed her eyes. 'I don't believe you.'

'He really was! Ask Grace!'

Joey's voice was colder than ever. 'I mean, I don't believe he was there by chance. It must've been planned. We all thought good old Seffy was givin' up her leave to help Grace but—' she shook her head and gave a hollow laugh '—you were doing it for yourself all along!'

What? This was a nightmare. She'd thought telling Joey about Callum would at least prove she had no interest in Ralph but now Joey thought she'd planned to meet Callum there.

She wasn't going to listen to any more of this nonsense. She turned towards the lorry, yanked open the cab door and climbed into the driver's seat. As she started the engine, she noticed Tattie, standing at the front door. How long had she been there?

Seffy called out of the window. 'Do you know anything about this letter business, Tattie?'

This despicable act had Angie's name written all over. And if Angie was responsible, Tattie had almost certainly been involved.

Tattie blanched. But that didn't mean anything. The girl looked terrified most of the time.

'No,' she said. 'Are yous coming in now or what?'

Joey jumped out of the way as the truck jolted into motion. There wasn't time to turn it around: Seffy glanced in the rear-view mirror and started to reverse up the drive.

'Where are you going?' Joey yelled.

As if you care, Seffy thought.

'Where's Persephone?' Captain Dilys asked, as Tattie returned to the drawing room with only Joey in tow.

Tattie bit her lip. 'She's driven off, in the truck.'

Captain sighed. 'Oh, for heaven's sake!'

'How will Grace get back to camp?' Enid asked. 'Someone'll have to gi' her a piggyback!'

Everyone laughed.

'Sounds like she's gone AWOL,' Angie said, rolling her eyes.

'Right, we'll start without her,' Captain said. 'If this were a real army she'd be up for a disciplinary.' She tapped her pen on the desk to call for order.

'Listen up! Next Saturday's training exercise!'

Tattie slid into the seat next to Angie. 'Seffy and Joey were rowing summat terrible,' she whispered.

Angie raised her eyebrows. 'Shame.'

'Aye, it IS!' Tattie shuffled nearer and put her mouth to Angie's ear. 'Joey thinks Seffy wrote the letter.'

Angie shushed her and nodded at Captain Dilys, who was in full flow.

'You'll be dropped off in the woods and left to navigate your way back to the village, in pairs.'

'From six miles away,' Lady Lockhart said.

There were a few cries of dismay.

'The men do more like twenty miles,' Captain said. 'It's a staggered start. You'll be dispatched in five-minute intervals and equipped with a water bottle, knapsack, rifle, map and compass. And you'll be blindfolded on the journey out!'

This was greeted with exclamations and excited chatter.

'The aim of this drill is to replicate a real mission in a field of battle!' Captain said, raising her voice over the din. 'But as we don't have the luxury of one gun each, it'll be one between two.'

'And will the rifles be loaded?' Angie asked.

'Goodness, no! We wouldn't want you to start taking pot shots at one another!' Lady Lockhart said. She laughed her tinkly little laugh and stopped abruptly, when Dilys glared at her.

'No,' Dilys confirmed. 'I do have to draw the line at live ammo. The pair that makes it to the finishing post in the shortest time, will be declared the winners!'

'And where is the finishing post?' Morag asked.

'Oh, didn't I say? It's the village hall, where Marigold holds the nursery, so everyone will be reunited and we'll have a bit of a do, to finally launch the WHD!'

The girls practically boiled over with excitement at the news but Tattie could hardly take it in. As the voices and laughter got louder, she glanced across at Joey, sitting with her head bowed and her hands clasped in her lap, and she felt a twist of guilt.

It was bad enough that she and the major weren't together any more but now Joey had fallen out with Seffy, too.

If Tattie had any backbone, she'd stand up and tell everyone that Angie had written the poison pen letter, that she, Tattie, had helped her and that all this upset was their fault.

But Angie would, no doubt, turn the tables. She'd put the blame on Tattie and everyone liked Angie, so they'd believe her. Then she'd carry out her threat to fib about Tattie having sold her travel warrant and Miss McEwen would have her guts for garters.

She knew she should tell everyone the truth but no one would believe her. She wasn't brave enough to even try. She couldn't do it.

Chapter 50

'Halt, who goes there?'

Golly, Seffy thought they only said that kind of thing in films. Mind you, the chap was pointing something that looked suspiciously like a machine gun, so perhaps she'd better not be flippant.

She'd pulled up outside the gates of Blantyre Lodge. The place had taken some finding – it was hidden deep within the rolling hills of the laird's estate – but hurrah, at last she'd done it.

She called down through the cab window, in her most authoritative voice. 'It's Lady Persephone Baxter-Mills!'

As the soldier stepped closer and looked up at her, his eyes opened a little wider.

'You're blocking the entrance, miss.'

'Correct. And I shall continue to do so until I've spoken to Major Stirling. This is a matter of national security!'

She turned off the engine, leaned back and put her feet up on the steering wheel, for all the world as though she were about to have a snooze.

The soldier muttered something and disappeared into the guardhouse, hopefully to make the necessary telephone call.

If her heart hadn't still been galloping, Seffy wouldn't actually have minded a nap. She was quite exhausted.

To think, only this morning, she'd been sitting quietly in that café, quite unaware of the emotional wringer that was to come: the shock and delight of seeing Callum, quickly followed by heartbreak at having to leave him, then cheering up a little on the train before – wham! Joey had accused her of the most terrible betrayal. It was hard to believe it had all happened in just one day.

Seffy opened her handbag, to check that Callum's cap badge was still there. Her heart lifted to see it. She must keep it safe. She certainly wouldn't be putting it in the suitcase under her bed, from which her money seemed to have disappeared. That's something else she should've told Joey: she wasn't the only one to whom bad things were happening.

She sat up and looked around. Over the high wall, topped with barbed wire, was the imposing Blantyre Lodge, where the commandos lived and trained. In addition to the large square house, there were rows of bell tents and Nissen huts with corrugated iron roofs and a collection of ropes and logs which was, presumably, an assault course.

Seffy jumped as the passenger door opened and Ralph Stirling hauled himself into the cab and sat beside her.

'Thought I recognised this beast,' he said. 'You need to move it down the lane. You're making my men jittery. And please, Seffy—' he shook his head '—don't mention the machine guns to your aunt.'

'And then we can talk?'

'Indeed.'

Five minutes later, they were ready.

'I understand you and Joey have . . . erm, had a spot of bother?' Seffy said, not looking at him.

Ralph shifted in his seat. 'I hardly think that's any of your—'

'It IS my business! She's my friend, she's distraught and she thinks I'm responsible for that ridiculous letter!'

He turned his dark eyes on her. 'And are you?'

Seffy sighed. 'Don't be silly. I have an idea who might've done it, though. But no proof.'

There'd been no point in telling Joey she suspected Angie, because Joey would only have pointed out that Seffy had had a grudge against her ever since she'd arrived. Which was true, but with good reason. Why was she the only one who hadn't been taken in by Angie Buchanan?

'Do you have any suggestions?' Seffy asked Ralph. 'Assuming we're ruling me out?'

He narrowed his eyes. 'I have remembered something. That wee scrap of a girl. What's her name?'

'Tattie.'

'Yes. She was hanging around me that day.'

Seffy opened her mouth to say it was hardly surprising – Tattie clearly had a pash on him – but thought better of it.

'Got it!' he said, thumping his thigh. 'I knew I'd seen her before. The railway station! I met her there, when I arrived. The lassie, as she turned out to be.'

Seffy frowned. She had no idea what he was talking about.

'Let's talk about you and Joey,' she said, firmly. She sounded such a bossyboots but there was no point in pussyfooting around.

'I've scuppered it completely,' Ralph said. He did, at least, sound regretful. 'I've apologised until I'm blue in the face. Once I found my way out of the forest, I went up to the camp to plead with Josephine but the place was deserted. I know she won't change her mind. She's headstrong.' He shrugged. 'Ironically, that's one of the things l like about her.'

'Like or love?'

He looked startled.

'Because, if I'm going to help you, I need to be sure,' Seffy said. 'Sure of your intentions, sure that Joey's not merely a challenge and absolutely positive—' she pointed at him '—that the letter hasn't made you doubt her, in the same way you doubted that nurse!'

Ouch, mentioning the nurse was a low blow. Perhaps she'd gone too far?

But Ralph didn't seem to have taken offence. He was rubbing his chin. 'I'm not good at this kind of thing. Feelings and words. I'm a soldier—'

'Try! Tell me what you love about Joey. One word at a time.'

He sighed and shook his head. Eventually, he said, 'Dimples.'

'Good!'

'And hair like a mermaid's.'

His face softened as he thought about her. 'She's funny. And, feisty, of course. And she likes . . . some girls are standoffish but Joey likes . . . she likes her hand held; she likes to cuddle and kiss.'

Seffy coughed. 'She's tactile.'

'Yes.'

'And I love how she's small. She's a neat little package and when I put my arm around her, she tucks in, underneath. She just . . .' He shrugged, sadly. 'She just, fits.'

Seffy nodded. 'Right, you need to woo her, all over again.'

'And how on earth am I meant to do that?'

'I have an idea,' Seffy said, slowly. In truth, it was only an inkling.

'Tell me!'

'I can't promise it'll work. But it's definitely worth a try.'

Chapter 51

A week later, Seffy was in the truck again, rattling around in the back with other members of the WHD.

They were being driven at breakneck speed by Captain Dilys at the start of their training exercise. They were blindfolded, which made every bounce and swerve even worse for being unexpected, and there was much un-military-like laughter and shrieking.

Everyone screamed as the lorry suddenly lurched off the road, bumped down a track and finally came to a juddering halt.

The girls ripped off their blindfolds and jumped out, blinking in the sunlight. They were in a completely unfamiliar part of the forest.

'I haven't a clue where I am!' Flora said. Which, as Seffy remarked, was rather the point.

It was another stiflingly hot day and Lady Lockhart urged everyone to drink plenty of water and to fill up their bottles from the bucket. Then, there was much excitement as Dilys finally revealed the pairings.

'Tattie and Enid!' she announced. 'Belinda and Flora!'

Joey wasn't here. She and Morag were on fire-watching duty and there was no ducking out of that, so at least there was no risk of Seffy being partnered with her. Things were still frosty between them. Apart from at work – when talking was unavoidable – Joey hadn't spoken to Seffy all week.

'Ailsa and Janet!'

And Grace's toe still hadn't healed, so she wasn't here either, although she'd be at the village hall later, for the celebratory tea.

The names of three more pairs were read out.

Seffy's stomach plunged. That just left . . .

'Seffy and Angie!'

Angie, of all people! Seffy was being punished, for certain, for skipping last week's briefing. After her dash to see Ralph, she'd driven straight back to Ballykinch but she'd missed the whole shebang. At least she'd been able to give Grace a lift back to camp. She'd offered a ride to the other girls too and most had been glad of it, but Joey had refused and had walked up the hill alone.

Now, Seffy looked daggers at her aunt.

'It'll do you good,' Dilys murmured. 'In wartime, we have to get along with those who mightn't be our natural allies.'

Angie was stony-faced and no doubt as unhappy as Seffy. She stepped forward to collect their map, compass and rifle and promptly disappeared into the woods, ostensibly to answer a call of nature but perhaps merely to sulk.

'You make a strong team,' Dilys said. 'You and Angie might even lift the trophy!'

Seffy huffed. She didn't give a fig about that. Imagine the smirk on Angie's face if they won! If necessary, Seffy would sabotage their efforts, to ensure they jolly well didn't.

'Everything happens for a reason,' Lady Lockhart said, nodding encouragingly.

Seffy shrugged. She'd been giving Angie the cold shoulder all week, convinced she was behind the letter that had caused so much heartache. If she could actually bring herself to talk to the girl, perhaps she might gather some evidence. She couldn't accuse her of anything without that. They were going to be together for the whole afternoon. She might as well make some use of it.

Tattie had been dreading today. And now she'd ended up with daft Enid for a partner. Neither of them could read a map or compass; they might as well give up now.

Unless . . . ? She pulled Enid behind a bush, out of earshot of the others and explained her idea. Enid was in favour. It'd certainly save trying to work out the map for themselves.

According to Jean, the map wasn't much cop, in any case. She'd turned hers around several times, frowned and said, 'It's rather rudimentary.'

To which Captain had replied, 'You're lucky to have maps at all! Imagine if one got into enemy hands? If it were up to me, you'd be relying solely on compasses but Lavinia took pity on you. Now, my final instruction: remember you're a team. Look after each other!'

A few others set off before Tattie and Enid, but finally it was their turn. They made a good show of racing into the woods but once out of sight, they ducked behind some thick brambles and waited for the last pair: Seffy and Angie.

When Angie marched past, the rifle was slung across her chest and she was studying the compass. Seffy was trailing behind, looking crabbit.

'Come on,' Tattie whispered to Enid. 'All we have to do is follow them at a safe distance. And keep quiet!'

But they'd only gone a few hundred yards, when Tattie spotted something on the forest floor.

She dropped to the ground, stifling a cry and cradled the little body in her hands. It hardly weighed anything.

'What is it?' Enid asked, looking over her shoulder.

It was a robin. Its beady black eye stared lifelessly up at Tattie, as its soft feathers were lifted by the breeze.

'Aw, the poor wee thing,' Enid said. 'What happened to it?'

Tattie looked around, as though the answer might lie here, in the woods. She shook her head.

Jock had told her robins sometimes fight to the death and although there wasn't a mark on this one, perhaps that's what had happened. Somewhere, another robin was flying around, victorious.

'Come on, we'd best go,' Enid said. 'Or we'll lose the others.'

Tattie placed the bird down carefully and covered it with a large green fern. '*Rudzik*,' she whispered.

She stood up, wiped a tear from her eye and ran to catch up with Enid.

Angie had commandeered the rifle, compass and map, so Seffy didn't have much choice but to follow her. At first, she didn't mind: it would all be Angie's fault if they got hopelessly lost.

But after a couple of hours trudging in her wake, Seffy was hot and bothered. She gritted her teeth as Angie consulted the map and compass yet again. Did she actually know what she was doing?

Seffy had no desire to win the race but neither did she want to traipse around unnecessarily in this dratted heat. If only she'd been paired with clever clogs Jean, they'd be halfway to the rendez-vous by now.

She was fighting the urge to take over. Didn't that prove she was naturally a leader, rather than a follower? Miss McEwen would have forty fits if she knew the lumberjills were involved in something as frivolous as the WHD but Seffy wished the supervisor could see her now, desperate to take charge.

Finally, she couldn't stand it any longer. 'Let me see that map,' she said.

Angie stopped with obvious reluctance and handed it over.

'This isn't right,' Seffy said, frowning. 'The stream's over there but according to this, we shouldn't be anywhere near it.'

Angie said nothing but simply snatched back the map and marched on, deeper into the woods.

'Oh, for pity's sake!' Seffy said. 'Didn't you hear? We're going the wrong way!'

Perhaps Angie was trying to lose her? Was that her plan – to make an utter fool of her? So that when Seffy finally reached the village hall, yonks after everyone else, Angie could roll her eyes and say, 'Here she comes at last, Dolly Daydream! I can't imagine where she got to!'

And everyone would laugh.

No chance! Seffy broke into a run. She'd soon catch her up. Whatever happened, she was going to stick to Angie Buchanan like a barnacle.

Chapter 52

Joey was sitting twenty feet high in the branches of a Douglas fir. The ladder she'd used to climb up was leaning against the truck and she had a pair of binoculars slung around her neck.

She and Morag were on fire-watching duty, keeping their eyes peeled for signs of smoke. The tree in which Morag was stationed was a hundred yards away.

Joey leaned against the trunk, hugging her knees and enjoying the breeze. It was cool up here, in the shade of the evergreen, the air full of the scent of pine. There were worse ways of spending the afternoon.

The WHD exercise would've been fun and she'd probably feel a pang, later, when the others enthused about their great adventure. But at least, by not going, she didn't have to consider how to keep out of Seffy's way. They might've been put in a team together. That was the kind o' sneaky thing Captain Dilys would do. Joey shuddered at the thought.

It'd been a miserable week. There'd been no sign of Ralph. Which was a good thing, of course. She'd only have sent him packing if he'd dared to turn up. And there'd been no possibility of making up with Seffy. How could she, when the girl was still proclaiming her innocence?

The others had been surprised when Joey had told them her suspicions. Grace and Tattie had spoken up for Seffy. They'd said she'd never do such a thing.

Tiny doubts were creeping in. Joey knew that the Seffy of old – the Seffy she thought she knew – would rather die than betray a friend, but no one else had known about Hamish. It had to be her.

Smoke! Seffy raised her head and inhaled. There! She'd caught another whiff of it. Who was stupid enough to light a fire in this heatwave? Everyone knew even a dropped match could start a blaze.

'Say, can you smell—?' She started but she was talking to herself. Angie had taken off again.

Seffy recognised this part of the woods. There was the bothy: the little wooden shack that held such happy memories. But there wasn't time to think about Callum now. She forced herself to concentrate. If they were near the bothy, they weren't far from the POW camp.

They must have walked in a huge semi-circle!

Her errant team mate was fifty yards ahead now, the rifle bouncing against her back.

'Hey, come back! It's this way!' Seffy yelled.

Then the acrid smell of smoke filled her nostrils, her stomach lurched and, with a sigh, she set off again after Angie.

Seffy saw the pall of black smoke first and then, as she got closer to the camp, she heard the ominous crackle of flames.

The perimeter fence was on fire!

She stopped a few yards away. The fire had already burned through several wooden poles, leaving the barbed wire charred and sagging.

Jakub and another guard were desperately pounding the flames with beaters but as the fire raced along, gobbling up the poles, they were clearly fighting a losing battle.

The fence was all but destroyed, which meant the camp was no longer secure! No wonder the prisoners had been corralled at the far end of the exercise yard. It was hard to see through the billowing smoke but it looked as though they were being ushered inside by the Polish guard, Tomasz. He was moving them away from the fire and, presumably, from any ideas of escape.

Seffy coughed, as the fumes and burning embers swirled around her.

When she was finally able to, she called out to the guards, 'Can I help?'

Jakub stopped beating. His blackened face was streaked with lines of sweat.

'No, miss! Go! Is not safe here!'

Seffy pursed her lips. There must be something she could do. The stream was nearby. If they had buckets, perhaps they could form a chain and douse the flames? Some of the more trustworthy prisoners could be drafted in, plus the guards and her and Angie. Goodness, Angie! She'd forgotten all about her. Where on earth was the wretched girl? So much for looking after one another. Seffy could be scorched half to death, for all Angie cared.

The guards were standing back from what remained of the fence, shaking their heads, defeated.

'We must go,' Jakub told Seffy. 'There is another fire. Look, there! We will try to put it out.'

He was right: in the distance, a plume of grey smoke hung over the treetops.

Seffy felt a sudden stab of fear. So many of her pals were out there, in the woods. She could only hope they weren't in danger.

'What about the prisoners?' she asked. Surely it wasn't safe to leave them here, as the fire encroached. Shouldn't they be evacuated?

'More soldiers and fire brigade are coming,' Jakub said. 'Prisoners are safe for now.' He nodded at the asphalt yard. 'That is fire break.'

Seffy followed his gaze. Was that right? Would the fire not cross the yard?

When she looked back, the guards had turned and were hastening away towards the forest, holding their beaters aloft.

A glowing ember landed next to Seffy's foot and immediately the tinder-dry undergrowth caught alight. She stamped the flame out, grateful for her sturdy boots. As she looked up again, she glimpsed Angie through the smoke.

What was she doing? Seffy watched, open-mouthed, as Angie stepped over the blackened wire into the camp and sprinted towards the prisoners who were still filing out of the yard.

Seffy was so shocked, she couldn't move or call out to her. She could only stare and shake her head in disbelief. Whatever Angie was up to, it wasn't good.

'Ma God, what's goin' on?' a voice called out from behind.

It was Enid, closely followed by Tattie. They were both breathless and wide-eyed. They must've got lost too, although Seffy now strongly suspected that Angie had deliberately misread the map. She'd intended to come to the camp all along.

One of the burning poles suddenly toppled over, falling with a thud onto the yard and Enid screamed.

'We cannae stay here!' Tattie said. 'The whole place is goin' up!'

'Angie's inside the camp!' Seffy said. 'Look!'

One of the Italians had broken away from the group. He greeted Angie with open arms and then, an embrace. As though he'd been expecting her.

'That's Luigi!' Enid said.

'Mebbe she wants to be sure he's all right,' Tattie said.

Enid tutted. 'I'd like to be sure ma Gio's all right but I wouldnae waltz into a POW camp like that!'

'Aye,' Tattie muttered. 'You'd have to be mad.'

Seffy's chest tightened. Had Angie abandoned the exercise merely to have a chat with her beau or was there more to it? After all, what were the chances of her and Angie arriving here just as the fire at the fence was causing such pandemonium?

It was too much of a coincidence. The prisoners must've been

308

out in the yard just before the fire started. Seffy had seen for herself how easily the parched grass could be set alight. Maybe one of the Italians had started the fire and – yes, that was it – Angie had been in on the plan! No wonder she'd been in such a hurry to get here.

Seffy had been right, all along. She'd known Angie was a bad apple, almost from the moment she'd met her. Pity she'd never been able to convince the others.

'We have to get her out!' Enid said. 'It's no' safe. We know our fellas wouldn't harm her but there are dozens of others in there. Wait! What's she doing now?'

Angie was lifting the rifle strap over her head. She was handing the gun to Luigi!

Seffy felt sick to the stomach.

'Thank God the rifles aren't loaded, eh?' Enid said.

There was a shocked silence. Seffy's throat had gone dry. Maybe, somehow, Angie's gun *was* loaded? Could she have stolen some ammo from Ballykinch House? When she'd disappeared into the trees with the rifle, before they set off, had she secretly been loading the gun? Otherwise, what use would it be to Luigi?

A gust of thick smoke blew into the girls' faces, forcing them to close their eyes. By the time they opened them again, there was no one left in the yard.

'I'm going in there!' Seffy said. She ran forward, stepped over the blackened wire and stopped again as she had another thought. 'Enid, throw me your rifle!'

Enid frowned. 'It's no' much use without bullets.'

But she threw it, nonetheless and Seffy caught it in one hand.

'We'll come wi' you!' Tattie said.

Seffy felt rotten for thinking it, but she'd rather have any of the girls than this pair: silly Enid and timid Tattie, who'd always been so loyal to Angie.

If she could pick a team, she'd have Grace – who'd once knocked a villain out cold – and Joey. The old Joey, before their falling-out; the Joey who was still her chum.

But she nodded nonetheless and accepted Tattie's offer, glad she didn't have to do this alone. For the last few minutes, a creeping terror had been rising up from her feet, threatening to envelop her, but now she was actually doing something, she felt better.

The girls raced towards the prison buildings. On every side, the perimeter fence was alight or smoking and Seffy prayed Jakub was right and that the fire wouldn't cross the yard.

They'd almost reached the gate when the crack of gunfire rang out. They stopped and stared at each other, open-mouthed.

The sound had come from the large wooden hut, just ahead of them.

'Maybe Angie's in trouble!' Tattie said.

No, Seffy thought, as they started running again. Angie *is* the trouble.

Chapter 53

Joey snapped out of her daydream and shifted on the branch, pulling her legs in.

Someone was down there, prowling about on the forest floor.

She raised the binoculars and peered through the tree canopy.

She could hear the hollow thud of horse's hooves and what sounded suspiciously like a man sneezing.

She knew that sneeze. It couldn't be . . . could it? Despite herself, her heart lifted.

The horse and rider walked into the clearing below and stopped. Joey saw a flash of grey and a horse's dappled hindquarters. The branch creaked as she leaned forward for a better look and the man gazed straight up at her.

Ralph.

Joey gave an involuntary, 'Oh!' and her heart squeezed before she remembered that she hated him.

He was red-faced and wheezing. What in heaven's name was he doing here? And riding Monty, all tacked up in a saddle and bridle? Had he come to torment her again? Or had he brought Monty to say goodbye?

Was Ralph Stirling a good 'un or a bad 'un? Her head was in a complete burl. She couldnae work the fella out.

'There you are, Josephine,' he said, sounding relieved. 'It would've been easier to find you if you had a proper lookout tower, you know.'

She wanted to tell him to get lost; she wanted to run away. But she was stuck up a tree; she couldn't go anywhere.

'A tree makes a pretty good lookout tower, if you ask me,' she said, coldly.

'Yes, but they're identical. Like rows of soldiers on parade. It's not an easy task, to find the right one.'

So he'd been looking for her then. But why? What had he come to say?

Monty threw up his head, which set off a volley of sneezes from Ralph.

'Has that horse had any water?' Joey asked. 'It's too hot out here for him.'

They must've come from the farm, which was a few miles away. She wasn't worried about Ralph – he could look after himself – but Monty was no youngster: he'd be worn out by now; he might even get heatstroke.

'Yes, he had a drink at Ballykinch, from the duckpond. I went there first. I thought you'd have your defence training. But no joy. Then I went to the camp and asked about you there.'

He'd had quite the run-around. Well, good, she was glad.

But she was also glad he hadn't given up; that he'd kept on searching.

'They said I'd find you here,' he said. He took his feet out of the stirrups and swung his right leg over Monty's neck, before jumping off. Joey frowned: that wasn't the right way to dismount.

'He's got a saggy old back, this fella,' Ralph said. 'It's like riding a hammock.'

Was that all he'd come to tell her? That dear, sweet Monty was an old nag?

He sighed and his tone changed. 'Josephine, please may I speak to you?'

'Aye, go ahead.'

He was rubbing his neck. He was getting a crick in it from looking up all the while. 'Can't you come down?'

Joey made a show of looking at her watch. 'Not for another hour. I'm on duty. Fire-watching, looking for smoke.'

She leaned back against the tree trunk and demonstrated with her binoculars, looking out over the trees. There was Morag in her tree, at a similar height to her. She was gazing out into the distance and clearly hadn't noticed Ralph and Monty's arrival.

Joey lowered the binoculars, let them fall in their strap onto her chest and peered down at him again.

'After all, you said yourself, there's no smoke without fire.' Aw, she hadn't been able to resist that one. 'So, whatever it is you've come to say, you'll have to say it from there.'

Ralph nodded. 'Very well. Firstly, I know who sent that letter.'

'Seffy!' Joey said, as he said: 'Not Seffy!'

Joey's stomach plunged. Had she been blaming the wrong girl, all along?

'It was the little thin one,' Ralph said. 'Tattie? When I thought back to that day at Ballykinch, I remembered seeing her, brushing up against my jacket on the chair. I couldn't swear to it, but I reckon she did it.'

Joey wrinkled her nose. 'Tattie? I don't believe it.'

He shrugged. 'I'm pretty good at remembering that kind of thing. All part of the training.'

But Joey wasn't convinced. Tattie knew nothing about her past and the lass had no motive. She'd have to think about that later.

'And what's the other thing?' she called down.

'I beg your pardon?'

'You said "firstly" – so there must be something else.'

She had to wait while he wheezed and coughed for a couple of minutes. It wasn't poor Monty's fault, but he wasnae doing Ralph any good at all.

'Right, secondly: I've bought the horse. For you. He's erm . . .

well, he's not going to—' he turned to face Monty and covered his ears '—he's not going to the knacker's yard, after all.'

Ralph had saved Monty!

Joey exhaled. She'd felt so rotten for so long and suddenly it was as though a cloud had lifted.

She was glad, even if she couldn't bring herself to say it. He'd bought Monty for her. Monty was her horse! Aw but wait. She could see problems ahead. How would she look after him?

'That's very kind,' she said. 'but I've nowhere to keep a horse!'

Or the money to do so. She and Ralph were still worlds apart. He was clueless. Horses were expensive to feed and care for, especially one that was past its best and couldn't earn its keep. It was just as she'd always thought: he and Seffy were two of a kind. They never had to think about money or how it felt to be without it.

'I've thought of that. It's all arranged,' Ralph said. 'He's to live at my cousin Lavinia's, on the estate.'

'What? Will he be on his own?' She knew that sounded ungrateful, but she couldn't bear it if Monty was lonely.

'No, I've checked. There are a couple of donkeys there and the laird's retired hunter. So he'll have pals.'

There was a pause, then Ralph said, 'If I might quote another proverb, Miss Wallace, "Don't look a gift horse in the mouth!"'

Joey's mouth twitched. That was almost funny. Almost.

But she was too choked up; she couldn't speak.

He sighed. 'You're clearly not in the mood for a chat and of course, you're working, so I'll clear off. Will the horse be all right if I leave him here? He won't run away?'

Joey felt a thud of disappointment. Ralph had bought Monty as a peace offering; he was really sorry for how he'd behaved, but now he was leaving and she didn't want him to go.

Her throat had closed up with emotion, but she needed to say something.

She'd been sore and cross and now she felt a little less so. She was glad to see him, she couldn't deny it. And if she was being honest, she still loved him, even though she hated him too, for doubting her and hurting her.

'Aw, he'll be fine,' she said. There was a catch in her voice. 'Leave him. He's not going anywhere.'

'Actually, neither am I,' Ralph said. 'I'm not going anywhere. Unless you tell me to.'

Joey rocked a little on the branch. She had to put out a hand to steady herself and when she glanced down she could see that he'd spread his arms and braced himself and oh, *ma God*, if she'd fallen then, he'd have caught her.

'I'm a fool! I've made a complete mess of this!' he said. 'I am sorrier than I've ever been in my life, but will you come down from that blasted tree now, Josephine? You're making me nervous.'

She laughed. 'You? I didn't think you were afraid of anything!'

He sneezed and held his hand out in front of him. 'Right at this moment, I'm shaking! Look!'

'I cannae see that from up here!'

'Well, use your binoculars, woman!'

Joey laughed. This was more like it: this was how it used to be.

She raised the binoculars and focused them on the forest floor where he was standing, legs apart. She traced his boots – as shiny as ever – and his legs, as strong as tree trunks, his khaki battledress, his broad chest and his face. Golly, he was very red and he was wheezing, like he could hardly breathe.

She moved the binoculars along his outstretched arm. No, he'd been fibbing. There was no sign of any shaking there. She inched further along. They were awful good, these wee binoculars. She could see the hairs on his arm, dark and thick. They made her stomach twist.

'Tell me, when you can see!' he said.

Aw, this was daft but it was a good daft; it was their kind of daft.

Then she saw it, held between his thumb and forefinger. A perfect ruby ring.

She gasped and pulled the binoculars away and in the second that she took to put them back up to her eyes, he'd gone down on bended knee.

'I'm a bloody fool, pardon my French. Will you forgive me and make me happier than I deserve to be? Josephine, will you—'

He took a breath. Joey tore the binoculars from her eyes and tried to calm herself.

Oh ma God. Wait! She'd just spotted it, out of the corner of her eye: a huge black cloud, over to the west.

She pulled herself up, stood on the branch and screamed, 'Fire! MORAG, over there! Can ye see that smoke? That's FIRE!'

Chapter 54

The girls stopped just short of the hut. The door was slightly ajar.

Seffy crouched down – beckoned Enid and Tattie to do the same – and they listened.

From inside came the sound of men's panicked voices. Oh, this was hopeless. They couldn't understand a word; they had no idea what was happening.

Seffy glanced down at the rifle hanging from her shoulder. It was too much to hope that it was loaded. She should've paid more attention in the shooting lesson; she had no idea how to check.

Enid and Tattie were looking at her, expectantly.

She bit her lip, quickly weighing up the options. Were they completely insane to think of venturing inside? Someone in there had a gun, after all, and they were prepared to use it.

It would be safer to leave and raise the alarm. Or look for a telephone. But where would they start? The camp was huge and roving around while there was a trigger-happy madman – or woman – on the loose probably wasn't the best option.

Besides, Jakub had said reinforcements were on their way. If they sat tight, maybe someone in authority would arrive and sort everything out?

Seffy sighed. She wouldn't hold her breath for that.

Aunt Dilys' words of all those weeks ago, when the WHD was first proposed, sprang into her mind. "I'm not sitting around, relying on them to save the day. I want to be able to do it for myself!"

'What'll we do?' Tattie whispered.

Enid held up a finger to silence her. She was concentrating on the voices inside the hut. 'That's Gio!' she said, standing up. Before Seffy could stop her, she'd kicked the door.

It swung open to reveal a crowd of prisoners in their familiar brown uniforms, gathered around something on the floor. Seffy recognised Alonzo and Paolo amongst the men. And there was Giovanni, crouched over a man's body, which was lying between rows of bunk beds.

The men turned as the girls walked in.

Gio straightened up. 'Enid, baby!' he said and she ran to him.

Tattie let out a strangled cry. 'Tomasz!'

Seffy glanced around, expecting to see the guard walking towards them. Then she realised, with a jolt, that he was the chap on the floor.

Tattie threw herself down beside him, frantically patting his hands and cheeks, as though that might bring him around.

There was a bloom of blood spreading over his uniformed chest and Paolo was gazing down, muttering a prayer and crossing himself.

There was a glimmer of hope then, Seffy thought: Tomasz was, for now at least, still alive.

She touched Paolo's arm. 'What happened?'

He looked at her with troubled eyes. 'When Captain Conti and Angelina come with the gun, Private Nowak try to stop them. They shoot him. And take his rifle, also.'

Seffy felt instantly light-headed. She grasped the frame of a nearby bunk, to steady herself. Captain Conti must be Luigi. Angie was in league with him; there could be no doubt about that now. But what on earth were they planning to do?

She looked around the hangar, with a pounding heart. Angie

and Luigi now had a weapon each. They could be training their rifles on them, preparing to shoot.

'Where are they?' she asked.

Paolo blew out his cheeks. 'They probably are letting the Fascists out.' He tapped the white armband on his sleeve and gave Seffy the gravest of looks. 'The black armbands.'

At that moment, a gun was fired somewhere deep within the camp.

Paolo nodded. 'I think they have just shot the bolt off their door.'

A minute passed, in which no one moved or spoke.

Seffy gritted her teeth. Was no one going to do anything? They were sitting ducks! They should make a dash for it; get out before the villains arrived. But then she looked at Enid, cuddled up to Gio and Tattie, fussing around Tomasz on the floor – and realised there was no point in even trying. The girls wouldn't leave their men and she wouldn't leave her pals.

A yell went up from the corridor and Seffy gasped as the men burst in. Luigi came first, brandishing Angie's rifle, followed by two others that Seffy vaguely recognised. One had an eyepatch; the other was a stocky, thuggish-looking fellow.

Seffy glanced at Paolo and he nodded. So, these were the black armbands. The Fascists. And they'd just been set free.

Angie was bringing up the rear. She looked flushed and more than a little pleased with herself. She was also holding a rifle – presumably Tomasz's – and as she scanned the prisoners' sullen faces, she held it up high, making sure everyone could see it.

Seffy's chest tightened. It was galling to think their Women's Home Defence training had helped prepare Angie for today. No wonder she'd been so keen to take part.

Angie's eyes widened in surprise when she spotted Seffy and then Enid. Tattie was still tending to Tomasz but when someone passed her a clean sheet to press against his wound, Angie noticed Tattie, too.

She nodded, looking strangely satisfied, as though she were glad they were here, to witness her moment of triumph.

Luigi was shouting and waving his rifle. His finger was on the trigger. He laughed manically, as the prisoners ducked and called to him in pleading tones.

Seffy clenched her fist. *Oh, please, someone wrench the blasted thing from him!* That gun would go off if he didn't calm down, and someone else would be shot.

Luigi finally tired of his sport. He called, 'Angelina!' and said something to her in urgent, rapid Italian. Angie replied without hesitation. My God, she was completely fluent.

Enid gave an ear-piercing shriek and pulled away from Giovanni.

'You're one o' them!' she said, jabbing an accusatory finger at Angie.

Angie simply smirked.

'Are you?' Seffy asked. 'Angelina? Is that your real name? Are you Italian?'

'Noo!' Tattie yelled from her position on the floor. 'She cannae be! Her name's no' Angelina! It's Angie! Angie Buchanan!'

Angie gave a supercilious smile. 'Aw, sweet Tattie. Faithful to the last.' She tilted her chin. 'Actually, my mother's Italian, my nonna – God rest her soul – was Italian. And my uncles!' She crossed herself. 'All Italian. I *am* Italian. *Viva L'Italia!*'

There was silence. No one – not even Luigi or the other thugs – joined in.

Seffy exhaled. It all made sense. Angie had transferred to their camp because she knew the Italians were nearby and she wanted to help them break out or lead a rebellion or whatever this was. She'd been right all along: she'd always known Angie was bad news.

Luigi and the two others were making for the door at the far end of the hut. They were escaping! Luigi beckoned to Angie again and she looked at Tattie, still pressing down on Tomasz's chest. The sheet was soaked and her hands were slick with blood.

'Come on!' Angie said. 'You can't do anything for him now. Leave him and come with us.'

Tattie looked exhausted. She couldn't even speak; she merely looked from Angie to Tomasz with tears in her eyes.

'Don't you dare, Tattie,' Seffy said. She stared straight at Angie. 'She's staying right here, you traitorous, murderous cow!'

She'd boiled over with fury, but now that she'd finally told Angie exactly what she thought of her, Seffy felt strangely calm. So much so that, when Angie's face twisted with rage and she pointed the gun straight at her, Seffy didn't even blink.

If this was how everything would end, then so be it.

Seffy touched the butt of the rifle, still hanging from her shoulder. There was no point even trying to lift it and take aim. Angie was five seconds ahead of her.

'Nooo!' Tattie was staggering to her feet and sobbing. 'Take me instead. Shoot me!'

Angie rolled her eyes but she let the rifle drop slightly and, for the first time since she'd charged into the hut, she looked uncertain.

'I'm your sister, after all,' Tattie said.

Angie's face clouded. She started to say something but stopped when one of the thugs called to her again from the door. A look of relief passed over her face. 'Aw, you're not even worth the bullet. Neither of you!' she said.

And with one last look of loathing, Angie lowered the gun and stormed out of the hut.

Chapter 55

Joey scrambled down the ladder, hardly noticing as her hands scraped on the bark of the tree. She jumped the last six feet, ignored the pain that shot through her feet on landing, and ran to meet Morag.

Morag stopped running when she saw Ralph and scowled. 'What's he doin' here? Is he bothering you?'

Joey grabbed Morag's sleeve and dragged her forward.

'Never mind him! You need to take this horse and go and raise the alarm. Run!'

Morag eyed them suspiciously but she did at least take Monty's reins from Joey. 'It doesnae bite, does it? And what'll you be doin'?'

'If I'm right – and please God, I'm not – that smoke's near the stables. The horses'll be trapped. They'll be—' She shook her head: it didn't bear thinking about. 'We have to rescue them!'

Ralph grabbed her hand and squeezed it tight. 'Let's go!' he said.

If Ralph hadn't been with her, Joey wouldn't have dared brave the fire.

It was like a snapping, snarling beast, gobbling up everything in its path with a terrifying roar. Flames licked the trees like huge burning tongues and as she and Ralph held hands and raced through the forest, branches cracked and crashed to the ground all around them.

'Stop a minute!' Ralph said, after a while, pulling up and panting.

Was he going to say they had to turn back? She'd refuse; she'd go on alone if she had to. The horses needed her; she couldnae let them down.

Ralph cupped her face in his hands. Her teeth were chattering even though she was hot.

He looked straight into her eyes. She'd never seen him look so serious.

'Listen. If the wind changes and the flames start coming towards us—'

'We'll turn and run like billy-o!'

'No! We can't outrun a forest fire. It's . . . it's impossible.'

'What, then?'

He swallowed. 'We'll find some barren ground, lie face down, cover ourselves with soil—'

What? Was the man completely crackers?

'And—?' she asked.

'We'll have to let the fire go over us.'

Joey was seized with fear. 'Nooo! I couldn't do that!'

He'd grabbed both her hands. 'Shush,' he said. 'I promise, I won't let anything harm you. I'm here. You're safe with me.'

As they got nearer to the stables, Joey could hear banging and neighing. The horses were kicking frantically against the wooden walls and whinnying in terror.

They must be able to smell the fire and feel the heat from the flames, which were only yards away. The stables were full of straw; there was a hayloft above them. If the fire reached them, they'd go up like tinder boxes.

She and Ralph flew into the yard.

Oh, the poor loves! Trapped in their stalls, the horses were wide-eyed and petrified.

'Shall we lead them?' Ralph yelled over the roar of the fire.

'No time! Just open the doors!'

Joey yanked at the bolt on Nelson's stable door. The metal was already getting hot.

She barely managed to get out of the way before Nelson charged out, snorting purposefully. Next, she ran to Storm's stable and let him out too.

Ralph had opened Nippy's stable door and she shot out next, following the first two horses in a thunder of hooves.

'God speed!' Joey called after them.

At least, now, they had a chance.

'Good work!' Ralph said, wiping the sweat from his brow. He held out his blackened hand to her. 'Come on, let's get out of here.'

They'd saved the horses. Now, they had to save themselves.

Chapter 56

Tattie's head was swimming; she thought she might pass out.

It'd been as quiet as a grave in here while Angie had been pointing that gun at Seffy. The only sound had been Tomasz's rasping breath and Tattie's own thundering heart. But once Angie and the wolf-men, as she thought of them, had left, the place had erupted.

Tattie crouched beside Tomasz as prisoners swarmed around them, yelling and waving their arms about. In the corner of the hut, a fight broke out. When someone insisted on lifting Tomasz onto one of the lower bunks, Tattie didn't object.

Paolo and Seffy were nearby, talking intently. It was too noisy to make out what they were saying but from the way Seffy had just gasped and put her hand to her mouth, it wasn't anything good.

Please, no more bad news. She couldn't take any more. She perched on the edge of the bed, looking down at Tomasz. His face was grey, his lips had a blueish tinge. If he died, it'd all be her fault.

Ma God, she'd been so stupid and feeble. A half-wit! Why hadn't she realised Angie was rotten to the core? Angie had bought her with a few kind words and the promise of friendship. It was pathetic.

Suddenly Seffy was there, squeezing her shoulder. 'Are you all right, Tattie?'

She shook her head. She'd never be all right again.

'I had no clue about any of this—' Tattie said, but Seffy was tugging on her sleeve.

'Come quickly. Paolo will stay with Tomasz. I need to talk to you and Enid.'

Seffy must've prised Enid away from Giovanni. She was leaning against the back wall, twisting her hands. Her face was pale and tear-stained.

Tattie looked at her – and at Seffy, so agitated and tense – and felt a wave of shame wash over her.

None of this would've happened if she'd only spoken up about Angie – if she'd only told them all the truth.

'I wouldn't have gone wi' her, you know,' Tattie said but Seffy only gave her a quick nod.

'Listen,' she said. 'Paolo overheard their plans. They're heading for the village hall.'

Enid gasped. 'But the bairns are there!'

Seffy bit her lip and nodded. 'Yes, indeed. They want the truck, the other rifles and . . . anyway, I'm off. I need to get there first.'

Tattie frowned. 'But the forest's on fire! You'll no' do it!'

'And they've got a head start!' Enid said. She clutched Seffy's arm. 'We'll come too!'

Seffy shrugged her off. 'No, I'll be quicker alone. I mightn't manage it but I have to try. I know the woods better than them. Tattie, stay with Tomasz. Keep him conscious. Help's coming, so just hold tight till then.'

She passed the strap over her head and gave Enid the rifle. 'Enid, you're in charge of this!'

'But it's not—' Enid started and Tattie nudged her.

'We don't know whether it's loaded,' Seffy said. Her voice had hardened. 'What's important is that you believe it is.' She nodded at the POWs. 'And so do they.'

'But they're our pals; I don't need to point a gun at them!' Enid said.

'That's no' true!' Tattie said. 'We only know a few of them. Half the others are already kickin' off! Look at them!'

'Tattie's right,' Seffy said. 'We've got to keep control, just until help arrives. Remember, Tomasz is their guard: they mightn't all be so keen for him to survive. And if any more men decide to go on the run, well . . . I can't even begin to imagine what might happen.'

A ripple of fear ran through Tattie. Seffy's confident voice might've fooled Enid but it hadnae fooled her. She'd heard that tremor. Mebbe Seffy was just as scared as them.

Enid was nodding, as though she finally understood. But in truth, how could they stop the Italians doing anything? They were lassies and all they had was a few men on their side and a useless rifle.

Alonzo – who was loud as well as tall – yelled out across the hut, calling for quiet.

Gradually, the prisoners stopped brawling and bickering. They followed Alonzo's instructions and clustered together. As they noticed Enid, a few started muttering. One or two laughed, until Paolo glared at them.

Enid was now standing on the bunk above Tomasz, pointing the rifle squarely at the prisoners.

Seffy was up there with her and once they had everyone's attention, Seffy nodded.

'Hands up!' Enid said. Her voice was quivering and no one moved a muscle. Paolo repeated the words in Italian but still no one moved.

Gio stepped forward and held out his hands. 'No, Enid, baby—' Enid stifled a sob.

Seffy grabbed the rifle from her and aimed it at the men. 'Hands UP!' she yelled. This time, they did as they were told.

'I know it's hard,' Seffy said to Enid, 'pointing a gun at your friends, but at this moment, they're not friends, they're foe!'

Gio had stepped back into line.

Seffy looked at him. 'And by the way, she is NOT your baby!'

She handed the rifle back to Enid. 'There. Act confident – that's the trick.'

Enid took a deep breath and this time, when she pointed the gun and gave the order, her voice was loud and unwavering. 'Sit on the floor, all of yous and put your hands on your heads!'

Paolo said it in Italian and everyone obeyed. You could hear a pin drop.

Seffy jumped down from the bunk and Tattie wanted to hug her. The girl was amazin'! It was surely too late for her to reach the village ahead of Angie and the men now. But on second thoughts, mebbe the lass would do it.

'Turn right out of that door,' Tattie said, nodding to the door in the corner. 'Straight on and then right again at the end of the corridor. It'll bring you out by the main gates.'

Seffy gave her a queer look.

Tattie didn't dare add, "Trust me". Why should any of the girls trust a word she said?

'Thank you,' Seffy said and turned and ran out of the door.

Paolo was saying something. 'Talk to Tomasz! You heard Miss Seffy. Keep him awake.'

Talk to him? What could she say? She'd hardly said two words to him in all the time she'd known him. All she could think of was, "Sorry" over and over again, which wasnae much good.

Then it came to her: she'd tell him a story. It had to be a good one, mind. The poor fella's breathing was so shallow now. But his eyelids were flickering. Hopefully, he could hear her. She hardly dared think it but what if her words were the last thing he ever heard?

'Go on!' Enid urged, from the upper bunk. 'It doesn't matter what you say!'

328

Tattie licked her lips. Her mind was blank. She closed her eyes. Think, think! At last, something came.

'Once upon a time,' she said, 'there was a hero. A man called William Wallace . . .'

Chapter 57

Seffy burst through the door at the end of the corridor. She'd followed Tattie's directions and – hallelujah – they'd brought her out near the main camp entrance. The metal gates and sentry boxes were just a few yards away.

She ran towards them, relieved that, although she could still smell smoke, there were no flames in sight.

The place was deserted, abandoned by all the guards except poor Tomasz. They must be out in the woods, fighting the fire, oblivious to the bedlam within the camp.

Suddenly, she heard men's voices.

Oh, thank God! Perhaps it was the reinforcements Jakub had promised. But in the next second, Seffy's heart plummeted again. That was a woman's voice. Angie!

The awful quartet was still here. Perhaps they'd changed their minds about heading for the village, or – more likely – were on the hunt for weapons or keys to a truck.

If they couldn't find them here, they'd get the other rifles from the village hall and take the lorry, to make their getaway. They might even have money. Is that what had happened to the money in her suitcase? Had Angie stolen it to fund this escape?

The voices were getting louder. They were coming her way!

If they saw her, she was done for. The men mightn't bother too much about a mere girl but Angie hated her: this time she might actually press that trigger.

She had to hide. There was a sentry box on either side of the gates. She slipped inside the nearest, pulled the door to – inwardly cursing that there was no way of locking it – and was immediately filled with a new terror.

It was horribly close in here and dark. Like a coffin. Seffy slid down against the back wall and crouched in the corner, hugging her knees and hardly daring to breathe. If she made so much as a peep, that blackguard Luigi might simply shoot through the door without even checking inside. She'd never see Callum again; she'd never make it up with Joey. She bit her lip hard to stifle a sob.

The voices were closer now. Seffy glimpsed figures and movement through a crack in the door. She couldn't understand their rapid-fire Italian but it sounded as though they were arguing. With any luck, they'd have a punch-up and knock each other out.

If only they'd move off, so she could get out. She felt like a fox, trapped in its den. She needed to get to the village hall.

She hadn't told Enid and Tattie the whole truth because she hadn't wanted to alarm them but, according to Paolo, Angie's gang were planning to take hostages – children – if their demands weren't met.

It was shocking but she didn't doubt they'd do it. The men were desperate and Angie was fanatical.

Seffy felt sick at the thought of Jock's grandson, wee Jock, and all those other sweet kiddies, in danger.

If anything awful happened, how would she face their mothers? The group of jolly young women who'd become her friends? They'd gamely signed up for the WHD and entrusted their children to Marigold's nursery, believing they were learning to protect their families, when in truth, they'd put them directly in the path of danger.

It was so hot in here. Sweat dripped down her neck and Seffy could feel the air thinning around her. She was trembling, her mouth was dry, the walls were closing in and suddenly, she was that little girl again, trapped in the trunk at school.

Her heart was pounding like a drum. She blinked hard. There were dark spots in front of her eyes. If she didn't get some air soon, she'd die.

Then – oh, the relief – the voices outside had stopped. She squinted through the crack in the door and could see nothing. They'd gone. But she didn't dare leave her hiding place. Not yet.

She had to pull herself together. She mustn't think about that awful time at school or that she was squeezed tight into an airless sentry box.

Perhaps, if she closed her eyes, she could imagine herself somewhere else; somewhere heavenly, like the pub with Callum, in Gretna Green. Laughing and teasing one another and feeling happy.

No, it was no good. She was getting dizzy.

She would count to ten, then, to heck with the consequences, she'd simply have to open the door.

They were the longest ten seconds of her life, but finally she pushed the door open a couple of inches, put her mouth to the small gap and breathed.

She peered out. There was the edge of the forest. Black smoke was still billowing in the distant sky.

There was silence. Angie and her gang must have set off to Farrbridge.

It was a relief that they'd gone, but Seffy's heart plummeted as she realised the truth of the matter: that even if she ran faster than she'd ever run in her life, she couldn't catch them up now, never mind overtake them and get to the village hall first. A wave of despair swept over her. She'd had visions of saving the day – or at least, of being able to warn everyone of the impending danger – but any chance of that had gone. She'd failed; she couldn't do it.

With a sigh and a heavy heart, she straightened up and stepped out of the sentry box.

She gave a jolt of surprise and then froze. She'd seen a flash of movement in the trees. She'd been wrong: they were still here!

The shape was getting nearer. It wasn't a person. It was something big and brown. A cow? No, it was a horse! It was Nelson.

Seffy almost laughed with relief. Not a gun-wielding Italian, then: only Nelson.

He was agitated, covered in foam and sweat, and trotting up and down through the trees, tossing his head. What was he doing here, alone and miles from his stable?

Seffy stepped forward carefully and held out her hand. Perhaps he was the answer to her prayers. If only she could catch him and keep him still for long enough to climb aboard.

She called his name, gently, praying he wouldn't suddenly take fright and gallop off.

Nelson stopped pacing, finally and turned to look at her. He was quivering. Did he recognise her voice? He stood still as Seffy approached, taking baby steps, talking softly.

Every fibre in her body was urging her forward, telling her there wasn't a moment to lose, but she couldn't rush this.

Eventually, she was near enough to reach out and grab his headcollar.

There, she had him.

Chapter 58

The first path Seffy tried was blocked by a wall of fire, like an angry, roaring dragon. Nelson reared up and Seffy almost slithered off his back. This was hopeless. If he bolted or reared again, she might fall off and find herself alone in the burning forest, trapped by a ring of flames.

So, even though the quickest route was through the trees, she urged Nelson onto the road. Without reins, she had to use her voice and legs to guide him. She yelled when he hesitated, pressing him forward with her heels, and praised him in soothing tones when he obeyed. Even though she was terrified, she tried to sound strong and brave so he wouldn't be afraid.

It was eerily quiet on the road and they passed no one. But occasionally, Seffy caught the reassuring sound of distant, clanging bells: fire engines. And finally, somehow, they'd made it. They were here.

As they clattered down the lane, just yards from the village hall, the woman who ran the shop put her head out of the door.

'Get in! Put up your shutters!' Seffy yelled, as she careered past. It had probably sounded like gobbledygook. She was so exhausted, she could hardly speak.

She'd been praying that commandos from Ralph's unit would be here – maybe even Ralph himself – and he'd say, 'Don't fret,

Seffy, it's all under control. We've moved everyone to safety and we'll have those reprobates the moment they step into the open.'

But no such luck. The door of the village hall was open and Seffy's heart sank as she caught a glimpse of bunting, balloons, trestle tables heaving with food and jugs of Marigold's special lemonade.

Giggling children and their mothers were tearing around outside, playing tag on the grass. There was Belinda and Jean and some of the other WHD girls. Flora was doing cartwheels.

Jean was the first to spot her. She looked up at the sound of Nelson's hooves and peered over the rim of her spectacles.

'Seffy is that you? That's cheating, turning up on a horse! And where's Angie? You're disqualified if you don't end the race as a pair.'

Flora laughed. 'You look like a chimney sweep! But dinnae fret: you're not the last. We're still waiting on Tattie and Enid, to start the tea. I wish they'd hurry. I'm starvin'!'

Nelson trotted up to the open doorway and Seffy slid from his back and almost collapsed. Her legs were like jelly.

A couple of children came running up to pat Nelson.

'Shall I fetch him a bucket o' water, missus?' one of the boys asked and Seffy nodded, gratefully.

Dilys and Lady Lockhart appeared, wearing aprons. Dilys' face was creased with concern. 'Persephone! What's happened?'

'They're coming! They're on their way!' Seffy managed to say. 'Someone run and get the police and, for God's sake get those children inside!'

But no one moved. No one was listening to her. They didn't understand it was an emergency. Dilys peered down the empty lane. 'Whatever do you mean? Who's coming?'

Seffy swallowed. 'The enemy!' she said.

'How many?' Dilys asked, a minute later, as she took Seffy to one side.

Once her aunt had grasped the gravity of the situation, she'd despatched Marigold to alert the constable and ordered everyone, except Seffy and Lady Lockhart, inside.

'Four of them,' Seffy said. Her throat was so rasping and dry, it hurt to speak. 'Three Fascists from the prison camp, plus Angie Buchanan.'

Lady Lockhart gasped but Aunt Dilys merely raised an eyebrow.

'Angie's a traitor,' Seffy said. 'And her rifle was loaded. Heaven knows how.'

'We should send the mothers and children home,' Dilys said.

'Goodness, we'll never eat all that food without them!' Lady Lockhart said and laughed, weakly.

Seffy shook her head. 'There's no time. The gang set off before me and took a more direct route. They'll be here any minute.'

The children who'd been playing so happily were in tears and throwing tantrums, as they were scooped up and dragged off the grass by their mothers.

Dilys winced, as a toddler who was being bundled inside by his mother let out an ear-piercing shriek, inches from her ear.

'What do they want?' Dilys asked Seffy. 'The Fascists?'

'The truck and the rifles, for starters,' Seffy said.

Dilys nodded. 'I'll remove the distributor cap and rotor arm from the truck. That'll render it useless and we'll send a couple of girls to hide the parts in the woods.' She pursed her lips. 'Should we hide the rifles, too?'

'No,' Seffy said. 'Let's double-check that none of them is loaded and then let's keep them with us. I've got an idea.'

'Very well. Lavinia, can you start checking all the rifles?'

'Aye, Captain!' Lady Lockhart said, and darted inside.

'There's something else,' Seffy said, gravely. 'The thugs discussed taking children, as hostages.'

'Over ma dead body!' Jennie McIlroy cried. She must've overheard, as she brought her kiddies inside. She was cradling wee Jock in one arm and holding a little girl by the hand.

She yelled to her friend. 'Mhairi! Bring all the knives out of the kitchen drawer in there! The sharper the better!' She turned to Dilys. 'We'll hide in the cellar with the bairns but if anyone so much as touches a hair on their wee heads, I'll no' be responsible for ma actions!'

Her eyes flashed and Seffy had no doubt she meant it. She was like a tigress, defending her cubs.

'That's the spirit!' Dilys said. 'Get yourself, Mhairi and the children down there now!'

Seffy grabbed Jennie's arm as she turned to go. 'Take the nursery helpers too. Barricade the door! Tell the children it's a game and they must be quiet as mice. But we'll need the other girls here, with us, so they'll have to trust you with their children.'

Jennie nodded and Seffy wheeled round to face her aunt.

'Come on, Captain. Disable the truck and, then, we need to talk to the troops!'

'Right, listen up,' Dilys said.

Seffy and the other remaining WHD members were clustered together inside the village hall. They'd closed the door and drawn the curtains. Grace, still on crutches, was at the window, as lookout.

Dilys' face was half in shadow. It was difficult to read her expression but her voice was calm and clear. 'As you've gathered, a group of enemy aggressors are heading this way. Amongst them, our erstwhile member, Angie Buchanan.'

Dilys silenced the shocked cries with a raised hand.

'I'm telling you that for one reason only: that you do not mistake the woman for a friend. Understood?'

Everyone nodded, solemnly.

'The good news is that the villains are outnumbered. There are only four of them and there are . . .' she started to do a headcount and frowned. 'Where is everyone?'

'We've catered for over twenty,' Lady Lockhart said. 'But they're somewhat dispersed.'

'Never mind,' Dilys said. 'We still outnumber them. There are ten of us. Twelve, when Bonnie and Ailsa get back from the woods.'

'Wouldn't we be better off slashing the truck tyres?' Jean asked.

'Absolutely not!' Dilys said. 'Once this hullaballoo is over, you'll need that vehicle for your essential war work. There's no rubber for tyres. You'd never replace them.'

Seffy nodded. Dilys was right: the truck was precious. They shouldn't even have had it today but Jock's daughter Jennie had talked her father round.

'There might only be four of them, but I've heard they're armed,' Belinda said.

Janet – another lumberjill – squealed. 'You know,' she said, 'before she went to fetch the constable, Miss Mackenzie said there was no shame in surrender.'

Dilys rolled her eyes. 'Marigold would say that. But there'll be no talk of surrender on my watch!'

Seffy sighed. Dilys was doing her best to rally them but could they really win a struggle against three vicious thugs, mean-spirited Angie and two loaded rifles? They needed a plan.

'Might I say something, Captain?' Seffy asked. 'We have one clear advantage: the element of surprise. The foe have no idea we're expecting them. So, here's what I think we should do. But first, Flora, would you go and put the kettle on?'

When Seffy finished speaking, a couple of girls blew out air from their cheeks but no one was panicking; no one said it was impossible.

They rushed about making their preparations and they'd barely finished when Grace called out, in a low voice, 'They're here! Two are coming to the door. Luigi's armed and is heading for the truck. Angie's armed and she's gone round the back.'

Could they do it?

'Positions, everyone,' Seffy whispered.

They were about to find out.

*　*　*

338

The door opened with a creak. The girls had deliberately left it unlocked and the Italians were, no doubt, expecting little resistance.

One muttered something to the other in a gruff voice. Then, through the gloom, they must've spotted the bait: the rifles were piled up on the floor ten feet inside the hall.

The men's voices were more urgent now, as they debated what to do. Eventually, they stepped inside, reaching out for the guns.

'Now!' Seffy yelled and the girls charged.

They mightn't have proper weapons but they had pepper from the kitchen and cups of boiling water and they threw them directly at the thugs' faces. While they were yelling in agony, the women threw tablecloths over the men's heads.

Seffy beckoned Grace and Belinda to the back of the hall, but not before she'd seen Dilys kick one chap in the back of the knees, sending him sprawling to the ground. Then Janet held him in an armlock.

'Don't move, you utter creep!' Dilys cried.

One down, three to go.

The other Italian – the one with an eyepatch – had made a run for it, pulling the tablecloth off his head and tearing back through the door, screaming blue murder.

Seffy glanced out of the window. Luigi was inside the truck, banging his fists on the steering wheel.

Then she heard the back door of the hall rattling.

'Stand to one side, quick!' she told Grace and Belinda, just in time.

Angie shot off the lock and stormed inside, rifle at the ready.

When she saw Seffy, her mouth dropped open. 'How . . . how did you get here?'

'Oh, I have a flying broomstick,' Seffy said. 'Which is precisely what you're going to need, you evil witch, if you think you're going to get away with this.'

Angie was distracted for a moment, as the yells of the first

Italian reached her from the other end of the hall. He was being rolled in a tablecloth and tied up with string, like a mummy.

Angie fixed her eyes – and her gun – back on Seffy. 'Where are the bairns? Tell me, else I'll shoot. And this time, I'll do it!'

Seffy lifted her hands slightly. 'All right. Step this way and I'll take you to them.'

Angie looked wary but without taking her eyes off Seffy, she took a step forward. Immediately, Grace and Belinda, who were crouching down, holding one end of a crutch each, lifted it and Angie tripped up.

She fell flat on her face.

The rifle skidded across the wooden floor and Seffy stopped it with her foot.

'That'll do nicely,' she said, bending to pick it up. 'Can you manage her, Grace?'

'Oh aye,' Grace said. 'It'll be ma pleasure!' She plonked herself down on Angie, who let out a wail. 'She's fair pinned to the ground now!'

Seffy braced herself. There was still the small matter of Luigi – thuggish, furious, armed Luigi – to deal with. At least now, she also had a gun.

She stepped outside and her head wheeled round at the sound of thudding hooves. It was the Italian with the eyepatch. He was riding Nelson and heading rapidly towards the woods.

Some of the other girls had run outside too.

'Shoot!' Flora yelled.

Seffy raised her gun and took aim. Her heart was pounding. She wouldn't try to score a direct hit: she just wanted to frighten him. But what if she hit him – or Nelson – in error?

'He's gettin' away!' someone yelled.

Seffy bit her lip, pressed the trigger and fired. Nelson bucked, catapulting the Italian though the air.

The girls cheered as he landed with a thud on the grass and Nelson continued to canter around.

'He's doin' a victory lap!' Flora said.

'Well done, Nelson, old boy,' Seffy muttered, as a group of girls ran forward to capture the Italian. He was winded and groaning. He wouldn't be putting up much of a fight.

'Persephone! Look!'

Seffy turned to see her aunt, looking suddenly stricken, pointing towards the truck. Luigi was standing next to it. He had a young boy in a stranglehold and with the other hand he was waving his rifle in the air.

It was the lad who'd brought the bucket of water for Nelson. How had he ended up out here and not in the cellar, with the others?

Luigi was shouting. It was all in Italian but the meaning was clear.

'He wants us to fix the truck,' Seffy said, feeling suddenly sick. 'And if we don't—'

There was an ear-piercing scream from nearby. It had come from Bonnie. She and Ailsa had only just come back from the woods where they'd been hiding the truck parts.

'That's my boy, Charlie!' Bonnie yelled. 'What the hell's he doin' with ma wee boy?'

Seffy looked down at the rifle in her hands. It was useless. Luigi was holding the child against his chest. She couldn't even think about trying to shoot.

Dilys shook her head. 'The game's up, Persephone. We have no choice. Bonnie, you stay here and try to be calm. Ailsa, go and get the parts for the truck. Hurry!'

Luigi had moved closer now. The boy was shaking with fear and Seffy's heart went out to him – and to his poor mother, Bonnie, who was beside herself. There must be something they could do. She took a step towards him and Luigi made a warning growl.

'All right!' Dilys said to Luigi. 'We're going to give you what you want.' She held up her index finger. '*Un minuto!*'

341

And then, it happened. Seffy watched in awe, as Lady Lockhart stepped silently out from behind the back of the truck and hurled a missile towards Luigi. It made a perfect arc before striking him clean on the back of the head. There was a splashing sound, then he fell like a stone, taking the boy down with him.

'What the hell was that?' Dilys asked, as they all ran forward.

Lady Lockhart had thrown a jug of lemonade at him. It hadn't quite knocked him out but he was dazed enough for young Charlie to scramble out from underneath him.

Someone screamed, as Luigi managed to stagger to his feet. He pushed the women roughly out of the way and, with a crazed grin, reached for his rifle.

But he'd reckoned without Jean.

The policeman's eyes were out on stalks when he arrived a few minutes later and saw the captured Italians.

'All you have to do is arrest them, Constable,' Dilys said with a satisfied nod.

He looked down at Luigi, who was lying on the ground, unconscious.

'Who's responsible for this?' he asked.

Jean stepped forward, pushing her spectacles up her nose. She looked a little sheepish.

'That would be me,' she said. And then turning to the other girls she mouthed, *Chin jab!*

In time, more police came from Inverness and took Angie and the Fascists away.

'Right!' Dilys said, clapping her hands. 'After that excitement, I think we can finally start our buffet tea! Let the children out of the cellar, Marigold!'

Soon the kiddies were tucking into the food, all – except Charlie – oblivious to the danger they'd been in. And young Charlie was amongst them, apparently none the worse for wear.

'He heard that baddies were coming, so he took the horse

342

round the back, to hide him,' Bonnie explained to Seffy. 'But look at him. There's nae bother on him, now!'

Morag was next to arrive, buoyed up by her part in raising the alarm, mobilising the fire brigade and summoning the commandos.

'I hear you've brought a horse too, young lady, is that right?' Aunt Dilys asked. 'Goodness, this place is turning into the O.K. Corral!'

Seffy couldn't think why Morag might have a horse but perhaps, in the same way that she'd found Nelson, Morag had come across a loose horse in the woods. Before she could ask, a shrill voice filled the hall.

'Have we missed the party?'

Seffy's heart lifted. That had sounded like Enid! Yes, it really was her, and Tattie was following close behind, head bowed. They looked a little weary but otherwise, unharmed.

'I hope you've left some cake for me!' Enid said, before introducing the commando who'd just driven her and Tattie back from the POW camp where everything, Enid assured them, was back under control.

'Aw, it wasn't so bad,' she added. 'My Gio would never have let us come to any harm!'

'How's Tomasz?' Seffy asked Tattie.

She shook her head. 'They've taken him to hospital. But . . . I dunno.'

'Here,' Marigold said, holding out an apron to Tattie. 'Why don't you put that on, dear?' She lowered her voice and waved her hand at Tattie's chest. 'It'll hide the blood.'

'So Angie's one of those, what do they call them?' Seffy said, as the WHD members sat together with their tea and cakes.

'A fifth columnist,' Jean said.

'Hardly,' Dilys said. 'There are British fascists, who, I can assure you, pose much more of a threat than the likes of Angie Buchanan.

But it seems, from what you've told me, Persephone, she was seeking retribution of some kind for what had happened to her family. This country wasn't a safe place for Italians when they declared war. But by helping the Italian prisoners with their escape – failed escape, as it turned out – she put everyone at risk. People who wouldn't hurt a fly; who'd been her friends.'

'It doesn't make sense,' Seffy said.

Dilys nodded. 'War doesn't make sense.'

Much to her surprise, Seffy felt a momentary pang of pity for Angie. It was as though she'd been driven mad by the thought of what had happened to her family. And by her infatuation with Luigi.

'What'll happen to her now?' Seffy asked.

'Prison, I expect. Who knows?' Dilys said.

'Who cares?' Grace said. 'As long as we never have to see her again!'

Seffy nodded and raised her cup of tea. 'I'll drink to that.'

The laird, Mr Strachan and a few other members of the Home Guard arrived then, holding their rifles and looking around cautiously.

'Can I help you, gentlemen?' Marigold asked.

'We heard there was some enemy action!' Mr Strachan said, hopefully.

'Too late, boys,' Dilys said. She glanced at the clock. 'You've missed it all by about an hour and a half.'

'But don't fret!' Lady Lockhart said. 'The Women's Home Defence Corps had it all under control!'

The laird's face turned puce. 'Lavinia? What are you doing here! Gracious! You're wearing slacks!'

'Yes. I'm a sergeant in the WHD!'

'Are you?' Dilys asked.

'Hmm. I think I need a rank.' Lady Lockhart turned back to her husband. 'Never had so much fun in my life! Now, think of your blood pressure, dearie, and do sit down. You're still in time for tea and cake.'

'Sorry, no cake left,' Flora said, wiping a few crumbs from the corner of her mouth.

'Tea, then,' Marigold said with a smile, picking up the teapot.

'Isn't this wonderful?' Dilys said, looking round. 'We're all reunited!'

But they weren't: there was one person missing. Seffy could only assume she hadn't wanted to come to the party, knowing that Seffy would be there.

'Have you seen Joey?' Seffy called down the trestle table to Morag.

Morag was chewing on a cheese sandwich. She swallowed it, finally and said, 'Last I saw, she was heading towards the fire with that major chappie. Is she no' here, then?'

A stab of fear sliced through Seffy's heart. She'd been going in the direction of the fire? Please God let her be all right. She couldn't bear it if anything had happened to her pal. Where was she? Where was Joey?

Chapter 59

Joey and Ralph sat side by side in the burn, with sooty faces. Delicious icy water lapped around their legs. The fire still crackled along the bank but with less intensity now. Ralph had tried smothering the flames with his jacket but they'd been too ferocious and, reluctantly, he'd given up trying.

They were safe here, for now. They simply had to wait to be rescued or until the fire ran out of fuel.

'Listen!' Joey said. In the distance, they could hear fire engine bells. She exhaled. The message had got through, then. Good for Morag.

'I expect my unit's been drafted in,' Ralph told her. 'We've been on stand-by for forest fires for a while.' He smiled. 'I should be with them, leading the way. If my men see me here, like this, I'll never live it down!'

Joey laughed and twirled her fingers through the water.

'How did you know about Monty?' she asked. 'That he needed rescuing?'

'Ah, well that was all down to Seffy. She sought me out. She wanted to help us patch things up.' He shrugged. 'She thought saving Monty from the knacker's yard might be a good start.'

Joey let out a groan, let her head fall back and looked up at the sky.

'Daft coo! Me, I mean. I was all wrong about Seffy, wasn't I?'

Ralph nodded slowly. 'Hmm. I think you might be eating humble pie for some time.'

Joey nodded. She'd do it, gladly, if it meant that she and Seffy could be pals again.

She glanced at her watch. The WHD expedition would be over by now and the lucky devils would be enjoying their tea party. If she and Ralph hadn't been cut off by the fire, they could've gone to the village hall and joined in. She could've apologised to Seffy.

'Aw, golly!' Joey said, as a horrid thought struck her. 'You don't think any of the lassies would've got caught up in that fire, do you?'

Ralph narrowed his eyes. 'Not unless they went in completely the wrong direction. I know where they started: I advised Dilys on the best place to make the drop.' He stroked Joey's arm. 'Don't fret, my love. They'll have been absolutely fine.'

Joey smiled.

She couldn't help wondering where that pretty ruby ring had gone. She hoped he hadn't lost it, tearing through the forest, fighting fires and splashing around in the burn.

It'd be an awful waste.

'You were sayin'?' Joey said, archly. 'Back there? Just before I spotted the smoke?'

Ralph looked blank. It was understandable: a lot had happened since then. They'd run, dodged fires, rescued horses, evaded more flames, run some more and finally, found sanctuary in the burn.

Thank goodness they hadn't had to implement Ralph's idea of burying themselves in dirt and letting the fire go over them, though. She wouldn't have minded lying down next to him – they could've snuggled up close – but not the fire part.

Suddenly, Ralph's eyes lit up. He realised what she meant and his mouth dropped open.

'You're not serious? Now?'

Joey shrugged. The bells were getting louder. They mightn't have too long.

'Why not? What else do we have to do?'

Ralph sat upright – or as upright as he could manage in a foot of swirling water – gave a small cough and took a breath before he restarted his speech from hours earlier.

'I should never have doubted you, never—'

'—have let me go,' Joey finished. She nodded. 'Aye, that's true.'

'Will you . . . I need to know if you can forgive me?'

The forgiveness part was tricky. Could she forgive him and allow herself to be happy?

Joey lay back in the water, dipped her head for a few seconds and sat up, sopping wet. 'I'm doing my best impression of a mermaid,' she said, laughing. 'Now, wasn't there another part, to what you were saying?'

Oh, she was enjoying herself.

Ralph grimaced. The fella wasn't half as brave now that she was right here in front of him, not perched high up in a tree. 'If you can forgive me, will you make me happier than I deserve to be? Josephine Wallace, will you—'

'YES!' she yelled, before he could even finish speaking. She leaped out of the water like a salmon, straight into his arms. 'Yes!' she said, kissing him. 'Oh, YES!'

Chapter 60

When Joey arrived back in camp in the early evening, Seffy was at the door of Macdonald hut to greet her.

'At last!' she said. 'I've been going out of my mind with worry!'

'Have you?' Joey was taken aback. She'd rehearsed how this would go and she hadn't expected this. 'Aw, that's nice,' she said. It was more than she deserved.

Seffy grabbed her hands and pulled her closer. 'Where've you been? And where's Ralph? Have you two—? Oh, come inside and tell us everything!'

Joey pulled back. 'Wait. First, I have to say sorry. For everything. I've been a total ninny! I should never have doubted you, Seffy, and I—'

'Enough! After the day I've had . . . well, life's too short for tiffs and fallings-out!'

They hugged.

'Chums again, right?' Seffy said.

'Chums,' she agreed.

'Ah, here she is, love's young dream,' Morag said, as they went inside. All the other girls were stretched out on their beds.

'I told them you were safe with your beau,' Morag continued, 'but they didnae believe me!'

'No, because last we heard, you hated him,' Enid said. 'And we all hate him too!'

Joey opened her mouth to say something but Morag was still talking. 'And dinnae fret about your wee horsey. He's safe and sound, with the other one.'

'With Nelson,' Seffy said.

'Aye. They're at my uncle's place. Willy Paterson: the blacksmith,' Flora said.

Joey was so tired, it was hard to take everything in but she'd grasped the good news: Monty and Nelson were safe. She thanked Morag, who seemed unusually chirpy and then she explained how the firemen had found the other horses – Nippy and Storm – and how she and Ralph, once rescued from the burn, had offered to take care of them.

'It was too risky to put them back in the stables, so we walked them all the way to the Blantyre estate. And Ralph's just escorted me back here.'

Ralph, her fiancé. Joey stroked the pocket of her breeches, in which the perfect ruby ring was nestling.

She exhaled. 'Which is why I'm so late and totally frazzled!' She flopped down face first onto her bed.

'Joey, whatever kind of a day you've had,' Enid said, 'I'll bet you ten shillings we can trump it!'

'Aye!' the girls chorused.

Joey frowned and turned her head towards them.

Tattie was lying flat out on her bed, but the others – Enid, Morag, Jean, Seffy, Grace and Flora – were all staring at her. No Angie. Where was she?

She pushed herself up onto her elbows. 'Well, I'm guessing, after your six-mile tramp through the woods, you all had a delicious afternoon tea?'

Which was more than she'd had.

'*Eventually*, we did!' Enid said. She sounded most put out. She looked across the hut at Seffy. 'Are you going to tell her, or shall I?'

In the end, they all told her. All except Tattie, who was lying motionless, staring up at the ceiling.

The others explained about the fire at the camp, the guns, the gang of four and the battle – as Jean insisted on calling it – at the village hall. They talked over one another, exclaiming and laughing and re-enacted confusing scenes with rifles, a jug, and Grace's crutches.

Joey listened, open-mouthed, barely able to take it all in.

'So the upshot of it all, is that Angie was a bad 'un, through and through—' Enid said, finally.

'And Seffy knew!' Grace said. 'Didn't you? From the very start!'

Seffy shrugged modestly. 'I suspected something was off with her, yes.'

'It stands to reason then, that Angie must've have written the poison pen letter,' Jean said.

Joey wrinkled her nose. 'I dunno . . .'

That letter had caused so much heartache, that although she was now reunited with Ralph and pals again with Seffy, it still needed resolving. It wasnae good enough to say, "It must've been Angie and there's an end to it." Tattie had been involved, for sure.

'Here,' Seffy said, handing Joey something wrapped in a tea towel. 'I saved you a few sandwiches from the tea.'

'Aw, thank you! You're an angel!' Joey said. She opened the little parcel and started tucking in.

'Joey, I've worked it out,' Enid said. 'I reckon Cora must've told Angie about you and the fella in Forres.'

'Who's Cora when she's at home?' Morag asked.

'I worked with a land girl called Cora!' Joey said. She was talking with her mouth full but she didn't care. 'How do you know her?'

351

'Angie always had a chat wi' her after church. They got quite pally,' Enid said.

That was it! The missing part of the jigsaw puzzle. Cora was one of the mean girls who'd been so jealous of her and Hamish. No wonder there'd been trouble, if Cora was behind it.

'Mystery solved!' Jean said, with a firm nod. 'Cora gave Angie the information and for whatever reason, Angie wrote the letter.'

'Out of devilment!' Enid said.

Joey shook her head. 'But Ralph thought he saw Tattie near his jacket that day.'

Everyone fell silent and looked at Tattie. She didn't give any indication that she'd even heard them.

'It was you, wasn't it, Tattie?' Joey said. 'You wrote that letter!'

Grace, on the bed next to Tattie's, shook her head. 'No, you've got it wrong. It was Angie! Tattie might've been instructed by Angie to put the letter in Ralph's pocket but she didnae write it.'

'How can you be so sure?' Joey asked.

It was typical of Grace, to be kind. But Joey wasnae going to let the lass get away with it. If it wasn't Tattie, let her say so.

Grace took a deep breath. 'For a start, Tattie never reads magazines.'

'Aye but she could've got hold o' plenty!' Morag said.

'And, she never writes or receives letters from home,' Grace said. 'You've none of you noticed, except me. Even so-called clever Angie didn't notice.'

Everyone gazed at Grace, puzzled.

'I'm right, aren't I, Tattie?' Grace said, softly. She turned to the others. 'Tattie can't read. And if she can't read, then she certainly can't write!'

As the girls gasped and exclaimed, Tattie leaped up from the bed and sprinted out of the hut.

'Guilty, as charged,' Joey said, with a satisfied nod.

Seffy frowned at her. 'But you just heard Grace. Tattie couldn't possibly have written that letter.'

'Aye, but she's not blameless! No one forced her to put it in Ralph's pocket. She should've told us the truth!' Joey said.

'Aw, cut the girl some slack,' Jean said. 'I think she's totally crushed by everything that's happened.'

'Aye,' Enid said. 'Her best pal turned out to be the devil in disguise and that Polish guard she's so fond of, well—' she shook her head '—she did her best to help him but I don't reckon he'll make it.'

'She's lost everything,' Grace said, quietly. 'And now she probably thinks we all hate her.'

Joey swallowed. The girls were right. She felt rotten now. She glanced at the door. One of them should mebbe go after Tattie and check she was all right.

Seffy sighed. 'Look, it's been a pretty awful day for all of us, one way or another. We're overwrought. Let's be nice to one another, shall we, and—' she looked at Joey '—perhaps let bygones be bygones?'

Everyone nodded and murmured their agreement.

'I've got some good news,' Joey blurted out. 'If you want cheering up?'

That ring was burning a hole in her pocket. She wasn't sure how much longer she could keep it a secret and yet, her stomach was churning; how were the girls going to react?

They were watching her and waiting.

'I'm engaged to be married!' she said.

'Who to?' Flora asked.

'To Ralph. To Major Stirling.'

'Sure you are,' Enid said. 'And I'm walking out wi' the Loch Ness monster!'

Everyone laughed.

Her heart plummeted. She wished she hadn't told them. It wasn't like this last year when Grace announced she was marrying Gordy. They'd all been over the moon.

Only Seffy believed her. She had the biggest grin on her face. 'You really are, aren't you?'

'But you hate him!' Enid said. 'He believed those horrid things about you.'

'And you made us hate him too,' Flora said.

Joey was blushing now. She felt daft. 'I did hate him, aye,' she said.

'And now . . . ?' Jean said.

Joey swallowed. 'And now, I love him.'

Enid squealed! 'It's true? You're getting married!' She ran up to Joey and ruffled her hair. 'You must've got Grace's bed! It must be the lucky bed. Everyone who sleeps in that bed gets married!'

'Aye, well I didn't get it, that's for sure,' Morag said.

Joey looked at Seffy. Her eyes were shining. Goodness, were those tears?

'It's very sudden,' Seffy said. 'Are you absolutely sure?'

'I am.'

'Then I couldn't be more delighted!' And for the second time that evening, they hugged. 'Joey Wallace,' Seffy said softly in her ear, 'I wish you all the happiness in the world!'

Chapter 61

Tattie was standing outside, in the moonlight, when Seffy found her.

'Hey, what are you doing out here?' Seffy said. 'The midges will eat you up!'

Tattie shrugged. She didn't care.

'You've missed all the excitement, you know,' Seffy said, nodding back at the hut.

Aw, very funny. She'd had enough excitement to last her a lifetime, ta very much.

'I've been thinkin',' Tattie said.

Seffy said nothing, just waited for her to carry on.

'I'm leavin',' she said. 'I'll be away at first light. Don't tell the others, will you? Not that they'll care, I'm sure.'

She'd been mulling it over for hours and this was the right thing to do. She'd been such a fool. Angie had been a wicked stepmother and an evil witch, all rolled into one. How hadn't she seen it?

'You're not embarrassed about . . . well, about the reading thing, are you?' Seffy asked. 'Because, I'm sure someone could—'

'No!' Tattie shook her head. She'd have liked the chance to send Ma a letter. Grace might've helped her with that. Ma hadn't heard hide nor hair of her since she'd left home and it would've been good to set her mind at rest. But it was too late now.

'What about Tomasz?' Seffy said.

Tattie frowned. 'What about him?'

'I'm sure he'd like a visit from you, while he recovers.'

Tattie didnae want to think too much about Tomasz. She still had his blood all over her shirt and she was expecting to hear the worst and yet . . . mebbe Seffy had heard summat else?

'Is he . . . going to be all right, then?' she asked.

Seffy sighed and patted her arm. 'Honestly, I don't know. But I'm sure a visit from you would help.'

'Aye, well I've some making up to do with him, first.'

When Seffy gave her a questioning glance, Tattie wrinkled her nose. 'Long story.'

That was one secret she wasnae quite ready to tell: how she'd gone into the camp, so Angie could have a date with Luigi.

'I have to go,' she said again.

Seffy stepped in front of her, blocking her path.

'No,' she said, softly. 'You're not allowed to leave. I tried it once and I was told, in no uncertain terms, that once you sign up to the Timber Corps, there's no getting out: you sign up for the duration. That's how valuable our work is.' She smiled. 'No other service will take you. Once a lumberjill, always a lumberjill!'

Tattie shook her head.

She wasn't planning on enlisting somewhere else. She was simply going to go, head back to the city, where she'd scrape out a living somehow and forget any of this had ever happened.

'We like you, Tattie,' Seffy said. 'You're one of us now. Oh, don't worry about that stupid poison pen letter. It's water under the bridge.'

But how could she not fret? She shouldn't have delivered it; she should've told the others it was Angie's doing.

'Look, Joey and I have made up and as for her and the major . . . well, Joey's just told us that he proposed to her.

Today, in the burn! Isn't that wonderful news? They're getting married, Tattie!'

That was good news, she had to agree. But it didn't change anything.

'You're all nice lassies,' she said. 'I don't fit in. I'm not the same as any of yous.'

Seffy nodded slowly. 'That's true, you're not the same, but none of us is the same.'

She was talking nonsense now. Tattie wished she'd get out of her way and let her go and pack.

'Jean's the cleverest person I know,' Seffy said, 'but she's also a little naïve at times. Enid's plain silly, although she's grown up recently and I have high hopes for the girl. Morag's miserable and Flora, well, she's going to be a child forever, that one. And Grace is constantly worried and yearning to be somewhere else and as for me, oh goodness, let's not get started with me!'

'You?' Tattie said. 'You're the bravest lass I've ever known! No—' She held up a finger. 'The bravest person!'

'But what about you? Tattie, you were brave today! When Angie wanted to shoot me and you offered to take my place?'

Tattie blew air out of her cheeks. At that moment, she hadn't cared if she lived or died.

'I don't know what you meant, when you said you were her sister,' Seffy said. 'But it did the trick, so thank you.'

Tattie tried to dodge around her, but Seffy moved fast and blocked her way again.

'But if you leave now,' Seffy said, 'you can never make amends. If that's what you feel you should do. And you'll never know the kind of girl – woman – you could've been, or what the Timber Corps could've made of you.'

Tattie looked at her.

'Kathleen Edwards . . . not Tattie, not the scruffy wee thing who stood on the platform that day, half-starved and terrified. Look at you! You're already a different person!'

Tattie put a hand through her hair. It was longer now and shiny and it had a natural curl. Seffy was right, she supposed. In some ways – on the outside, at least – she was different.

She shook her head. 'But you all know what I did! You know I helped her. I didnae take your money, mind, I swear. But I got flour so she could make glue and stick the letters on the paper and I put the letter in the major's pocket and I . . . I helped her get closer to Luigi. But I honestly didn't know what she was planning.'

'Is that what you're worried about? That we're all going to hate you forever? Come on, no more defeatist talk! Shed your skin, like a snake!'

'Like a snake? Like Angie?'

There, she'd said her name aloud. And nothing terrible had happened.

'Yes, she was a snake,' Seffy agreed. 'But she's gone now. You're free of her! Now, come back inside. Will you come? Kath? Not Tattie. I'm calling you by your proper, grown-up name: Kath. So, what do you say, Kath? Will you stay?'

Chapter 62

Seffy and Grace were sitting barefoot in the warm sun, next to the burn. Grace's toe had finally healed and she was no longer wearing a bandage.

The girls were under strict instructions not to move a muscle – unless it was to paddle their feet – until they were called back to camp.

Certain arrangements had to be made and Seffy wasn't allowed to see.

She exhaled. Everything had turned out all right. She and Joey were reconciled; Joey and Ralph were a pair again – engaged to be married and more lovey-dovey than ever; Tattie – or Kath, as she was now to be called – had agreed to stay; and against all the odds, Tomasz the guard was recovering.

All the bad people had been removed and life was hopefully going to calm down a little now.

'Seffy?' Grace said. She licked her lips and looked tentative.

'Nothing's the matter, is it?'

'I've had a letter in the post this morning.' Grace held out a piece of paper filled, Seffy could see, with Gordy's loopy scrawl.

Seffy waved her hand. 'Oh, you go ahead and read it. If they come to get me, I'll go and you can always catch us up.'

Grace nodded but she still looked uncertain. 'Gordy wrote this just after we went to Gretna Green. It's taken more than a fortnight to arrive.'

'Oh, it's such a drag. The postal service is terrible at the moment. I haven't heard from the parents in yonks but I know they write, religiously, every week.'

She glanced through the trees, towards the camp. How long were they going to be?

She didn't want to be rude. It was lovely that Grace had another letter from Gordy and she couldn't be happier that she and Grace were on good terms again, but her stomach was churning. It really was impossible to concentrate on anything. She was about to have her big moment.

Lord and Lady Lockhart had – finally – come to carry out an inspection, not only of the lumberjills but also of the Women's Home Defence Corps. It was a huge honour.

Not only that, but Aunt Dilys had dropped a heavy hint that Seffy might be getting a "mention in despatches".

'For bravery,' she'd said, which had made Seffy's heart soar. Maybe she wasn't so lily-livered, after all.

'But Nelson should be there,' Seffy had said. 'He needs a special mention too!' And Dilys had promised it would be arranged.

Her aunt had also warned Seffy she probably wouldn't get all the praise she was due.

'Everyone in Farrbridge knows what happened but it won't make the nationals, mark my words. Or, else it'll be downplayed. It'll be a jolly jape about a group of harmless Italian chaps making a half-hearted bid for freedom.'

Seffy had frowned. 'No mention of Angie or the Fascists or Tomasz getting injured? Or the WHD?'

'Doubt it. They won't want to frighten the populace. And don't forget—' Dilys had waggled her finger '—the enemy reads our newspapers!'

Seffy supposed it made sense, national security being

paramount and all. And although it was rather disappointing that she and the other women wouldn't get their crowning moment, their family and friends knew the truth and perhaps that was all that mattered.

Today wasn't all about her, in any case. The girls were going to plant a tree, to remember Hazel by. It'd been Seffy's idea. It was a hazel sapling, courtesy of Jock, who was so grateful to her for – as he put it – "saving wee Jock" – that he'd have done anything.

Grace was shaking her head. She put the letter from Gordy in her lap and sighed.

'I didn't know, I swear. In fact, I could swing for him. We promised we'd never have secrets from one another.' She raised her voice suddenly, in a very un-Grace-like manner. 'Seffy, will you stop daydreaming and listen to me?'

'Oh, sorry, yes. Go on. I'm all ears!'

Grace sighed again. 'It turns out that my scheming husband sent a wire to Callum Fraser on the very day that you and I arrived in the Borders. I wondered why he wasn't there when I woke up in bed . . . erm, that afternoon.'

She blushed.

Seffy had heard Callum's name: she was on high alert now. But she still didn't understand.

'He says he didn't tell me at the time in case he raised false hopes,' Grace said. 'Or in case he'd read the situation wrong. But, do you see?'

What on earth was Grace talking about?

'Gordy told Callum you were in Gretna Green!' she said. 'That you'd come with me!'

A swirl of thoughts and images ricocheted around Seffy's mind. Then, like fog lifting, everything cleared and made sense.

'What . . . ? You mean, he wasn't at the Borders to see his folks?

'No!' Grace laughed. 'He went all that way – he must've got special dispensation. He—'

'—caught a train all the way up there to see me? For two hours?'

'Aye!'

The girls looked at each other.

It could only mean one thing.

'He must really like me!' Seffy said.

'Aye, he must.'

'SEFFY! Come on! It's time! You're needed!' It was Joey, hurrying towards them, grinning. Her smile faltered when she saw them. 'Is everything all right?'

'YES!' Seffy said. 'It's never been better.'

'Good! Now, make haste. Lady Lockhart's wearing an amazin' hat decked with flowers and Nelson's already eaten half of them! And the man from *The Courier*'s here, with a photographer and they're no' interested in anyone but you, Seffy! The heroine of the hour! Your auntie's telling them all about how you rode through an inferno, risking life and limb to raise the alarm, and aw, come on, you daft moo! What're you waiting for? You know you've always wanted to be a star!'

Grace laughed. 'She already is. Especially in the eyes of a certain someone.'

Joey shook her head. She was jiggling on the spot now.

'Miss McEwen's gonna make a speech and this, I have to hear!' Joey said. 'I cannae wait for the auld dragon to apologise and squirm and beg you on bended knee, to be our leader girl again!'

Seffy put her forefinger to her chin and raised her eyes to the sky. Which was as blue as Callum Fraser's eyes. 'I might say no.'

'I dare you!'

Seffy wrinkled her nose. 'I probably won't.'

'Nah!' Joey turned and started to run back the way she'd just come. Then she stopped and waited for Grace and Seffy to stand, brush the grass from their breeches and catch her up.

'You're looking very pleased wi' yourself, you wee Sassenach,' Joey said, narrowing her eyes. 'And you, too, Grace. What's goin' on, eh? Some good news, is there?'

Seffy laughed. 'Maybe!'

Today had barely started but she thought it might just be turning into the best day of her life. So far.

'So what is it, then?' Joey asked. 'Pals don't have secrets from one another!'

'Very true,' Seffy said. 'I promise I'll tell you later. Not now. Everyone's waiting for us!'

She linked arms with Grace on her left and Joey on her right.

'Let's skip!' Seffy said and they laughed and skipped, in perfect unison, all the way back to camp.

Gripped by *The Highland Girls on Guard*? Don't miss *A Wartime Secret*, another unputdownable novel from Helen Yendall. Available now!

A Letter from Helen Yendall

Thank you so much for choosing to read *The Highland Girls on Guard*. I hope you enjoyed it! If you did and would like to be the first to know about my new releases, you can follow me on social media or via my website. (Details below.)

I hadn't planned to write a *Highland Girls* series, but as I came to the end of the first book (*The Highland Girls at War*) there was still so much to tell and it seemed an obvious step to continue the lumberjills' stories. There are plans for a third book, and after that, who knows?

I had great fun writing *The Highland Girls on Guard*. I lived out my dream of galloping along a beach (one day I'll do it for real!) and I enjoyed turning the girls of Macdonald hut into real action women.

As you may know, women weren't permitted to join the Home Guard until 1943 and then only in auxiliary roles.

In response to this, Dr Edith Summerskill formed a national Women's Home Defence (WHD), comprising of several women's defence organisations (Venetia Foster's 'Amazon Defence Corps', for one). In the book, Dilys meets these women in London and is inspired to form her own unit.

The real wartime WHD was never recognised by the War Office.

If you're keen to brush up your unarmed combat skills, everything that Ralph Stirling teaches the girls came from a natty little manual (written by Major W C Fairbairn and first published in 1942), entitled, *Hands Off! Self-Defense for Women*, which is still in print.

I will admit to using a little poetic licence with the weather. The summer of 1943 in the Scottish Highlands wasn't bad but it wasn't quite the scorcher that I've portrayed. However, the rest of the book is very much based on fact.

British commandos trained in the Highlands during the war, as did other nationalities (including Dutchmen and Norwegians). There were also Polish soldiers guarding POWs.

And while you may wonder at the relative ease with which Tattie enters and exits the camp on the night she stands in for Luigi, I took my inspiration from the Northill POW camp in Mearns, Scotland, from which Italian prisoners regularly slipped out for the night, to meet girlfriends or hunt rabbits. At least one local used to stand in for his Italian friend, playing dominoes and wearing his great coat in the camp, so that if a guard did a headcount, nothing would seem amiss.

And what of Angie ('Angelina') Buchanan and the experience of the thousands of Anglo-Italians living in wartime Britain?

When Italy declared war on Britain in June 1940, the estimated 20,000 Italians living in the country were immediately classified as 'enemy aliens'.

Owners of Italian businesses – cafes, hairdressers, ice cream parlours and chip shops – were terrorised by mobs who smashed windows, looted and set fire to buildings. The terrible irony, of course, was that many of their victims were British citizens, having lived here for decades and many had sons serving in the British armed forces.

Then came internment. Italian men aged between 16 and 70, who'd lived in Britain for less than 20 years, were immediately considered for this type of detention and many of them were deported overseas.

Tragically, on 2nd July 1940, the SS Arandora Star, bound for prison camps in Canada, with hundreds of Italian Scots (and other internees) on board, was torpedoed by a German U-boat and sunk off the coast of Ireland. Hundreds perished, including 486 Italians.

I've imagined that these were the experiences of firstly Angie's Italian grandmother – who owned an ice cream shop – and, later, of Angie's Italian uncles.

I have no idea what might have happened to Angie once she was arrested. Would the authorities have shown leniency, given what had happened to her family? I doubt it somehow, but I will leave it up to you to imagine her fate.

I hope you loved *The Highland Girls on Guard* and, if you did, I would be so grateful if you would leave a review. I always love to hear what readers thought, and it helps new readers discover my books too.

Thank you

Best wishes

Helen Yendall

Twitter/X: @Helenyendall

Facebook: https://www.facebook.com/helen.yendall

Website: http://www.blogaboutwriting.wordpress.com

https://harpercollins.co.uk/blogs/authors/helen-yendall

https://www.instagram.com/helenyendall23/

A Wartime Secret

England, 1940. Can Maggie keep her family – and her secret – safe? An emotional and heartbreaking wartime novel for fans of Diney Costeloe, Dilly Court and Mandy Robotham.

When Maggie's new job takes her from bombed-out London to grand Snowden Hall in the Cotswolds she's apprehensive but determined to do her bit for the war effort. She's also keeping a secret, one she knows would turn opinion against her. Her mother is German: Maggie is related to the enemy.

Then her evacuee sister sends her a worrying letter, missing the code they agreed Violet would use to confirm everything was well, and Maggie's heart sinks. Violet is miles away; how can she get to her in the middle of a war? Worse, her mother, arrested for her nationality, is now missing, and Maggie has no idea where she is.

As a secret project at Snowden Hall risks revealing Maggie's German side, she becomes even more determined to protect her family. Can she find a way to get to her sister? And will she ever find out where her mother has been taken?

The Highland Girls at War

Scotland, 1942.
The lumberjills, the newest recruits in the Women's Timber Corps, arrive in the Scottish Highlands to a hostile reception from doubtful locals. The young women are determined to prove them wrong and serve their country – but they're also all looking for something more . . .

Lady Persephone signed up to show everyone she's more than just a pretty face – but it'll take more than some charm and her noble credentials to win handsome Sergeant Fraser over.

Tall, strong Grace has led a lonely life working on a croft, with just her mother for company. All she wants is to find her place in the world – even if that's a thousand miles from home.

And Irene misses her husband terribly, so until he returns home from the front line, she's distracting herself with war work. But one distraction too far leads to devastating consequences . . .

Can the lumberjills get through their struggles together – even when tragedy strikes?

Acknowledgements

A published work of fiction is always a team effort, so thank you to my agent Robbie Guillory and the team at HQ, particularly Abi Fenton, Seema Mitra and Helena Newton, for helping to make *The Highland Girls on Guard* the best it could be.

Many thanks to fellow writer – and 'Sicilian Mama' – Stefania Hartley, for checking my Italian and for laughing at the football match 'basta' joke.

"Thank you, thank you, thank you!" to my extra-special cheerleaders, Wendy March and Jane Wharmby.

A large chunk of this book was written in Evesham library (a handy halfway house between home and Gloucester, where my mum was in hospital and then rehab' for a total of 10 weeks). I was so grateful to have a warm, welcoming and (mostly!) quiet space in which to work. Thank you to all involved in providing and maintaining such a valuable resource.

When I was researching the lumberjills of the Women's Timber Corps, one aspect of their experience cropped up time and time again: the camaraderie, the fun and the lifelong friendships made. That was a big part of why I wanted to write about these amazing women, because there's nothing quite like the bond you form with friends in the workplace.

I've been lucky enough to make what Seffy would call 'super chums' in many places that I've worked. Many thanks to: Derry Hughes, Jo Orme, Claire Smiley, Sue Barnes, Emma Jones, Paul Keeling and Zosia Bernad, for all the laughter and support and for still cheering me on, after all these years.

Often the brightest part of a day in the office, was spending it with you.

Dear Reader,

We hope you enjoyed reading this book. If you did, we'd be so appreciative if you left a review. It really helps us and the author to bring more books like this to you.

Here at HQ Digital we are dedicated to publishing fiction that will keep you turning the pages into the early hours. Don't want to miss a thing? To find out more about our books, promotions, discover exclusive content and enter competitions you can keep in touch in the following ways:

JOIN OUR COMMUNITY:

Sign up to our new email newsletter: http://smarturl.it/SignUpHQ

Read our new blog www.hqstories.co.uk

🐦 https://twitter.com/HQStories
f www.facebook.com/HQStories

BUDDING WRITER?

We're also looking for authors to join the HQ Digital family!
Find out more here:

https://www.hqstories.co.uk/want-to-write-for-us/

Thanks for reading, from the HQ Digital team